"A perfect romance novel . . . funny, h
I can't wait to devour everything Sara

—Jasmine Guillory, *New York Times* bestselling
author of *Drunk on Love*

"Ridiculously charming and irresistible. This delightful slow burn romance has it all: sizzling chemistry, phenomenal banter, a voice that's both hilarious and vulnerable."

—Lana Harper, *New York Times* bestselling author of *In Charm's Way*

"With voice-y narration and whip-smart humor, Sarah Adler has concocted a delightfully original screwball rom-com. This book had me at 'fake medium helps a goat farmer with a ghost problem'—yes, please, and thank you."

—Megan Bannen, author of *The Undertaking of Hart and Mercy*

"*Happy Medium* is a sincere and sincerely funny romance populated by a higher-than-average number of goats and ghosts. I stayed up late to finish it and fell asleep smiling."

—Alix E. Harrow, *New York Times* bestselling
author of *Starling House*

"Adler dazzles yet again with a voice that leaps and twirls off the very first page. Equal parts hilarious, whimsical, and utterly unique in the best way, Gretchen, Charlie, Everett, and the goats stole my heart and ran away with it."

—Amy Lea, international bestselling author of *Exes and O's*

"Hilarious! This is exactly the kind of rom-com I love to read—the perfect alchemy of romance, humor, and quirky originality. Gretchen is now one of my favorite heroines. This book is going to be huge."

—Sophie Cousens, *New York Times* bestselling author
of *This Time Next Year* and *The Good Part*

"What an absolute delight. *Happy Medium* is quick, clever, and fantastically fresh. Sarah Adler just earned herself a spot on top of my auto-buy list." —B.K. Borison, author of *Lovelight Farms*

"It was a *delight* to watch morality-zigzagging Gretchen get herself into situations that—keep in mind that they would make anyone else sweat—excite her in a wily, hilarious way. She and Charlie have sizzling opposites-attract chemistry, and her interactions with the resident lovable himbo ghost are laugh-out-loud funny."

—Sarah Hogle, author of *Old Flames and New Fortunes*

"A funny and flirty tale of redemption, both in this life and the next. . . . A warmly addictive story of finding yourself and what you want in the most unexpected of places."

—Sara Goodman Confino, bestselling author of
Don't Forget to Write and *She's Up to No Good*

"A total delight from the first sentence to the last . . . an utterly winning romance. . . . Sarah Adler knows how to spin a story that's exactly what her audience wants—and needs—to hear."

—Laura Hankin, author of *The Daydreams*

Praise for **Mrs. Nash's Ashes**

"The ultimate rom-com alchemy. . . . Full of zippy banter, gorgeous prose, and tender-hearted characters who give the novel a deep, emotional core, it's a complete delight."

—Carley Fortune, #1 *New York Times* bestselling author of
Every Summer After and *Meet Me at the Lake*

"Soft, sweet, and utterly enchanting, *Mrs. Nash's Ashes* by Sarah Adler is a delightfully funny and poignant romance that sticks with you like a warm and gooey cinnamon roll."

—Ashley Poston, *New York Times* bestselling author of
The Dead Romantics and *The Seven Year Slip*

"Brilliantly constructed and full of unforgettable characters, *Mrs. Nash's Ashes* is an unequivocal delight. Fans of Emily Henry and Sarah Hogle, you've found your newest obsession."

—Ava Wilder, author of *How to Fake It in Hollywood*

"With an unforgettable voice, Adler crafts a tale full of humor and heart, proving that love sometimes finds us when we least expect it."

—Ashley Herring Blake, *USA Today* bestselling author of *Astrid Parker Doesn't Fail*

"Instantly addictive! . . . Pure rom-com gold. Witty, fun, and yet also deeply affecting, this remarkably strong debut from Sarah Adler is sure to win hearts."

—India Holton, bestselling author of *The League of Gentlewomen Witches*

"This is a road-trip romance at its best, with all the forced proximity, unexpected intimacies, and questionable music playlists that come with it. . . . A journey I didn't want to end."

—Jen DeLuca, *USA Today* bestselling author of *Well Matched*

"Adler perfectly mixes humor, heart, and steam to create a flawless rom-com. If you're in the mood for a true rom-com, you cannot go wrong with this book!"

—Falon Ballard, author of *Lease on Love* and *Just My Type*

"At turns both zany and heart-wrenching. . . . This is a treasure of a story that lived and breathed inside my heart."

—Anita Kelly, author of *Something Wild & Wonderful*

Also by Sarah Adler

MRS. NASH'S ASHES

HAPPY MEDIUM

SARAH ADLER

BERKLEY ROMANCE

New York

BERKLEY ROMANCE
Published by Berkley
An imprint of Penguin Random House LLC
penguinrandomhouse.com

Library of Congress Cataloging-in-Publication Data
Names: Adler, Sarah, 1991- author.
Title: Happy medium / Sarah Adler.
Description: First edition. | New York: Berkley Romance, 2024.
Identifiers: LCCN 2023031108 (print) | LCCN 2023031109 (ebook) |
ISBN 9780593547816 (trade paperback) | ISBN 9780593547823 (ebook)
Subjects: LCGFT: Romance fiction. | Novels.
Classification: LCC PS3601.D5748 H37 2024 (print) | LCC PS3601.D5748
(ebook) | DDC 813/.6—dc23/eng/20230714
LC record available at https://lccn.loc.gov/2023031108
LC ebook record available at https://lccn.loc.gov/2023031109

First Edition: April 2024

Printed in the United States of America
1st Printing

Book design by George Towne

For my parents

*Thank you for setting me up for success
while always letting me define it.*

Author's Note

This book has scenes involving a relative living with dementia. If this is a potentially sensitive topic for you, please read with care.

HAPPY MEDIUM

1

GRETCHEN ACORN IS A BULLSHIT ARTIST.

The talent for it runs in her family—her daddy's a bullshit artist, as was his daddy before him, and his before him. And so on, all the way back to Fritz Eichorn, who scammed his way into first class on the ship that carried him to the US by posing as a recently heartbroken Austrian count. But while great-great-great-grandpa Fritz and most of his male descendants gravitated toward the hasty brushstrokes of shell games and selling landmarks to tourists, Gretchen has found her own, more *sophisticated* medium.

No pun intended.

"Ah." Gretchen presses two fingers to each of her temples. She winces as if her mental call to the spirit realm has conjured nothing except a headache. "I feel Ronald trying to be here with us, but the connection is fragile. Too fragile to make anything out, I'm afraid."

"It's my aura, isn't it?" The elderly woman across the table unclasps her hands and sets them atop the plum brocade table-cloth. She still wears her platinum and diamond wedding set, the swell of her arthritic knuckle the only thing keeping the too-large rings in place. "I've been told before that it's a problem, but no matter how many Reiki experts I've consulted—"

"No, no," Gretchen interrupts. "You have a *beautiful* aura, Mrs. Easterly. The most gorgeous"—*Pick a color, any color*—"vermillion I've ever seen. Don't let anyone do a thing to it."

The idea of some opportunistic asshole swindling a nice old lady like Janice Easterly makes Gretchen's jaw tense. Perhaps that seems hypocritical given that she herself relies upon dishonesty to make her living (and that she can't even remember if vermillion is a shade of green or red). But the difference is that Gretchen only takes people's money if she's certain she can leave them better off than she found them. That's the one Rule that governs everything she does. Her singular guiding principle. It transforms her work from a con into a business transaction, her morally gray impulses into something mutually beneficial. That's why she turns away potential clients if she knows she won't be able to provide what they need, and why she's building up to telling Mrs. Easterly that her telephone line to the spirit world is currently generating nothing but a busy signal.

Her code of ethics may not win her a Nobel Peace Prize, but it's been something of a compass since Gretchen struck out on her own almost seven years ago. She has the skills of her forefathers in her back pocket at all times—her father made sure she could lie, cheat, and steal with the best of them before she could even spell her own name—and it would be easy enough to fill the rest of Mrs. Easterly's half-hour session with the cheap tricks that make up the bread and butter of most supposed spirit mediums and psychics. No doubt Mrs. Easterly would confirm, tears cutting through her caked-on face powder like an icebreaker navigating the Baltic, that the two-story house with a chimney Gretchen describes (not too specifically, of course) must be her husband's childhood home. A woman with a name beginning with H? Well, her sister's name was Harriett, could that be it? And oh my word, she does indeed own a heart-shaped piece of jewelry! A long-ago gift from her late husband, in fact, from before he made his fortune buying and selling laws or whatever it is people in this town do to get so damn rich.

But Gretchen Acorn didn't become the most sought-after spirit medium among Northwest DC's high-society set by throwing generic guesses at the wall, assuming something would be bound to stick. It takes extra effort—extra *artistry*—to win over the rich old ladies who reside in this part of the city. Gretchen's clients know that when they come to her, they aren't going to get the preschool crayon drawing version of a séance, where you have to squint and tilt your head to make out what the medium is telling you they see. No, they can rely on her to paint them a vivid picture, full of detail and symbolism that gives them permission to fully buy into the belief that they aren't as alone as they feel. She's the bullshit artist equivalent of a Renaissance master, and as long as what she produces is pretty and reassuring, her clients never think too deeply about the process that went into creating it.

Unfortunately, Mrs. Easterly barged in without an appointment, which Gretchen allowed only because the woman introduced herself using the magic words: "I'm a good friend of Deborah Van Alst." So she went into this séance without the usual mental dossier of information that acts as her canvas.

She drops her chin as if the weight of summoning Mrs. Easterly's dead husband has become too heavy for her mind to bear. Her head lolls for effect, which also has the added bonus of stretching out a little twinge in her neck. "I'm almost certain the problem is me," she says wearily. "I'm feeling . . . weakened this afternoon." Also hungry, according to the growl of her stomach. Mrs. Easterly's unscheduled appearance at her little basement-level shop on MacArthur Boulevard interrupted Gretchen's lunch plans. She thinks longingly of the Cup Noodles still sitting inside the microwave in the back room.

"I hope you're not ill?" Suspicion sneaks into Mrs. Easterly's voice, as if she's now concerned that Gretchen may secretly be several infectious diseases masquerading as a spirit medium.

"No, nothing so mundane. There seems to be a disturbance in the veil." Gretchen glances up as she speaks, but doesn't meet Mrs. Easterly's rheumy eyes. Instead, she stares slightly off into the distance, finding a cobweb in the corner that makes an excellent focal point for moments like this (the reason, she tells herself, she hasn't cleaned it despite first noticing it weeks ago).

True Believers—of which Mrs. Easterly is clearly one—*love* this kind of drama, so Gretchen is unsurprised to see her lean forward and nod as if she's all too familiar with the fickle whims of the veil between the living and spirit worlds.

"As a highly intuitive soul, I'm particularly sensitive to such fluctuations. Especially on Thursdays." Thursdays don't have any particular occult significance that Gretchen is aware of, but it *sounds* good.

"Oh. I see. Yes, now that you mention it, I also feel that something is quite out of alignment."

"Out of alignment, exactly! Of course you sense it, given that lovely vermillion aura of yours." The large emerald and diamond brooch at Mrs. Easterly's throat twinkles in the candlelight, and the mink stole draped over the woman's bony shoulders prompts Gretchen to add, "But it always falls right back into place in time. Perhaps we can try again next week?"

By then, Gretchen can gather enough information on Ronald Easterly to make this worth his widow's two hundred bucks. Maybe she'll even cultivate her as a long-term client. Because while her initial instinct might've been to turn Mrs. Easterly away (and only partially because she's currently hangry), the old woman's penchant for real fur and gaudy-but-fine jewelry acts like a siren song, calling to all of Gretchen's . . . ahem, artistic instincts. Surely, she can find a way to make herself useful.

"Of course," Mrs. Easterly says. "That sounds— Yes, next week. I'll call to make an appointment."

Calling ahead, Gretchen thinks. *What a novel concept.*

When the woman reaches for her vintage Chanel purse to pull out her wallet, Gretchen takes her hand to still the action. Mrs. Easterly's skin is fragile and clammy, as if it's made of half-dried papier-mâché.

"No charge for today, ma'am. I cannot accept payment when I was unable to provide you with the requested service," Gretchen says, flashing a rueful smile.

An answering expression stretches across Mrs. Easterly's thin lips, emphasizing the tiny estuaries of red lipstick traveling outward in every direction. "No wonder Deborah speaks so highly of you." Gretchen allows her hand to be patted affectionately before she draws it away.

"I appreciate how many of Mrs. Van Alst's friends trust me to assist them." Considering Deborah Van Alst's referrals make up almost a third of Gretchen's business these days (and Mrs. Van

Alst herself another third), this is not only sincere, but somewhat of an understatement. Gretchen allows her earnestness to show in her expression; it's smart to lean into the truth whenever she can.

"Oh. Oh no, it *is* Thursday." Mrs. Easterly's smile falls, then transforms into a concerned purse of the lips. "Deborah is supposed to see you today, isn't she? I hope the disturbance"—her voice drops to a whisper on the word as if trying not to offend the spirit realm—"doesn't prevent her from speaking with Rachel."

Gretchen guides Mrs. Easterly toward the doorway with a hand hovering over her back. "The veil to the spirit realm is notoriously capricious. But I'm certain if Rachel has anything to say to her mother this afternoon, she'll find a way to come through. Those who pass young tend to be stronger spirits, and Rachel is even stronger than most. I barely need to exert any energy to get her chatting away most of the time."

Rachel Van Alst died at age thirty-three in a skiing accident. She left behind Instagram, TikTok, and Twitter accounts, *and* never deleted the LiveJournal she kept from ages twelve to fifteen—a veritable buffet of personal information that's made convincing her mother that her deceased daughter is communicating with her from the afterlife one of the easiest jobs Gretchen has ever pulled off.

"Yes, Rachel always was a big presence, you know." Mrs. Easterly glances back over her shoulder as she shuffles forward. "Still had so much life ahead of her. Such a shame."

Gretchen hums her agreement and at last wishes the old woman farewell. She retreats to the back room that serves as her office. It's actually a closet with a beaded curtain for a door, but the size doesn't matter as much as the fact that it's somewhere she can be Gretchen Eichorn, twenty-nine-year-old (mostly) ethical bullshit artist, for brief moments in between being Gretchen Acorn, purported ghost microphone. Also somewhere she can finally reheat her Cup Noodles and shovel them into her mouth in peace before her next appointment.

While the container circles in the ancient microwave and Gretchen curses Mrs. Easterly's interruption for making her pathetic lunch even more pathetic, she thumbs through the stack of mail that was piled under the front door's slot when she showed the woman out. Bill, bill, bill. Swiss Colony catalog addressed to the accountant's office on the house's main floor. Envelope with a handwritten address . . .

The microwave beeps, but Gretchen's stomach no longer growls so much as lurches.

Well. Her father was bound to track her down eventually. She just didn't expect him to take so long. Then again, knowing Ned Eichorn, it's all part of the plan. She originally braced herself for this moment fourteen months ago when she learned he was out on parole. But when no unknown numbers called and no letters like this one arrived, she slowly, slowly let her guard down until she forgot why she should have it up at all.

It's the way she would have done it too, were she him. But she's spent several years trying to prove to herself she *isn't*. And she's *not*. Her Rule makes sure of that. But there's certainly a part of her that suspects that, without it, she wouldn't be inclined to be much better.

Ned Eichorn is extremely skilled at spotting a person's weaknesses, and hers are no exception. So she can predict with some accuracy what this letter says. Its arrival sends much more of a message than whatever words are inside. It's pointing out her sloppiness, her complacency. It's not a threat, exactly, but the *suggestion* of one. Yet instead of throwing it straight into the small trash can in the corner, Gretchen tucks it away under the bottom of the pile of bills before placing the whole stack of mail on the nearest horizontal surface.

As Gretchen twirls noodles around her fork, she forces her thoughts to turn from her father to her upcoming afternoon meeting with Deborah Van Alst—only a marginally less stressful topic. "Talking" to her daughter has been a crucial part of Mrs. Van Alst's grieving process; Gretchen wouldn't allow her to come in twice a week for the last nine months if she wasn't convinced she was doing the woman some good in exchange for her money. But based on Yolanda's reports, Mrs. Van Alst has turned a corner in her grief. The neighborhood chatter is that she's come out of hiding, no longer only leaving her bijou mansion on Glenbrook Road to visit Gretchen's shop. She's been spotted at restaurants, charity events, the University Club. Then, this past weekend, according to the gossip Yolanda gathered for Gretchen at Salon Apolline, she participated in a bridge tournament in Potomac and was later seen getting drinks with a handsome (and much younger) man.

Getting the woman back out into the world was always the goal, but it's a bittersweet development. It's becoming more difficult to justify Mrs. Van Alst's twice-weekly séances. Still, Gretchen keeps procrastinating on doing anything about it. Not because she's learned to *like* the absurd woman or anything. It's just that her landlord is unlikely to accept good deeds in lieu of rent on the basement space and the only slightly larger apartment on the converted house's top floor, and without Mrs. Van Alst's biweekly appointments, Gretchen's monthly income will be reduced by several hundred dollars. Not exactly a drop in the bucket, especially in an expensive city like Washington.

Gretchen side-eyes the letter from her father hidden beneath the stack of bills. She can only see the corner of the envelope, the empty one where there should be a return address. Her father would advise her to keep up her current schedule with Mrs. Van Alst. Shit, he'd suggest she try to get her to come in more often. The woman has the money, and if she's stupid enough to want to waste it like this . . .

Gretchen shakes her head. It's certainly tempting, but that's why she created her Rule in the first place. And said Rule dictates that it's time to gently nudge Mrs. Van Alst into relying on her less.

Just maybe not so much less that Gretchen won't be able to pay her bills.

The last time they spoke, her dad called her out for being on a high horse. But Gretchen's always pictured it as more of a stubby-legged pony, elevated off the ground just enough to keep the worst of the dirt off. She's above *some* things . . . but not *all* things . . . and even then, not by a significant margin.

So when the sixty-eight-year-old canned goods heiress-cum-ultra-wealthy divorcée arrives in the shop—her once gray-streaked hair now shiny, blonde, and meticulously coiffed—and takes her seat, Gretchen intends to call upon the Mother and the Father and the Heavens and her Spirit Guide to let Rachel come through like she has dozens of times before. Today, though, instead of reaching into the mental grab bag of information she's compiled via Rachel's amazingly thorough documentation of her life (the woman had recently started a *podcast*!), she fully intends to regale Mrs. Van Alst with the good news that her daughter has noticed her recent progress, and that now that she's certain her mother will be okay, she's going to go spend time enjoying everything the afterlife has to offer. She'll be harder to reach from here on out, so Mrs. Van Alst shouldn't take it personally if Gretchen can no longer deliver Rachel's messages as regularly. In fact, might as well only come in once a month to preserve her strength and ensure the strongest chance of contact. No, better make it twice a month; Rachel will miss her too much otherwise (because, seriously: rent).

But, despite her intention to do the right—okay, right*ish*—thing, Gretchen doesn't get further than greeting Mrs. Van Alst and making their usual small talk about the weather before the woman interrupts. "Instead of speaking with Rachel today, there's something else I would like to discuss with you."

"Oh?" Gretchen dabbles in palm reading, tarot, and the occasional psychic prediction when a client is amenable, but Mrs. Van Alst has never shown interest in anything except communicating with her daughter's spirit. Unless . . . No. It's unlikely Mrs. Van Alst has discovered she's a fraud. Or who her father is. Gretchen's heartbeat stutters at the thought.

Luckily, she isn't left in anticipation for long. Mrs. Van Alst launches right in without further prompting. "I would like to hire you to help a friend with a particular . . . problem."

The way she says it makes it sound like Gretchen's about to be propositioned to cure someone's impotence, and her eyebrows are hoisted by a mixture of curiosity and bemusement. Her interest is certainly piqued. "And the nature of this problem?"

"I would like you to perform . . . an exorcism."

Well, that is certainly a less awkward request than where her mind initially went, but still not on Gretchen Acorn's usual menu of services. Other than having seen *The Exorcist* (way too young, by the way, at one of the few sleepovers she ever attended), she doesn't particularly have any experience with that sort of thing. Is an exorcism even something she could do? Or rather, pretend to do?

"You believe your friend is . . . possessed?" she asks, finding herself mimicking Mrs. Van Alst's cadence. That pause does feel natural when discussing the topic. Obligatory, even.

"Goodness, no. As if I believe in *that*." She says this dismissively, like she hasn't paid Gretchen thousands upon thousands of dollars to channel her dead daughter. "My bridge partner, Charles Waybill, has a goat farm in Maryland. Historic little property that's been in his family for eight generations. But personal and financial circumstances have convinced him it's time to sell."

"Ah, I see." Gretchen isn't entirely sure she does, but Mrs. Van Alst seems to be waiting for a response.

"He's had several offers since he put it on the market in February, but they keep falling through at the last minute. There have been some . . . unexplained phenomena." There's that pause again. "Lights turning off during open houses, doors slamming in home inspectors' faces, spots of extreme cold in otherwise warm rooms, a sense of being watched. It all points to a haunting. Wouldn't you agree?"

Gretchen nods. That's definitely some stereotypical ghost shit. Things for which there are also a million other, more rational explanations, of course. But it's not really in her best interests to point that out when her business relies upon people believing in the afterlife.

"I told Charles about you and how you've been helping me communicate with Rachel since she passed. I assured him you would know how to rid the property of its spirits, or at least that you could speak with them to see if they have some issue with the farm's sale and persuade them to allow it. That *is* something you could do?"

Could she? It's been a long time since Gretchen used her skills outside the safety of her shop. Probably why she's been feeling a bit stuck lately, like she's just going through the motions. Maybe this is a chance to experience that excitement again, the feeling she fucking *loves*, the reason she does this instead of waiting tables or grooming poodles. The only way she can describe it is like the atoms that make up her body start a game of freeze dance, and when the music stops they're in an entirely new arrangement that makes her feel a little bit invincible. Her father always called that high from successfully pulling off a con "gotcha euphoria." And she hasn't felt the full force of it in a long, long time.

If she can manage a convincing enough exorcism to help an old man sell his struggling farm? That just might be the pinnacle of her career as a bullshit artist. Her masterpiece. The gotcha euphoria would be overwhelming—a high she could ride for a good long while.

Also, she hasn't forgotten the bills on the shelf in the back room. Those might begin to haunt her themselves soon, especially once she convinces Mrs. Van Alst to stop coming around as often. Which she really does still intend to do, just as soon as the right moment arises . . .

But then Gretchen also remembers the letter beneath those bills, the one she assumes says something like, *We're peas in a pod, kid, whether you want to admit it to yourself or not,* and her selfish, mercenary thoughts make those words too close to the truth for her liking. So she clings to the resulting compunction, accepting it as a sign from her subconscious. "Mrs. Van Alst, I appreciate your faith in me, but I'm not sure if my schedule can accommodate such a—"

"Oh, but Charles is such a dear friend. If you don't help him, I'm afraid he'll never be able to move on with his life. He's all alone now. It's no way to live . . ." Mrs. Van Alst's voice trails off, as if perhaps she's unsure if she's speaking about Charles Waybill or herself now.

A twinge of empathy makes Gretchen bow her head. Not that it's the same, really. Gretchen is also alone, sure. But it's by choice. Not having anyone is different from having them and losing them.

"I'll of course compensate you for the trouble," Mrs. Van Alst adds, reaching for her purse. Her instinct (like many other exorbitantly wealthy people's, in Gretchen's experience) is to throw money willy-nilly at every problem that arises, hoping the right amount of it will magically relieve her burden. And why not, when it nearly always works?

Except Gretchen's supposed to be weaning Mrs. Van Alst *off* of her services. That is the right thing to do. And if she doesn't do the right thing, then her dad wins the long, drawn-out battle that his letter reminded her is still quietly raging between them. "I'm not certain I'm—"

"I'd like you out there right away. I understand that it may take several days, and I know you usually have clients on the weekends. You'll have to reschedule several appointments, find transportation and lodging." She pauses a moment as if mentally calculating, then writes out a check. "I believe this will cover both your losses and expenses, as well as provide for your time and expertise."

It's slipped Gretchen's mind that many of the people around here have an odd, detached relationship with the cost of things

outside of property and fancy wine. So when Mrs. Van Alst slides
the check over the brocade tablecloth toward her, she nearly chokes
on the number she sees.

"Have I underestimated?" Mrs. Van Alst smiles, closemouthed,
as if she's uncomfortable with the vulgarity of speaking of money
and would really rather be finished with this part of the conversation.

"No, you— That's *much* too generous," Gretchen forces herself to say through the odd combination of giddiness and nausea
the number of zeros trailing the one inspires.

It could be nice to get away for a few days . . . give her time to
think about how to handle her father before he comes barging into
the life she's so carefully constructed for herself. Time to get one
more job in the books that she can point to as evidence that she's
able to survive without completely stomping on her moral compass.

"I assure you, Charles's happiness is worth anything. He's a
dear friend."

Well, then. If he's *that dear* of a friend.

Gretchen starts making a mental packing list. Looks like she's
going to be spending her weekend in the countryside, making an
old farmer very, very happy.

2

MRS. VAN ALST WRITES DOWN THE FARM'S ADDRESS ON A sheet of personalized embossed stationery from her purse and hands it to Gretchen. "Now, Charles may be a tad reluctant when you arrive—he's somewhat skeptical about these sorts of things—but I'm certain he'll warm to the idea once he experiences your gifts for himself."

When she tucked the check away and formally accepted the job, Gretchen didn't consider that she might be performing this fake exorcism against the property owner's will. Not that it will be a problem getting Mr. Waybill on her side. She's convinced her share of skeptics since the five years since she set up her shop. In fact, she admires someone who is reluctant to believe; it shows intelligence. And she assumes the eventual gotcha euphoria when she wins the farmer over will be all the sweeter if she has to work a little harder for it.

"Thank you for agreeing to do this," Mrs. Van Alst says, as if the amount of money she offered Gretchen really gave her any choice in the matter. "Oh, and I'm leaving for France tomorrow. I'll be staying with friends in Provence for a few weeks, but I want to hold my spot in your schedule in case my plans change, so I'll have Shruthi send your monthly payment as usual. Contact her if you need anything else. And please give Charles my regards."

"Of course," Gretchen answers as Mrs. Van Alst heads for the exit.

Provence? Well. That all but confirms that the bridge tournament and outings weren't flukes. Mrs. Van Alst is fully back in the world (or, well, the extremely rich–person version of it). That means Gretchen has officially conned Mrs. Van Alst into being better off than when she first met her. A rousing success. She waits for the gotcha euphoria to hit but, once again, only gets a whisper of the old feeling. More like a gotcha wistful contentment.

Well, since their appointment finished early, she may as well get started on researching this guy and his goat farm. It's been a long time since she's had to rely solely upon the internet to get a feel for what she's going into, having organized her business around the high-yielding local rumor mill and her roommate Yolanda Ortiz's strategic positions within it. Hopefully, this Charles Waybill has a public Facebook page or something she can use, even if it does mean having to scroll through a bunch of highly artifacted chain letter graphics and bizarre political memes.

After Gretchen extinguishes the candles around the room and snuffs out the incense, she locks the door and heads up to her small apartment on the duplex's second floor. Yolanda is in the kitchen, a can of cold brew in one hand and her keys in the other. Gretchen's eyes rake over her roommate's clothing for clues as to her destination. Off to one of her jobs, but Gretchen can't be sure which, since black leggings and a black shirt is her uniform for working the front desk at both Salon Apolline and Balasana Yoga.

"I thought you weren't scheduled until four today," Gretchen says as she toes off her pointed flats.

"Wasn't," Yolanda answers, reaching for her bag—also black. "But Candy's daughter needed to be picked up from school early, so I offered to fill in at the salon until my shift at the studio."

"Well, before you head out, I had a potentially lucrative walk-in today. A woman named Janice Easterly. Wants to talk to her husband, Ronald. Ring any bells?"

"Easterly," Yolanda repeats, glancing up at an old water stain on the ceiling that looks a little like a dinosaur. "White lady in her late seventies or early eighties, gigantic black-framed glasses, wears too much makeup and real fur year-round?"

"Yep, that's her. She's been to the salon, then?" The brittle woman she met today would no doubt snap in half if she tried to do a sun salutation, so it seems like the more likely option.

"She gets her nails done at Apolline when her usual 'girl' isn't available to make a house call. Last time, she had on this fox coat that gave me the heebie-jeebies. Had the heads attached and everything. When she handed it to me to hang up for her I nearly dropped it and ran." Yolanda shudders at the memory. "I think Lex was her tech. I'll fish around and see if they know anything."

"Excellent, thank you." Gretchen pauses, stripping the teasing tone she wants to use from her next question before she asks it. "Penny'll be there tonight?"

"I don't know." Yolanda fiddles with her keys to avoid making eye contact. "Probably."

Gretchen knows Yolanda has the pretty yoga instructor's

schedule memorized down to the second, but doesn't give in to the temptation to call her out. Instead, she takes a seat on one of the stools at the breakfast bar and opens up her laptop.

"She's teaching a seven thirty and a nine," Yolanda concedes almost immediately anyway. "And I think . . . I think I'm going to see how she feels about me coming over after."

Gretchen's response slips through her defenses like a rogue. "All right, I won't wait up, then. Hope you have fun with your *girlfriend*." It's hard to regret the moment of weakness when Yolanda's light bronze cheeks pinken ever so slightly.

"She's not my— We're not dating, it's just a casual—"

"Yeah, yeah, sure. Mark my words, give it a month and you'll be moving into her bungalow and adopting a cat together."

"And what makes you such an expert on how this is going to play out, Miss Hasn't Been on a Date the Entire Three Years I've Lived Here?"

"That's way too long of a nickname. And I don't need to date to know what's going to happen between you and Penny. I have a gift, remember?" Gretchen places her fingers to her temples and flutters her eyes closed. "It'll be a long-haired calico. Name her Mitsy. That's her soul's true name."

Yolanda laughs. "Yeah, yeah. Save it for the paying customers. Hopefully, soon to include Madame Dead Fox. You're going to be doing the planet's soft and fluffy animals a big favor, taking that woman's money."

"That's my good deed for the year already sorted, then," Gretchen mutters. The urge to go back over and wrap her red-wood tree of a roommate in a tight hug strikes as she watches Yolanda gather up her fleece jacket and tuck it under her arm. That's enough to shake Gretchen out of this easy banter, to hastily rebuild the walls around her heart and remind her of the reasons they're there.

Yolanda is someone Gretchen knows could easily become a friend. That's why it's so important to keep her emotional distance. Because when their relationship eventually comes to its end—which it will, because business transactions are always finite—it's going to be hard enough to figure out what to do without the cornerstone of her operation. For Yolanda, collecting information for Gretchen is just another of her streams of income. In exchange for reporting back everything she hears at the salon and the yoga studio—jobs that each give her incredible access to all of the most gossipy wealthy women in Georgetown, the Palisades, and Spring Valley—she lives in the apartment's den for the extremely low price of $300 a month. But one day this arrangement will no longer serve her, and she'll leave. So if Gretchen allows herself to indulge in things like affection and loyalty . . .

Well, that generally has not worked out super for her in the past.

Yolanda's dark brown eyes dart to the oven's digital clock. "Shit, I better get going. I told them I'd be in by one thirty."

"See you tomorrow." While waiting for her spreadsheets to load, Gretchen types "Gilded Creek Goat Farm" into Google, prompting her to remember she's about to spend the weekend elsewhere. "Oh, actually, I probably won't. Deborah Van Alst hired me to go exorcise her bridge partner's historic farm in Maryland. She's convinced it's haunted."

"Exorcise it? Don't you need, like, an old priest and a young priest for that?" Yolanda jokes, attempting to swipe a strand of her long black hair from her face with her shoulder since her hands are still full.

"I don't expect to find any possessed, barfy children on this farm. Sounds like it's just an old guy and a bunch of goats." An assumption supported by the fact that Gilded Creek has zero internet presence.

"And a ghost, don't forget." Yolanda smiles, lips pressed hard together to suppress her laughter.

"Allegedly."

"So how long will you be gone? Do I need to take care of anything with the shop?"

"Probably until Sunday or Monday." With Mrs. Van Alst's ample funds and her father's letter sitting in the back room like a placeholder for his imminent arrival, it seems like a good idea to make this surprise job into a mini vacation. Give her a few days to strategize. But she's not about to unload her daddy issues on Yolanda, so she says, "Mrs. Van Alst is paying me ten thousand dollars 'to cover my lost business and expenses,' so I figured I'll find a nice hotel somewhere nearby and make a couple trips out to the farm over the course of the weekend. Put on a real show. That way she feels like she got her money's worth when she hears about it. Probably wouldn't hurt to have extra time to build some trust with this guy anyway. Mrs. Van Alst seemed to think he might be resistant to the whole thing. The way she talked, I doubt he even knows she hired me."

"Whoa, whoa. Back up a sec. Ten thousand dollars?" Yolanda's mouth drops open so wide Gretchen hears her jaw click. "Girl. That's . . . an insane amount of cash for a weekend of you fucking around with some sage in a farmhouse."

"Yeah, I know. Absurd, right? But Mrs. Van Alst insisted. And it's not like I can't use the money, especially since I plan to cut her down to twice a month . . . soon. It doesn't go against the Rule, so . . ."

Yolanda knows about Gretchen Acorn's Singular Rule for Bullshitting, though nothing about its origins. In fact, the Rule's existence was one of the reasons Yolanda agreed to become Gretchen's informant in the first place—she appreciated that the gossip she gathered would be put to use helping people more than harming them. Well, that and the fact that she really needed a place to live when her extremely religious parents kicked her out of their house after discovering that she had both a girlfriend and an OnlyFans account.

Yolanda shrugs her shoulder toward her ear in an attempt to adjust the purse strap there. "Okay, well, you be careful out there in the boonies. Don't fall in love with the farmer and move to the countryside or anything."

Gretchen wrinkles her nose. "I think Mrs. Van Alst would have something to say about that. She referred to him as a '*dear* friend,' so there may be some history there. Besides, considering he's her bridge partner, I'm pretty sure this guy has to be in his sixties at least."

"So is Daniel Day-Lewis, though, and we both know how you feel about him."

This time it's Gretchen's cheeks that turn pink—a rare occurrence, but one that never fails to happen whenever Yolanda brings this up. "How many times do I have to tell you, I wasn't—"

"You were watching *There Will Be Blood* with your hand in your pants, Gretch. I know what I saw."

"I was *scratching* an *itch* on my inner thigh," Gretchen says, watching as Yolanda's lips drain of color as she presses them even harder together. In these moments, teasing each other over crushes and (alleged) masturbatory habits, it's so easy to see what it would be like to be friends instead of simply roommates and business associates.

Tempting. Terrifying. "Also, I'm pretty sure he wasn't in his sixties when that film was made."

"Whatever. Just make sure you pack your vibrator. You know, in case the farmer's got a big, bushy mustache and you can't stop fantasizing about him drinking your milkshake . . ." After a burst of laughter, she adds, "Text me when you get there so I know you're alive," blows a kiss, then wiggles her fingers in farewell as she walks out the door.

The subsequent silence in the apartment brings Gretchen abruptly back to reality—that she's alone. It's almost reassuring, in a way. Because the other rule she lives by, the one that's unwritten but perhaps more important, is that the beautiful, masterful pictures she paints are only for other people. Not for her.

3

OF COURSE GRETCHEN EXPECTED HER DESTINATION TO BE rural. It's a farm after all. But as the scenery shifts from the suburban sprawl of gas stations and fast-casual restaurants to long expanses of gently rolling pastures dotted with cows, freshly tilled fields, and still-shuttered-for-the-season roadside produce stands, it registers just how far from the hustle and bustle of DC she's headed. When she looked up Derring Heights, Maryland, last night—the town in the farm's address—she found one of those places so diminutive that Google Maps doesn't even deign to label it until zoomed in almost to the street level. There isn't much more than a church, a post office, a 7-Eleven, and a string of impressive old Victorians along the main thoroughfare. Gilded Creek Goat Farm is located another fifteen minutes west. Even though Gretchen spent her childhood moving around thanks to her father's own bullshit artist career, she's never lived anywhere that could be classified as remote (not a lot of worthwhile marks in these sorts of places). Now, so accustomed to the conveniences of city living, she can't imagine willingly settling anywhere that it takes half an hour round trip just to get a Slurpee.

When her Lyft driver, Sulayman, pulls off the main road and onto a long dirt-and-gravel driveway, he meets Gretchen's eyes in the rearview mirror. At first, the look is one of inquiry: Is she certain this is where she wants to go? Perhaps her finger slipped when entering her destination into the app and mistakenly entered Gilded Creek Goat Farm instead of Trader Joe's? But as his previously spotless white Toyota Corolla gets flecked with mud thanks to last night's storm leaving large puddles along the tire-worn path, Sulayman's look transforms into an overtly annoyed one that warns Gretchen she should plan to tip enough to cover the cost of a car wash.

She grabs hold of her trusty canvas backpack's strap, ready to make her getaway. "Thanks. You can just let me out here." No need to make him drive all the way up to the house and completely tank her passenger rating.

Sulayman does a hasty three-point turn and speeds back down the driveway as soon as Gretchen is out of the car, more mud flying up in his wake. Hopefully Mr. Waybill doesn't notice the tire tracks in the grass. Not that he seems to be particularly precious about appearances. Gretchen spots a broken-down, rusted, two-wheeled . . . *thing* parked beside a large tree stump off to the right, and the barn in the distance isn't particularly photogenic with its walls overtaken by ivy and the white paint on the wooden areas faded and chipped off in a pattern that looks like a giant creature scratched its claws down each board.

Is she more likely to locate Charles Waybill inside said barn, or in the brick farmhouse at the end of the driveway?

If she were a farmer and it was close to noon on a Friday . . .

Unfortunately, her knowledge of farmwork is limited to having read *Charlotte's Web* as a child, leaving her with very little practical information to help her finish that sentence (unless an unusually gifted spider is going to appear and spin her an answer). Well, the barn is slightly closer, so she might as well check there first.

Animal smells assault her nose as she approaches. When she walks around the side of the barn to what she presumes would be considered the front, a small herd of goats in the nearby pasture start up a chorus of aggressive *mehhh*ing, startling her into taking several steps backward. Gretchen has never interacted with a goat—at least not as an adult. She vaguely recalls a field trip to a petting zoo at one of the six elementary schools she attended and assumes there could have been a goat involved then. Luckily, she's here to deal with ghosts, not goats, and she's much more familiar with pretending to understand the former. Because the animals she can see are, frankly, intimidating even from afar. Very . . . unpredictable-looking. And can't they, like, eat your hair off or something?

Does that brown-and-white one by the side fence have . . . tennis balls stuck to its head?

A woman appears inside the barn, her silver-gray braid swinging against the back of her long-sleeved tie-dye T-shirt with every step. Gretchen calls out a greeting, and the woman turns around. With her forearm shielding her eyes from the sun since her gloves are covered in dirt (or worse, considering the variety of smells present in this space), she takes Gretchen in from head to toe. Then she frowns, adding a few more wrinkles to her heavily freckled, sun-worn face. "You lost, hon?"

Gretchen glances down at her outfit, reassessing the burgundy pleather jacket, short black swing dress, heeled suede boots, and layers of assorted dangly crystal necklaces. Maybe showing up to a goat farm looking like Alexis Rose gone goth wasn't the most practical idea. Then again, it's important to maintain the right vibe no matter the atmosphere; no one's going to put their faith in a spirit medium wearing overalls.

"I'm actually looking for Mr. Waybill. Do you happen to know where he might be at the moment?"

"Oh." The woman glances at the smartwatch on her wrist. "A little after noon? He usually breaks for lunch about this time," she says. "Check the house first. But nice day like today, he could be by the creek."

Gretchen already knows about the creek that gave the farm its name. The sale listing for the property—priced at $800,000, by the way, and the livestock and equipment all convey—included no less than twenty different photos of the narrow stream during different seasons and at various times of day (including at sunset in the summer, when it does admittedly take on a golden hue). She figures she can claim its presence as a potential reason why spirits are drawn to this place. That sounds like a thing.

"Thanks so much." Gretchen gives a smile and a small wave that's almost more of a salute, then turns and begins walking toward the brick house.

"Hey, hon, wait!" the woman calls out before Gretchen makes it more than a few steps.

She turns back around. "Yeah?"

"A bit of advice—stick to the paths."

She says it like she's an old local in a Yorkshire pub warning a young American tourist to *keep off the moors* and *beware the moon*. The side of Gretchen's mouth slides up. "Well, that sure sounds ominous!" she says.

The woman reaches her forearm over her eyes again, but still has to squint with the bright sun directly above. "Nah, there's just lots of dog shit in the grass and you're wearing those fancy little shoes."

"Oh. Right, thanks."

Gretchen is careful where she steps as she continues following the driveway. As she approaches, she takes in the tiny details of the farmhouse the same way she studies each person who comes into her shop for a séance. Her daddy taught her the importance of noticing the little things—chewed fingernails, the imprint of a removed wedding ring, under-eye bags—that can tell a great deal about a person. It applies to places too. Like here: The roof looks to be on the older side, but the white of the porch and trim is vivid and clean as if it's been repainted recently. A sign that Mr. Waybill has put some effort into the improvements he can afford in hopes it will help sell the property. Mrs. Van Alst subtly implied his financial situation is strained, which is why time is of the essence. Perhaps in his desperation, he'll be glad to have Gretchen here after all, True Believer or not.

She wishes she knew more about what she's getting herself into. But for someone usually quite chatty—Rachel must have gotten her penchant for oversharing from her mother—Mrs. Van Alst didn't provide Gretchen with all that much information about Gilded Creek or her *dear* friend Charles Waybill. Two hours of internet research last night turned up only the basics: Charles R. Waybill is seventy-eight (over a decade older than Daniel Day-Lewis, for the record!), he lost his wife, Ellen, two years ago, and he's lived in Derring Heights his entire life besides the year he served in the Navy during Vietnam.

Even without a ton to go on, Gretchen figures there are several different ways she could play this. Maybe she can claim the "ghost" preventing the sale is Ellen. Or an old war buddy. One of the prior generations of Waybills who ran the farm. A Union soldier who succumbed to illness on the property during the retreat from Antietam. Maybe it's all of them, working in cahoots. An ensemble cast! Go big or go home, right?

Usually, for her séances, she prefers to work out her strategy ahead of time. But this particular job isn't one she's run before. There are variables she can't anticipate. That's actually kind of exhilarating. She'll have to rely solely upon her instincts and people skills to convince Mr. Waybill to buy into the exorcism. Just like old times, with her dad. Except now she's doing someone a favor instead of stealing from them. And she's doing it alone, of course.

Which is for the better, really. She's gotten used to flying solo over the past few years.

She shoves away the memory of the letter from her father buried under the bills back in DC by focusing on how the farmhouse's front door is painted the same crisp, new white as the porch and the trim, with a rather charming old W-shaped brass door knocker. Before Gretchen can determine if there's also a doorbell, a dog sitting in the grass just inside the fenced area holding the goats lets out a loud, deep bark that makes her heartbeat falter. It's a huge white cloud of a dog—a fluffy marshmallow that could probably eat her in one bite. It lets out another bark, and she turns to knock frantically at the house's door.

Please answer. Please answer. Please answer.

She keeps her eyes on the dog, as if she might warn it away with her gaze alone. It's not that she's *afraid* of animals, exactly; they just make her *uneasy*. Gretchen is good with people. They're mostly predictable, and she's spent her whole life observing them. She understands them. Animals . . . well, she's pretty sure she once read an article about a monkey in a zoo biting the head off a seagull, Ozzy Osbourne–style.

The terror—no, not terror, because she's *not* afraid—the *unease* she feels as the dog continues barking at her absorbs all of her attention momentarily. So when the door finally swings open, she startles and takes a step backward.

Oh.

The man standing in the doorway isn't really that tall—several inches shorter than Yolanda's six-one, for sure—but Gretchen's petite stature and his slight elevation on the threshold contribute to the illusion that he towers over her. He stares down with hazel eyes that question who she is and why she's here, though the scrutiny manages to come across as more curious than unfriendly. His blond-brown hair has shampoo-commercial body that gives it a spectacular wave, his beard is short and neat and a tiny bit darker, more like caramel but with strands of a cinnamon color that—

"Hi." He looks left and right, as if searching for the source of what might have startled the strange woman at his door and then caused her to look at him silently for a truly uncomfortable amount of time. "Everything okay?"

"Is your dog going to eat me?" Gretchen blurts out.

The man peeks out from the doorway to stare at the dog, as if considering the question. When he looks at her again, he asks, "You an undercover pork chop by any chance?"

"Am I a . . . No. No, I'm a . . . human person."

"Ah. Probably not, then." He leans farther out of the doorway, causing Gretchen to take another step backward, and shouts, "Clyde! Get back to work, you bozo!" The fearsome giant cotton ball ignores the order and instead plops onto his side, tail thumping against the ground. "Useless," the man says to himself, rolling his eyes fondly. Then he turns back to Gretchen. "Sorry about that. So . . ."

"So?" she repeats.

"Can I help you with something?"

Gretchen shakes her head as if to clear it, but then realizes she's inadvertently implied that no, he can't help her, and quickly pivots into a nod. This is, she admits, not the smoothest first impression she's ever made. "Yes, actually. I'm looking for Charles Waybill?"

The man tucks a hand into his jeans pocket, and the movement draws Gretchen's attention to a large hole in the shoulder seam of his extremely ugly sage-green and neon-pink sweater, revealing a white cotton T-shirt underneath. "Yeah, that's me," he says. "I'm Charlie Waybill. What can I do for you?"

This man is, in no universe, anywhere close to seventy-eight. Gretchen estimates him to be in his early thirties, tops. "Oh. And you're sure there are no other Charles Waybills living here?" She glances past him, as if she might catch a glimpse of an elderly man hiding inside the foyer.

His eyes narrow slightly, and Gretchen suspects she's already misstepped. Maybe she's grown a bit rusty. When was the last time she met someone new anywhere that wasn't within the safety of her shop? All the better that she came out here, then. She's gotten too comfortable over the years—as her father's letter was surely meant to remind her—and that's no good. Gotta keep sharp.

"Yes," he says. "I'm fairly certain I'm the only Charles Waybill currently living here. What is this about?"

"Sorry, that was a stupid question. It's only that . . . Well, I'm looking for Deborah Van Alst's bridge partner? And—"

"Right. That's me."

Gretchen is aware of Mrs. Van Alst's tendency to avoid nick-names (Yolanda once reported her going on an absolute diatribe at the salon while relaying how a nurse at the dermatologist's of-fice dared call her *Deb*). So her not mentioning that Charles is ac-tually a Charlie isn't what's unexpected about this. It's more that Gretchen's public records search last night said this farm is owned by a septuagenarian Vietnam vet, not a handsome man with great hair and concerning taste in sweaters.

Also, who would ever guess that the person in front of her with his youth, beard, and broad shoulders would be a member of a bridge club? Bridge isn't exactly a stereotypical pastime for mil-lennials; Gretchen had to watch two YouTube videos and read the Wikipedia page to even figure out what it was, and still ended up with a lot more questions than answers.

"You know Deborah?" Charlie—and Gretchen has to admit that the diminutive definitely fits him better than the staid and formal *Charles*, whatever Mrs. Van Alst's opinion on such things—tilts his head and flashes a polite, pleasant almost-smile. There's suspicion lurking behind his eyes now, and her instincts bristle in response.

She takes a deep breath through her nose, trying not to let on that the way he's looking down at her makes her want to run in the opposite direction. Maybe even hide in a bush for good mea-sure. It's been a long time since she felt so . . . nervous? Is that what this clammy-hand, chest-tight feeling is? She's decidedly not a fan.

"Yes. My name is Gretchen. Gretchen Acorn. Mrs. Van Alst sent me here to help you sell Gilded Creek."

"Gretchen . . . Acorn." He says her name as if hesitantly tasting an ice cream flavor that's a little bit out there—olive oil, or sweet corn, maybe. Something he isn't sure will be to his taste, but he feels compelled to sample anyway. "You're a real estate agent, then? Sorry, I'm already working with someone at Coldwell—"

"No, I'm a spirit medium. Mrs. Van Alst told me you're having some . . ."—she finds herself incorporating that pause again—"paranormal activity around here and that it's affecting your farm's salability. She asked me to cleanse the property for you."

Charlie's sigh is audible. His chin drops so he's staring down at his bare feet. Gretchen takes a surreptitious glance at them too. They're several shades lighter than his tanned face, a little bony. Strangely handsome, she decides, though she isn't sure when she developed personal criteria for judging the attractiveness of men's feet. She forces herself to focus on the hole in Charlie's sweater instead, keeping her face neutral. But inside, her blood is buzzing, as if all of her Eichorn ancestors are chanting a warning: *danger, danger, danger*. Sure enough, when Charlie's eyes meet hers again, the suspicion that was there before has morphed into something colder and harder. No longer curious. Definitely unfriendly.

"Ah. So *you're* the charlatan," he says, crossing his arms in front of his chest.

DANGER, DANGER, DANGER!

That quiet warning crescendos into a scream that bounces around her skull, and her heart races as if trying to get a head start on fleeing the scene. She's able to keep the panic at bay enough to be vaguely surprised that it's occurring at all. This isn't the first time she's been accused of being a fraud. Especially early on, when she first set out on her own and started playing around with mediumship, there were a few unhappy marks who began hurling accusations. But she was always able to keep her cool and smooth those over. None of them triggered the fight-or-flight response coursing through her now. Flight isn't a real option, though. Not without looking guilty as hell. So, she decides, fight it will have to be.

Gretchen raises her eyebrows. "Sorry, I'm the *what*?"

"Oh, I think you heard me just fine," he says, voice full of venom. "Why don't you say it again? Just so I can be sure."

But Charlie doesn't repeat the word that sent her into a tailspin. Instead he says, "You're the . . . the . . . bullshitter taking Deborah's money, making her think she's been talking to Rachel."

And *that* makes Gretchen's heart do a weird little flip-flop. Because the way he's described her is so close to how she views herself that she feels suddenly exposed. Like she's standing naked on the porch in front of him. She should be frightened by how easily and quickly he's seen right through her, seen to the very essence of what she does, but instead it makes her . . . perversely excited? *He sees me.*

Charlie presses his lips together and shakes his bowed head. "You should really be ashamed of yourself. Stealing from people when they're grieving."

Or maybe he doesn't see anything after all if he thinks what she's doing for Mrs. Van Alst is the equivalent of theft. Gretchen puts her hands on her hips and leans slightly forward. "Hey, what gives you the fucking right to—"

"What gives me the right?" he interrupts. He leans forward too, the scent of citrus and crisp spring air and something earthy that might be hay drifting over with the movement. Now he isn't towering over Gretchen so much as . . . looming. "I've known Deborah practically my whole life. She's like family to me. I care about her."

"Yeah, whatever, sure you do."

He leans in even closer. "What's that supposed to mean?"

"If you care about her so much, where were you for the last nine months? Did you even visit her after the funeral? Because Mrs. Van Alst never once mentioned you, not until yesterday." She moves an extra inch toward the threshold and maintains eye contact. It's a little like staring into the eyes of a tiger while armed with nothing but a Nerf gun. "And Rachel's never mentioned you at all."

Such scant space separates them now that Gretchen has a front-row seat to the responding twitch in Charlie's jaw. But then his eyes dart away from hers, and his head drops again, de-escalating everything so suddenly it's almost more disorienting than an actual blow. "I've had my own stuff going on," he says to the porch. "Deborah understands."

"Excuses, excuses." Gretchen's instincts tell her she isn't going to get anywhere with this stubborn man unless she can rebuild the momentum of their argument. And win it. "Well, whether you like it or not, I *have* been there for her. She was in a bad place when she lost Rachel, but *I* helped her find the way back. And yeah, she pays me. But that's because she appreciates my gift, and that I use it to help people like her feel like they aren't so alone during some of the darkest moments of their lives. A gift Mrs. Van Alst asked me to come out here and share with you, though it really doesn't seem like you deserve my help, to be quite frank. If she hadn't already paid me, I would've been out of here the minute you started in with the insults and accusations."

Charlie's eyes once again pierce hers. They really are beautiful, she thinks, forcing herself to look past the intensity of his glare. So many shades of brown and gold and green, all marbled together. They remind her of the rainforest jasper she recently added to her stock of crystals at the shop.

"Goddammit. She paid you for this scam already?" He runs a hand over his face, suddenly looking like someone whose already overflowing plate has been filled with another unasked-for helping of a vegetable he doesn't even like. Gretchen almost feels sorry about it. "How much?" he asks, his voice quiet now in concession. "I'll write you a check. You might need to hold it for a few days but . . . Use it to refund Deborah's money. And then you have to tell her you can't do readings or whatever for her anymore."

"Ten thousand."

"Excuse me?"

"Ten thousand dollars," Gretchen repeats. "That's what she paid me to come out here and rid you of your ghost."

Charlie brings both hands to his head and pushes his fingers through his hair. "Jesus Christ, Deborah, what have you done?" he mutters, staring up at the place where the porch's roof meets the brick of the house. The position makes his biceps bulge under his horrible sweater, and the dark gold strands of his hair fall right back into place as soon as he lets go.

It takes a moment for Gretchen to refocus on the matter at hand, her brain as reluctant to pull itself away from watching his movements as an extra strong magnet resisting removal from a refrigerator. "Plus, if I'm going to tell Mrs. Van Alst she can no longer be my client, I'll lose . . . well, two hundred dollars twice a week . . ." He doesn't need to know that she was already planning on persuading Deborah Van Alst to come see her less frequently. "That's twenty thousand dollars for the year, rounded down. And a majority of my other business comes from her referrals, which I'm sure she'll no longer provide if I cut her off all of a sudden with no explanation, so let's make it forty to account for the harm to my reputation. Plus the original ten thousand. So sure, for fifty thousand dollars, I'll leave right now, refund Mrs. Van Alst's prepayment for this service, and cancel all her future appointments."

That muscle in his jaw twitches again, this time joined by a vein throbbing in his neck. "This is extortion," he says, voice so full of rage that Gretchen has to keep herself from flinching at the rawness of it.

"When it comes down to it, I run a business same as you, Mr. Waybill. And my time is valuable." Gretchen waits, watching as Charlie's hands clench into fists at his sides. She should probably be afraid of his anger, but instead finds it only emboldens her. "I also accept credit cards. If that's more convenient."

Then Charlie's fury breaks into something else, something more subdued on the outside but with a barely leashed quality that does actually scare her. He clutches the doorframe in either hand and leans in as close as possible. He looks past her, out toward the road, as if he doesn't trust himself to meet her eyes. "Get off my property," he says, his warm, peppermint-scented breath against Gretchen's forehead. "*Right now*, Ms. Acorn. Or I'll have you arrested for trespassing."

And the bright white door slams in her face.

4

THE CONFRONTATION WITH CHARLIE HAS GRETCHEN'S BODY
overflowing with energy, and if she doesn't find a way to discharge
it, she's worried she might explode like a can of soda forgotten in
the freezer. She tugs at the ends of the dark brown hair that falls
over her shoulders and lets out a guttural scream. Then she stomps
her feet on the porch a few times as if she's a large toddler, letting
the block heels of her boots make strong, loud contact. It helps,
but only a little.

"Fine!" she shouts, turning back to face the closed door. "I'd
rather lick a goat's asshole than help you anyway!"

Well. That was a very weird, very gross place to go with that.
Hopefully, Charlie got the gist of her fury without actually hearing the specifics of it.

She puts extra weight into each step to maximize the clomp
of her heels against the porch's wooden boards as she leaves. Once
she makes it back to the long driveway, her strides pick up speed;
the sooner she leaves this stupid farm, the better. She'll email Mrs.

Van Alst's assistant while she waits for a Lyft and inform Shruthi that she tried her best, but that Charlie's intense negative energy prevents her from doing the job. Which isn't far from the truth, anyway.

Gretchen figures she'll refund half of the ten thousand as a goodwill gesture. Maybe even two-thirds (she was supposed to be here for three days, after all). Whatever it takes to ensure Mrs. Van Alst continues telling everyone how honest Gretchen is and sending that word-of-mouth business her way. And to keep her from believing Charlie when he insists that Gretchen's a thief.

So much for getting ahead on next month's expenses. *This was such a waste of time.*

Her escape down the driveway feels infinite, even with Gretchen moving at such a brisk pace. If she requests her ride now, it'll probably arrive by the time she reaches the main road. The app connects Gretchen with Sulayman again, who she supposes couldn't have made it very far in the remarkably short time it took for this to all implode. Great, what luck. He's apparently fifteen minutes away. *Getting a Slurpee, maybe.* Fifteen minutes feels like too long of a wait to leave this place. Charlie might call the cops on her before then, or come out to shoo her away with a shotgun like some handsome live-action version of Elmer Fudd. She isn't up for playing the role of Bugs Bunny today. Not in this outfit.

Something in Gretchen's peripheral vision urges her to glance up from her phone just in time to see a man standing directly in her way. Her brain doesn't process it fast enough to slow her forward momentum, though, and they collide.

Except . . . they don't actually collide at all?

And then, all of a sudden, she's cold. *Painfully* cold. She chills easily to begin with, but this is a different level. It's like being encased in a block of ice. Gretchen clutches her arms, attempting to pull some minuscule amount of warmth from the brisk outside air and gather it closer to insulate her freezing bones.

Holy shit.

What the actual fuck.

The man is still there when she regains enough blood flow to turn around, confirming he wasn't a figment of her imagination. His young face is clean-shaven and ultra pale, not at all like the bearded and tanned Charlie's. He's dressed like a *Peaky Blinders* extra—newsboy cap, breeches, knee-high boots. As if Gretchen's attention on him is a physical thing, a tap on the shoulder or a smack on the back, his head bolts up. Bright blue eyes take her in from head to toe as a slow, crooked smile spreads across his face.

"Well, *hello* there," he says.

"What just— How did— Who are—" Gretchen's lips clamp shut, confusion and the lingering chill leaving her unable to produce a full, coherent string of words.

"Speechless, huh? I always did have that effect on the ladies." He winks cartoonishly and clicks twice with his tongue. "Been a while, though. Nice to know I've still got it."

I just— Who is— What— Gretchen has to remind herself to breathe. This is some kind of illusion, a trick. A rather impressive one, admittedly. But once she figures out what is going on here, everything is sure to make sense.

"I went *through* you," she says. It comes out like an accusation, which it sort of is. Just of what, she's not quite sure.

"Yep, that'll happen. Most people assume I'm a random cold spot and go on with their day. But you . . . you can see me, huh? Really, you can?" He waves a milky-white hand a few inches from her face and cackles at the way she flinches. "Isn't that swell! Ha!

Ha ha ha!" His laughter is strange, disbelieving. Almost as if he's as shocked to have encountered her as she is to have encountered him. "Oh, how I'd love to pick you up and swing you around right now, but, well . . ." He pokes Gretchen's shoulder and his finger disappears somewhere *inside* her body. Another severe chill results, frozen darts piercing her skin.

"What the fuck kind of trick is this?" she demands. Because it's becoming even more convincing by the second, and whatever is happening would be a complete game changer if she could figure out how to incorporate it into her séances. Except none of this makes any sense. Who would be trying to fool *her*? Here? And how? Why? Also, *what*??

This can't be real. It can't be.

"Ooh, salty language for such a cute little gal." The man's dark eyebrows shoot up. "But no tricks here! Just me, doin' my thing. The name's Everett. I'm Gilded Creek's resident ghost, and oh so very pleased to meet you." Everett holds out a hand to shake, then glances at it, lets out a chuckle and an "Oh, right." He dips instead into a deep showbiz-style bow.

This is frankly unbelievable. Therefore, Gretchen decides, she is not going to believe it.

Everett's smile inclines a bit farther as he waits for her own introduction. Instead, she stares at him with her lips pressed together, still trying to figure out how the hell this is being pulled off. She's read every book out there on nineteenth- and early twentieth-century séance tricks, along with the more modern hoaxes. But whatever this is? It's next level. Especially because the almost bluish tint of his skin looks like it's moving, something swirling like wispy clouds just under the surface. It would take CGI or holographic technology to make this so realistic, probably, and . . . well, Gretchen has to accept that the likelihood of someone flawlessly executing big-budget movie effects inches away from her face on a rural Maryland goat farm is approximately zero. The alternative is only ever so slightly more probable but . . .

Ghosts are real. Ghosts. Real. This is a ghost, standing in front of me. And he's real. A real . . . ghost.

"No. No, no, no," she protests, though to whom, she isn't quite sure. "It was all fake. The séances, the communicating with dead people. I was pretending. It was a fucking con! I was never actually *doing* it, so I can't be doing it now. You can't be . . ." Gretchen reaches out a hand to tug on Everett's sleeve, one final test, but her fingers find only air and come away numb as if she's been holding an ice cube for several minutes.

"Dead? As a doornail. Yep, sure am. Going on almost a hundred years now, I think? Time works kinda weird here in the In-Between, so I'm never exactly sure from minute to minute. Anyway, it's been a real lousy time without anyone to talk to. Doesn't stop me from talking anyway, of course. Just no one ever responds. Until now—until you!" He waves his hands in excitement, then throws one up toward the sky and slowly turns, gyrating his hips as he chants, "Ooga-chaka, ooga-ooga . . ."

Gretchen's knees wobble. All of her feels a little shaky, really. *This is a dream, all a dream. It's the only explanation that makes any sense.* She pinches her own arm to test that hypothesis and winces at the resulting pain—and at this weird, wild situation that is almost definitely actually playing out in her waking life.

"Were you alive when *Ally McBeal* was on?" Everett asks, still dancing. "I wasn't. Fun show, though."

Okay, it might not be a dream, but there is one last possibility: Gretchen has officially lost her mind. Maybe punishment for using her brain to deceive others instead of figuring out how to solve world hunger or something. That or all of her wasted good-person potential has turned into a subconscious-constructed specter sent by karma to kill her with irony.

"Sorry, I'm not doing . . . whatever the hell this is. I'm out. Peace." She resumes her walk down the driveway to the main road, walking with purpose even though what she really wants to do is run as fast as she can. Putting distance between her and the . . . ghost—*oh god, it's really a ghost?*—seems to be the best course of action. There's no way it's been fifteen minutes yet, but she hopes that by some miracle Sulayman and his Toyota Corolla will be waiting—

The cold smashes through her body again before the sight of Everett in front of her even registers.

"Ahh! Dammit fuck!" Gretchen shoves her hands into her armpits, trying (and failing) to find any lingering warmth there to ease the sudden severe ache in her joints.

"So . . ." He flashes another handsome, crooked smile. Under other circumstances, she thinks she might've appreciated just how much charm he manages to exude with that puckish tilt. "What's your name, doll?"

Gretchen doesn't say anything; if she refuses to talk to Everett, maybe he'll disappear. Then she can pretend this never happened and that she's still completely sane, or that the universe doesn't hate her, or whatever it is that's caused this reality derailment.

He claps his hands soundlessly and rubs them together. "Oh, are we playing a guessing game? That's fun. Though I suspect the names that were popular when I was alive and well aren't quite the thing anymore. Time marches on and all that. No problem! I've been keeping somewhat up-to-date. Let's see. Lucy? Maude? Uh, Monica? Phoebe? Oh! What about Pam? Angela? *The Office* was this century, right?" Gretchen maintains her silence. "Hm, maybe not a TV name, then." He taps his chin. "Charlie brought a Kayla around a few times recently. I say recently, but that might've been years ago for all I know. But I suppose it's unlikely you're also a Kayla. And he knows a Jess—oh, have you seen *New Girl*? Winston's my favorite."

Nope, she's already reached her limit. "Gretchen! Okay? My name is Gretchen. And as fun as this has been, I am not going to stick around and talk sitcoms with . . . with a *ghost*. So, my sympathies on you being dead and stuff, I guess, but I've gotta go now."

Everett holds out a hand before she can put one foot in front of the other, effectively blocking her from moving forward if she doesn't want to experience that bone-deep chill again (which she very much does not). "Wait, wait, wait. Gretchen. Doll. You cannot, you just *cannot*, leave."

"Oh yes, I can. In fact, I have to, since I'm technically trespassing right now. Charlie made it abundantly clear that if I didn't get off his property ASAP, he'd have me arrested. And I don't think he or the cops are gonna believe that the farm's resident *spirit* invited me to stick around. I'm not even fully sure *I* believe it. So if you'll please excuse me . . ." She makes a move to go around Everett, but—

Cold. So fucking cold.

"Stop doing that!" she yells when her vocal cords are thawed out enough to cooperate. "Jesus, you're like a person-shaped freezer."

"Freezer, what's a . . . oh, right, the extra cold part of the icebox. Where Charlie keeps those sad little one-person meals. And ice cream. I really miss ice cream." He stares off wistfully as if the mountains in the distance are large, unreachable scoops of mint chocolate chip. His head tilts as his focus returns to Gretchen. "I also miss pickles, of all things. Those big dill ones from the barrel. Didn't even like them that much when I was alive. Who'd have thought?"

"What do you *want* from me?" Gretchen's voice comes out as a combination of a shout and a whine. "I have a life. A business. I need to go back to DC. I can't stick around here for your amusement."

He pauses as if considering the question. "While there's a lot about you that I'm sure I would find *very* amusing . . ." The way Everett looks at her lands somewhere smack-dab in the middle of charming and overly intense—really his vibes in general. "What I actually want from you is your help."

"My help?"

"Yes. With Charlie."

She shakes her head. "Ha, well, sorry to break it to you, babe, but that guy hates my guts. There is no way I can help you with anything regarding Charlie."

Gretchen's phone vibrates, informing her of Sulayman's imminent arrival. Five more minutes. *Thank god.* She continues forward. This time, she decides, she isn't going to stop no matter how many times Everett makes her feel like she's been cryogenically frozen.

"Pleeeeeease," Everett begs from somewhere directly over her shoulder. A slight chill radiates from him the same way heat would off a living person. "What if I told you it's a matter of life and death?"

"Yeah, well, you're already dead, so I wouldn't be too concerned about it, to be honest."

"I might be, but Charlie isn't."

Gretchen stops in her tracks, as frozen as if Everett had touched her even though it was only his words that reached her ears.

"Not yet," he continues. "But he will be soon if we don't stop him from leaving."

5

GRETCHEN SPINS ON HER HEELS TO FIND HERSELF NOSE-TO-nose with Everett. Or, well, not nose-to-nose, since he's quite tall. Also, he kind of floats an inch or two off the ground, adding to their height difference. It's actually more nose-to-not-exactly-corporeal-chest.

"Ah, so that got your attention," he says.

Gretchen steps to the side to put space between them. "Explain," she orders.

"I'd love to." His focus drifts to something behind her. "But is that jitney here for you?"

"That what?" Sure enough, when she glances over her shoulder, a mud-speckled white sedan is waiting at the mouth of the driveway. *Five minutes, my ass.* "Shit," Gretchen says under her breath. Except this is good. Because now she can get in Sulayman's back seat, speed away from Everett and Gilded Creek Goat Farm, refund some of Mrs. Van Alst's money as penance, and leave this nonsense behind. Possibly even convince herself it never happened at all.

She pauses, half-turned toward the car.

If Charlie's life really is in danger and Gretchen is the only living person who is aware and therefore able to do something about it . . .

Ugh.

Having a conscience and something to prove is truly the worst combination for someone in this line of work, she thinks. No wonder her dad didn't want to do jobs with her anymore.

Sulayman sighs through the open passenger window. "You again, huh?"

"Yeah, me again, but . . ." Everett watches, a fist to his mouth as he waits to see what choice she'll make. His eyes light up, and he starts doing that damn *Ally McBeal* baby dance again as soon as Gretchen says, "I'm so sorry to have wasted your time, but I actually don't need a ride anymore."

Sulayman frowns more deeply. "There's a fee for that, you know."

"Yes, I know, but something came up just now and I can't leave yet."

His responding glare effectively communicates his mixture of ire and boredom and doesn't leave her until after he's rolled his window back up.

Gretchen calls out one final apology as the car pulls out of the driveway and onto the road. The rideshare app alerts her to the resulting charge to her credit card.

"You're *staying*! Woo-hoo!" Everett finally ceases his spinning and hand-waving. "We're going to have so much fun, you and me. Ev and Gretch on a mission. Like a buddy cop show."

"We are not going to have *any* fun together. The only reason I'm still here is to find out what the hell you're talking about. There is absolutely no guarantee—in fact, the likelihood is infinitesimally small—that I am sticking around longer than another few minutes. So you better get talking."

"Right." He nods. "Charlie. Gotta save Charlie."

"Tell me what you meant when you said he'll be dead soon if we don't stop him from leaving."

Everett strolls over to the post and rail fence—also freshly painted—that separates the property from the road and . . . well, he doesn't sit so much as he hovers above the top rail in a seated position. *Neat trick*, Gretchen thinks for a moment before remembering it's not a trick. Just the physics of being spectral, apparently.

"It's a sad, sad story," he says, his wide, delighted grin detracting somewhat from his words. "I suppose I should start at the very beginning." Instead of continuing with his explanation, though, he stares at Gretchen, waiting for permission.

She gestures for him to get on with it already.

"Right. So. As you can see, I'm a rather handsome fella." He waits again.

Anything except a confirmation is probably going to sidetrack this conversation and draw it out even longer, so Gretchen mutters, "Sure." Besides, she will admit that he is easy enough on the eyes. Well, if dead *Great Gatsby* stage production understudies are your thing, at least. They aren't really hers, but she could comprehend how someone might've been into Everett's whole vibe back when he was alive.

"Everyone was always saying, 'Everett, you could be the next Valentino, you have such an expressive face, you should be in

Hollywood pictures.' And oh, I *loved* the movies. Almost as much as I love television—though of course we didn't have that yet when I was alive. Such a neat invention, the television. But movies! They were really starting to pick up back then, simply spectacular stuff." He puts his hands out as if praising the film gods, then clasps them together again. "There was this gorgeous little tomato, Betsy Chandler—her family had a horse farm up the road a ways—and one time I took her out to the Opera House. But the whole time she kept trying to sneak kisses in the dark, can you believe it? She didn't even want to watch the picture! I had to say, 'Betsy, now, stop that, I'm trying to see what this Nosferatu fellow is getting up to—'"

"What does this have to do with Charlie, exactly?" Gretchen asks.

"Oh, right. Yes." Everett's smile returns, as if it's how he re-sets his focus. "So I thought about it for a while and realized every-one was onto something. I *should* be an actor in Hollywood." He counts off on his fingers as he says, "I had the looks. I had the talent. I had the drive. Especially the drive. In fact, I wanted it more than anything. But I was stuck here working this damn farm. The place was supposed to be the responsibility of my older brother, Robert, but he got himself killed during the war. Right at the end. Meuse–Argonne. And our parents passed soon after." His voice remains casual. Yet if there's one thing Gretchen knows (other than how to bullshit), it's how to spot grief. She clocks how it transforms Everett's face for a fraction of a second before he continues. "Left me . . ."—for a moment he pauses, then continues—"*trapped*, taking care of everything. And not just the farm, but also our ancient great-aunt, Lucretia Thorne—who man-aged to outlive us all, by the way, the witch. Did I ask for that responsibility? No! Didn't want it, not even a little bit. So one day I said to myself, 'Now, ol' boy, why are you simply accepting this life you've been saddled with? You have free will, don't you? At least, according to that pastor your mama used to drag you to every Sunday, and probably some philosopher or another. If you want to make something of yourself, do it! Go West, young man! Pursue your dreams!'"

Gretchen stares blankly. "Okay . . . And what does this have to do with—"

"I'm getting there, I'm getting there. So I told Aunt Lucretia, 'Auntie, I'm going to sell the farm, take you to live with Cousin George and his brood, and move out to California. I'm gonna be a film star.' And, well, Aunt Lucretia didn't like that, not one bit. Kept saying, 'There have always been Waybills at Gilded Creek.' She insisted that the property must be kept in the family. That I mustn't go, but stay, marry, and reproduce like my ancestors before me. That's what her grandfather intended when he built this place, she said. It was to be passed down through the generations, not sold off for quick cash to a railroad tycoon. Then she looked me in the eye and said—nay, she hissed!—'A terrible fate will befall you, Everett Waybill—'"

"I don't think you can hiss that. But wait. So you're a Waybill? You're related to Charlie?"

"Yeah. He's my . . ." Everett looks up and to the side as if counting, then draws some imaginary lines in the air with his finger. "It's something like first cousin three times removed? I never quite understood how all that works. It doesn't really matter. This is the important part, doll. Listen." His lips purse and his eyes narrow. Gretchen has to admit, his face *is* incredibly expressive. "Aunt Lucretia hissed, 'A terrible fate will befall you, Everett Waybill, if

you ever take one step off this farm without the intention of returning. A terrible, terrible fate.'"

"And then you left anyway?"

"Yep. Tried to, at least. Fell onto the tracks right as my train
was approaching the station in Harpers Ferry. And, well, splat!"
He must notice the way Gretchen's face contorts as he chuckles
at his gruesome death, because he shrugs and says, "If you can't
laugh about your mistakes, what can you laugh about?"

"Then what happened?" she asks.

"I kind of . . . poofed back here. And I've been hanging around
as a ghost ever since."

Gretchen considers the story. She has a lot of questions, and
it's challenging to settle on one, but eventually she starts with,
"How did the farm stay in the family? Hadn't you already sold it?"

Everett shakes his head. "The sale wasn't complete yet when
I left—the railroad fella who wanted to buy it was still dotting
some i's, crossing some t's and whatnot. He told me we could do
the final signatures through the mail once everything was together.
But then I was dead, so the property went to my next of kin, Cousin
George. Conveniently, he already had Aunt Lucretia at his place,
since I dropped her off with him just before going to the train
station. And I suppose *he* took the whole curse thing seriously,
because he immediately canceled the sale and brought his family
to live at Gilded Creek. Ol' George's progeny have been running
things here ever since. It was George, then Charles, then . . . well,
it skipped a generation with Chuck, since he had no interest in it.
And now Charlie."

Gretchen maps out this family tree in her head. She wonders
fleetingly what the deal is with Chuck, who is presumably Charlie's father. But of all the questions floating around her brain, that

seems like it belongs in the "low priority" pile. "So you think if Charlie tries to leave he'll get killed like you did?"

"Not only get killed but . . ." He trails off and looks around. "Do you see any other ghosts around here?" he asks.

"Uh . . ." Considering this seeing-ghosts thing is quite a new development, Gretchen isn't entirely sure if there are others about or not.

"No, you don't. And I'll tell you why. Because everyone else who died before and after me got to move on. They got to go Up. Understand?"

She tilts her head. "Not really, no."

"The terrible fate Aunt Lucretia cursed me with wasn't death. It was being stuck here, haunting this place." He pauses and his eyes shift back, forth, back again, with the dramatic intensity of someone who's been assigned the role of Street Crosser #1 in a movie. Apparently deciding it's safe, he bursts out with, "For *eternity*! I wanted to leave, so now I have to stay forever. And that's what will happen to Charlie too if he sells the farm."

"It's certainly a poetic punishment. Props to Aunt Lucretia for that, I guess." She bites her lip as she runs the story back over in her mind again. "But how are you so sure Charlie will meet the same fate? Has anyone else tried to leave in the decades you've been here? What if the curse only applied to you, or it expired or something?"

Everett scoffs. "I think I understand the terms of my own damnation, thank you. It's my job to ensure Gilded Creek stays within the family as long as the Waybill line exists, to keep my relatives—to keep Charlie—here and safe."

"So all that spooky shit was you? You *have* been intentionally scaring away everyone who wants to buy the farm?"

This is all getting wilder and wilder. First a ghost, now a family curse with life-and-death stakes? Gretchen pinches her arm again. *Ouch.* Nope, still not dreaming.

"Yes, and that's why I need your help. I've been successful so far, but one day I'm gonna encounter someone who isn't put off by a little haunting and my luck'll run out. No matter what I do, Charlie comes up with boring, alive-person explanations for it. Oh, it's the wind, it's old wiring, it's poor insulation, a lack of sleep. I tell you, the man's ability to rationalize is almost irrational. Only a matter of time until he finds a buyer who's the same way and Charlie leaves, heading straight for death and, well . . ." He stands from where he was float-sitting and gestures to his body and its cloudlike undercurrents. "This. *Forever.*"

Gretchen folds her arms and gives it one last shot. One last-ditch effort to convince herself she doesn't need to involve herself in this. "Is it really so bad? Aren't there some upsides to being a ghost?"

A seriousness comes over Everett's features, made startlingly more effective by its contrast with his previous demeanor. "I wouldn't wish it on my own worst enemy, much less a good guy like Charlie."

A sigh falls from her mouth. She won't be requesting another ride for a while (if she'll even be able to find another one once Sulayman is out of the area), so she tucks her phone into her backpack's front pocket. "How do you expect me to help you? I'm the last person in the world Charlie Waybill is going to believe about anything, much less *this.*"

Everett shrugs. "You'll make him."

"What?"

"You'll make him believe you," he repeats. "I'm sure you can figure it out. You said before you were only pretending to talk to the dead? That it was a con. So I assume you're some kind of fakeloo artist? A flimflam lady? And such a lovely one at that. I bet you've got some tricks up your sleeves."

Gretchen's instinct is to lament, *Why me, though?* But the more she turns it over in her mind, she starts to think maybe saving Charlie from death and eternal unrest is the perfect opportunity to test out her Rule—the ultimate way to prove that she can use her natural talents without doing more harm than good in this world. Then her father can say whatever he wants and she'll know, deep inside, finally and without a doubt, that he's *wrong* about her. Besides, this could be the challenge she needs to reboot her system, to get back the excitement that used to come with pulling off a job.

Really, the possibility of her gotcha euphoria returning might be worth it alone. That, and the ten thousand dollars she could definitely keep with a clear conscience.

"True," she admits, smiling at the thought. Charlie is certainly a tough customer, but Gretchen has confidence in her skills. She'll make it happen. Whatever it takes. Why her? Because she's great at what she does, that's why.

"Attagirl." Everett grins back at her. For a second, it feels like Gretchen's a kid again, her daddy humoring her by letting her take the lead on planning a simple job. Her heart twinges at the mix of memories—so many highs and so many lows intertwined with them. Maybe if she pulls this off, she could open that letter waiting for her back in DC. Maybe she could even throw it away.

With a shake of her head, she clears the unwanted thoughts of her father and walks back toward the house, examining the property and idly searching for inspiration as she goes. Everett follows like a seagull trailing someone eating french fries. "If this has any chance of working, I need to find a way to get Charlie talking to me again," she says. "Our last interaction ended . . . not so great." She should stop and google to see if this Charles Waybill has any social media. Then again, perhaps she has a much more valuable resource right here. "What do you know about him?" she asks.

"What do I know about Charlie? What *don't* I know about Charlie! I've been around since he was a baby visiting his grandparents here. I watched him grow into the strapping young man he is today. It all started when his father was born, back in January of '63. There'd been a snowstorm, and—"

"Can we speed this up?" she asks. "I know time is meaningless to you, but some of us still have, you know, lives to live."

His smile droops, and a stab of remorse prompts her to hold up a hand. "I'm sorry. That was insensitive of me. I would really appreciate it if you could tell me a bit about Charlie, what he's like when he isn't threatening to call the cops on people."

Everett looks to the sky, contemplating how to answer the question. "Hm. Well, the first thing you need to know about Charlie Waybill is that he's a genuine good egg. And his yolk's real runny."

Gretchen grimaces. "What's that mean? It sounds gross."

"It means he's got the softest heart."

"Oh. I see."

"He can't help himself from helping people, no matter how big of an inconvenience for him or how much they don't deserve it. He'd give his worst enemy the shirt off his back. And if he loves a person, well . . . pretty sure he'd give them anything in the world. His grandmother, Ellen—she was the same way. Compassion always won out over everything else."

"Interesting," she says. "So you think he'd help me if I needed it, even though he doesn't like me?"

"Oh, Gretchen, sweetheart, I'm counting on it." He grins. "Sorry in advance."

"Huh? What are you—"

Then she's jerked forward, and the cold overtakes her before she hits the ground with a *splash*.

6

THIS MUST BE WHAT IT FEELS LIKE TO DO THOSE POLAR
Plunge events where people run into bodies of water in the middle of the winter. Except instead of the ocean or a lake, Gretchen's face down in one of the largest muddy puddles bordering the driveway. Which is kind of warm thanks to the midday sun, so it must just be her blood that's frozen.

With her head elevated enough that she won't swallow dirty water if she opens her mouth, she shouts, "Did you just fucking *push* me?"

Everett doesn't respond, the coward.

Her attempts at getting up are almost Sisyphean, her hands and boots unable to find traction in the slippery mud. It's reminiscent of quicksand, the way she sinks deeper into it the more she struggles. Plus, her clothes are now thoroughly saturated. Eventually, exhausted and certain the damage is already done, Gretchen gives up and rolls over like a rotisserie chicken until she's sprawled out in a dry spot of grass. She stares up at the cloudless sky, its blue antagonistically similar to that damn ghost's eyes, and wonders again if this might be a dream after all—no, a nightmare. And also if it's possible to strangle someone who's already dead.

The thin, wet fabric of Gretchen's dress clings to the tops of her thighs. Her knees are thoroughly caked in mud and slivers of dead grass. And her hair feels as if a large snake/rodent hybrid drowned and its corpse was laid to rest upon her forehead. She's going to need to do some research to figure out if her pleather jacket is salvageable. No googling necessary to determine that the suede of her boots will never fully recover. At least she has a few changes of clothes—*Ah, shit!* Her backpack still rests in the deepest part of the puddle. She scrambles to her knees and grabs it, but the canvas is as muddy and soaked through as she is. Her wallet, phone, and phone charger have thankfully escaped undamaged in their external pocket, but even at first glance she can tell that almost everything inside the main compartment of the bag is contaminated with puddle gunk.

"Dammit fuck, Everett Waybill, I'm going to—"

Except Everett is nowhere to be found. In fact, no one, living or dead, is in sight. A goat bleats in the distance as if to say, *You're on your own, lady.*

So . . . Everett pushed her and then he *disappeared.* That's somehow more insulting than if he'd stuck around to point and laugh.

The way her satin underwear squishes against her skin as she moves is something she'd be happy to never experience again. And it's a reminder that even if she could leave now, there's no way Sulayman would allow her inside his car in this state.

The whole point of this, she assumes, was to give her an excuse to approach Charlie again. A fairly smart idea, she concedes, though it doesn't erase her anger at Everett for the way he executed it. Still, she might as well head back to the farmhouse and hope this drenched and pathetic version of herself elicits enough pity to earn her an invitation inside.

"You better've been right about this," she grumbles in case Everett has gone invisible somehow and is still able to hear. (After everything that's happened so far today, she's not sure what all is within the realm of possibility, and she figures it best not to discount anything.)

Gretchen takes the shortest path to the house, cutting diagonally through the grass because really, who cares about dog poop when she's already looking like something that would crawl out of a swamp in a low-budget sci-fi film.

She breathes a sigh of relief to see that Clyde, the menacing marshmallow by the fence, has followed the goats to another, farther-away part of their enclosure. Her next breath hitches momentarily as she spots Charlie standing on the porch as if he's been waiting for her to come slinking back. His features soften as he takes in her unfortunate state, and his lips part to speak. Then his extreme dislike of her must kick in again, his eyebrows sinking into a V as his expression sours. The transformation takes only a fraction of a second, and Gretchen finds herself torn between bracing for his animosity and wanting desperately to know what he was going to say before he thought better of it.

"Pretty sure I told you to leave," he calls out, folding his arms over his chest to add an extra dose of hostility. His body language and his words deliver the message that he's completely on guard, but Gretchen catches his eyes doing a quick sweep over her messy body one more time, as if double-checking her for overt injury.

Everett was right; Charlie Waybill is softhearted, no matter how much he might hate her at this very moment. That's something she can work with.

She stops at the bottom of the three steps leading to the porch, daffodils on both sides, and gazes up once again into his hardened stare. "You did. And I was leaving. I just . . . I . . . Well . . ." Then she drops her bag and bursts into tears. Crying on demand was one of the first skills Gretchen mastered while apprenticing with her father. She uses it much more sparingly as an adult, but still, it does have its place.

"Hey, now, hey," Charlie says, leaping from the porch to the ground without bothering to take the stairs. In Gretchen's experience, a crying woman sends most men into a tailspin, and she suspects that for someone as compassionate as Everett said Charlie is, this is absolute torture. He puts a strong hand between her shoulder blades and guides her to the porch. The touch makes her feel dry and warm and okay until he takes his hand away and she remembers she is none of those things at the moment.

"Sit," he orders. "Breathe."

Gretchen lowers herself to the top step, her dress squishing under her weight and releasing a small pool of water beneath her bottom. Charlie stands on the opposite side of the stairs, leaning against the railing and drying his palm on his jeans. The motion draws her attention to his thighs, and—wow. Manual labor makes a man *sturdy*. But the position also creates the illusion of him looming over her again, and she feels so . . . small. At a disadvantage. Something she rarely is and doesn't particularly like to be.

She chokes down a tiny bark of laughter as she thinks about how the man always seems to be looking down at her. It's funny.

But also not, because the thought of how poorly Charlie thinks of her and how clear he's been about it pulls a melancholy *something* to the forefront. More tears slip down her cheeks, these not quite as fake as the ones that came before. Weird.

"I . . . There was a big, gross puddle," she says, deciding to skip how she wound up making full-body contact with it for the time being.

"Are you hurt?" His tone now sounds less concerned about her than about his homeowner's insurance premiums.

"No, but I'm . . . I'm really wet and cold and muddy, and all of my stuff is soaked, so I can't— I just— I really was going to leave, but now I can't get in a rideshare like this and—" Gretchen feels herself running out of air and leans into the absolute overwhelmingness of this afternoon. Of her initial confrontation with Charlie, and this one. Of meeting Everett and learning that ghosts are indeed real and that she is, for some reason, able to communicate with (at least) one of them. And also that she is now responsible for saving another person's *life*. That's . . . well, that's a fucking *lot* to deal with, even for someone good at rolling with punches. Which she used to be, but her spirit medium gig hasn't exactly thrown her many lately, and she's coming to realize she's out of practice.

Charlie lets out a sigh and goes to retrieve her discarded, sopping-wet bag from the walkway. He holds it out to her, and the corner steadily drips onto the stair's tread—one, two, three times—before she takes it from him. "Come on," he says. "Get up."

"But I—"

"You can take a quick shower, change clothes. Then you're out of here. Got it?"

Gretchen hauls her bag onto her shoulder, smiling to herself as Charlie turns away to open the front door. Everett's still on her shit list for pushing her into the puddle, but his plan did work. She's inside the house now, which is farther than she got on her own.

I still want to kill him, though. Or, re-kill him, rather.

She follows Charlie into the narrow foyer, then up a flight of creaky stairs to the second floor. He leads her to an open door at the top of the landing. Gretchen peeks inside. A bathroom, painted a pale yellow color reminiscent of the daffodils along the porch. The floor is covered in small, white tiles, and a claw-foot tub sits at the far end, the curved rod around it holding up a navy-blue floral shower curtain, scrunched to one side. The fixtures are on the older side, but it's all well-kept and clean, especially considering this farmhouse seems to be a bachelor pad.

"Towels are in the corner cabinet," Charlie says.

Gretchen continues inside, then turns around. There's the beginning of a strange sensation swirling around in her chest, something that feels like vulnerability. She latches onto it, detaching herself enough to use it as a mental exercise. *This is what a person feels in this situation.* She hugs her bag to her chest. *And it makes her want to shield herself.* It was one of the things her father taught her from the very beginning: Put your emotions to work for you, let them advise your behavior, but don't let them take control. Because looking vulnerable is great; actually *feeling* it is a liability.

"Thanks," she says. "I really appreciate your help."

"Yeah, well, this is probably a huge mistake." Charlie turns to leave, but pauses with his back half to her. "Just do me a favor and try not to steal anything, okay?"

He closes the door at the same time the insult registers. "I'm not a thief!" Gretchen shouts. But for all she knows he's already long gone and her protest doesn't reach him.

She drops her backpack onto the toilet's lid and unhooks its closure. As she anticipated, the puddle did a number on her belongings. Thankfully, one bra and a pair of underwear have been left unharmed. And there's a T-shirt and pajama shorts that are slightly damp in spots, but serviceable enough.

"Wowza. Women's unmentionables have really changed, haven't they?"

Gretchen spins around at the sound of the voice, simultaneously surprised and not surprised to find Everett in the bathroom with her. "Jesus! Don't sneak up on me like that."

"That lacy black thing you're holding—wooo." His eyebrows jump, then his head tilts as he examines the thong in her hand. "How does it . . . work?"

"No. No commenting on my underwear. Actually, no talking to me at all. I'm extremely pissed off at you."

"At me?" He places a hand over his heart with the affectation of an offended southern lady. "What did I do?"

"What did you do? Seriously? You pushed me into a gigantic puddle."

"Oh, right. That." Everett attempts to casually lean against the bathroom door, his elbow going through the wood. "Sorry, doll, but I had to do it. And it worked, didn't it? Got you inside the house."

"But *how* did you do it?" Gretchen asks, remembering the frigid push against her lower back and the terrifying rush of falling forward as that painful cold burst into her limbs. "Whenever we came into contact before, we went through each other. You go right through everything solid." She gestures to the situation with his elbow and the door. "But I felt you touch me."

"Right. So I, uh, actually *can* touch things, if I focus real hard," he says. "But it takes a lot of effort and energy, and it kind of hurts to do. Not physically but like, psychically? And it makes me poof."

"Poof?"

"Yeah, into the Nowhere. Which is unpleasant. So I don't do it too often." He scratches at his dimpled chin. "Oh, by the way, how long was I gone? I've always wondered."

"I don't know. Ten minutes, maybe?"

"Oh, not that long, then. I never could tell if it was a minute or two months. Time is confusing enough in the In-Between, but in the Nowhere it's like it doesn't exist at all. Disorienting as heck when I come back out the other side."

Gretchen's curiosity annoyingly wins out over her desire to end this conversation and peel off her soggy clothing. "What, exactly, is the Nowhere?" she asks.

Everett shrugs one shoulder. "It's, well, it's nowhere. It's dark, except also light. And so, so loud. But also silent? Mostly it's like I simply cease to exist for a bit. I'm not a big fan. I enjoy existing, even if it's only as a ghost." He looks her up and down as if assessing the damage, and then his eyes stop on the muddy backpack atop the toilet's lid. "Anyway, sorry about your bag there. I would've moved it out of the way, but that would have poofed me before I could push you. And, well, needs must and all that."

The wet fabric of her clothing chafes her clammy skin as she reaches for the towel cabinet. "You could've just told me what you were thinking and I could've fallen in myself. And spared my bag."

"Hey, now, that would've been a good idea." Everett stands

straighter. "Say, you should definitely be the brains of this operation."

Gretchen rolls her eyes. "I have to admit that the thoroughness of the damage is probably more convincing. But no more touching me without permission. Got it?"

"Aye, aye, captain," he says, grinning. "Say, you showering now? Mind if I stick around?"

"What? Yes, I absolutely mind. Get out."

"Aww, but I asked so nicely! And I usually don't even have to ask, so I think I deserve some credit for bothering."

Gretchen is actually talking to a ghost after years of pretending to do just that, and he's trying to convince her to get naked in front of him. *Men.* "Is that how you get your kicks? Watching people shower?"

"Look. People just come into the bathroom when I happen to be in here and . . ." Everett mimes someone disrobing. "It's not like I *request* to be privy to their skivvies."

"Right, and you're just hanging out in the bathroom because . . . ?"

He shrugs. "Flattering lighting?"

She gives him her most judgmental look, even though she'd probably do the same in his circumstances. In fact, Gretchen decides, anyone who says they wouldn't take advantage of being invisible in a somewhat gross way at least occasionally is probably lying. "You're a pervert, Everett Waybill," she chides as a formality.

"Hey, being dead is a real snore. I take what I can get. Besides, people can't even see me—except you, of course—so no one's the wiser. No harm, no foul, right?" He pauses. "So, um . . . that's a no on sticking around while you undress, then?"

She takes off a soggy boot and throws it at his head. It sails right through and hits the door behind him, leaving a splatter of mud in its wake. "Out!"

"Fine, fine, I'm going," he says, then walks through the wall into the next room.

Even though any remaining doubts Gretchen had that Everett is truly not among the living were thoroughly squashed by him poofing out of and back into the physical plane, watching him do things that shouldn't be possible still takes a massive mental toll. So her brain is stalled when a knock comes at the door. Considering knocking would apparently cause Everett to disappear again, that must be Charlie.

Gretchen answers the door, half expecting an inquisition regarding to whom she was talking. Maybe an accusation that she was calling some accomplice to give a status update. But instead Charlie averts his eyes (despite her only having removed a single boot so far) and says, "I didn't hear the shower yet and I thought I should . . . I thought you might need . . . for your wet things," then thrusts a kitchen-size trash bag in her direction.

"Thank you. That's very thoughtful."

His tan from long days working outside does little to hide the blush that overtakes his cheeks as he meets her eyes. "I'll be in the kitchen." He turns and hurries away, stomping down the stairs like he's taking them as fast as possible.

Well, that was interesting.

Could it be that Charlie Waybill is attracted to her? Or is it only pent-up hatred that has him all flustered? Perhaps it's a combination of both. Regardless, it gives Gretchen a potential advantage. Only a fool would pass up the chance to use it, especially when the conversation she's about to have is going to be tricky, to say the least.

So she turns the water on, then gathers up the few remaining semidry clothes she has and shoves them under the showerhead until they're also soaked through.

7

EVERETT IS WAITING IN THE HALL WHEN GRETCHEN COMES out of the bathroom wearing nothing but lacy thong underwear and a damask-patterned towel.

His blue eyes descend her body in businesslike assessment this time, nodding in approval when he reaches her legs. "Nice getaway sticks." He rubs his hands together. "Are we going to talk to Charlie now? Ooh, can we do good cop, bad cop? I'll be Stabler, you can be Benson."

Gretchen frowns.

"No, you're right. You should be Stabler. You're definitely the more believable loose cannon."

"Neither of us is going to be Stabler," she says.

"We're doing Benson and Amaro? Hm, interesting choice."

"We're not doing Benson and anybody."

Everett pokes at the dimple in his chin. "Briscoe and Green, then?"

"Oh my god." Gretchen groans. "No one is going to be anyone from any branch of the *Law & Order* franchise."

"Got it." Everett rocks back and forth on his toes, half an inch above the floorboards. "What about Starsky and Hutch?" Gretchen's face must adequately convey her feelings on this because he holds his hands up in capitulation as he floats backward down the stairs. "Okay, okay. No good cop, bad cop. So what are we doing?"

"*We* aren't doing anything," Gretchen says, the old stairs letting out a veritable symphony of squeaks and creaks as she descends. "*I* am going to go into the kitchen to ask Charlie if I can borrow some clothes, hopefully distracting him from how much he hates me with my—what did you call them?—my 'getaway sticks,' and then I am going to tell him everything you've told me and hope for the best. *You* will stand by in case I need further information, but otherwise you are to be completely silent."

"Except for when—"

"*Completely*. Silent," she reiterates, narrowing her eyes.

Everett does a pirouette around the end of the banister, passing through the bottom steps so that the lower half of his body is momentarily inside the staircase. "Mm, yeah, not sure that's going to work for me."

"What do you mean it's not going to work for you?"

"Well, I haven't had a reason to be quiet in a looooong time, doll. And now you expect me to be able to keep my yap shut on command?"

"Yeah, that's exactly what I expect. And if you want my help fulfilling your cursely obligations, you'll try your best not to distract me when I need to focus." She glances around the foyer. "Kitchen?"

"Right this—ah—" Everett presses his lips together and mimes locking them with a key, which he then pretends to throw over his shoulder before sweeping his hand in front of him and bowing his head like an obsequious butler in a period drama.

He leads her to an open doorway, through which is a large kitchen with dated appliances, butcher-block counters, and a square oak table in the center of the room. The walls are covered in wallpaper that features apples or maybe cherries—some fruit, it's hard to tell, really, given how faded it is. It isn't chic. Definitely not the "farmhouse" decor Gretchen has seen on HGTV. But it's so, well, *cozy*, that it makes Gretchen immediately imagine the numerous pies and scrambled eggs and pot roasts produced here over the years. The kind of home cooking she's only ever really experienced at hole-in-the-wall family restaurants on the road, never at anyone's actual *home*. Her stomach growls at the same time her heart aches. Probably hunger-induced indigestion.

Charlie sits at the table, his chair turned to the side. He has his left ankle propped on his right thigh and an open hardback book resting at the junction. With the afternoon sun coming through the window over the sink highlighting the gold of his hair and turning the amber strands in his beard into tiny streaks of fire, he looks like some sort of fierce angel. Maybe the one that would have warned Gretchen that this was a bad idea if she hadn't evicted it from her shoulder back in 2005, leaving a flashing vacancy sign that seems to have attracted an extra devil.

Speaking of, Everett wanders past her into the kitchen. He hunches behind Charlie, staring down at his book. Charlie's shoulder twitches, a small shiver at the slight change in temperature. The family resemblance is undeniable now that Gretchen sees the men together; their coloring is different—Everett pale, blue-eyed, and dark haired under his tweed cap; Charlie sun-kissed, hazel-eyed, hair straddling that line between blond and light brown. But they have the same slightly too large nose, matching wide mouths.

Gretchen can't help but wonder if Charlie's smile would also be charmingly crooked. But given the animosity between them, it seems unlikely she'll ever find out.

Not that she cares anyway.

She clears her throat.

Charlie glances up from his reading half-heartedly. Then, as he absorbs the reality of Gretchen Acorn in apparently nothing but a towel, she wins his full attention. He uncrosses his legs, and the book falls with a loud *thump* to the floor.

"Why aren't you dressed?" he asks, directing the question not to Gretchen but to the book—*The Great Pyramids of Minnesota* by Hollis Hollenbeck, she recognizes, having recently read it herself after an exuberant redheaded woman foisted a copy upon her in the National Archives cafeteria—as Charlie leans down to grab it from where it's tented itself on the yellowed linoleum.

Attracted. He's definitely attracted to her. And she's sure he doesn't want to be, because it's not like she wants to find him appealing either. It isn't exactly convenient. That the sleeves of the awful green-and-pink sweater are now pushed up to reveal strong forearms (and are those tattoos?) makes her downright annoyed. But this is ultimately good, in a way. Because if he's attracted to her, it's another thing she can use to draw him in and convince him to trust her. She's certainly not above subtly exploiting Charlie's weaknesses to ease her way. As long as hearts never get involved—which, why would they?—a little light seduction doesn't break her Rule.

Everett wanders over to the counter and does his freaky float-sitting thing atop it. He has both hands pressed to his mouth, covering his wide grin. The scene playing out between Charlie and Gretchen might be some of the most interesting non-television drama he's witnessed in years, if not decades.

"My changes of clothes are all wet too," she says, wrapping her arms around her chest to ensure the towel stays put. It also pushes her breasts together more, emphasizing the cleavage peeking out over the top. "I was hoping I could maybe borrow—"

Before she can finish the sentence, Charlie springs up and leaves the room. The sound of his heavy footsteps stops a short distance down the hall. There's a slight creak as a door opens.

Everett leans over until his head is sticking through the wall. "He's in the laundry room," he says, straightening again. Then adds, "Oh, right," as he remembers he's supposed to be quiet and refastens his lips, throwing away a second imaginary key. This one imaginary-lands near the fridge.

Charlie returns to the kitchen and hands her a red-and-black buffalo plaid flannel shirt. Pretty staid, considering she was half expecting another crime against color theory. The soft, worn material is still slightly warm from the dryer.

"Keep it," he says, retaking his seat at the table and picking up his book again.

"Oh. Thank you." Shirt off his back, indeed.

"Only because I don't want to give you any excuse to come back here ever again."

"And to think I was starting to consider that you might not be a jerkass after all." That gets his attention. Charlie's eyes meet hers with that same look from earlier that makes her blood simmer.

"Gretch, I don't think this is—" Everett starts, but as soon as she shoots a quelling look his way, he claps his hands over his mouth again, muffling the rest of his sentence into "ummummfrur-fururmurmm."

If Everett was about to warn her this isn't the best way to lead into the whole curse discussion, she doesn't need to hear it. She can already tell by the responding furrow of the farmer's brow and the way his arms cross over his chest that he has his hackles all the way up again. Angering him might earn her his full focus and make it feel like there's something hot and carbonated running through her veins. But it's certainly not going to make him receptive to what she has to say. She should know better—*does* know better. *Get your head in the game, Gretchen, geez.*

"Sorry," she says, biting her lower lip. His eyes catch the movement and linger on her mouth for one second, two seconds, three before he remembers to glance away. "Today's been . . . unexpected, to say the least. Though I realize that's not an excuse for being rude, especially when you've been so kind to me. I know you've asked me to leave, but I can't until I talk to you about something. Something really important. Like, life-and-death important."

As she speaks, she maneuvers the flannel shirt over her arms and grabs it at the center to close it. Once she has a few buttons buttoned at the top, she allows the towel underneath to fall to the ground. Charlie's Adam's apple bobs as he swallows, and he redirects his focus to the book in his hands as if it's a life preserver and he's noted the sea looks particularly choppy today.

Well, at least he seems to like *something* about her. She bends over to pick up the fallen towel, aware that the shirt's hem rides up to reveal a tiny sliver of butt cheek in the process. Charlie can't look away quite fast enough this time when she stands back up and holds the towel between her fingertips. *Caught you.* Suppressing the wolflike grin that tugs at the corner of her mouth, she asks innocently, "Where should I put this?"

He clears his throat. "Throw it over a chair. I'll take care of it later. What do you need to talk to me about? Make it quick. I have a lot of work to do and you've already taken up almost an hour of my day."

She looks to Everett. *Here goes nothing.*

"Right. Sorry. So, um, funny story. Sort of. Maybe not." Her attempt at sheepishness doesn't soften Charlie's stony expression, so she seamlessly drops it, adopting a more direct tone to signal she isn't trying to waste his time. "I was on my way to the main road to catch my ride back to the city and I literally ran into the ghost who's been causing trouble around here. His name is Everett. Everett Waybill. He's your distant cousin, actually. A contemporary of your great-grandfather's. And he's right over there." The spirit himself, still atop the counter, gives a little wave even though Gretchen is the only one who can see it. "He, uh, says hello."

Charlie doesn't bother looking where she's pointing. Instead his eyes narrow, and his lips part. To say something cutting, no doubt. Gretchen holds up a hand to stop him. "Wait, let me finish before you start calling me names and threatening to have me arrested or whatever, okay?"

She gets a slow blink in response that's probably the closest thing to assent she can expect.

"So it turns out Everett is stuck haunting the farm for eternity because he tried to move to Hollywood in the 1920s and his great-aunt cursed him for it. Like, actually cursed him. The reason he's been sabotaging your efforts to sell Gilded Creek is because the same fate will supposedly befall you if you leave. The curse dictates that this place has to stay in the Waybill family, and anyone who tries to abandon their responsibility to it by leaving with no intention of returning without another Waybill taking over meets with an immediate tragic death and becomes a spirit tied to the land forever." Gretchen gestures Vanna White–style toward the ghost on the counter. "Which is what happened to Everett. Did I miss anything, Ev? Was that all correct?"

Everett opens his mouth, remembers his vow of silence, and instead gives her two thumbs-up and a nod.

"Yeah, that's about the whole of it," she says. "So, you see, Mr. Waybill, I know I came here saying I was going to help you sell your farm, but actually, you need to take Gilded Creek off the market immediately. And assuming you don't have a Waybill relative willing to move in, you're gonna need to stick around for . . . well, the rest of your natural life. Anyway, sorry to be the bearer of bad news, but that's what Everett said I needed to tell you. I actually wound up in that damn puddle because he pushed me in, so I'd be forced to come back to the house and talk to you. And now that you know everything, I'm more than happy to be on my way. Unless you have any questions before I go?"

Every inch of Charlie's body is so tense she wouldn't be surprised if a speck of dust settling on his person would be enough to crack him into a thousand pieces. "I have to hand it to you, Acorn," he says after what feels like minutes but must be only a few seconds of silence. His voice is deep and quiet, that barely leashed tone from the porch earlier that makes something inside her crackle and pop like Rice Krispies in milk. "You have some real goddamn nerve." He's half standing now, palms flat on the table. It's not the right thing to focus on at the moment, she knows, but Gretchen is completely entranced by his forearms again, the way the muscles there flex as he leans slightly forward. There's a baby goat tattooed on his left one, and a sunflower beneath it, above his wrist. Both are in a traditional style with bright colors, reminiscent of a stereotypical old-school sailor. Charlie starts speaking again, pulling her attention back to his face before she can make out the letters printed beneath the goat. "I tell you to leave, so you throw yourself into a puddle and come here all teary-eyed with a story about a ghost and a family curse to get a second chance at trying to scam me?"

"I am not trying to scam you." Gretchen looks him directly in the eye to make it clear she's being genuine. Never mind that she would do that even if she were lying; she's very good at it. Sometimes at night when she can't sleep, she stands in front of a mirror and says things she knows are untrue to reassure herself she has no tells. If she does, she hasn't spotted them yet. "Whatever you might think of me, it's imperative that you believe I am being one hundred percent honest with you right now."

He stands fully, again somehow feeling like a larger presence than he actually is. Even at the opposite side of the table, her heart thumps as if he's only inches away and staring down at her.

DANGER, DANGER, DANGER!

"So you're being honest with me *right now.* Which means you weren't being honest earlier. Which is it, Acorn? Am I supposed to trust you or not?"

She doesn't particularly appreciate the cheap gotcha in the way he asks the question, though she reckons it's fair. "Yes! You are supposed to trust me—*need* to trust me—because I am telling you the truth. And if you didn't hear me earlier, your *very life is at stake*, so it's kind of super important that you take this seriously, regardless of your completely unfounded negative personal feelings about me."

Gretchen never particularly enjoyed the story of the boy who cried wolf. Probably because when she read it in their fables unit at whatever elementary school she was in at the time, the teacher took away her recess privileges after she raised her hand and pointed out that none of this would have happened had the boy not tried to pull off the same con on the same group of people over and over (seriously, that's Grifting 101). But she's starting to think that maybe she understands the moral of the story after all— albeit twentysomething years later.

"How can I prove it to you?" she asks. "Would it help if I told you things that only someone who's been creeping around here for a hundred years would know? Everett, hit me with some little-known facts about our friend Charlie here."

Everett's face lights, overjoyed at the opportunity to speak. He jumps down from the counter and taps at his chin. "He still sleeps with a teddy bear."

"You sleep with a teddy bear," she tells Charlie.

Charlie's eyes widen, but his hands come to his hips. "I can't believe you went into my bedroom. I knew I shouldn't have left you up there alone."

"No, Everett told me. Just now. And its name is . . ."

"Teddy," Everett supplies.

"Teddy," she repeats.

Charlie pauses before saying, "And how could you possibly guess that?"

"Hey. Not my fault you chose something so unimaginative. What else do you have for me, Ev? Preferably something that he can't write off as a lucky guess."

Everett makes a series of *hmm* noises as he thinks. "Charlie's left-handed."

She shakes her head. "Too obvious." In fact, Gretchen already noted that when he reached for the book earlier.

"But he always uses his right when he's doing the ol' one-two."

"What does that—"

"You know," Everett says, curling his fingers and pumping his fist a few times near his hips.

"Jesus, Everett. Not that sort of information," she says as heat washes over her face.

"You said a little-known fact! It doesn't get more little-known than that."

It is . . . too easy for her to imagine that for some reason. Now she can't *not* imagine it, in fact. She spent enough time studying Charlie's hands and forearms a minute ago that it's not that much of a challenge to fill in the blanks and paint a very vivid mental picture of what he might look like bringing himself right to the edge of— "Ah, give me something else. Something appropriate. Quick."

"Um . . . he's afraid of clowns?"

"Who isn't? I need something more unique here."

Everett paces frantically. He looks like he'd be sweating if that was a thing his spectral form could do. "I can't work under this kind of pressure!"

"What about his family? Did anyone have any unusual habits?" she prompts, thinking of the details that she's whipped out during séances to convince clients that their loved one is really speaking through her. "A favorite food?"

"Oh, oh! Lemon meringue pie," Everett says, then wipes his brow in relief now that the pressure is off. "Ellen—Charlie's grandmother—loved lemon meringue pie."

"Lemon meringue pie," she says, lightly smacking the table in victory. "That was your grandmother's favorite."

For a fraction of a second, Charlie's face takes on a pained expression, like he's holding back some emotion. *Did that do it?* He shakes his head as if answering her mental question. "Deborah told you that, I take it?" His voice is quiet, more hesitant.

"No, Everett did. Just now." She tries to keep the frustration from her voice, but it doesn't work. Usually, Gretchen finds it easy to remain in control of her emotions. Why is this man so . . . so . . . ? "What do I have to do to get you to believe me? I'm trying to save you from a real shitty fate here, pal, but all you've done since I arrived is malign my character—"

"Character!" He scoffs. "What character?" Charlie takes a few steps toward Gretchen and throws his hand out, gesturing to her with a swift, dismissive movement. The way someone might to a pile of dirty laundry that should've been picked up days ago. Something inside her stomach shrivels at the look of disgust on his face; she's seen that expression before, years ago, back in Chicago. It doesn't bode well. "What is there to you except smoke and mirrors?" Charlie continues. "Because I highly doubt there's a genuine bone in your body, much less any concern for the people whose money you steal."

"I don't steal anything from anyone," she reiterates, moving closer and jabbing a finger into his chest. Gretchen Acorn is many things, but a thief is not one of them. If anything, she *gives* much more than she takes. It's immensely important to her that Charlie understands that. After all, it's the principle for which she gave up everything and started her life over, the reason she's endured being alone for so long. And if she doesn't have that going for her, well, what does she have? "I help all of my clients, and I care deeply for their well-being." And she does . . . at least as it relates to hers.

Based on his glower, he isn't convinced. "If you cared for Deborah, you'd stop taking advantage of her."

"This again? I'm not taking advantage of Mrs. Van Alst." Or rather, not for much longer. She still fully intends to cut back her appointments after all of this is settled. Therefore, the accusation is untrue. Also genuinely hurtful. Gretchen's surprised at how it digs its claws into her in a way that forces her to suppress the urge to squirm.

Like earlier, Gretchen wants to flee. Distance is the only thing that will relieve all of these new and unpleasant sensations. Usually, she'd welcome them as resources, but for once she can't grab hold firmly enough to any of them to figure out how they might be made useful. Until she can get away, she'll have to convert the discomfort into anger—the language that seems to come most naturally to both of them in each other's company, apparently. "She paid me to look into the ghost that's here, I found the fucking ghost that's here. Payment for a service—that's capitalism, babe. If you don't want to listen to me about Everett and the curse, fine! I tried. Happy hauntings to you both, then. I'm going home."

"Don't let the door hit you on your way out," Charlie mumbles.

Gretchen huffs as she turns to march out of the kitchen, but Everett appears in front of her, blocking her dramatic exit. Thankfully, she stops right before she can step through him and freeze her ass off again.

He clasps his hands in front of his chest. "You can't leave, Gretchen. Not until he starts taking this seriously."

"Oh yes, I definitely can. Move. Now." She attempts to dodge the ghost, but he shifts directly into her way whenever she tries to circumvent him. Forget acting, Everett Waybill would have made a decent power forward. She can only imagine how ridiculous this must look to Charlie, her bobbing and weaving around his kitchen while emitting annoyed growls.

Taking a different tack, Everett drops to his knees. "Please. Please. You're my—*our* last chance. Our only chance."

"Sorry, Ev. I tried, but he doesn't want to hear it. I'm going home now. Where my skills are *appreciated*." She says this with a sideways glance at Charlie.

"Gretchen, you're a good person. You're meant to help people. I see it in you. You can't let this happen to him," Everett pleads at the same time as Charlie says, "You seriously expect me to believe you're talking to a ghost right now?"

"Yeah, as a matter of fact, I can," she says to Everett. Then to Charlie, "That ghost is trying to convince me not to give up on you, FYI."

Charlie shrugs. "I'd really prefer it if you did."

"Yeah, I would too." She stares up at the ceiling, unable to resist whatever swirls inside her soul the way those cloud things swirl right under Everett's skin. If he sees something in her, then maybe it's there after all. Maybe it's something she can get Charlie to see too. And if she can get him to believe it—this man who clearly hates her—it'll be as good as true, as far as she's concerned. Then she'll be able to face her father's letter and whatever it might say armed with absolute certainty that she's doing just fine on her own, thanks. Convincing someone like Charlie that she's able to use her powers to better lives instead of destroying them will be indisputable proof. Ned Eichorn's insistence that she's useless if she isn't willing to play the game his way anymore will be so, so easy to ignore then. What's more useful than preventing someone's demise? So maybe Everett's right: She can't leave Gilded Creek just yet. Not without doing everything she can to save Charlie first.

"Unfortunately, it seems that my conscience isn't going to allow me to do that," she says. "Because you're wrong, Charlie. You're wrong about Everett not existing, but mostly you're wrong about me. I don't leave anyone worse off than I find them, and I'm not about to start now. Even if you are rude and have bad taste in sweaters."

He stares down at his torso, then back up at her with his brows knitted tighter together. "I'll have you know—"

Gretchen takes a few steps forward until she's inches away and tilts her head up. Charlie refuses to meet her eyes, so she ends up mostly staring at his mouth. It's nestled between his beard and mustache like a framed work of art. Good thing she isn't the thief he accuses her of being, or it would be real tempting to steal it. She frowns at that distressingly fanciful thought before continuing. "You don't want to believe me yet? Okay. That's fine. But at least give me a chance to prove to you that the curse is real."

"And why would I want to do that?"

"You mean other than the obvious preferring-not-to-die part? I really thought that'd be enough." Gretchen looks to Everett, silently pleading for a reason Charlie might be willing to allow her to stick around for a few days. "Because . . ."

Everett's blue eyes spark as the answer strikes him. "Oh! Because it's the height of kidding season. He could use an extra pair of hands around the farm, but he can't afford to hire anyone," he says excitedly.

"You need help around here for kidding season," she says, not really knowing what that even means, "and you don't have enough money to hire anyone. So let me stick around and . . . help." Gretchen isn't quite certain how this wound up with her offering to do manual labor on a farm. She isn't exactly experienced with—or comfortable around—animals. And the most strenuous workout her spaghetti arms are used to is carrying her groceries up the stairs to her apartment once a week.

"What do you even know about goat farming?"

"Nothing," she admits. "But I'm a fast learner."

"I don't care how fast of a learner you are, you aren't going to pick up enough to be helpful to me over the course of a few days."

"Then I'll stay longer. How long's kidding season?" she asks Everett.

"About a month," he and Charlie answer simultaneously.

A month is a long time to be away from DC. She'd need to cancel on a lot of clients. But Mrs. Van Alst's ten thousand dollars will cushion the blow of any lost business (and she can certainly justify keeping that money if she spends four whole weeks on this job). Not to mention her father won't be able to track her down out here, not for a while at least, which means a longer reprieve from having to find out what, exactly, he wants from her. Besides, her stubbornness has fully kicked in at this point, and she's not about to back down now. "Okay. It's March twenty-ninth. I'll stay through the end of April."

"Or . . ." Charlie says, "I could send you on your way right now and be done with all of this."

If there's one thing Gretchen knows how to do, it's identify people's weaknesses, and Charlie's is clearly his desire to take care of people—especially his people. So she needs to offer him a way to feel like he's doing that by accepting her proposition. "Tell me if I'm wrong, but I don't think free labor comes knocking on your door every day. Still, if that's not enough to persuade you, how about this? If we get to April thirtieth and you're still not convinced, I'll give Mrs. Van Alst her money back—all of it. The ten thousand she gave me to come out here and help you, plus the additional amount she's planning to pay me this month to cover her appointments while she's out of the country. *And* I'll drop her as a client going forward."

This is a huge gamble. Perhaps the biggest of Gretchen's life, and one she maybe wouldn't have made if she had longer to think about it. That's a *lot* of money. Money she definitely doesn't have on hand, especially if she spends the next few weeks out here in rural Maryland instead of meeting with clients back in DC. But Charlie looks at her with something in his expression that assures her that he's not quite as closed off to the proposition as he was a second ago, and she knows it was the right way in. The way that will let her save him. And maybe, in a way, save herself too.

"I'll need room and board," she adds, transferring her attention to the practical aspects of staying at Gilded Creek for a month. "Even then, I'm sure it's a lot cheaper than hiring someone."

There's a long silence as he contemplates this. "And if I say no?" he asks, although she's pretty certain he's going to agree at this point. He'd be stupid not to, and he doesn't strike her as stupid in the least.

Gretchen shrugs, as if the outcome of this makes no difference to her. She isn't quite sure why it *does* make a difference to her, except that the thought of the man in front of her coming to harm makes her feel a little panicky. Though she would feel that way about anyone coming to harm, she reminds herself. Because, like Everett said, she wants to help people. Even when it bites her in the ass. Like with Lawrence Biller, back in Chicago. And right now, with Charlie.

"Then I'll keep all of Mrs. Van Alst's money and my future appointments with her. Plus you'll still be short-handed around here, not to mention you'll probably wind up dooming yourself to an eternity as a spirit who can't go any farther than the end of the driveway, which Everett assures me gets old pretty quick."

A strand of Charlie's hair falls over his forehead, and she has to resist a bizarre impulse to tuck it back. Instead, she flashes the smile she's spent hours practicing since she was twelve, her *trust me, I'm harmless* one. It's been the downfall of much greater men than Charlie Waybill. (There was this one time, with a Yankees shortstop . . . and well, anyway . . .)

"The better question is: What do you have to lose by letting me stick around?" she asks.

"My valuables?" he grumbles.

The flippant accusation reheats her temper, and her smile drops as quickly as she put it on. This has never been her button before, but it apparently is now, with this man. With Charlie. And boy, does he keep pushing it and *pushing* it.

"Ten thousand dollars is a lot of money, isn't it? Then again, Mrs. Van Alst is a very rich woman . . ." She lets the statement trail off for effect. "If she gave me that much to come out here for a weekend to rid you of a ghost, imagine how much she'll give me when I tell her there's a whole dang family curse. And it will take me some *time* to convince you, since you're such a stubborn ass . . ." See, the thing is, Gretchen knows Charlie's button too. And if she needs to hold it down steadily in order to get him to agree to her staying, so be it. He doesn't need to know she would never in a million years actually follow through on her threat; despite what he thinks of her, she really isn't out to take advantage of anyone. Especially not Deborah Van Alst, who has been nothing but generous and kind to her.

"Are you . . . threatening to blackmail me?"

"Blackmail involves the threat of revealing information, and that's not what this is at all. So no, not technically."

"Then what is it?"

Gretchen plops into the chair Charlie previously vacated and crosses her legs, fully aware that the position shifts the hem of her borrowed shirt upward, revealing more bare thigh. "Just another facet of the situation for you to consider. Mrs. Van Alst really cares about you, for whatever reason. She said your happiness is worth, and I quote, 'anything.' I highly doubt she's going to give up trying to help you out because you sent me away. Especially once she knows how dire the situation actually is. And you know that even if you don't believe me about any of this, she absolutely will. So how about you make it easier on all of us and let me stay? Then we won't have to get her involved at all. She can enjoy her vacation without worrying about any of it. Won't need to trouble her."

Charlie lets out a frustrated growl that sounds a little too close to his big fluffy dog for Gretchen's comfort. Her shoulders tense.

"Room and board. For a month. That's all I need from you," she says. "And, well, for you to keep your mind slightly open to the possibility that I'm not trying to screw you over."

He's silent again, head bowed as he considers the situation. At last, he looks her in the eye. "Fine. Room and board. But I'm going to work you so hard, every single day, sunup to sundown." Charlie pauses as Gretchen's eyebrows raise and a suggestive smile spreads over her face. He swallows hard and quickly adds,

"If you insist on nagging me about family curses, you better be useful as hell while doing it. Not that I have any expectations that you'll even be able to do all that much." His quick inspection of Gretchen's body is that of someone evaluating livestock, which is certainly enough to throw cold water over his inadvertent innuendo. "You don't get any more money from me or Mrs. Van Alst under any circumstances. And you're giving her everything back at the end of the month when you haven't convinced me. Every single penny she's paid you since the beginning of the year—"

"Hey, I said one month. You can't just—"

"January through April, or no deal," he emphasizes. "Do I make myself clear?"

"Crystal," she says through gritted teeth. How sure he is that she's going to fail! Well, she won't. She can't. Neither her pride nor her bank account can afford it, especially since he's insisting on an extra three months of repayment. The ten thousand Mrs. Van Alst gave her will cover all of her April expenses and then some, but if she has to give it (and oh god, another six grand) back, she'll be absolutely fucked. It's not going to be a problem, she tells herself. Because if Gretchen is so good at making people buy into her lies, surely, convincing them of the truth shouldn't be much harder.

Right?

8

THE WALLS OF THE SMALL BEDROOM UPSTAIRS ARE COVERED
in a red floral paper that's curling in a few spots, and the ceiling's
gentle slope creates a cozy nook that's a perfect fit for the full-
size bed and its wrought iron headboard. Charlie pulls linens
from an antique steamer chest in the corner—including a golden-
yellow, lime-green, brown, and cobalt afghan that's even more
distressing to Gretchen's eyes than his sweater. It looks like one
of those Magic Eye images, but in blanket form. He waves off
Gretchen's half-hearted attempt to help make the bed, which
frees her to slip away and check out the hallway. She gestures for
Everett to follow.

On the way upstairs, she noticed some photos hanging here—
including an odd space to the right where one clearly used to hang
but no longer does. "Tell me who's in these," she says quietly so
Charlie doesn't overhear. Everett's eyes bounce from side to side,
prompting Gretchen to roll hers. "You can talk."

He lets out a gasp, as if his brief stint of silence since they left the kitchen required him to hold his (nonexistent) breath. "Oh, thank god. I was *dying*. Get it? Dying? But I'm already dead?" Gretchen does not laugh, so he continues. "Okay. So, um . . ." He gestures to the one in the middle. It's an older photo that's been colorized, so it has a strange, otherworldly quality to it. "That's Charles and Ellen on their honeymoon. They went to Niagara Falls." Everett looks from the picture to Gretchen. "Hey, you look a little like her, don't you? The brown hair and the brown eyes."

"They aren't exactly rare attributes," Gretchen says. She's always been grateful for her generic prettiness. Most people would be hard-pressed to pick her out of a crowd. Or a lineup. A real asset for someone in her family's line of work.

"Anyway, Charles and Ellen. And then this one beside them is my cousin George Waybill and his wife Enid, along with baby Charles there, and his twin older sisters." Everett clears his throat, which Gretchen assumes is for effect considering she's pretty sure he can't generate phlegm. "And the old ghoul lurking off to the side is Aunt Lucretia Thorne. She lived to be a hundred and three, the mean ol' bat."

"Why didn't you sell the farm to George in the first place?" Gretchen asks. "It sounds like he was happy to take it over after you died."

Everett shrugs. "The mac from the railroad was going to pay me more."

Gretchen wonders if the irony of this all was intentional. She kind of wishes Aunt Lucretia were haunting this farm too so she could find out more about how she managed it. A chill shoots down her spine when she takes another glance at the desiccated Strega

Nona look-alike at the edge of the photo. On second thought, it's probably for the best she isn't hanging around.

"Room's ready." Gretchen turns, startled, at the sound of Charlie's voice. His eyes do a quick sweep over her body, so fast that she would've missed it if she hadn't been watching him. Then they narrow again, remembering they should be suspicious of the stranger in his house—even if she does have nice legs. "What are you doing?" he asks.

"Everett was telling me about your family." He might have dismissed everything she said in the kitchen earlier, but surely this level of detail will convince him. "Your grandparents, Charles and Ellen, and your great-grandparents, George and Enid. Aunt Lucretia Thorne, who lived to a hundred and three." She gestures to the photos in their simple gold frames. "And . . . the missing one is . . . ?"

Everett takes a moment to realize she's asking him. "Oh, that was a picture of Charlie with his mom and dad. But he, uh . . . knocked that one off the wall after he had a pretty heated telephone call with Chuck."

"Hm . . . Interesting. What was the fight with your dad about, Charlie?"

"I—" Charlie's surprise wears off too quickly, though, and the anger from earlier comes roaring back. "You must get a lot of use out of that Ancestry dot-com subscription while defrauding people. Do you deduct it as a business expense when doing your taxes?"

Yes, actually. "I don't know what you're talking about."

"His dad's kind of a sore subject at the moment," Everett says unnecessarily.

Charlie shakes his head. "I have to go back outside and actually work now. I'd tell you to come with me, but . . ." He glances at Gretchen's bare legs and feet. "You're not really dressed for it. Throw your stuff in the washer—laundry room's next to the kitchen. You can start learning the ropes tomorrow when you have something more suitable to wear."

"What, exactly, would be suitable?" she asks. "Because all I brought are two dresses and a pair of pajamas."

He gives her a look of derision.

"I didn't exactly plan on all of this happening."

"I'll ask Lori if she has any of her daughter's farm clothes from when she helped out last summer. I think you're close enough to the same size."

Charlie doesn't notice the way Gretchen bristles at the idea of wearing a stranger's hand-me-down overalls, but Everett spots the look on her face and says, "Hey, doll, at least you can change clothes." He picks at the fabric of his shirt. "I've been wearing the same outfit for *decades*. Imagine how stupid I feel wearing breeches in the twenty-first century."

And because Gretchen is appreciative of an interaction with someone who doesn't despise her, she quips, "I'd rather wear those. I bet they'd do good things for my butt."

"Uh, what?" Charlie asks.

"Oh, sorry, nothing. Talking to Everett."

He ignores that, instead saying, "Help yourself to whatever in the kitchen." Charlie turns, but stops with his hand on the newel post. "And, uh, Acorn?"

Gretchen shivers, though Everett isn't all that close to her. "Yeah?"

"Don't make me regret inviting you into my home."

The tone of his voice is somehow both biting and vulnerable, and Gretchen swallows a sudden lump in her throat. She gives a brief nod, and he continues down the stairs.

"Wooooooooo!" Everett screams once the front door slams shut. "Woooo wooooooo!"

Gretchen claps her hands over her ears. "Ahh! Why are you doing that? Stop shrieking like a sorority girl."

"Sorry, I just . . . I've got a lot of pent-up noise in me! Being quiet is *hard*."

A small smile lifts the corners of her mouth, despite her efforts to appear stern. *This ghost is like a little kid*, she thinks. *Well, except for the part where he's six feet tall and kinda pervy.*

"And you! You were brilliant, Gretch. Absolutely brilliant. Now all you have to do is get him to believe you about the curse and we'll be hitting on all eight! Woooo!"

"All right, all right, that's enough with the yelling."

"I haven't been this excited since Charles accidentally left the TV on the entire weekend." Everett smiles wistfully. "It was just the Weather Channel, but it sure beat sticking my head into the creek and making up soap opera plots for the tadpoles. Though I am rather proud of some of their character arcs. Oh, hey! I have an idea!"

Well, that sounds like trouble. "What is your idea?"

He climbs onto the bed, although his knees don't quite touch the duvet. Still, he manages to bounce a little as he says, "We should go downstairs and watch TV!"

"Mm, I don't know. Isn't there a better use of our time right now? Like, I don't know, trying to figure out how to convince Charlie to believe in this life-threatening family curse of yours?"

"Hey, that makes it sound like *I'm* responsible for all of this mess."

"Aren't you?"

"No," he says, elongating the word to give it a sense of attitude. "It's all Aunt Lucretia's fault. Have you even been listening to me?"

If the curse was supposed to teach Everett Waybill a lesson, Gretchen isn't sure he's learned it yet. Well, he still has . . . the rest of eternity, she supposes. Maybe he'll have a light bulb moment at some point.

"Based on his reactions so far, I don't think any amount of information I shouldn't know but do is going to be enough for Charlie. We're going to need a different approach."

"What about something like those Greek fellows did, hiding in that horse?"

Why is this happening to me? she thinks for the twentieth time over the last hour. "And how, exactly, do you conceive of that working in this particular situation, Everett?"

The ghost ponders this for a moment, starting and stopping a few sentences before throwing his hands in the air. "I don't know! Why are you asking *me*? We've already established that you're the brains of the operation."

"You said a Waybill has to be here, but it doesn't have to be Charlie, right? Is there someone else in the family who would be willing to take over? Then Charlie can leave and it wouldn't even matter."

"Nope. Charles's sisters both passed, neither ever had children. Chuck's the one pushing for the sale in the first place. So unless you're volunteering to become a Waybill, or help make some new ones . . ." He winks.

"*Hard* pass, for so, so many reasons."

Everett begins pacing again, more leisurely than he did in the kitchen. He stops abruptly and holds up a finger. "What if . . . you told Charlie the truth?" His eyebrows raise, waiting for Gretchen to applaud his genius.

"I've done that already. It didn't work."

"No, you tried telling him the truth about me and the curse. But not the truth about *you*."

Gretchen blinks a few times, letting this idea permeate her brain. It both terrifies and perversely excites her. What might it feel like for someone like Charlie to know her secrets? Would he recognize just how damn good she is at all of this? No. No, he would hate her more, and punish her for it. It would be Lawrence all over again. And if there's one thing about Gretchen Acorn, it's that she learns from her mistakes.

"Absolutely not," she says at last. "That would ruin me. My business. My life. Charlie already thinks I'm a fraud, and if I confirm it, then . . . then . . . I'm done for. He'll make sure of it. No. We need another way to convince him that doesn't involve me admitting that you're the first ghost with whom I've ever actually spoken."

Everett stares blankly for a moment, opens his mouth to speak, then closes it again as if nixing his own idea. Then he apparently reconsiders. "Flash mob?"

"Okay, well, this has been completely unhelpful. Thank you."

"You're welcome," he replies cheerily. "So can we watch TV now?"

"OH MY GOD, JUST KISS ALREADY," GRETCHEN GROANS AT the television.

"This is getting painful," Everett agrees from where he float-sits beside her on the beige-and-navy-striped living room sofa. "If I were James Herriot, I guarantee I would have had Helen rolling around with me in a haystack within a week."

"Well, she *is* dating someone else," she points out.

Everett shrugs. "So?"

They're on their fifth episode in a row of *All Creatures Great and Small*, which Everett originally chose because he liked the way the actors looked. Once he realized it was about a country vet and included lots of animals, he insisted it would be a good introduction to farm life for Gretchen. That it's set in England and in the 1930s does not detract from its relevance, in his opinion.

"Animals are animals," he said authoritatively. "That's one thing that hasn't changed in all the years I've been hanging around here."

After watching James Herriot shove his hand up various creatures' hoo-has over the last five hours, Gretchen can't say she's particularly eager to get out there and interact with the goats tomorrow. There seems to be a lot of dirt and fluids involved in animal husbandry even during the best of times, and despite the way she handled getting dunked in that mud puddle today like an absolute champ (RIP to her boots and maybe also her jacket depending on how it dries), she's never really been a fan of getting her hands dirty. Especially not literally.

"Charles would love this show," Everett says with a sigh as the episode's end credits roll.

"He probably already knows about it, but I can ask him when he gets back in if you want."

"No, not Charlie. *Charles*," he repeats, enunciating the *s* at the end. "Charlie's grandfather."

Oh, right. The elder Charles Waybill—the septuagenarian Vietnam vet she thought she'd be meeting today. "I meant to ask you about that. My research implied Charles Waybill is still alive, but clearly, he doesn't live here anymore . . ."

"Yeah, Charlie moved him to a place a while back. Don't ask me when, because—"

"Yes, time is confusing for you. So you've said. By 'a place,' you mean like a nursing home?"

"I guess? It's called . . . Meadowwood, Meadewood, something like that. The brochure was on the table for a while after Charlie moved in. Front of it said something about 'assisted living and memory care.'"

"After Charlie moved in? When was that?"

"Moved in *again*, I should say. This was basically his second home as a kid. He was here every summer, every school break. But he didn't come to live at the farm permanently until after Ellen died. Charles was forgetting stuff more often, needed help with everything. I don't know where Charlie was living before that. He traveled a lot as part of his job. Ellen and Charles had a big board in the laundry room where they pinned all of the postcards and photos he sent from his adventures."

Gretchen summons a mental picture of the small space where she did her laundry before they got deep into their binge watch, but doesn't find anything on the walls. "It isn't there anymore."

"Yeah, the night after Charlie moved Charles into the place, the boy got absolutely blotto and pried the thing off the wall with his bare hands like some kinda David Banner. It was actually pretty impressive." Everett chuckles. "You know, Charlie wouldn't hurt a fly, but he's really been doing a number on the wall decorations."

Gretchen's been too distracted by the whole ghosts-and-curses-are-actually-real thing to give much thought as to how Charlie wound up running the farm solo when his grandfather's still alive and the legal owner (according to her online property search), but Everett's insight makes it seem like a responsibility Charlie had to take on without a lot of time to adjust. No wonder he's trying to get rid of this place if his old life was full of travel and excitement. If only she could tell him that she understands how he feels; didn't Gretchen also struggle to untie herself from familial expectations? But there isn't really a way to share that part of herself without sharing *all* of it, which she obviously cannot do.

Besides, why would I want to share any part of me with that jerk? That's not strictly true, of course. There are many parts of her she would not mind sharing with Charlie Waybill. They just all happen to be the parts currently underneath the borrowed flannel.

She pauses the TV. "I need to go to the bathroom," she explains before Everett can protest. "I'll be right back."

On the way, she notices a text from Yolanda, sent hours ago.

All good??

Things are not, actually, all good. Part of Gretchen wants to respond with the long, long story of everything that's happened over the last few hours. About Everett and the curse. About Charlie. The immense amount of money she's risked in pursuit of saving him and proving herself. If anyone would believe her about all of this and understand everything it means to her, it's Yolanda. Instead, she sends a simple:

Situation changed. Staying until end of April. Will send $ for rent and bills soon.

Straightforward. Professional. *Good job*, Gretchen tells herself.

There's a teeny-tiny half bath under the stairs, barely big enough to hold a toilet and a miniature sink. Gretchen feels like an absolute giant inside of it, which is delightfully novel. "Fee, fi, fo, fum," she jokes to herself as she slips back into the foyer.

At that exact moment, Charlie comes back inside. They stand face-to-face, a few feet apart, both as still and assessing as if they're two burglars who came across each other trying to rob the same house.

"Done for the day?" Gretchen asks.

"Mostly. As long as none of the other goats start showing signs of labor."

"Cool. Cool." So now they're just going to be . . . in the house. Together. For the rest of the night. Why's that thought so intimidating? *Come on, Gretchen, you are good with people. Put him at ease. Pretend he's a client.* "So . . . do you enjoy . . . goats?" she tries, but her usual talent for seamless small talk is conspicuously absent from her mental tool kit.

Charlie looks at her as if she's flung another insult his way, then grabs a jacket from a hook on the wall and walks right back out the door.

"You are very rude, you know!" she shouts. This time, she hopes he *can* hear her through the door.

Gretchen returns to Everett on the couch. "Where's Charlie going?" she asks him.

"Um, I don't know, maybe I'll go hitch a ride and see if— Gretchen, how am I supposed to know where Charlie is going?" He rolls his eyes, allowing Gretchen to see that the strange swirling clouds beneath his skin are also in his sclera. *Creepy.* "You know I can't leave the property much less follow Charlie around like I'm Magnum, P.I., from *Magnum, P.I.*"

She throws herself into the same spot on the couch she previously occupied. "Sorry, sorry, I didn't mean to rub it in. Just thought you might know his routine."

"All I know is he goes out some nights and comes back pretty late. No idea where he goes. He doesn't exactly say where he's been when he gets home. Not the talking-to-himself type."

"Is he seeing someone? You know, romantically?" It would make sense. Charlie is young, admittedly handsome. Considering the way she called him a "*dear* friend," Gretchen even suspected for a moment that Mrs. Van Alst and he might be . . . well . . . She highly doubts that now, having met him and heard the way he speaks of Deborah as if she's a beloved aunt. But even if that's unlikely, it doesn't mean Charlie isn't involved with *someone*. His sudden departure without bothering to shower after a long day of work makes a date seem somewhat improbable, but maybe this is just how rural folk live. What's a little livestock residue between friends?

Everett tilts his head, contemplating, before shaking it. "Don't think he's got anyone right now."

"Why do you say that?"

"As we discussed previously, I'm aware of most things that go on in this house, and the guy's, uh, *alone time* has only increased in recent months. If you get what I'm saying."

She forces the mental image of Charlie Waybill with his cock in hand out of her mind for the second time today. "Yeah, yeah, I get it. So probably not dating anyone. Maybe he's—"

"Gretchen, sweetheart," Everett says. "Don't take this the wrong way. But you talk *a lot*."

She blinks a few times in disbelief. "I talk a lot? *I* talk a lot? Ha! That's a good one, babe."

"Look, I understand. I do. I'm a wonderful conversation partner. A treasure trove of interesting insights. It's only natural you'd want to make the most of my company now that you have it."

She scoffs.

"But let's take a break from chatting and watch more of our show now. Okay, doll?" Everett hovers his hand over her knee, motioning up and down. "Imagine I'm patting your leg affectionately," he says, "to demonstrate that I hold you in great esteem despite your flaws."

She rolls her eyes and picks up the remote.

9

"GRETCHEN! GRETCHEN!"

Her eyes fly open to find Everett's face only a few inches from her own. "Oh, good, you're still here," she mumbles. "Guess it was too much to hope that you were just a particularly vivid bad dream."

He rears back. "Wow, you're kinda mean when you wake up."

Gretchen yawns, covering her mouth with her forearm. "Well, you yelling in my ear repeatedly doesn't exactly make for a pleasant alarm."

"What else was I supposed to do?" he asks. "Tenderly caress your face and whisper, 'Time to wake up, my sweet darling girl'? First, I'm not your mother. Second, you're neither sweet nor darling at the moment. And third, I can't touch you without poofing. So yelling is what you get."

"And why, exactly, did you need to wake me up?" She blinks to clear the sleep from her eyes. The clock on the cable box says it's a little after midnight. "Is Charlie home?"

"No, still out," Everett answers. "I woke you up because I have an idea."

"You woke me up because you have an idea," Gretchen repeats, her tone much less enthusiastic.

"Yes. And also the show stopped playing to ask if I'm still watching, so I want you to fix that. But that's not as important."

"At least you understand the concept of priorities. So what's the idea?"

"Okay, ready?" Everett pauses, and Gretchen glares at him until he realizes that's her version of yes. "Make Charlie fall in love with you."

"... What?"

"Make Charlie fall in love with you! When *All Creatures* stopped playing, my mind drifted to this other show I watched with Charlie a few ... months? ... ago, about these Soviet spies pretending to be an American family."

"*The Americans?*"

"Yeah, that's the one. Good, you've heard of it. So the dad spy, he cozies up to this woman who works for some agency—"

"Look, if you're saying I should fuck Charlie to get him to listen to me, I have to stop you right there. I'm sure I'm fine at sex, but even my best performance is not going to change hearts and minds."

Everett rolls his eyes as if annoyed with Gretchen's inability to keep up with his thoughts. As if *she's* the one who suggested earlier they consider somehow using an actual Trojan horse. "No, not sex. Although maybe that should be a part of it. I'm talking about *love*. Charlie will do absolutely anything for the people he loves, so if you make yourself one of them, he'll have to listen to you when you tell him not to sell."

"And I'm supposed to make him fall in love with me . . . how, exactly? I'm a fake spirit medium, not a hypnotist."

He does a brief assessment of her features. "You're a pretty little dish, so that'll help. And . . . well, I would say you're nice, but you did call me a bad dream a minute ago. Still, I'm sure you could *pretend* to have fine qualities that would win Charlie's heart."

"Gee, thanks. You sure know how to make a girl feel good, Ev."

"Oh, I do," he says with an eyebrow wiggle and his trademark crooked smile.

"Gross." Gretchen shifts on the couch and pulls another afghan—highlighter yellow, maroon, Kelly green—up to cover more of her. "I'm not making Charlie fall in love with me. It goes against my Rule."

"Your . . . rule?"

"Yeah." The only person she's ever told about this is Yolanda, but Everett might as well know if they're also going to be working together, so to speak. "I have one Rule I live by, so I don't wind up doing anything I'll regret in the pursuit of money. I always have to leave people better off than I found them. Making Charlie fall in love with me, if that's even possible, would have to end in breaking his heart. Which would almost definitely violate the Rule. So it's a no."

Everett stares at her, unblinking, long enough that it starts to creep her out. "It's a good idea," he says at last.

His feelings are hurt. "I'm not saying it's *bad*," she reassures. "And it's certainly better than some other ideas you've had that I won't name. But we're gonna have to go back to the drawing board and find another way in. Now, I know you probably don't remember what this is like, since I presume you don't need to sleep anymore, but I'm tired. So I'm going to head up to bed."

"Will you at least put something else on TV for me first? Something that won't question my endurance." He scowls at the screen's *Are you still watching?* prompt.

"Fine," Gretchen says, switching over to regular live television to ensure it'll continue playing all night. It's mostly infomercials this late on basic cable, but eventually, Everett brings a stop to their channel-hopping with a shrieked, "Oh, oh! That's what I want! *The Golden Girls*! I love *The Golden Girls*!"

"Okay, I'll put it on, but then you're not going to disturb me again for the rest of the night. Deal?"

"Yes, sure, deal."

She confirms the channel is showing back-to-back-to-back episodes, then heads to the laundry room to check on her jacket (not looking good) and collect her dry things before trudging to the second floor. Upstairs, she examines the doors lining the hallway—Charlie's room to the left, the bathroom straight ahead, her room and the office to the right. Now would be a good time to sneak around up here and learn what she can about Charlie to help her better convince him of her honesty. She hoped Everett would be a valuable source of info, but so far he hasn't proven himself particularly reliable, especially when put on the spot (not that Charlie has been at all receptive to the info she has managed to get out of him anyway). Plus, there's gotta be stuff up here Everett hasn't seen because he can't open drawers or comb through piles of papers . . .

Except . . .

Well, Charlie is already so suspicious of her. What if he left a booby trap somewhere? Not like an *Indiana Jones*–style boulder one, but something that will give him the evidence he needs to prove that Gretchen went into his bedroom or office, the door to which is cracked open just enough to see that the small space is mostly taken up by a large antique desk. As much as her fingers itch with the desire to get her hands on the mountains of paper-work in there, and as much as she would love to check out his bedroom and meet Teddy the teddy bear, the thought of losing even more of Charlie's already limited esteem by doing exactly what he expects of her—and the way her toes are starting to go numb as the old farmhouse gets chillier—has Gretchen heading straight to bed.

But she doesn't sleep right away. Her brain won't let her. It's too busy continuing to scheme, plot, *think*. Not that Gretchen minds too much; this is, after all, her default state of being, and it's actually nice to return to something familiar after the bizarre day she's had. Not to mention the fact that she's in a strange bed, in a strange room, in a strange place—which used to be par for the course for her, but hasn't been something she's had to accli-mate to recently. So she embraces her instinct to work on the prob-lem at hand: Charlie Waybill.

He's going to be a tough nut to crack, that much is certain. Maybe she's become too used to the grief-stricken old rich ladies who come to her already halfway (or fully, in the case of True Believer clients like Janice Easterly) convinced of her abilities. But Charlie's so resistant to her spirit medium persona that it al-most seems like more of a burden than a boon. Everett was right that honesty would no doubt get her farthest in this situation, but there's a limit to just how honest Gretchen is willing and able to be. Strategically and maybe even biologically.

So what are her other options? *Make Charlie fall in love with you.* Gretchen scoffs at the memory of Everett's voice, so matter-of-fact, as if he was proposing wearing a sweater on a chilly day instead of manipulating a person's strongest emotion. What would it be like to have someone like Charlie love her? She allows herself to imagine it. Safe. Warm. Right. "Yeah," she says to herself, mentally crumpling the picture her brain starts to paint. "Great plan. A-plus-plus. Nothing could go wrong there."

And yet the idea echoes in her brain, getting quieter with each reverberation but not fully disappearing until sleep finally overtakes her. She wakes briefly sometime later at the sound of the front door closing, and Everett's subsequent, "Gretchen! Help! Charlie turned off the TV! And in the middle of a St. Olaf story. Help!" But it's been a long, long day, and tomorrow is bound to be even longer, so she clutches her pillow over her head to drown out the shouting and drifts off again.

10

A SOUND—SOMEONE KNOCKING AT HER DOOR?—PULLS
Gretchen from the deepest sleep she's had in years. As her eyes
flutter open, she takes in her surroundings. *Right.* She isn't in her
apartment in DC, she's in the farmhouse's guest bedroom, with
its startlingly bright afghan and wrought iron headboard and a
pair of bright blue eyes staring at her from the other side of the
bed and—

"Jesus, Everett!" she says, springing up to escape from the chill
emanating off him. No wonder she dreamed about living in an
igloo last night.

"And a good morning to you too," he says grumpily.

Morning seems like an exaggeration, considering it's still dark
outside. Gretchen slides out of bed, wrapping herself in the afghan for extra warmth. "What are you doing here?" she demands.

"Um, okay, I thought we already went over this, but . . . I'm
the victim of a family curse that has me stuck at Gilded Creek—"

"Not what I meant. Why are you sleeping with me?" She speaks in her angriest whisper, aware that Charlie is probably able to hear anything louder through the door. And while she does want him to believe her about Everett in general, she doesn't need him knowing that she apparently shared a bed with a freaking visitant last night.

"I told you this was my room," Everett counters. "So really, when you think about it, *you* were sleeping with *me*."

The knock comes louder and more urgently, along with a deep-voiced, annoyed, "Acorn, get up," that makes Gretchen's skin tingle in a way that she can't tell if she likes or not.

"This conversation isn't over," she warns Everett, and reaches for the doorknob.

Charlie stands there, already dressed in worn jeans and a long-sleeved T-shirt with the sleeves pushed to under his elbows. He's wearing socks but no shoes, and he has a pile of clothes thrown over his shoulder. He dumps it into her arms. "Lori brought you a few things. Will they work?"

A quick glance through the stack reveals two pairs of overalls—one olive-green twill and the other light-blue-and-white-striped like a train engineer costume—and a dark tan duck canvas jacket. "Thanks. They should. So . . . should I wear these with just a bra underneath or . . . ?"

A blush sweeps over Charlie's cheeks. He grits his teeth, as if annoyed with himself for not resisting that mental image. "Hold on," he says.

He disappears into his own bedroom and comes back with a plain white cotton T-shirt like the one Gretchen spotted under his sweater yesterday. "Here," he says, holding it out, the scent of laundry detergent wafting toward her. His other hand busies itself with scratching at his beard while he avoids direct eye contact. "That should work for now. We couldn't figure out footwear, though. Lori's daughter has real big feet, so we doubted her shoes would work for you."

"I can wear the ones I came here in," Gretchen says. "They're already ruined anyway."

Charlie quirks an eyebrow. "Didn't those have heels?"

"Just a three-inch block. It's fine."

"If you break your ankle, you're going home." He points a finger at her. "I'm not letting you stick around here if you aren't going to be useful. Understand?"

Wow, that's almost exactly what my father said to me the last time we spoke. She nearly says that aloud, but catches herself just in time. The reminder stings, but perhaps she needed it: Her usefulness is the only thing she has to offer anyone, and there's little reason to keep her otherwise. Her father might have been the most explicit iteration of that fact of life, but it's a lesson she's learned time and time again. But that's not something she can tell Charlie. Instead she goes with, "Yes, sir," and sinks her top teeth into her bottom lip as she looks him directly in the eye.

The remnants of pink in his cheeks rebrighten, and, oh, Gretchen experiences a miniature version of the gotcha euphoria then. Just enough of that familiar heady rush to make her want to bring that flush to Charlie's face again and again. It's not quite the same as the feeling she's been missing, but it's . . . almost better. Thankfully, she thinks, it's not exactly difficult to fluster him; the man can't seem to look at her for more than a couple minutes without presumably picturing her either naked or being marched away in handcuffs. Maybe both at the same time.

"There's cereal in the pantry. Eat some and meet me at the barn," he says, looking down again as if it's important he watch his feet in case they make a move forward without his permission. "Don't dilly-dally."

"Wouldn't dream of it," she calls after him as he hurries down the stairs.

Everett is still lounging on the bed, arms folded behind his head, legs stretched out and ankles crossed. "Wow, the sexual tension between you and Charlie is really bomb-dot-com tasty."

"Oh my god, where did you learn that term?" she asks, tossing the T-shirt and olive overalls on the bed. Maybe if she rolls up the legs a couple times and adds in one of her dangly necklaces . . .

"The spiky-haired guy on the food show says it. Didn't I use it right?"

She thinks for a moment. "Do you mean Guy Fieri?"

"Yes, him! Ellen loved her some Triple D. I like it too. That cat is really money."

Gretchen opens the dresser to retrieve a pair of the clean underwear she put in there last night, and grabs her now-clean bra from where she left it drying on one of the drawer pulls. "Mm, yeah, no. I can't deal with you using Guy Fieri catchphrases."

"Well, that's not very Flavortown of you," he says, frowning.

"Besides, the tension between me and Charlie isn't sexual." Okay, maybe it is. Gretchen is willing to admit that much to *herself* at least. But it doesn't matter, since they don't like each other. And even if they did, this isn't a conversation she wants to have with the ghost currently chilling on her bed. Speaking of which . . . "It's all animosity-based. And if you want to talk about something that isn't 'very Flavortown,' it's that you slept in my bed without my permission."

Everett opens his mouth to speak, but Gretchen cuts him off with a, "And if you're about to say it's actually your bed, don't."

He takes a moment to think, since that clearly was what he was about to say. Finally, he settles on, "I suppose me pointing out that I didn't actually sleep doesn't change your opinion?"

"Nope. That makes it worse, actually. What were you doing then? Staring at me all night?" A horrifying thought enters her mind. "Oh god, this isn't a weird sex thing for you, is it?"

His eyes go wide in response to her expression. "Of course not! I already think of you like a sister. A hot sister, sure, but a sister all the same."

Well, the hot-sister thing is still pretty disturbing, but better, she supposes, than the alternative. Then again, the last twenty-four hours have really raised the bar on what she's willing and able to mentally accommodate.

"Usually at night I lie down in here, close my eyes, and pretend to sleep until I hear the neighbor's rooster," Everett says. "Helps time feel a little less wobbly if I stick to a living-person routine, more or less."

That pinches Gretchen's heart in a way she doesn't appreciate. "I guess that makes sense."

"But last night I did mostly stare at you," he admits.

"That is extremely creepy."

He shrugs. "You make funny noises in your sleep. And since Charlie turned off the TV when he got home—you need to talk to him about that, by the way—how else was I supposed to keep myself entertained?"

She's about to protest that she *does not* make *any* noises in her sleep, funny or otherwise, but it's possible that she indeed does. No one's been beside her in a bed overnight in . . . she can't even remember how long. Maybe she's never actually spent the night with another person since reaching adulthood. All of her hookups (not that there have even been many of them) over the last few years have been of the hit-and-run variety, neither party interested in lingering for more than a few minutes after the fun was over. How sad is it that her first time sharing a bed with someone was with a Prohibition-era ghost who thinks of her as a hot sister? Maybe "sad" isn't the word for it. "Absurd" probably fits the situation a little better. But, well . . . it's kinda sad too.

"From now on, you do your weird nighttime power down elsewhere," she says.

"I can pretend-sleep on the couch, I guess." Everett's face is penitent, like he actually understands he crossed a line and is embarrassed about it.

His expression reminds Gretchen that this—having someone else see him, talk to him, even be aware that he's in their space at all—must be a huge adjustment for him too. She supposes it's a challenge for him to figure out what's appropriate. Not only have societal standards changed immensely since he was alive, he hasn't had to think through his interactions with anyone in almost a century. She should probably cut him a tiny bit of slack as they both adjust to this strange new arrangement of theirs.

"Thank you," she says. "I'm sorry to have displaced you. But while we're at it, let's also agree that you never come into this room without asking and getting my express verbal permission first."

"You told me you have one rule, but it seems like you actually have a lot of them."

"These aren't rules, they're boundaries, and they're healthy." She holds the overalls up to her body to check the length; the pant legs reach the floor. Definitely going to need to roll them. "Now, if you'll excuse me, I've gotta get dressed and head out to the barn before Charlie has a conniption."

"Go ahead," he says. "Don't mind me."

"Everett."

"Right, right. I'm leaving, I'm leaving." And he floats through the door.

GRETCHEN MAKES IT APPROXIMATELY THREE-QUARTERS OF the way to the barn before she fails to notice a divot in the grass and winds up doing something to her ankle. *That bitch karma is really trying to send me a message*, she thinks as she tries not to cry.

"Why didn't you warn me?" she whines to Everett as she hobbles along.

"How was I supposed to know the ground was uneven? It's not like I walk on it."

He has a point. "It huuuurts."

Everett moves from beside to in front of her, forcing her to come to a stop. "Hmm. This is great, actually," he says, putting his index finger to his chin dimple as he considers it.

"It's great that I'm injured and in pain?"

"Yes, because now you can tell Charlie you're hurt and he'll send you back to the house to rest. He'll feel sorry for you and dote on you while we lie on the couch and watch *MacGyver*."

"I absolutely cannot let Charlie know that I've done the exact thing he just warned me not to do. Sorry for me is not what he will feel." Gretchen did not suffer through Everett summarizing all of the major plotlines of late-nineties *Days of Our Lives* (which Ellen apparently used to tape daily to catch up on before bed) while eating flavorless bran cereal with the funky-flavored milk she found in a mason jar in the fridge this morning to go home already.

"Maybe it'll get better the more I walk on it. I think that's a thing in . . . sports?"

A few steps are enough to tell her that's definitely the opposite of what's going to happen, but she doesn't see another option.

Charlie's brow furrows immediately when she appears outside the barn. "What's wrong?" he asks, his tone accusatory as opposed to concerned.

"He knows," Everett says in a panic, and crouches down for some reason. "Oh no. Don't let him send you away. You can't go. Don't leave me alone, Gretch—"

"Nothing's wrong. Everything is wonderful. Sunshine, fresh air—" Gretchen makes a show of taking a deep breath. It smells strongly of animals and excrement, and she gags. "I'm so excited for . . . hard . . . work?"

Charlie openly evaluates her as she moves toward him, as if he wants her to be aware he's paying attention so that she might crack under the pressure of her lie. Joke's on him, though; it would take a whole lot more dishonesty before the weight of it would even register, much less exert any pressure on Gretchen's conscience. Her ankle feels like someone's tied a rope around it, lit the rope on fire, and is now tugging it in the opposite direction of where she's trying to make it go, but she flashes a carefree smile and takes several more steps, careful to put her full weight into each one without the pain showing on her face so he can't accuse her of anything.

"Wow. My biggest regret," Everett says, watching Gretchen walk toward Charlie with the bold strides of someone whose ankle isn't probably swelling exponentially every second, "is that we couldn't have acted in a production together. We both missed our true callings."

Interesting how that's his biggest regret, not the whole getting-cursed-to-eternally-haunt-this-farm thing. But Gretchen doesn't particularly feel it's her place to judge.

"What's my first task, boss?" she asks Charlie. She does a great job of making her lean against the fence surrounding the pen look casual and cool as opposed to the metal rail's support being the only thing keeping her from crumpling to the ground. The goats' bleating is distant, and Gretchen follows it with her eyes to the pasture. She spots the herd congregated around an area of over-growth at the far end of the enclosure, munching on the weeds and low-hanging branches that obscure the fence there. At least she won't have to face any actual animals yet. Right as she has that thought, something brushes against her leg and she screams.

"Oh my god!" She clutches her hand to her chest as an orange tabby circles her—*like a shark*, she thinks. It's purring, but maybe that's just a trick it's using to get her to let her guard down.

Charlie ignores her and leans down to scratch the cat under the chin. "Fill up the water troughs, and then the plastic drums," he orders without taking his attention away from the feline. *Laying it on a bit thick, aren't you?* Gretchen thinks as she watches it flop over at Charlie's feet and purr even louder.

Gretchen finds a hose in the nearest corner, then picks up the nozzle and carries it over to the large black plastic trough in the open pen. Each step makes her want to collapse, but she's sure that Charlie's watching her every movement even if he does seem distracted by the cat. So she forces herself to keep walking normally. The return journey over to the hose valve isn't more than a few feet, but the pain makes it more like a mile. She keeps herself motivated by telling herself she can lean against the wall for support once she gets there. But of course Charlie is still examining her for signs of weakness, so she doesn't get to actually carry out this plan after all, instead forced to remain freestanding while she opens the valve. As water rushes through the hose and spills into the trough, Gretchen realizes she has no way of knowing when it's full without walking back over there. She considers asking Everett to monitor it and shout when it's getting full, but he's wandered off somewhere. *Of course he isn't here when I could actually use him.* And it's not like she can discreetly call for him. So back over to the trough she goes.

When the water level reaches the halfway mark, Gretchen heads for the valve, figuring the trough will be full by the end of her leisurely stroll. She turns off the hose and allows herself a nice, long lean against the wall at last. Then she moves the hose from the one trough to the other inside the barn and drags herself back to the valve.

Charlie walks over to the first trough and stares into it just as she's about to turn on the water again. "Fill this one up a little more," he says, as if it's a matter of simply walking over there and doing it. Which, of course, it is.

She manages to move the hose back over to the trough in the outside pen, but when she pivots to go through the barn to turn the water on again, a new, more severe pain makes her cry out and fall. She lies there atop the straw-and-who-knows-what-covered ground, staring up at the sky.

Oh my god, I am going to die. I am going to die during my very first farm chore.

To add insult to injury, the cat comes over and pounces on her ponytail. Gretchen shrieks.

"You're hurt, Acorn," Charlie says, fury buried just under the surface of his voice, as he gently nudges the cat away from Gretchen with the edge of his boot. "Admit it."

"No, no, I'm just . . . resting here a minute. That cloud up there looks a lot like a bunny, don't you think?"

Everett reappears then and crouches beside her. "I see Don Knotts," he says, glancing up.

Charlie doesn't look at the cloud, much less provide his opinion on what animal or beloved television star it looks like. "This is ridiculous. You're really going to risk doing lasting damage to yourself because you're too stubborn to admit I'm right?"

"Look who's talking. Must I remind you that you're the one willing to *die* and get stuck here forever because you don't want to believe I'm telling you the truth about Everett and the curse?"

"Oh, please. Save it. I don't have time for this," he says. "Gilded Creek is a working farm. That means we have to actually *work*."

"Give me a minute and I'll get right back to it."

"No, you will not." His voice and the way he stands there with his hands at his hips makes it clear he's made up his mind. But Gretchen can't give up, cannot let him send her home after less than twenty-four hours. Risk to Charlie aside, that would absolutely murder her pride. Or what's left of it, considering she's fairly certain she's lying within inches of a goat pee puddle.

"I . . . Okay, I admit I might've tweaked my ankle a *teensy* bit during the walk from the house, but it's fine. It barely hurts. Let me rest here for like, two seconds, and I'll—"

He gets closer, stopping right where the toes of his boots meet the soles of hers. "Stand up," he orders.

Thanks to an upbringing that didn't particularly hold the concept of authority in high regard, usually Gretchen has the immediate urge to defy anyone telling her what to do. But with Charlie, she gets this tingly sensation that spreads from her stomach to her legs. *Then* she has the urge to defy him. So she sits up but stays seated. If she's going to get kicked off the property, she's at least going to make him put in some effort to make it happen.

"Can you walk?" he asks.

Everett bounces around them. "Ooh, ooh, say no! Maybe he'll carry you! Ask for a piggyback ride!"

Getting to loop her arms around this man's neck, his citrus-and-hay scent stuck in her nose while her entire front bumps against his back with every step, tempts Gretchen in a way that makes her certain it's a bad idea. Her job is to exploit *his* weaknesses, not her own. Not that it matters, since he's about to put her in a cab back to the city anyway. "Yeah, I can walk," she says to Charlie. Everett grumbles, but she ignores him. "I'm telling you, it's basically nothing. I swear I can keep working if you would just let me—"

"Stand up," he repeats, and extends a hand out toward her. She stares at it stupidly for a second, as if she can't comprehend this thing attached to his arm. The calluses, the faded scar bisecting his life and fate lines, show a hand used to getting its way through strength. This is a hand that makes things happen. Unlike Gretchen's soft, manicured one, which only lends its support to her mind while it does the bulk of the work. The same mind that stops functioning at peak efficiency around this man, apparently. That's the only explanation she has for why she lays her palm on his and allows him to pull her to her feet.

She stumbles forward with the motion, unused to standing flamingo-style, and Charlie's other hand automatically comes to her waist to steady her. His grasp is warm and strong, almost uncomfortable as he digs his fingertips into her side, somehow expressing punishment more than support. Gretchen's nerves stand up and take notice of the touch, unsure whether to feel it as pain or pleasure. Before they can decide for sure, Charlie adjusts her until she's solidly upright and moves to her side.

He grabs her arm and throws it over his shoulder. The physical contact between them is extensive—he has one hand on her wrist and one again at her waist—but it lacks the intensity of a moment ago, when they were face-to-face. Probably because relatively few sexy things could be accomplished in this side-by-side position. Not that Gretchen's brain is drawing a *complete* blank. As soon as they move deeper into the barn, though, she recalls that this is not a positive development and resumes her protest.

"I'm sure it'll be better in no time. I'll go rest in the house for like, an hour, maybe? Ice it or whatever. And—"

"No."

Fuck. How did Gretchen Acorn, someone who hasn't bungled a job in years, screw this one up? And so quickly! She can't get sent home, can't leave without having accomplished what she's here to do. How will she face her father if her most ambitious attempt to prove her decentness fizzles out so anticlimactically? Turning in his grip, almost falling again, she resists being led toward the early-morning light shining in through the barn's doorway. "Charlie, wait, it's . . . I think it's actually, yep, all better now! Look, let me show you—" It's some of the least convincing lying she's done in her entire life, and she resents this sloppy, panicky desperation that's spilling out of her.

"I'm not sending you back to DC, if that's what's got you in a tizzy," he says, turning her back around. His voice is softer, gentler than it usually is with her. It's more like how he talked to the dog, Clyde, yesterday—exasperated but warm. "You're gonna take it easy for the rest of the day and *observe*. Don't think I'm letting you get out of this deal of ours that easily, Little Miss Fraud."

To Gretchen's surprise, when she glances over at Charlie, a closemouthed smile plays on his lips. And, oh my, she almost collapses again, because it's slightly crooked.

11

GRETCHEN SUPPOSES IT WAS INEVITABLE. SURELY, SHE could not help out around a goat farm for a month and never once encounter a goat. But does it really have to happen right now? She basically *just* got here, and she's limping, and really, she should probably go back to the house and rest—

"All right, Acorn, what's going on now?" Charlie asks, leaning over the top wooden beam of the fence.

She blinks at him.

"Let me rephrase. I'm on this side of the fence, and you're still on that side. Even though I told you to follow me. Why?"

"My ankle?" Gretchen tries, already surveying the area for another excuse since she's sure that one isn't going to cut it. All she finds around her is a beautiful, peaceful morning. The sun's still making its way over the low mountains in the distance. The air is crisp. And thin, new blades of grass hint at the verdant season ahead. A truly idyllic place to be murdered by livestock.

Charlie shakes his head. "You've been hobbling around, but

you managed fine up until now. Are you . . ." An astonished chuckle tumbles out of him as he studies her face. "Are you scared or something?"

"Of course I'm not *scared*."

One of the goats milling about nearby rears up on its hind legs and shoves its snout through a small opening in the fence. Gretchen squeals as she takes another step backward.

Charlie laughs again, deep and full of humor. Gretchen's body zings with that sensation that's like the gotcha euphoria she got after making him blush, except way stronger. She can't decide if the feeling is welcome or traitorous, considering he's laughing *at her*.

"Jesus," he says, bowing his head. "Wish I knew you were afraid of goats. Could have just sicced the herd on you when you showed up yesterday. You would've been off my property like—" Charlie snaps his fingers.

Gretchen grabs the gate and swings it open. As soon as she steps inside the pasture, a black goat with a bulging belly attempts to shove its way out, prompting a still-laughing Charlie to lunge forward and slam the gate closed. "If you let them escape, you're paying to replace the neighbor's azaleas," he warns, working the latch and ensuring it's secure.

But Gretchen isn't listening, because other than the apparent Houdini of the bunch, still staring at the gate as if she's hoping it might open again, all of the goats now have their weird eyes on her. And they are coming her way with alarming speed. She can imagine it now: bleeding out in the bright green grass after being gored by fifteen dairy goats (or, fourteen, rather, because the one with the tennis balls on its horns won't gore her so much as smack her around a little) as they stand over her, staring down at her with their eerie rectangular pupils. Gretchen's spine goes ramrod straight as the herd surrounds her. Where is Everett *now*? He should be here to help her. It's in his best interests that she remains alive, isn't it?

The goats jockey for position, probably all wanting to be first in line to impale her. Gretchen blames her hubris; she's flown too close to the bullshit-artist sun. A square-toothed mouth comes at her, and she squeezes her eyes closed, unwilling to witness the carnage. But instead of the slicing bite she expects, there's a tug at her sleeve. And then one at the hem of her jacket. And at the leg of her overalls. And then her other leg. And the back of her jacket, and—

"Ahhh!" she screams when she opens her eyes again and sees several goats gently nibbling at her clothing. "They're eating me!"

In response to the commotion, the two—oh no, there are *two* of them?!—giant white herding dogs dance around the gathered goats, barking merrily as if cheering on their wards' murderous rampage. Gretchen screams again. "Charlie! *Help!*"

But there's no answer from Charlie. She looks over to where he's using one of the fence posts to remain upright as his laughter shakes his body.

The goat with the tennis balls on its horns manages to open one of her jacket pockets and tries to shove its entire face inside. The others notice and want in on the action, and Gretchen is quickly in the middle of a shoving match between several hip-height animals who clearly consider her a necessary civilian casualty in their battle. An unexpected push at her leg—the one with the injured ankle—knocks her off-balance, and Gretchen finds herself on the ground for the third time in less than twenty-four hours.

The laughter stops abruptly, sliced by a panicked shout. "Shit! Acorn!"

Charlie must have sprinted over, because he's there in seconds. Gretchen's covered her head like they taught her to do during tornado drills in school, but she turns her face up enough to see him part the goats like he's Moses and they're the Red Sea. He lifts her by the arms to standing.

"You should have warned me they were bloodthirsty!"

"They weren't after your blood," Charlie insists, although the way he looks her up and down frantically as he checks for damage makes the statement less convincing. Then his gaze catches on her side, and his lips press together in vexation. "They were after this." He reaches out and pulls a plastic bag full of almonds from her jacket pocket.

"I found them in the pantry when I was getting my cereal. Thought I might get hungry later," she mumbles.

"Well, you happened to choose one of their favorite snacks." His face goes softer, and he opens the bag. Charlie grabs a few almonds and holds them out to her. "Why don't you give some to them? Show them there are no hard feelings."

"No thanks. There *are* hard feelings."

He rolls his eyes and grabs her hand, turning it upright and prying open her fingers until her palm is flat. The almonds transfer, along with a bit of warmth from his skin. Then, to Gretchen's surprise, Charlie wraps his fingers around her wrist and extends her arm out toward the closest goat.

"Keep your palm flat so your fingers don't get in the way." His voice is low, gentle. "They won't hurt you. They're sweet girls. Yes, even you, Thistle." He runs his free hand down the spine of a dark brown, enormously pregnant goat that's attempting to nab the rest of the bag out of his hand.

The goats surround Gretchen's outstretched hand, and the nuts are gobbled up in an instant. It tickles, and she lets out a yelp mixed with a laugh in response.

"There you go," Charlie says with a smile that's even warmer than the emerging sun. "See? Nothing to be afraid of."

Gretchen huffs, offended. "I wasn't afraid."

"Oh, my mistake," he says. "Guess you've got this under control, then." He drops the rest of the almonds in her hand and strolls away, whistling, as the goats once again close in on her.

"Charlie . . . Charlie, no, wait!" Her attempt to sprint after him is much more of a frantic zombie shuffle, the goats and dogs all following as if she's leading the world's oddest and most chaotic parade.

12

THE NEXT MORNING FEELS LIKE DÉJÀ VU—IT'S A KNOCK AT the door that wakes her, and Charlie's voice, deep and gruff from overnight disuse, commanding her to get up. There are important differences, though. This time, when she opens her eyes, she doesn't have a ghost staring back at her; Everett presumably kept his word and stayed out of her room. Also, this morning she's aware of a slight ache in her ankle as she attempts to move it.

"I'm up, I'm up," she says, moving cautiously.

But when she opens the door, Charlie has disappeared. In his place are three paper Walmart bags sitting on the floor. "What's this?" Gretchen calls across the hall, assuming Charlie's still within earshot. The house isn't that big, and he couldn't have gotten too far in the last minute.

"Just some stuff," he replies cryptically from somewhere within his bedroom, the door to which is open just enough that a crack of sunrise shines through. It projects a glowing line onto the hallway's old hardwood, like someone took a highlighter to the floor.

She brings the bags inside her room and drops them on the bed. The first contains a pair of bright yellow rain boots. The next has a pack of six plain white cotton T-shirts like the one she borrowed yesterday, but a size smaller; a few pairs of women's crew socks; and a compression brace for her ankle. The last bag includes some utility gloves like she's seen Charlie and Lori wearing, and . . .

Did Charlie Waybill seriously buy Gretchen three bulk packs of underwear? *With more moisture-wicking power!* according to the package.

She finds herself smiling as she limps her way to Charlie's room. Resting her head on the doorframe, she says into the crack of sunlight, "Thanks, boss. How much do I owe you?"

Charlie's voice comes from closer than she's expecting, like he might be right on the other side of the door. "Consider it included in room and board."

"Thank you." And then, because she can't help herself, she says, "The, uh, underwear were especially thoughtful."

She can imagine Charlie's subsequent blush as he replies. "I figured you probably hadn't packed enough for a whole month. And they're, it's, um, important. To be comfortable while working. Hopefully, they're . . . right. The right size, I mean. Lori suggested . . . Anyway—"

"They'll do," she says. She should really thank him one last time and go back to her room. But it's too tempting to continue, to get more of a reaction from him. She's greedy for that little euphoric zing. "But really, I appreciate you thinking of that. I only brought four pairs with me, all very lacy. Actually, that's not true.

One pair is sort of a satin and mesh combo. Still, not ideal for farmwork. So I'm grateful—"

The door swings open. Charlie stands there with cheeks pinker than a theater kid's after doing their own stage makeup for the first time. Gretchen's grin is slow, expanding along with the deep satisfaction she gets out of affecting him. His gaze sweeps down her body as if he can't help himself, eventually landing on her bare feet.

"Looks like your ankle is better today," he says, drawing her attention to the fact that she's been standing with most of her weight on that foot this whole time.

Oh, great. Now he probably thinks she was lying about her injury, even though she really was in a lot of pain yesterday. "I told you it was nothing. *I* wanted to keep working. You're the one who made me spend the day mostly on my butt."

His expression is more skeptical than she'd like, but he says, "Probably a mild strain. Still, you should wear the brace for a few days to be safe." Then Charlie stares at her for a long time, as if contemplating something. He seems to come to a decision that he's not all that excited about based on the tone of his voice. "Go get dressed. You're coming with me."

"Coming with you where?"

"Farmers market."

For some reason, the idea of leaving the premises with Charlie never crossed her mind. Which is stupid, now that she thinks about it. It's not like Gilded Creek is the Hotel California. Well, at least not for *her*. "Oh. Um. Okay."

"Meet me at the truck in half an hour."

"Sure thing, boss." She's about to turn and go back to her room, but something makes her pause for a moment. "Everett told me you're a good egg. Keep this up and I might have to start agreeing with him."

"Just get ready," he says, and slams the door closed.

"WHERE ARE YOU OFF TO, LOOKING SO, UH . . . LIKE THAT?"
Everett asks, his head peeking over the back of the couch when Gretchen comes downstairs.

"What's wrong with it?" she asks defensively. She's wearing a short black velvet dress she brought with her, along with two crystal necklaces she was able to de-mud. Just the sight of her heeled booties made her ankle throb again, so she decided to break in the new yellow rain boots, which she admits don't exactly match the rest of the outfit. And okay, yes, she's wearing the flannel Charlie gave her as makeshift outerwear since her jacket is still out of commission. It's very . . . gothic grunge Gorton's Fisherman. And based on the face Everett is making, it isn't particularly working.

"Nothing, nothing. You just . . . nothing."

"Whatever, I don't have time to change. I'm going to the farmers market with Charlie." Gretchen finger-combs the ends of her hair, trying to work some body into it. Two showers with the farm's well water combined with Charlie's citrusy three-in-one has made it lie so limp it almost looks like she flat-ironed it. "I'm not sure why he wants me there, but it's a good opportunity to work on him a bit."

Everett doesn't say anything, just continues to stare at her.

"What? I know my hair isn't great, but—"

"Don't worry about it," he says. "Go ahead. Have fun. I'll just . . . be here. Doing the same thing I do every day. Alone."

"Everett."

"It's okay. Go. Enjoy."

"Are you seriously trying to guilt me?" She walks around to the front of the couch to get a full view of the ghost, who has his legs crossed primly as he hovers an inch above the cushions.

"Of course not."

"You want me to save Charlie, right? Well, to do that I'm going to need to spend time with him. And he isn't particularly inclined to give me a ton of opportunities to do that. I need to take them where I can get them. Hey, I'm sorry you'll be lonely, but—"

"Ha, lonely?" Everett scoffs. "I won't be lonely. I have . . . *so* many other friends."

Gretchen rolls her eyes. "Yeah, okay. I'm the only person who knows you exist, but you're Mr. Popular, huh?"

"I managed just fine before you showed up, didn't I? So go. Have a good day with *Charlie* at the *farmers market.*"

"Why are you saying it like that?"

"I'm not saying it like anything." Everett throws his upper body down hard enough on the couch that part of him disappears inside, leaving only an arm and his face sticking out of the cushions.

"Okay, well, whatever is going on with you this morning, I don't have time for it." As if to corroborate her words, Charlie calls from the porch for her to get a move on. Gretchen turns to leave the living room, but Everett's expression—framed by the beige and navy stripes of the couch's upholstery—makes her pause. She's seen it before, on her own face when she looks in the mirror sometimes.

"Ev," she says, taking a step closer. "I'm going to be back in a few hours, okay? I promise. I'll come back."

He considers for a moment. "I know. You think I was worried

or something?" The scoff he produces is some of the worst acting she's seen. Ironic, considering the aspirations that led him here.

"It's okay if you were. I know that being alone . . . it really sucks." Gretchen suppresses the laugh absurdly rising up in her throat in response to the too-simple description of the aching, all-encompassing emptiness with which she's quite familiar. She glances down at the jute rug beneath her feet. The words are meant to reassure Everett, but as they come out of her mouth, they feel strangely like they're buoying her as well. "But I'm not going anywhere. At least not yet."

Charlie yells for her again, then opens the front door a crack to poke his head inside. He glares at her. The man's patience is already gossamer thin, and they've barely started their day.

Gretchen grabs the remote and turns the TV on to a random channel. "I'll be back soon," she mutters, and then heads for the door as quickly as her tender ankle will allow.

13

THE FARMERS MARKET IS IN A SHOPPING CENTER PARKING
lot in Leesburg, Virginia—a town about half an hour away that's
on the smaller side but practically a metropolis when compared
to the nanoscopic Derring Heights. Most of the other vendors
are already set up by the time Gretchen and Charlie arrive. Unsurprising, considering Charlie spent nearly the entire trip harp-
ing on how late they're running thanks to Gretchen's supposed
lack of haste in getting ready to leave.

Thankfully, their booth at the end of a row is under a small
tent, since the clouds are looking ominous. Charlie tosses a
wooden sign reading GILDED CREEK FARM—GOAT CHEESE,
MILK, SOAP onto the table, wordlessly ordering Gretchen to set
up while he grabs the large cooler from the back of the truck. She
sits the sign directly in the middle of the gray plastic surface. Not
the most glamorous setup. She wonders how much it would cost
for a banner to affix to the front of the table, and maybe a cute
gingham check fabric tablecloth would add a certain charm—

"Hello!" A sunshiny voice makes her head snap up, and a woman with blonde milkmaid braids stands in front of the booth. There's a slight luster to her peachy skin even on this overcast day— probably thanks to some sort of body lotion or sunscreen, but she wears it so effortlessly that Gretchen can't be sure it's not a natural radiance. A customer already? No. Gretchen has been away from her shop for a few days, but a bullshit artist is always working. Which means that, even as she bickered with Charlie about who was to blame for their lateness as they arrived and unloaded their things, she took note of the other booths and the people manning them. Her memory clicks this woman into place behind a burlap-covered table across the aisle. Yellow candles, jars of honey, and tubes and tubs of lip balms and lotions covered the surface. The sign attached to the corner of the tent with twine read JOHNNY BEE GOODS.

"Hi there," Gretchen says, adopting a folksier cadence and her sweetest smile to match the one in front of her.

"I noticed you're running a bit behind schedule this morning. Would you like some help with your table?"

"Oh, um . . ." The idea of Charlie thanking this literally dazzling woman for her assistance makes Gretchen's fist clench around the bar of goat's milk soap she's unpacking from the crate. She loosens her grip so as not to indent it, and adds it to the display she's constructing as she formulates a polite way to turn down the offer.

The woman points to the soap, currently laid out in a row of small stacks. "Oh, Charlie likes those stacked as a pyramid, actually."

Gretchen's hand slips off the next bar altogether. It shoots across the table and falls to the ground.

"Oh no," the woman laments as she picks it up from the asphalt in front of her feet. The light gray-purple soap is indented at the corner, a chunk of gravel embedded in the side. "Can't sell this one now." She brings it to her nose and inhales deeply. "Sage-lavender. My favorite. Such a shame."

Charlie sets down the large cooler filled with ice to keep the milk and cheese chilled behind the table. He glances up. "Oh, hey, Hannah."

The woman—Hannah—passes the soap back to Gretchen and flashes her beautiful smile in Charlie's direction. "Hi, Charlie. I see you . . . brought help today?" Her eyes dart over to Gretchen and linger awkwardly.

"Yeah. This is Gretchen Acorn. She's my, uh, my intern. At the farm. Just started the other day."

"Oh, wow. An intern. That's exciting. I bet you're learning so much!" Hannah's voice drips with condescension. She casually brushes her fingers along Charlie's arm and leans in closer. "Would you like some help setting up?"

Charlie shoots that charmingly crooked smile Gretchen has only gotten out of him once so far back at her. For someone who seems to see right through Gretchen's whole schtick, she wonders why he's so oblivious to what Hannah's doing. Which is . . . um . . . well, she isn't exactly sure, but the pretty blonde woman is up to *something*. And Gretchen would know, so often being up to something herself.

"I think we're about done, actually, but thanks so much for offering," he says as he takes off his dark green baseball cap with GILDED CREEK GOAT FARM embroidered in white on the front and smooths back his hair.

"Just in time." Hannah's smile seems to have increased in wattage throughout the conversation, the way a light bulb flares briefly before exploding. "Well, have a great one!"

"You too, Hannah," Gretchen says, unable to say her name without emphasizing the two syllables separately, almost mockingly. "And hey, I know it's a little banged up, but do you want this? Since it's your favorite scent and all." She holds out the damaged bar of soap in both her hands, as if intending it to be a peace offering. *It's not.*

"Oh, no thanks. I already have a *ton* of Charlie's soap at home." This sounds oddly territorial to Gretchen's ears, which she's pretty sure is intentional. "Happy selling!"

Charlie gives Hannah another smile and a nod of acknowledgment, and she does an annoyingly cute little happy nose-scrunch in response before turning away and practically skipping over to the Johnny Bee Goods booth.

"What's the holdup with the soaps?" Charlie asks, his voice back to the low growl he reserves solely for Gretchen. He reaches over the small pile to grab the bar that fell victim to her . . . jealousy? Anger? No. It may have seemed like a reaction to Hannah's apparent familiarity with Charlie, but it wasn't. It was run-of-the-mill clumsiness. *Just clumsiness.* A new affliction for her, but a more palatable explanation than that she's suddenly lost her ability to distance herself from those sorts of emotions. "And what the hell happened to this one?"

"Deduct it from my pay," she snaps.

"You don't get paid."

"Most sought-after spirit medium in one of the wealthiest areas of DC to unpaid farm intern." Gretchen continues straightening the soap into neat little stacks, despite Hannah's warning of Charlie's preferences. "My, how I've fallen in life, and so quickly."

Charlie reaches under the table and drags something over— the closed large cooler by the sound of it—and says, "Ankle."

"Huh?"

"Sit and rest your ankle. I'm not going to let you overuse it today so you can get out of doing work again tomorrow."

She obeys the order, despite her instinct not to, because her ankle is starting to twinge ever so slightly. That and because this looking-out-for-her thing Charlie's been doing, however begrudgingly, is kinda nice.

They sit in silence as customers start to mosey onto the lot. None are heading toward the Gilded Creek table yet, focused more on the booths toward the market's entrance.

"Why did you do it that way?" Charlie's voice startles Gretchen with how close it is. He must have leaned toward her at some point while she was watching an elderly couple holding hands as they made their way up the row.

"Do what what way?"

"Stack the soap like that. You barely put any out. I brought thirty bars and you only put out, what, seven?"

"Scarcity," she replies, returning her gaze to the shuffling little elderly couple. Looking at Charlie from this angle, mere inches away, feels too intense for a Sunday morning. It makes her heart swallow its next beat, as if she were standing directly in front of an amp at a concert.

He leans back in his chair. "What are you talking about?"

"Especially somewhere like this, people walk through and browse, and they say, 'Oh, I'll come back and buy this later,' but how often do they really? Not that often. They get distracted, or tired, talk themselves out of it, forget about it completely." Gretchen adjusts the way she's sitting to get more of her leg on the cooler under the table. "But if it seems like the thing they want might be gone if they don't jump on it now, they're more likely to buy it on the spot."

"Mm, and how do you know this?"

"My dad works in sales." It's a lie she told hundreds of times growing up. Sometimes she changed what Ned sold to suit the conversation, or just on a whim. Insurance, cars, hot tubs, even space shuttle parts when they lived near Cape Canaveral one summer. "He taught me a few tricks of the trade."

"Did he." Charlie says it flatly, not really a question.

Gretchen's never worked retail, exactly, but she assumes she'd be a natural. Sales and bullshit artistry really aren't that different; when it comes down to it, both require convincing someone that you understand their needs and can offer them a solution to a problem—even if the problem is one you created for them. And she's always been excellent at that.

Well, usually. As long as the someone isn't Charlie Waybill. She can't even seem to convince him there's a problem to solve in the first place.

"Anyway," she says, "I'll replenish the stock as we go so we don't actually run out."

"I don't usually sell more than a couple bars. Mostly people want cheese."

"Leave it to me," she says with a smile. "I'm gonna move some fuckin' soap today. Just watch."

"All right. You do that."

After a minute more of silence as they wait, Gretchen finds herself asking, "What's the deal with Hannah?" It wasn't her intention to bring it up, and she usually doesn't say things without thinking them through. But something about the woman and the way she keeps glancing over at the Gilded Creek Goat Farm booth like she's trying to catch Charlie's eye makes Gretchen feel a little . . . impulsive? Sure. Let's go with that.

"What's the *deal* with her? I don't know that she has a deal. Her family owns an apiary in Lovettsville. Her uncle takes care of the bees, her mom and aunt make the products, and she does all of their selling and marketing stuff. We trade sometimes to get local honey for the honey chèvre and the oatmeal soap."

"It seems like you're . . . friendly."

Charlie gives Gretchen a mean little smile—not crooked. "I'm friendly with most people."

Gretchen sighs. She thought his asking her to come to the farmers market with him was a sign he was thawing, but apparently not. Annoyingly, his hostility does nothing to dissipate her desire to learn more about his relationship with Hannah.

"Have you ever gone out with her?" she asks. "Like on a date?"

"Not sure how that's any of your business, but no."

"She likes you."

Charlie shrugs, his hostile expression replaced with a carefully blank one. "So?"

"So she's really pretty," Gretchen concedes. "Like *really* pretty. The big eyes, the silky gold hair. I mean, her skin practically *glows*."

"If you think she's so pretty, maybe you should ask her out."

"I don't date," Gretchen says, which for some reason feels safer than admitting that Hannah rubs her the wrong way. Because she's fairly sure the only reason for that is the blonde bee lady's blatant interest in the man sitting beside her. Maybe it isn't so strange that she feels . . . protective over Charlie, though. It's part of her job to save him from his family's curse, after all. She might as well have his other best interests at heart. A good person would probably throw that in for free.

He glances at her. She assumes he's noticed that Gretchen said she doesn't date, and not that she doesn't date women. And she doesn't, but only because she doesn't date anyone. Gretchen is an equal opportunity not-dater. Sex? Sure. Once or twice a year, if the opportunity arises. Dating? Never. Too much trouble, too much risk. But if Charlie has any questions about the people she does or doesn't not-date, he doesn't ask them.

Customers finally reach their booth, which Gretchen appreciates since it means the end of this conversation. It's two men in their early forties, a chubby baby strapped to each of their chests. One baby is wearing a yellow sun hat, the other an identical one in orange.

"Oh my, look at you," Gretchen coos to the one nearest her. She isn't particularly interested in babies, but parents are always more likely to warm to you if you fawn over their children. "I love the little hats."

"Probably didn't need them today," one of the men jokes, gently bouncing back and forth as if afraid to cease movement for even a second. "Supposed to start pouring any minute."

"Fingers crossed it holds off," Gretchen says, crossing the fingers of both hands emphatically.

The baby in the orange hat has a bumpy red drool rash on its chin, and Gretchen sees her opening. "Have you ever tried goat's milk soap with them? It's extremely gentle and so, so moisturizing. All natural ingredients. Great for sensitive baby skin. A ton of our customers with young children swear by it."

"Hm, no, we haven't tried that yet," the other man says, his attention moving from the cheese display to the small stacks of soap. He picks up a deep purple-red bar—blackberry vanilla, Gretchen remembers from arranging them—and sniffs it. The face he makes says he either doesn't like the scent or finds it overpowering.

Gretchen picks up a bar of the oatmeal soap, which is made with Johnny Bee Goods honey, apparently, and hands it to him. "This one's our bestseller," she says, having absolutely no clue if that's true or not. "The oatmeal is a natural soothing agent, and we use local honey."

He gives it a sniff. "Oh, that's lovely. Subtle and clean. Maybe we'll swing back by to get some on our way out?" He directs this question to his partner.

"Oh, you certainly could, but we don't have too many of that one left," Gretchen says, glancing down at the two bars she arranged on the table. "Like I said, it's our bestseller. I would hate for it to be gone by the time you come back around."

"Ah." The man looks at his partner again and they have one of those brief eye-contact-only conversations. "Okay, let's get it now." He holds out his credit card, which Charlie runs through the reader attached to his cell phone.

Gretchen finds the stack of small brown paper bags under the table, and slips the bar of soap inside one. "I hope you love it," she says as she hands it over. "And that we'll see you again soon."

"We actually live in Frederick, just here visiting family," the other one says. His bouncing has transitioned into a sort of cha-cha movement. "Are you at any of the markets up that way?"

Charlie shakes his head. "Only this one at the moment."

"Well, your mom is always saying we should visit more often . . ."

One man nudges the other affectionately, as his partner rolls his eyes.

They each hold up one of the babies' chubby hands to have them "wave" goodbye, and Gretchen waves goodbye back (although it feels kind of ridiculous).

"You only do one farmers market?" Gretchen asks. "I thought this was the main way you sell your products."

"It is." Charlie takes off his cap and pushes his hair back again before replacing it. "But I'm only one person, and I can't be everywhere at once."

"What about Lori?"

"She already works as many hours as I can pay her to work, and I need her help back at the farm a lot more than I need it here. Besides, Lori is an excellent cheesemaker, but she isn't exactly customer-service oriented."

Gretchen snorts. "That's true." Her limited interactions with the older woman so far have been what she can only describe as brusque.

She wonders how Charlie makes any money at all without doing more than he currently is. But she senses he's not especially inclined to talk about the whys and hows of his business decisions at the moment.

"How did your grandparents manage it all?" she asks instead.

Charlie hesitates before answering. "I imagine it was a lot easier with the two of them, plus they had a few seasonal employees and me during summers and long weekends. Grandpa managed the farm, and Grandma made the products with some help from Lori and took care of all the markets. Three or four a week, spring through fall, and one in the winter. Plus she knew all of the people at the local mom-and-pop stores and got them to carry Gilded Creek products. I think they even had relationships with a few restaurants." He stares into the distance for a moment, lost in thought or maybe a memory, then brings himself back. "They were such a good team. I don't . . . can't . . . do it all half as well as they did."

A genuinely good person, Gretchen presumes, would feel sympathetic. Instead, she feels a tiny jolt of excitement hearing the undercurrent of emotion flowing in Charlie's voice. It rises to a nice steady buzz when she sees something in his eyes that makes him look young and vulnerable. His feelings of failure, of not being able to carry on his grandparents' legacy. *This is my way in.* But it all evaporates as quickly as it arrived, like a few raindrops falling in the desert on a hot day.

"So why don't you date?" Charlie asks. The subject change isn't exactly subtle, but he manages to make it sound completely devoid of curiosity, which both is impressive and gets under Gretchen's skin. "Is it because relationships are challenging when your entire life is built on lies?"

And there it is. A step forward, a step back. Just like the man with the baby doing the cha-cha. Ironically, she thinks his accusation that she's nothing but a liar is a necessary reminder that she can't tell him the truth. Because, for a split second, she wanted to tell him. She wanted to say that, yes, it is actually difficult for her to let people in. But not because of the way she lives her life. No, it's because, in her experience, love isn't worth her time or the inevitable heartache; she's a person who isn't meant to keep anyone she loves. They leave her, or she's forced to leave them, and it always hurts just a little more than she wishes it did. She thought maybe, when she met Lawrence, it would be different.

But even he dropped her once he knew who she really was. Or rather, who she wasn't. And every loss feels like the deepening of an existing wound, getting nearer and nearer to piercing the vital parts of her that she won't be able to survive without.

Gretchen's not about to tell Charlie any of that. He's made it clear that they are still at odds here, and she's not going to let her guard down in some foolish attempt to feel temporarily close to someone—to him especially. Not when there's so much at stake.

So she says, "No, it's actually because I don't see a point in going out and bothering with other people when I can just stay home and make myself come better than anyone else ever could."

Charlie's attempt to swallow his surprise at her bluntness seems to go awry just as the next customer stops in front of the booth. And while he's busy coughing into his elbow and taking swigs of water, Gretchen sells an extravagantly bedazzled woman who looks like she could be Mrs. Easterly's country cousin ten bars of goat's milk soap.

14

THANKS TO GRETCHEN'S COMMENT, HEIGHTENED SEXUAL
tension hangs around the rest of the morning, as unacknowledged
but obviously present as the darkening clouds overhead. The latter finally give in and burst around eleven, and all of the remaining customers hurry back to their cars. At first, Gretchen and
Charlie remain at their table, watching Hannah buzz around like
one of her family's bees as she puts her cutesy rustic decor and
products into storage containers and shoves it all into the back
seat of her SUV. But then there's thunder, which even Gretchen
knows means there's bound to be lightning—not ideal when out-
doors under a metal pole tent. So now she and Charlie scramble
around too, trying to load everything into the truck without getting completely soaked. It's mostly futile.

As she hoists herself into the passenger seat, she's happy to note
that her velvet dress dries much more quickly than the gauzy one
she was wearing the day she arrived at Gilded Creek. She sheds

the now-wet flannel, and squeaks the toes of her rain boots together. It turns out the gothic grunge Gorton's Fisherman ensemble was quite practical if not fashion-forward.

Charlie tucks his drenched Gilded Creek Goat Farm hat between his seat and the cupholders, leaving his damp and mussed hair uncovered. Seeing it messy instead of in its default wave does something strange to Gretchen's heart. Nothing worth paying attention to, she's sure. Probably just some sexual attraction that got lost on its way from her brain to her vagina.

She clears her throat at the same time Charlie clears his. Both go silent, waiting to see if the other will speak.

"Thank you for your help," he finally says. "I have to admit you, uh—how did you phrase it? Oh right. You did 'move some fuckin' soap today.' We only have, what? Five bars left?"

"Something like that." Four, actually.

"It's a lot more than I've ever sold." He taps his fingers on the edge of the steering wheel. "It was interesting. Seeing you talk to people, I mean. You're good at it. Though I probably shouldn't be surprised by that, given your profession."

They both know that he's using "profession" as a euphemism. While it most likely is standing in for "charlatan," not "spirit medium," Gretchen doesn't allow herself to take offense, because she hopes it might be his clumsy version of an olive branch. And also because he isn't wrong (not that she can admit it).

Then Charlie says, "I got some asparagus before we left. From a friend who sells produce. It's in season." The way he blinks after he finishes talking makes him look bemused, as if he's surprised himself with the non sequitur.

"I'm . . . happy for you?"

He opens his mouth again, then closes it, fishlike.

They pull off the road and onto the farm's long, winding driveway. The rain makes the rusty junk and dead tree near the entrance look particularly sinister. *We should do something about that*, she thinks. The truck bounces as it rolls over small potholes and ruts where the gravel needs to be replaced. *And that.*

But her plans for improvement are pushed to the side as Gretchen catches Charlie sneaking a glance at her chest as it jiggles around the seat belt. *He wants me too.* A pleasant reminder that all of this tension between them isn't just torture, but another weapon in her arsenal. She's under no illusions that sex would be all it takes to leave Charlie spellbound and willing to do whatever she says.

But god, would it be fun.

GRETCHEN HAS JUST FINISHED CHANGING OUT OF HER damp clothes and into the T-shirt and sleep shorts she brought as pajamas when Everett sticks his fist through the door to her room and pounds rhythmically in the air. "Knock, knock," he says. "Can I come in?"

She stifles a smile as she says, "Sure." Because despite Everett's faults—of which she has already discovered several—he is genuinely making an effort to respect Gretchen's boundaries. He may not have been her first choice for a partner in this unconventional mission, but maybe they can make it work.

"You've gotta talk to Charlie." Everett has his arms folded over his chest and looks surprisingly serious as he steps through the door and into the room.

Gretchen barely glances at him as she takes down her ponytail and runs a brush through her hair. "Yeah, I know. That's why I'm still here," she mumbles around the elastic held between her lips.

He shakes his head. "No, not about the curse. I mean, yes, about the curse, but also about the TV. You gotta talk to him about it," Everett says, tugging at the tuft of dark hair protruding from under his newsboy cap. "You gotta tell him to leave it on for me. I can't live—I mean, I can't *haunt* like this anymore."

"How, exactly, do you recommend I approach that conversation, Ev? Charlie doesn't even believe you exist, much less give a shit about whether you're adequately entertained."

"Pleeeaaaaase. Charles bought his mom—that's Enid, George's wife—a television in 1955, and it completely changed my afterlife. But I've always been restricted to watching when and what someone else wants. Now you're here, making my dreams come true. Don't let Charlie crush them."

She figures she could mention it to Charlie, but not tonight. Tonight she plans to stay in her room, email her clients to inform them of her unforeseen monthlong absence, touch base with Yolanda about paying the outstanding bills and rent, and head to bed as early as possible. And if she just happens not to see Charlie until tomorrow morning because of how busy and tired she is, well . . . that's fine.

"I'll try to talk to him about it at some point," she says, hedging as much as she can.

Everett steps in front of her. "Or now? Now would be good."

"If I talk to him now, will you leave me alone for the rest of the night?"

He looks up, considering. "Turn something on for me, talk to Charlie, and you won't hear a peep from me till morning."

Now, that's too good of an offer to pass up.

After setting up Everett with an *NCIS* marathon in the living room, she finds Charlie in the kitchen. He stands at the stove, stirring something in a pan. Delicious food smells fill the air, and Gretchen's stomach rumbles.

"You're cooking," she says stupidly.

"I am," he responds without looking at her. "Why do you sound so surprised about it?"

"Everett told me you eat a lot of frozen meals, so I figured . . ." It's frankly embarrassing how little she knows about this man despite unprecedented access to his life. She has a spy who is *literally invisible*, and yet she would probably have to turn Charlie Waybill away were he to come into her spirit medium shop, she has such an incomplete picture of what he values and needs from her. It's like his ability to see through her has given him some boon that makes him extra opaque when she tries to do the same to him.

"Mm, right, the ghost told you. Not that you looked inside my freezer and saw them all stacked in there."

She sits backward in one of the chairs around the table, folding her arms over the back so she can rest her chin there and watch Charlie move about the kitchen. "I didn't look in your— well, I did, because I made myself a Marie Callender's last night for dinner since you left me here alone, but that was after Everett told me that's what you eat. Seeing them only corroborated what he said."

Charlie shrugs, choosing to ignore the parts about his ghostly relative. "Sometimes it's easier to pop something in the microwave after a long day than make a whole meal from scratch. Especially since it's just me here now and I get tired of leftovers." He grabs a cutting board piled with asparagus and dumps it into the pan, then scoops up something that looks like a pile of pale yellow ribbons from the counter and drops them into a pot of boiling water.

"But tonight, you cook."

"Tonight, I cook," he agrees. Gretchen suspects he's smiling, but he still doesn't look at her, so it's hard to tell for sure.

She leans forward to get a better view of what he's doing. "Give me the play-by-play. What's happening here?"

"I'm sautéing the asparagus from the farmers market with some garlic, butter, and lemon juice to go over the fettuccine I made."

"Sorry, that you *made*?" The man makes his own pasta! Gretchen isn't sure what she could have done with this information had she had it earlier, but she's still annoyed that Everett didn't bother telling her about Charlie's talents in the kitchen. That frozen potpie she had to eat last night feels like even more of an insult now.

"My grandmother taught me," he says. "She was a great cook. She loved trying new recipes. Watched a ton of Food Network shows."

"*Diners, Drive-Ins and Dives*," Gretchen says quietly, almost to herself.

"Um, yeah."

"Well, it smells delicious," she says, changing the subject before he can accuse her of a good guess. Her stomach growls loud enough that she's sure he hears it. "I suppose I better select my dinner from the freezer and get out of your way."

"You— We— I figured we would share this? Unless . . . Do you have any allergies? Or, uh, plans? Guess I should've asked before, I shouldn't have assumed—"

Gretchen smiles at the way Charlie stumbles over his words.

"No allergies. Or plans. I just didn't expect you to want to share your dinner with me, given, you know, your general dislike of my presence."

He gives the pan another stir. "Your presence isn't what I dislike about you, Acorn." She's still trying to decipher if that's a compliment or an insult when he continues, "Besides, I made too much. You might as well have some."

"Thanks. Um, can I help with anything? Keeping in mind my kitchen skills are extremely limited."

"Think you can handle zesting a lemon?"

Said lemon, the grater, and a bowl are sitting on the counter on the opposite side of the stove, so she walks over and gets to work. This might be the longest interaction Charlie and Gretchen have had without one or both of them resorting to name-calling. Progress! Now, if they can just keep it going through an entire meal, then—

Ah, fuck, shit.

"What happened?" Charlie asks. Gretchen must have said that aloud.

"Grated myself." The blood wells up into a tiny dome on the tip of her index finger. "I don't think it's too bad, though?" She holds it up for his inspection and he takes it between his own fingers to study the injury.

"You'll likely pull through," he says, releasing her. He turns back to the stove. "Clean it off and wrap a paper towel around it for a minute."

She sticks her finger under the faucet as directed, the sting of citrus oil in the open wound diminishing as it's diluted. "I swear I'm not usually this incompetent," she says.

"Oh, I don't think you're incompetent at all." Charlie turns off the burner under the pasta. "You're just pretending so I'll assume you're harmless and let my guard down."

He says it in a tone that could be taken as teasing, but she's fairly certain it's another accusation. Which is funny, because Gretchen actually hasn't been hurting herself on purpose. But is that something she would do? Absolutely. She's honestly a bit surprised she didn't think of it earlier. Like she told Everett, he didn't need to push her into that puddle; she would have fallen into it herself. Then again, how long could she really coast on being pathetic? Probably not that long before Charlie would catch on and harden his heart. Even a softy like him has his limits. She feels dangerously close already without even trying to test them.

But really, this man sees through her so much more easily than anyone else ever has. And why doesn't that scare her? Okay, it does scare her—rather a lot, actually. But shouldn't it scare her *more*? The urge to flee is still there whenever he gives Gretchen that look that says he knows she's a liar. Except what if maybe she doesn't want to run away so much as be chased? And maybe . . . maybe caught? Now, *that's* a frightening thought.

"So how does a young guy such as yourself wind up as a sixty-something-year-old woman's bridge partner?" she asks.

The way he finally glances over at her before responding says he wants her to be aware that he knows she's changing the subject and he's doing her a favor by allowing it. "Deborah and I only really played together a few times before she lost Rachel and I got too busy with everything here. But when she called the other week and asked if I was interested in partnering again, I was glad for the opportunity to catch up. She actually used to be Grandma Ellen's bridge partner. They were close—Grandma used to babysit her back when she was a little girl living around here."

"Wait. Deborah lived around . . . here?" It's difficult to reconcile the fancy rich lady who throws thousands of dollars around with someone who would live out in the boonies.

"Yeah. You wouldn't think it, considering how hoity-toity her life is now, but she was born a country girl. A wealthy country girl, but a country girl nonetheless. Her parents owned a horse boarding facility out this way." Charlie lowers the heat on the burner and leans back against the counter. "Anyway, when Grandma died, I took her place in the next big bridge tournament. She'd taught me to play when I was a little kid staying here for the summer. She was always teaching me stuff. Probably to keep me out of mischief." He smiles fondly. "Joining up with Deborah when she needed a new partner felt like a good way to honor Ellen and all of the love she gave me when I needed it. And a good way to support Deborah now."

"That's . . . really sweet."

Charlie shrugs, then takes hold of both sides of the pasta pot. He dumps its contents into a colander in the sink, steam billowing up and temporarily obscuring his face. "Deborah was a good friend to my grandmother, and she's become a good friend to me. Up until she dropped you into my lap, at least. She and I are going to have a . . . serious conversation about that when she gets back from France. Grab plates, would you? Top corner cabinet."

Gretchen abandons the small hill of zest she's produced and opens the cabinet, trying not to think too intensely about the mental image of being in Charlie's lap. The dishes are stacked on the second shelf—a few inches too high for her to reach. Standing on tiptoe gets her closer, but she's still not tall enough. Plus, the odd angle sends a twinge through her ankle. Then suddenly

Charlie is there, the warmth of his body pressed against the back of hers, one hand on the counter so close to her waist that his thumb almost brushes against her as his other hand reaches above and over her head to grab two plates. He lets go of the counter, and that's it, he's about to step away. Except he doesn't. He lingers there, their bodies still millimeters apart.

"Acorn?" Charlie whispers, and his breath flutters the flyaway hairs near her ear.

"Hmm?" It comes out higher pitched than Gretchen expects.

"Why do you . . . smell like me?"

"Oh. Ha ha. Um, yeah. I packed my bag counting on those little hotel toiletries, so I've had to borrow your shower stuff. Is that a problem?"

"No. Not a problem." He hands her the plates.

They barely speak as they eat dinner, his demeanor closed off yet again, and as soon as the last dish is washed, Charlie grabs his jacket and leaves.

THE LAST TWO NIGHTS WHEN CHARLIE WENT OUT, HE didn't come back to the farm until well after midnight. So when Gretchen literally runs into him in the upstairs hallway after coming out of the bathroom just after nine, she shrieks. Not because she's startled to run into him so much as startled to actually run *into* him instead of *through*. She's already gotten too used to hanging out with Everett.

"Sorry, sorry," he says at the same time she manages an, "Ope!" Apparently, those four months she lived in Wisconsin really made an impression on her.

"I wasn't expecting you," she says to explain her initial over-reaction to his presence. "Back so soon, I mean. You stayed out later the last couple nights, so I figured—"

"I just went to pick up a few more things at the store. Here." Charlie shoves a full plastic bag toward her, then brushes his hair back with his fingers as if he isn't sure what else to do with his hands now that he isn't holding something.

"More gifts? You spoil me, sir." The bag is surprisingly heavy. Gretchen opens it and peeks inside. "Shampoo?"

"And conditioner and stuff. So you won't keep using mine."

"Oh. Um, thanks?" She isn't sure why her using his cheap Suave Men's 3-in-1 is such an issue that he had to immediately drive an hour round trip to the nearest store to remedy it, but regardless of his motives, this is so *considerate*. Better for her hair too. Except . . . "Why are there . . . so many?" Gretchen counts ten travel-sized bottles, plus a bulk pack of disposable razors and two mini cans of shaving gel. How much shower stuff does he think one woman needs for a month? It's like how NASA tried to send Sally Ride to space for one week with a hundred tampons "just in case."

Charlie scratches the back of his neck. "I, uh, didn't know what kind you'd want. They had a lot of options. You know, extra body, color treated, moisturizing. So I figured I would just get a bunch to be safe. And then tell me if there's one you like best, and I can . . . we can . . . I'll grab a bigger bottle next time I go into town."

"That's really . . . Thank you." She wonders for a moment why he didn't simply ask her what shampoo and conditioner she usually uses. Maybe he didn't know he was going to do this until he was actually doing it? Like getting carried along a wave of kindness he had no choice but to ride if he didn't want to drown be-

neath it. She pictures him standing in front of the bins of tiny
toiletries at the store, unsure how he got there but knowing he
can't leave until he's gathered a truly ridiculous number of them
to give her. The mental image forces her to stifle a smile.

"You're welcome." He starts to turn toward his room, but stops.
"Oh. I should have asked . . . is your bed comfortable enough?
Do you need anything?"

Yeah, she thinks. *You in it.* "It's great. Really comfy. Except . . ."

"Except?"

"Well, it's been a little chilly at night. Do you have any extra
blankets?" Even without Everett beside her last night, she woke
up shivering. But mostly she's fishing for an opening to ask about
the color-clashing handmade projects sprinkled around the house.

"Sure, yeah."

He disappears into his bedroom, then returns a minute later
with another visually challenging afghan. This one is in a diamond pattern, featuring red, light pink, neon pink, and a truly
horrific brown-yellow shade.

"This is really . . ." She searches for a word to describe it and
lands on "fun." She takes the blanket and runs a finger over the
outline of one of the diamonds. "Kind of looks like the one in
my room."

"Yeah. Grandma Ellen really enjoyed knitting."

"She made them all? The one on the couch too?" As if these
were something someone would *purchase*.

"Yeah."

"Wow. A real talented lady," she says. And she means that,
because though the color combinations are . . . unique . . . it
doesn't negate the skill and care it took to create them. Certainly
not something Gretchen would know how to do.

Charlie folds his lips into his mouth and chews on them before responding. "She was. Grandma could do pretty much anything."

The choice of words feels heavy, how much that *anything* speaks to the magnitude of what Charlie lost when his grandmother died. He bows his head, staring at the floor. A flash of selfishness has Gretchen wishing she could take away his pain, replace it with something he wants, something he can use. And she can, the way she has for the people who come to see her in DC. Before she thinks better of it, she's reaching for his hand. It's warm, rough with calluses that kiss her own palm.

Charlie looks up. Their eyes meet. Gretchen takes a step closer.

"She misses you too, you know," she says. "And . . . she wants me to tell you . . . that she's so proud of you."

His face loses its softness as his stare becomes instantly imbued with that quiet anger yet again. He pulls away, wrenching their hands apart. "Be out at the barn by six tomorrow morning," he says, turning back toward his bedroom. "Set an alarm."

15

A SHINY RED PICKUP TRUCK BUMPS DOWN THE DRIVEWAY around noon on Monday. Gretchen doesn't think much of it— some neighboring farmer, perhaps, coming to trade kale for goat curds or whatever (she should really get a better handle on how, exactly, this all works). But then the truck is followed by a black Mercedes sedan. *That* catches her attention. She can't imagine luxury cars are particularly abundant (or practical) in these parts.

She hurries toward the house, where she planned to grab a quick lunch while doing her best to avoid Charlie in the process. Things between them have been weird since last night when she . . . well, after she screwed up whatever kind of moment they were having. They've reverted to how they were before: snide comments about her being a fraud and a thief, his disdain making her snap back at him before she thinks it through. All the progress she might have made with him so far, erased just like that. Stupid.

When Gretchen reaches the farmhouse, though, she realizes

there's no avoiding Charlie if she wants to get inside. He's standing in front of the porch, talking to a middle-aged white woman in dark jeans and an ivory ruffled blouse. The woman shakes his hand and goes over to the couple getting out of the red truck. Charlie spots Gretchen and heads her way before she can find anywhere to hide.

"Potential buyers," he explains.

Where's Everett? *Shit. Shit shit shit.* "Um, I'll just make my lunch quick . . ."

But he stops her forward movement with a hand on her shoulder. The touch makes her feel like a snowman that unwisely booked a trip to Cancun. "We're supposed to let them tour without interfering. Besides, the last thing I'm gonna do is let you go in there and put a bug in their ear about how the place is haunted."

"Well, it is haunted. So."

Charlie rolls his eyes.

"This is a mistake," she tells him. "A big one. If you sell, you *die.* I don't know how to make it any clearer to you that you need to take this seriously. Take it off the market, Charlie. Please."

He turns on her, pointing a finger in her direction. "Pretty sure the only big mistake I'm making is letting you stay here. If it weren't for the possibility of getting Deborah her money back, I would have kicked you out twenty times already. I have been very patient, Acorn. But my patience, even in matters of looking out for my friends, has a limit. Remember that." Charlie starts to walk away, then returns after a few steps. "Actually, you come with me. I'm not leaving you unsupervised near these people. God knows the lengths you'll go to fuck me over."

"I have no intention of fucking you *over.*" Whoops, she did not mean to emphasize the last word there. Maybe she can course correct without him noticing? "I want to *save* you, you asshole."

"Don't need saving," he says. Thankfully, he seems to have missed her Freudian slip. Or is at least ignoring it like a gentleman.

"Yes, you do," she responds, mimicking his petulant tone.

"Sure, yeah. Tell me, Acorn: Where's your ghost right now? Is he walking along with us, telling you embarrassing stories about my childhood?"

"No, he's . . . I don't know where he is, actually. He's probably—"

A horror movie–worthy scream comes from inside the farmhouse.

Gretchen smiles, relief flushing the worry from her system. "Yep, he's in there."

The couple rushes out the front door, the man's arm protectively circled around the woman's shoulders, her face buried into his chest. The real estate agent glances over her shoulder repeatedly as she trails behind them. Charlie hurries over to catch her, the engine of her Mercedes already remote started.

"Everything okay?" he asks.

"Oh, yes, fine." The nervous smile pasted on her face says otherwise. "You have a lovely property here, Mr. Waybill. My clients just . . . uh . . . decided farming isn't a good fit for them after all. Sorry for the inconvenience."

"But—"

The agent and her clients speed away as fast as they can without damaging their vehicles on the unpaved road, a cloud of dust obscuring their getaway.

"What the hell was that about?" Charlie asks the farm at large.

"Everett must have done something to really freak them out."

As she says this, Gretchen is struck by an immense sense of pride. If she and Everett are a team, she suspects that ridiculous ghost just won them their first match.

Charlie makes a sarcastic *after you* gesture, so she opens the door and steps into the foyer. "Ev?" she calls out. "Where ya at, babe?"

No response. No handsome, annoying man in 1920s garb chilling half-inside the couch. No trace of him at all.

"Hmm. He must've touched something and poofed," she says, peeking around into the other rooms on the first floor to see if she can find anything broken or out of place.

"He what?"

"Poofed. Disappeared into the Nowhere. It's what happens if he uses too much energy at once to make physical contact with something, like when he pushed me into the mud puddle." Gretchen speaks with authority, as if she didn't only learn about this herself a couple days ago. She strolls to the kitchen, Charlie following behind. "He'll be back in ten minutes, give or take." She turns around, almost hitting her nose on Charlie's chin. He's standing so close, looking so intense. Gretchen has the sudden urge to reach up and smooth his furrows and stroke away the clench of his jaw, but she knows her touch would have the opposite effect. Strange how much she wants to ease this man's burden when he's made it very clear that she currently makes up a significant chunk of it.

"Well, since we're both here and it's lunchtime, how about a fancy grilled cheese?" she asks instead. Maybe feeding Charlie will be enough to scratch this annoying itch she has to take care of him. Pay him back in some way for all of the small ways he's taken care of her since she arrived. "And by fancy, I mean I can put some tomato on it."

He doesn't respond, only watches as her lips stretch into a practiced self-deprecating smile.

His voice comes out as a whisper. "If you could just be honest with me . . ."

"I know it's not exactly easy to believe, but I *am* being honest with you, Charlie."

"Are you? I doubt you've ever been completely honest with anyone in your life." One of his hands slowly comes to her face, and he tucks a strand of hair that's freed itself from her ponytail back behind her ear. The contrast between the tender gesture and the harshness of his words is almost painful, like coarse grit sandpaper rubbed against the delicate skin of the inside of a wrist. "Maybe not even with yourself."

Gretchen swallows, attempting to suppress the emotions rising inside her. That isn't true. It can't be. The part about not being completely honest with anyone? Maybe. Maybe that's the case. Yolanda is the closest thing she has to a confidant, and she still keeps so many things from her. Or sometimes she tells her half-truths, just to maintain the distance between them when she worries they're at risk of growing too close. But Gretchen is not lying to herself. She would know if she's been lying to herself.

Wouldn't she?

"So is that a no to the grilled cheese?" she asks, trying to sound vaguely amused instead of shattered.

Charlie lowers the hand he hovered over her cheek and tucks it into his pocket. "Yeah, I'll take one if you don't mind. Thanks." He somehow manages to imbue the polite words with bitterness.

Gretchen turns to open a drawer and pulls out two paper plates, avoiding having to try to reach the stoneware ones in the cabinet again. The silence feels open, like Charlie might still choose to fill it. But then the window for more shuts tight and she's left with her head in the fridge as she searches for sandwich ingredients.

Everett's head joins hers in there after a moment, though his comes in from the side. "Hey, doll. Looking for me?"

"Why would I be looking for you in the fridge?" She whispers so Charlie won't overhear. "No, I'm looking for the mayo."

"Back here," he says, pointing to a blue-lidded jar.

"Thanks."

Gretchen balances the cheese, mayo, and an anemic out-of-season grocery store tomato in her arms and closes the fridge door with her hip. Charlie's footsteps signal his departure from the kitchen, which hurts her feelings more than it should. At least now she can talk to Everett without worrying about how he might react to their conversation.

She drops her sandwich ingredients on the counter. "Those people left in quite a hurry. Great work, whatever you did."

"Ha, yes. Good job . . . me." The way he says it, with a light, forced-sounding chuckle and an odd hesitation, makes Gretchen turn to face him.

"Everett. What was it that you did, exactly?"

"I, uh . . ." Everett reaches behind him and rubs his neck—a gesture that he either picked up from or passed down to Charlie. "I might have . . . sort of . . . pushed the lady down the stairs?"

Gretchen freezes with her hand inside the bread bag. "You what?"

"Not the whole way down! Just . . . three steps, give or take?"

"Everett! You cannot push people down the stairs, that could *kill* someone!"

"I know, I know, it's not great. But I panicked! They were loving the place. Talking about making our room into a nursery, how their future children would have so much fun growing up with the goats, color options for redoing the kitchen cabinets. They could really see themselves here, and none of the repairs the property needs seemed to worry them so . . . I . . . well . . ."

"So you panicked and pushed a woman down the stairs?"

"Yes. Pretty much . . . that's—" He nods. "Yes."

Gretchen looks Everett in the eye. "You cannot hurt people," she says, emphasizing her words with the butter knife in her hand.

He flinches despite the knife's dullness and the fact that he can't be stabbed (much to Gretchen's current chagrin). "Okay, okay." He pauses. "Although . . . a mysterious death would probably make this place pretty hard to sell, huh?"

"Everett Jebediah Waybill." Though it seemed morbid at the time, Gretchen is grateful she agreed to stroll out to the small family graveyard on the edge of the property this morning to see his headstone. Scoldings really are more potent when you include a middle name.

"I'm just saying! I watched this episode of *Dateline* once and—"

"That's it. No TV for the rest of the day. It's clearly rotting your brain."

"But Gretchen," he whines. "I wanted to start *Bridgerton* tonight."

She stabs the knife into the mayo. "Attempted murderers don't get to watch *Bridgerton*."

"I was just trying to help."

"Well, you took it way too far."

Everett puts his hands on his hips. "It's your fault, you know."

"Excuse me? It's *my* fault? How do you figure?"

"I wouldn't have needed to do anything if you were doing a

better job of convincing Charlie not to sell. Geez, Gretch. You've spent the week you've been here—"

"Four days," she corrects.

"—bumbling around, just hoping Charlie will suddenly believe you, and it's not going to happen. Some flimflam lady you are! I thought you would be able to help, but so far there doesn't seem to be any point in having you here."

"Go to your—our—*my* room," she shouts, gesturing toward the stairs with the knife. A glob of mayonnaise catapults across the kitchen. "I don't want to hear a word from you until after dinner." Gretchen feels like she's playing the mom in a family sitcom. Except instead of a rebellious teenager, she's dealing with an inadvertently malicious himbo ghost. One apparently quite skilled at homing in on the barely healed part of her heart and ripping off the scab.

"Fine," he shouts back. But since he can't stomp off to express his displeasure, he reaches out and waves his hand through Gretchen's arm. Cold bursts through her bloodstream, and her fingers go instantly numb. She barely manages to direct her hand back over the counter before the butter knife falls from it, hitting the butcher block with a *konk*.

"Dammit!" she yells as his lips form a perfect O of shock at her anger. "That's the way you wanna play this? Fine! No TV for a *week*!"

Everett dashes away, and only when he's somewhere on the second floor does Gretchen hear, "That's not fair! You're so mean!"

At the same time, Charlie returns to the kitchen and asks, "What the hell is going on in here?"

"Your ghost cousin a million times removed or whatever is a dickbag." It feels like she's really glossing over the whole Everett-could-have-killed-someone-today thing, but why would Charlie believe her about that when he hasn't believed her about anything else? "He's banned from TV for a week. So if you see it on and I'm not around, turn it off." She remembers suddenly her unfulfilled promise to talk to Charlie about leaving the TV on for Everett and hastily adds, "But, uh, don't otherwise. After his punishment is over, I mean. It's the only thing that keeps him entertained and away from me."

"So you're the one who keeps leaving the TV on all the time?"

"Like I said, it keeps Everett busy and out of my hair. So please leave it on. Except for this week. When you should turn it off."

Charlie leans against the counter. "Because you're punishing the ghost. For being a dickbag."

"Right."

He shakes his head and grabs a paring knife from the knife block. "Give me that tomato," he says. Her hand is visibly trembling when she picks up the too-firm fruit, Everett's chill still making it feel like she camped outside overnight with no sleeping bag in the middle of January.

Charlie's fingers brush against hers as he lifts the tomato from her palm. "God, Acorn, your hands are freezing."

"I, um, I tend to run cold," she says. Which is the truth, just not the reason for her current temperature-regulation issues. But when she looks into Charlie's eyes, there's a tiny ember of softness there, something she suspects could grow and glow into full-blown interest in her welfare. It's the same one from last night when he gave her the bag of mini shampoos and conditioners—before she opened her mouth and reminded him of the reason she's here, the reason he hates her. Whether it's because Everett's right and she does need to hunker down and be more strategic, or because part of her wants nothing more than to be the recipient of some of that softness, Gretchen knows that, whatever she does, she cannot let that ember burn out again.

16

SHE'S AT THE KITCHEN COUNTER, DOING . . . *SOMETHING*.
It's unclear. Or maybe her task keeps shifting. And then there's
Charlie, suddenly behind her. His strong forearms come to either
side of her, caging her in. It's like when he reached for the plates,
except this time he's pressing up against her, pressing *himself* against
her lower back, and his hand leaves the countertop to travel up
her arm, brush over her bare shoulder (wasn't she wearing clothes
a second ago?). His touch is gentle, but he bows his head to place
his lips beside her ear and his tone is desperate, angry. "God, I
need you," he says like it's an accusation. "Do you need me?"

"Yes," she sighs.

"Acorn."

Maybe he didn't hear her the first time. After all, it was barely
more than a word-shaped exhale. "Yes," she tries again.

"Acorn!"

"I said YES!" But by the end of the sentence she realizes she's not in the kitchen, about to do something deliciously debauched, but sitting up in bed in the farmhouse's guest room.

Charlie *is* there, though. And he's wincing in response to her unexpectedly intense wake-up.

"Yes? Yes to what?" he asks.

"Nothing." Gretchen rubs the sleep in her eyes away with her fingertips. "Why are you in here?" It sounds more hostile than she intends, but going from such a wonderful but confusing dream to this reality with no time to ease into it has her brain scrambling to sort out what's real. She's almost certain none of the good parts were.

"I need you," Charlie says.

". . . What?"

He blinks as if trying to determine if he said something nonsensical that warrants her confusion, then repeats slowly, "I. Need. You. In the barn. Now."

Gretchen's brain is still playing catch-up, trying to figure out why they're going to have sex in the barn of all places. *No, no, that was the dream*, she reminds herself. So what does he mean, he needs her in the barn now?

She must still look adequately baffled, because he explains, "One of the goats is in labor, but the kid is in an awkward position. So I need a hand. Literally. And yours are smaller than mine."

"You want me to . . ." Gretchen recalls the animal birthing scenes in *All Creatures Great and Small*. *Oh no*, she thinks. *He wants me to James Herriot it*. "But I don't know how to—"

"Get dressed and meet me out there."

She throws on yesterday's outfit and slips into her rain boots as quickly as she can, though her movements feel like trying to swim through pudding, thanks to the interruption of her REM cycle.

When she arrives at the barn, Gretchen is struck first by the strange metallic smell, and then by the pained bleats cutting through the otherwise quiet night. She goes over to join Charlie inside one of the birthing pens.

"So . . . what, exactly, am I—"

"Take off your coat," Charlie orders. "Thoroughly wash your hands and arms up to the elbow. Then grab a pair of gloves from that box over there."

Gretchen does as told, feeling like a surgeon in a medical drama. That makes her think of Everett. Where is he anyway? She hasn't seen the ghost since their fight in the kitchen earlier. He's probably roaming around the property, grumbling about how mean she is because she won't let him have any fun killing people.

"Okay. Where do you want me, boss?" she says, joining Charlie and an extremely uncomfortable-looking black goat. Its name is . . . something with a B, she thinks. Beulah, maybe?

"Behind her. Just reach in there and feel around until you find the kid's head. It's bent backward a little, which isn't going to work coming out. So you need to guide it into a different position. I'm fairly sure there's only one in there, so it should be pretty easy to—"

"Am I going to hurt it?" she asks.

Charlie shakes his head. "Nah. But work with the contractions if you can. Easier on everyone that way."

Gretchen thinks back to the episode where James Herriot delivered a horse, how each of the intense contractions crushed his arm. "Is it going to hurt *me*?"

"I promise you, any discomfort you might experience pales in comparison to what Beulah is going through," Charlie says, impatient.

"Right. Okay. Right." She hesitates, staring at—okay, yes, Beulah—Beulah's angry backside. It has a . . . bubble sort of thing sticking out of it. Gretchen chokes back a combined sob-gag. "Shouldn't we call Lori? Or a . . . a . . . vet?"

Charlie shakes his head. "It would take too long to get someone else out here, and they'd just do the exact same thing I'm telling you to do. Get in there, Acorn, before things get dire."

It's only been a handful of days since she arrived at Gilded Creek, and to go from hesitantly feeding a goat for the first time on Friday to helping one give birth on . . . well, she assumes it's currently the early hours of the morning on Tuesday . . . feels like too speedy a progression.

I can't do this. I can't do this. Her feet move her backward, away from Beulah, in response to her rising panic. But Charlie catches her, his hands taking her by the shoulders.

"You *can* do this," he says, as if reading her mind. "I know you can. I believe in you, Acorn."

It's easy to tell herself he's just saying this so she'll do what he needs her to do. Yet she thinks back over the last few days, and how working on the farm with Charlie has shown her that he cares about the goats the way he cares about the people he loves—with all of himself. And she knows he wouldn't let her do this if he didn't trust her on some level. He does believe in her. Perhaps she can do it after all.

Still. *I don't* want *to do this. I don't want to do this.* Her brain continues repeating the sentiment as Charlie gently guides her forward, releasing her when they reach Beulah's backside again. He nods encouragingly. Gretchen takes a deep breath, trying to ignore the way her stomach roils as her fingers, then hand, then wrist meet all sorts of new and alarming textures through the paltry barrier of her gloves. Her eyes squeeze shut, as if that might help. It doesn't. It only heightens all of the sensations.

But then her fingertips find something that feels like . . . a nose, maybe? Inside a balloon sort of thing. She follows the curve downward, understanding what Charlie meant by the positioning. The kid's head is bent back like it's been looking up this whole time, and the resistance to her initial gentle probing seems to indicate it isn't thrilled about looking elsewhere.

"I think I feel its face," she says, swallowing to avoid the increasing nausea creeping up her throat as the bubble beside her wrist shifts around.

Charlie is beside her, and he bends, bracing his hands on his knees as if trying to match her position. Whether it's a sympathetic unconscious gesture meant to communicate that he would help if he could, or a frustrated one that she isn't doing this right, Gretchen isn't sure. She decides to take it as the former.

"See if you can get your hand behind the head and bring it down," Charlie says, talking quietly and in a singsong sort of voice as he strokes Beulah's gigantic, heaving side.

A contraction squeezes around Gretchen's hand, and it's tight but not finger-breakingly so. She takes Charlie's advice and tries to use it to work her hand to the right place to bring the kid's head forward. When the tension releases, she feels movement like closing the lid on a box, though it's hard to tell, considering it's still within the balloon thing, which she assumes must be a different part of the bubble sticking out of Beulah. *Gross.*

"I think . . . I think I got it?" she says, feeling around again and finding the nose pointing toward the opening instead of up now. Gretchen removes her hand, and the nose immediately shifts into the part of the bubble sticking out. "Is that . . . good?"

"Yeah," Charlie says with a little chuckle, and he pats her on the back in a way that isn't at all erotic but still makes Gretchen's face heat. "That's good. You did it, Acorn. Great job. Beulah can take it from here."

Gretchen would be lying if she said what comes next isn't one of the most disgusting things she's ever seen. But it's also somehow one of the most magical. *Life is freaking magical.* And Charlie puts his hands back on her shoulders, less to keep her from bolting and more as if he can't help but want to connect in this moment, releasing only when the kid is mostly out and needs some help clearing its mouth of . . . whatever that is. Gretchen doesn't—nor does she want to—know. Magical or not, she isn't particularly hungry for details.

With one last push, Beulah's kid drops to the straw-covered barn floor in an awkward heap, and Gretchen is surprised to find herself gasp and take a step forward to help it up. But Charlie gives her a peaceful, crooked smile and the slightest shake of his head. *It's all right*, he seems to say. So she stays where she is and watches as the slick, shiny black-and-white kid rights itself.

"A girl," Charlie says, doing a quick inspection so as not to interrupt Beulah's efforts to clean her baby of blood and other gunk that Gretchen still doesn't want to think too hard about.

"What's her name?" she asks, realizing too late that it's a ridiculous question. *Goats aren't born with names, you nincompoop.*

Charlie's smile is still intact, and he points it in her direction, making her heart thump harder. "I think that's up to you. You were the one who helped get her out, you get to name her."

"Really?" Gretchen's never named anything in her life (well, except herself a few times).

Watching Beulah with her kid makes her think of her own mother, who disappeared from her life when Gretchen was two. She doesn't remember her much, which she supposes is why she's never felt the loss all that keenly or cared to try to find her. Except at this moment, when she thinks about the circle of life and mothers and daughters and all sorts of things that probably belong in the lyrics to an old folk song. This gush of emotion isn't something she's eager to welcome, but there doesn't seem to be any fighting it. Tears well behind her eyes at the one memory she does have—one she isn't sure is real, even; her mind could have made it up somewhere along the way—a woman's sweet voice singing "Daydream Believer" softly as Gretchen drifted to sleep, warm and safe in her arms.

"Sleepy Jean," Gretchen says. "I want to name her Sleepy Jean."

"All right. Welcome to the world, Sleepy Jean," Charlie says, wrapping the kid's now-fuzzy body in a towel. And then he scoops the kid up and hands her over to Gretchen, who isn't sure if she wants to hold her, but takes her nonetheless. Sleepy Jean lets out the most pathetic little bleat—almost like a meow—and Gretchen responds with a stunned, incredulous laugh. *I helped bring something into the world. That's so weird. That's . . . amazing.*

"Glad you're here," Charlie says.

Gretchen's head snaps up, surprised at the compliment, only to find him staring at Sleepy Jean. *Oh. Right.* "Ha, I thought you were talking to me," she says, unsure why she's even admitting it aloud.

"I wasn't not," Charlie responds, his cheeks pinker than they were a moment ago, and their eyes meet for a split second before another distressed bleat from the stall next door catches his attention. "Sounds like Clotilda might have a second one on its way out."

And Gretchen assists while the miracle of life is repeated. Again. And again. And, it turns out, again before dawn.

———

EXHAUSTED YET WIRED, GRETCHEN SINKS ONTO A HAY BALE
on the floor of the little stone outbuilding where Charlie brought
the newborns to sleep for the night with the four other kids born
last week. She watches the tiny new goats wiggle around and get
comfortable in a big pile in the corner, never taking her eye off
Sleepy Jean for more than a second. But soon the adrenaline of
sticking her hand inside of a goat and maneuvering its offspring
wears off, and she's left wrung out. Her eyes flutter closed and
she's about to fall asleep when the goose bumps on her left arm
alert her to Everett's presence.

"Hi," he says, staring at the toes of his boots.

"Hi," she says.

"I saw you helping with Beulah. You did great."

"Thanks. It was super gross." Her eyes search for Sleepy Jean
among the other goats. Strange how her heart soars as soon as
she spots the tiny black-and-white kid half-buried under a slightly
larger, two-day-older tan one.

Everett fiddles with his cap. "Gretch. I'm sorry about earlier.
With the, you know, attempted murder." She swings her head to
aim her stare at him, causing him to promptly add, "Not that I
was actually *attempting* to murder anyone! Anyway. It was . . . it
was an error in judgment. And I understand why you're mad at me."

Gretchen sighs.

"And it was wrong of me to accuse you of not trying with Charlie," he continues. "It's just that it seems pretty easy to me. Let him
in enough to get him to care about you. Make him fall in love. Then
he'll have to believe you."

"I can't do that, Ev. I can't. My Rule."

Everett reaches for her as if about to drape his arm over her shoulders, then remembers he can't without turning her into a popsicle. Instead there's silence, broken finally when one of the goats lets out an annoyed bleat as another accidentally steps on its face.

"I would argue," Everett says, "that Charlie will definitely not be better off if you allow him to leave the farm and he *dies tragically*."

Gretchen ignores this and continues, "It's . . . important to me. Not to hurt him. Not to make him think I'm . . . I'm . . ." *The bad person he already thinks I am. That I could so, so easily be if I stop being careful.*

Everett shakes his head. "Look. Charlie is going to be cursed regardless of what happens. Right now, he's likely to be dead and haunting this place within a few months instead of working the farm and annoyed about it but *alive*. You don't want to leave him worse off? Well, I don't see how you could possibly leave him worse off than he is right now, unless you do nothing at all and let this play out how it would have had you never shown up."

"That's unusually articulate of you," Gretchen says.

Everett grins. "I don't really know what that means, but thanks, I think?"

What if I'm the one who gets hurt? What if I'm the one who winds up worse off? What if I can't make him love me at all? But she doesn't voice these thoughts, because ultimately the goal of the Rule is to keep the selfishness her father taught her was one of her best assets from dictating her actions, and aren't these fears about what happens if she makes Charlie care about her just another form of being selfish when it comes down to it?

"I promise I'll try to behave myself going forward," Everett says. "But the rest of the month is going to fly by. We're already—what, three weeks in?"

"Less than one week."

"Okay, but still. No more waiting around for inspiration to strike. Find a way. Let's get this done. We need to keep him here. *Safe*."

As much as she agrees her current strategy (which isn't even a strategy so much as a hope that something will magically change) isn't likely to pay off within the allotted time, Gretchen also isn't ready to accept that the only way forward is the one most likely to leave at least one of them brokenhearted. "Yeah. I'll . . . keep thinking."

"Why don't you go get some sleep?" Everett suggests. "You look tired."

"Gee, thanks." She watches as Sleepy Jean wiggles deeper into the cuddle puddle. "I think I'll stay out here a little while longer."

"Want some company?"

Gretchen is surprised to find that yes, actually, she does. And specifically Everett's. Because he's kind of a nightmare, but he's also someone she can count on being there. He also knows that she's a bullshit artist, and considers it a feature instead of a bug. She's willing to admit that it's . . . sort of nice to have him around.

She settles in, letting the goats nibble at her clothes and fingers like little weirdos, and Everett tells her about how Ellen and Charles used to call Charlie "Chick" when he was a boy because of how his baby hiccups sounded like a just-hatched bird cheeping. That somehow leads to when Ellen accidentally used salt instead of sugar in a batch of Christmas cookies. The time a goat got into the house when no one was home and ate all of the labels off the cans in the pantry ("Preparing dinner became quite the adventure for the next six months or so!"). And other Waybill family stories that Gretchen decides to pretend half belong to her too, if only for tonight.

17

GRETCHEN AWAKENS WITH A SORE NECK AND TWO BABY goats chewing on her ponytail. Despite her intention to go back to the house to shower and sleep, she must have drifted off on the hay bale in the little outbuilding. She lets out a quiet groan as she straightens and moves to shoo the kids away. There's someone still sitting to her left—Everett, she assumes. Except in the process of shifting her body, her arm brushes against heat instead of cold.

Charlie.

Once her eyes are completely open and her neck is willing to participate, she turns her head slightly to confirm. Everett is absent, but Charlie is indeed seated beside her on the hay bale, scratching Clyde's (or is it Bonnie's? Gretchen struggles to tell the two dogs apart without Everett's help) head and watching two babies attempting to simultaneously climb atop each other.

"Hey," she says, yawning at the end of the word so it comes out stretched.

Charlie glances over at her as if he hadn't noticed she was awake, which seems unlikely considering how noisy she was while trying to get her neck to cooperate. "Oh. Hey."

"How are they doing?"

"Good. We'll take them back to their moms soon, let them eat. You should go to the house, clean up. Get some real sleep."

She shakes her head. "Nah, I'm okay." The dog—Bonnie, she's pretty sure—stands, walks over, and plops down in front of Gretchen. Hesitantly, she reaches out and, determining her hand isn't about to get chomped off, gives the fluffy head a few tentative pats.

"Did you stay out here all night?" Charlie asks.

"Yeah. I didn't want to leave them alone. I thought . . ." This sounds ridiculous, but she makes herself say it anyway. Testing how it feels to be vulnerable with him. For purely strategic purposes, of course. "I thought they might be scared if they didn't have a familiar face nearby."

He gives her a playful nudge. "Trying to get the goats to imprint on you, Acorn?"

"You've caught me. I'm hoping they'll think I'm their leader and do my bidding."

Charlie chuckles. "At least you aren't afraid of them anymore."

"I was never *afraid*," she insists. She stretches her arms above her head, and her back gives a satisfying crack. When she's done, she shifts a few inches farther from Charlie, suddenly self-conscious of how dirty she is, how much she must smell like goat fluids and dried stress sweat. "I, um . . . mostly, I didn't want to leave Sleepy Jean. I was worried she might . . . I don't know."

"I can't make any promises, because nature does what it wants," Charlie says slowly, studying the little black-and-white goat still sleeping half-buried under one of her friends. "But based on my experience, I fully expect her to thrive. She's healthy—in part because you did what you needed to do. You don't need to worry about her."

"Good. That's good." Gretchen swallows a lump in her throat. She doesn't know if it's relief or a kind of subtle dread. Maybe because she helped usher Sleepy Jean into the world last night, life suddenly feels a lot more fragile. A sudden memory of scrolling through Rachel Van Alst's Instagram feed, full of photos and videos of someone so young and lively, makes her breath feel caught in her throat. And the full extent of what could happen to Charlie if she fails fully hits her in a way it hasn't before.

"It's normal," Charlie says after a long pause filled only with the kids' occasional bleats and a rather noisy yawn from Bonnie, "to fret over the first one you help deliver." He stretches his legs out in front of him and crosses his ankles. Gretchen notices now that he's wearing gray joggers instead of jeans. He has on that hideous sage-green and neon-pink sweater again, the one from the day she arrived, one she now knows his grandmother made. "Mine was named Stu." His fingers slide under the cuff of his left sleeve, pulling it up to his elbow. Charlie points to the tattoo of the goat on his forearm and the cursive letters beneath. "S-T-U, not S-T-E-W."

And now he's smiling. *Oh god.* Gretchen isn't sure if ovaries can flutter, but hers seem to be doing exactly that.

"I was eight years old, visiting for a long weekend around Easter. I didn't really do all that much. It was an easy birth, but we had six in one night and a few were tricky, so they let me take care of one on my own. Grandpa let me name her."

Charlie's smile fades to something more pensive. She's caught this look on his face several times since her arrival, and she would bet everything she has that it signals he's thinking about how he's selling the farm and, therefore, letting his grandparents down. At first, she thought his selling the farm was an attempt to get out from under his family's expectations—the way she tried to rebuild her life into something else after parting ways with her father. But now she sees that his desire to be rid of the place is deeply tied to his inability to meet the expectations he had for himself. It makes sense that he might feel like he's failed. But Gretchen hates that he does. She definitely doesn't look at him and see a failure.

"Her? Why did you name a girl goat—"

"A doe," he corrects.

"Why did you name a doe Stu?"

Charlie scratches at his beard. "Ah, this is kind of embarrassing, but . . . I had a crush on a girl at school. Her name was Brittany, but there were four Brittanys in our class, so we called her by her last name, Studebaker, which got shortened to Stu. So . . . yeah."

"And what did Brittany Studebaker think about having a goat named after her?" Gretchen asks.

"I don't really remember her reaction when I told her, to be honest. But considering we were in the third grade, she probably just said, 'Cool,' and went back to reading a *Baby-Sitters Club* book. Besides, I was considered the weird kid. Most of the other students at the private school I went to in DC didn't understand why I liked to go to my grandparents' farm for breaks instead of Monaco or whatever."

They exchange smiles, and it feels like, at least for this moment, there's a connection. This is her opening, she realizes, and she should take advantage of it.

"You seem to have a lot of happy memories here," Gretchen says carefully. "So why do you want to leave?"

The old irritation returns to his voice as he says, "It's just . . . it's time. It's past time. I need to move on."

He exhales noisily, then closes his eyes. When he opens them, he seems to have fought off the instinct to shut her down. A tiny spark of excitement flares to life inside her when he clasps his hands together between his knees and keeps talking. "I always knew I would take over the farm one day. God knows my dad wasn't interested, much to my grandparents' dismay. He's a corporate lawyer. About as far away from agriculture as you can get, unless you count representing Monsanto." Charlie pauses for a beat. "He could make all of this go away. So, so easily. My parents have spent their entire adult lives focused solely on the accumulation of wealth. They have more than enough money to pay for my grandfather's care out of pocket. But they won't do it."

"Why not? It's your father's father. Is there bad blood between them, or is Chuck just an asshole?"

"The latter, primarily." He reaches over and plucks a piece of straw from Gretchen's sleeve.

"Thanks," she says, watching the straw fall to the ground as he releases it from between his fingertips.

"You asked me that first night what my dad and I fought about." Charlie stares at an unremarkable spot on the stone wall across from him. "I called him to ask for help, for money. When I realized my grandfather needed specialized care, I talked over the financial aspects with my dad. I told him my priority was keeping the farm. I needed him to pay for the nursing facility so we wouldn't have to sell off Grandpa's assets. He asked me a bunch of questions about profit and loss, then pronounced that Gilded Creek wasn't worth keeping. As if it was a simple matter of addition and subtraction and not a family legacy spanning centuries. He said it was a bad business decision and he wouldn't support it, even indirectly. So I wound up paying for Grandpa's care with my savings. I'm running out now. So."

Charlie shifts and clears his throat. Gretchen subtly inches her hand closer to his on the hay bale until their pinkies are a hairsbreadth apart. To her surprise, he closes the small gap, forming a small connection between them.

"As much as my dad can be an asshole, maybe he's onto something. Because this . . . this is so much harder . . . than I thought it would be. The money stuff . . . it's just . . . I need to invest more into the farm to get the kinds of profits we need to stay afloat, and I don't have that kind of cash to put back into the business because of my grandfather . . ." Charlie pulls his hand away, breaking the contact. He runs it through his hair and lets out a heavy sigh. "You're too easy to talk to, Acorn. You know that?"

"I've never heard it used as an insult before," she says, still flattered despite the censure in his voice.

"Not an insult. Just an observation. Sometimes I forget I need to be extra careful around you."

Gretchen frowns, ready to counter that he doesn't need to be careful at all, that she's not going to do anything to hurt him, that she doesn't do anything to hurt anyone. But she somehow doubts he'll believe her even if she says it. Besides, what if it isn't true? What if she does have to hurt him in order to save him?

Regardless, she's figuring out that Charlie is a man of action, not of words. Nothing she can say is going to make him believe her.

Which gives her the seed of an idea, actually.

"If you could make enough money to get the farm in the black so your dad would cover your grandfather's care, would you want to stay?"

Charlie stares at a kid who's made its way over to try to burrow its head into the side of the hay bale. "I . . . I don't know. I like the work fine, but I don't . . ." He runs a hand over his face. "I don't think I realized until I started running this place alone that the main reason I enjoyed being here when I was younger was because I got to work with my grandparents. The family part of it being a family business was what I loved. And without that . . . I'm starting to wonder if I only ever loved it because I was expected to."

That taps into something deep inside Gretchen's heart. Would she be a bullshit artist if it hadn't been expected of her? If she hadn't been raised to expect it of herself? Doing it without her father has actually been freeing, for the most part, but there's still a large part of her that misses what it used to be like back when she had someone to count on. Someone she *thought* she could count on. "So is there something else you'd rather do? Maybe what you were doing before you had to take over here?"

At this he smiles. "I'm not sure my body could handle going back to what I was doing before. I'm feeling a bit too old and rickety for the high seas." Her expression must show that her mind has immediately dressed him in a stereotypical pirate's outfit, because his smile widens and he explains, "I spent my twenties working for a few different tall ship cruise companies in the US and Europe."

"A tall ship," she repeats. "Is that like . . . the kind with all the sails and . . . poles and stuff?"

Charlie lets out a small laugh, the first she's really heard from him since the day the goats almost devoured her in the pasture. It snakes through her and squeezes. "Yeah, with the sails and poles and stuff."

She recalls Everett's mention of Charlie traveling the world, the board that used to be in the laundry room. "You sent your grandparents postcards from everywhere you went," she says quietly.

"How did you . . ." He trails off and shakes his head, unwilling to follow her down that path. And Gretchen is grateful, because this conversation . . . it's nice. She wants it to continue.

"Anyway," he says. "Whatever I do next will ideally involve more sitting around than sailing and farming allow. I've always thought I might like being a librarian."

"A librarian? Really?" It seems incongruous at first, but then it becomes so easy to imagine Charlie shelving books and shushing people. The man can pull off a ridiculous sweater like no one's business; she can only imagine how well he might wear a dress shirt and cardigan. The mental image has her feeling a little flushed.

"I've always loved to read. I was pretty seriously looking into MLIS programs right before . . . I didn't expect—well, I thought I had a bit more time before this all would become my responsibility." His voice goes quiet on that last sentence, as if he's talking to himself.

She's about to tell him he still could be a librarian if he wanted, but that isn't true. He can't walk away from the farm and survive, and there isn't enough money to have someone else run the farm while he pursues a new career. A different life is truly out of reach for him. The unfairness of it sends a jolt of anger through her. Charlie shouldn't have to stay here doing work that's begun feeling like a burden when there are other things he wants from life.

The very least she can do, as the person (well, living one) he will probably blame for forcing him to stay here, is increase his cash flow to get him through the worst of it. To her surprise, she's been subconsciously compiling a few ideas over the last several days. Charlie might not like them—especially the ones that involve him shirtless on the internet—but it's something. Something she can offer to ease his stress. One less thing for him to worry about.

But before Gretchen can ask any questions about the farm's accounting or propose Charlie let her take over the business side of things for the next few weeks, he stands and holds out a hand to help her up. She shouldn't take it, because she's starting to think she's the one who might need to be extra careful around *him*. The feelings he sparks in her aren't necessarily new, but they've grown much stronger. Harder to slip a rope around to lead them somewhere more useful.

Except as she tries to rise on her own, her body reminds her that she's been sitting on a hay bale for several hours, some of them asleep in an awkward position. Against her better judgment, she grabs Charlie's hand to keep herself from falling atop the several baby goats now swarming them. The warmth that permeates her skin feels like both a reward and a punishment, straddling the line between too much and not enough.

Maybe Charlie feels the heat of their connection too, because he visibly swallows once they're face-to-face. "Let's get these kids back to their moms for the day," he says, and gives Gretchen's hand a light squeeze before releasing it.

18

GRETCHEN HAS CONSIDERED CHARLIE'S SUSPICIONS something of a cinder block wall between them since she arrived at Gilded Creek. But after their conversation in the outbuilding Tuesday morning, she wonders if perhaps the wall has been replaced by a . . . privacy fence? Something tall and still extremely difficult to make her way over, but at least now there are cracks of light shining through. It's like she's found a way to look through the slats and see to the other side.

Simultaneously, there's now a sense that something is surrounding her, squeezing her just tight enough that she's always aware of the constriction. She's become tangled in something she can only describe as a fierce affection and . . . yearning. Convincing Charlie of the curse no longer feels like the centerpiece of her bullshit artist career, but something she *needs* deep inside in order to feel complete. Because the way he looked at her as he sat there on the hay bale, as if maybe she's someone he could confide in, maybe even learn to care for . . . now that's all Gretchen wants. A voice is whispering to her that if this man, this *good* man, can see through her and find something somewhere in there to like, maybe she can put to rest this constant need for reassurance that she isn't ruthless, like her father. That she's—at her core—good too.

She'll need to do some reconnaissance. Everett doesn't know much about the farm's business dealings. When she interrupted his recitation of all the local women he wished he had managed to kiss before kicking the bucket to ask if he had any information about how the farm got to be in such a precarious spot financially, he simply shrugged and returned to the M section of his list, picking right back up with Margie Halifax, who apparently wore thick spectacles but made up for it with—Gretchen stopped listening there, to be honest, and instead came up with a plan to seek out information from another person she figures knows a lot about Gilded Creek and the Waybills.

"So. You've been here awhile," Gretchen states as she helps Lori wrap cheese in the barn's second-floor cheesemaking room Friday afternoon. It took some sweet-talking (and pretending that Gretchen possesses a strong desire to learn more about the cheesemaking process) to be allowed in here. "Working here at Gilded Creek, I mean."

Lori raises her eyebrows. "You calling me old?"

"No! I'm just saying, you're a fount of knowledge about this place, about the Waybill family. I doubt there's anyone around who knows more than you, really." Gretchen has noticed over the last week that Lori is a sucker for a well-placed compliment, and indeed, the gruff woman almost preens.

"Probably true," Lori concedes, trying not to show how much she appreciates being recognized for her experience. "Though I bet the ghost around here knows a good bit too."

Gretchen freezes mid-motion. "The ghost?"

"Yeah, this farm is haunted as shit." Gretchen doesn't even need to ask Lori to elaborate. She throws her rubber-gloved hand in the air dismissively. "I don't like to make a big deal about it, especially 'cause I know Charlie thinks it's a bunch of nonsense, but I'm kinda sensitive to that type of stuff. And this place definitely has a ghost."

"Really?"

Lori glances at her expression, mistaking her shock for incredulity. "Great. Now you think I'm a kook too."

"No! I . . . definitely believe you." She pauses. "I, um . . ." The truth is on Gretchen's tongue—that she knows the ghost exists because she herself can actually see and talk to him, and also, by the way, there's a family curse that might result in Charlie's death. But she stops herself. Because she sees that Lori is a True Believer, and she will accept what Gretchen tells her without too much of a fight. On one hand, she sure could use an ally in convincing Charlie. On the other, she's seen the way Charlie and Lori interact, the way they care for each other like they're related by more than shared memories of this place. How, on the days Lori works, Charlie greets her with a kiss on the cheek. How Lori ruffles Charlie's hair like he's still a little boy and not a grown man the same height as her. Gretchen couldn't bear it if she strained their connection, seemingly one of the few that Charlie still has here. And that's exactly what would happen if Lori tried to get Charlie to believe in Everett and the curse. Not to mention the way it would slice right through the silk-thin thread of trust she's managed to build with him.

She settles on, "I'm kinda sensitive to it too."

"I knew there was a reason I liked you," Lori says, which

absolutely blows Gretchen's mind. She kind of assumed the older woman tolerated her at best. "So what was it you wanted to ask me about?"

"Oh, right. How did Ellen and Charles make this all work? Charlie told me they were a great team, but there's more to running a business than that. So what's different now that's making it such a struggle for Gilded Creek to turn a profit?"

"Why do you wanna know?" Her hesitance makes sense. Lori might get paid for cheesemaking and light farmwork, but it's unlikely that she's worked here for thirty years and not developed some sense of loyalty and affection toward the Waybills. Gretchen respects that, especially since what she feels for Charlie and his family is starting to be something close to the same.

"I'm trying to figure out how to boost the business side of things, to help Charlie out so maybe he won't have to sell after all. But I sense there are parts of it he doesn't want to talk about."

Lori sighs. "If he doesn't want to talk about it, then it's not really my place . . ." But by the way she trails off, Gretchen knows the older woman is thinking that if there's even a remote chance of keeping Gilded Creek under Waybill ownership, it increases the likelihood of her continuing to have a job here. So she's pleased but unsurprised when Lori begins again a moment later. "About five years back, Charles's memory started to go. Small stuff, here and there, easy to write off as regular forgetfulness. But it got a lot worse after Ellen died. Charlie came to help out, figured he'd stay for a week or two to get things back in order, but he realized pretty early on that Charles couldn't run the place on his own anymore. Then he took a look at the books and found a complete mess. A bunch of discrepancies. Turned out Charles got scammed by some guy posing as a handyman who was supposed to do repairs to the house and barn. Fifteen thousand dollars, gone, with no way to get it back. And it's not like the farm was making beaucoup bucks at that point anyway. Retail and wholesale had mostly fallen to the wayside, what with Ellen being sick for a while before she passed. So, you see, Charlie inherited this place in the red. He's done his best, started up the farmers market again, cut the herd down to a third of its original size. But he's drained his savings trying to take care of his grandfather without selling the farm. Then, of course, guess that's what it's come down to anyway."

"I had no idea the situation was that bad," Gretchen says.

"Charlie isn't exactly going around screaming it from the rooftops. The man's absolutely sick over it all. Blames himself for not being able to keep the family business going."

"He shouldn't."

Lori huffs. "You don't gotta tell me. A miracle he's kept everything afloat this long, really."

They store the wrapped cheese in the fridge and do a deep clean of everything. Once that's taken care of, they close up and head back into the large empty space on the barn's second floor. Lori leans against the stair railing. "You know, Ellen and Charles used to have barn dances up here."

Gretchen isn't exactly sure what a barn dance is. Just a dance in a barn? Some sort of ritual? But she says, "Oh, really? Cool."

"Yeah. Gilded Creek was really part of the community, back in the day. Dances, seasonal tours, even hosted a few small weddings in the early 2010s when everyone was nuts for 'shabby-chic.' It was a fun place. Always lots of people around." Lori lets out a *hmph* that sounds to Gretchen like, *not so much nowadays.* Then Lori slaps her on the back, just a little too hard. She has to grab the banister to save herself from face-planting, but it's somehow the warmest gesture she could imagine from this woman. "Welp, gotta run. Daughter's coming home for spring break. Flying into Dulles right at rush hour, Lord help me."

Other than a snoozing cat spread out atop a tower of grain sacks, Gretchen is soon alone. She sits on a dusty wooden bench shoved up against a wall and takes in the space. Now that she knows to look for it, it's almost as if she can see the imprint of couples slow-dancing, wallflowers leaning in corners with little plastic cups of punch, children playing an impromptu game of tag weaving in and out of the crowd. It feels a bit haunted. Which, speaking of . . .

"I've got it," Gretchen says, startling Everett out of his *Frasier* trance when she comes back in from outside. She's spent the hour since her conversation with Lori coming up with more concrete ideas for making money—almost all of them completely on the up-and-up, even. She is inordinately proud of herself. Who knew there were so many transferable skills between conning people and doing legitimate business?

"Ah! Don't sneak up on me like that. God." Everett clutches at his chest, as if his heart is racing. She's pretty sure he doesn't even have a functioning one of those anymore, so it's rather overly dramatic. "Now, what is it that you've got, exactly?"

"How to win Charlie over."

"You're going to make him fall in love with you?"

"No. I told you that wouldn't work."

"And I told you that it would one thousand percent work."

She rolls her eyes. "No. I'm going to help him make more money."

Everett frowns. "And that will convince him to stay?"

"I . . . I don't know, to be honest. The farm's financial issues seem to only be part of what's making him want to sell at this point. But if I do manage to show him how to turn a profit, I think he'll have to recognize that I'm truly trying to help and he'll be more receptive to what I have to say."

"Orrrrr," Everett says, turning to hover-sit cross-legged on the couch. "You could say, 'Charlie, you're right that I'm a liar but I'm not lying this time,' and put your tongue in his mouth."

"I'm not talking to you anymore."

Everett shrugs and goes back to watching Niles bicker with Frasier about wine.

Just then, Charlie comes in from outside. He looks into the living room, where Gretchen is staring at Everett disapprovingly. So to him, it probably appears that she's just really angry at the couch.

"Uh, hey," he says as he takes off his boots.

"Hey, I want to talk to you about some ideas I have for the farm," she says. "Maybe over dinner tonight? I could cook . . ." What she could cook, she doesn't know. Grilled cheese with some tomato is pretty much the extent of her repertoire.

"Ah, I wasn't planning on eating here. I was going to go shower and then head out."

"Oh. Another Friday night out on the town. Hot date or something?" She says it like a joke, although the thought of him saying yes in response makes her stomach feel like she's riding a carnival Tilt-A-Whirl that may or may not be fully up to code. Whatever that's about, she isn't a fan.

He scoffs, as if he thinks she's being sarcastic. Which she was. Probably. "Awfully interested in my comings and goings, aren't you?"

"Wish she was more interested in your coming," Everett mutters from the couch. "Maybe then we'd make some quicker progress here."

Gretchen gives him a death stare. It's ineffective (unsurprising, considering he is already dead).

"It's not that I'm *interested*," she says to Charlie.

Charlie doesn't bother looking up from where he's peeling off his socks as he says, "Oh? What are you, then?"

"Curious. Just curious."

"Mm. Curiosity killed the cat, you know. You should be careful, Acorn." He stretches his arms up toward the ceiling, then brings them back down to untuck his flannel shirt. But he doesn't stop there! Her eyes are on his nimble fingers as he slips the shirt's buttons through their holes. All of the saliva in Gretchen's mouth disappears until her tongue feels like an old sponge left in the sun. "And why, exactly, are you so curious?" he asks once his shirt is open, and his voice just barely manages to pull her eyes away from the muscles hiding beneath his undershirt and back to his face.

"Probably because of the boredom. I've spent every single night here at the house while you're out gallivanting—"

"Mostly I went out to Walmart," he corrects.

"You know what? I'm so bored that a trip to Walmart sounds *thrilling.*"

He smiles. "Well, how about this. Go change out of those dirty overalls, put on one of those ridiculous little dresses you brought with you, and we'll see what we can do to make you a little less bored."

She can hardly believe her ears! Charlie is opting to *spend more time with her*? Take that, Everett. This is definitely progress, and she didn't even have to go all femme fatale to achieve it. "Are you sure? I didn't mean to intrude on your Walmart run . . ."

"Don't *question* it, Gretch, geez. How did you ever successfully con anyone?" Everett says from the couch, while Charlie says, "We're not going to the store tonight." And oh my god, he pulls his undershirt over his head, revealing an impressive chest and torso, slightly paler than his arms and face and lightly dusted with hair the same caramel color as his beard. The tattoos on his left forearm actually go all the way to his shoulder, where the branches of some kind of tree that begins on his bicep extend down onto his pectoral muscle, over his heart. "Be ready by eight," he says, and heads up the stairs.

19

"WHY ARE YOU BEING SO SECRETIVE ABOUT THIS?"
Gretchen asks as they bump down the dirt-and-gravel driveway.
This is her second time in Charlie's truck, but the first time she's
noticing that it smells like him after a long day of working on the
farm—citrus and outside and exertion with a hint of hay. The scent
really has no right being so alluring. She's going to need to have
a serious conversation with her brain about that.

"I'm not being secretive," he says.

"Then what are we doing?"

The corner of his mouth kicks up, smug. "You'll see."

When you make your living knowing things you aren't supposed to know about other people and their lives, you get used to
having all the information. Since Gretchen arrived at Gilded Creek,
Everett has been able to fill in some of the blanks for her, and the
rest she's mostly figured out by getting Charlie to slowly open up
to her—those little revelations that she holds in her heart like a
firefly carefully cupped between her palms. So this mystery of

where Charlie Waybill goes when he wants to have fun is driving her fucking crazy, and she's fairly certain he knows it. He's loving having the upper hand. That's probably the reason he invited her along in the first place, to watch her squirm; she can't think why else he would choose to be around her.

His cell phone rings through the truck's speakers, connected by Bluetooth. The screen reads: *Meadewood Assisted Living.*

"Shit," Charlie says, pressing the button on the steering wheel to answer the call.

It's just past eight, which seems late for his grandfather's assisted living facility to be calling. No wonder he's gone as pale as a—well, not a ghost, because even Everett may not be this pale.—

"Hello?"

"Hi, Mr. Waybill. It's Wendy from Meadewood."

"Is he okay?"

"Your grandfather is fine, but . . . he's having a bit of a rough night," Wendy says. "Would you be available to come by and talk to him?"

"Of course." Charlie pulls the truck onto the road's narrow shoulder and turns on the hazard lights. "I'll be there in twenty minutes."

"I'm sure seeing you will help immensely."

"Yeah, thanks for calling me. See you soon."

Charlie pushes both hands into his hair and takes a deep breath, eyes closed tight. "I'll drop you back at the farm on the way," he says.

"No, don't worry about it. I don't want to hold you up at all. I can just wait in the truck or whatever."

"It might take a while. When he gets like this it can be . . . It might be a couple hours."

"Charlie Waybill, I would go to a paint-drying expo if it meant not having to spend a third night in a row listening to Everett's ideas for a *Friends* reboot."

Gretchen shouldn't have mentioned Everett. They haven't talked about him or the curse all day, and she's certain that's at least part of the reason Charlie invited her along tonight. Maybe he forgot that he doesn't like her, that he doesn't fully trust her. And she just reminded him why. *Good job, Gretchen. Very smooth.* What is it about this man that both puts her on edge and relaxes her too much? Very discombobulating.

"Okay," Charlie says, voice quiet. He turns the engine back on and makes a wide U-turn that takes them momentarily into the grass on the other side of the road.

Neither of them speaks as they drive to Meadewood, a small campus of squat buildings in Germantown. They park in the near-empty visitor parking lot near the main building's front entrance.

"I'll come in with you," Gretchen announces, unbuckling her seat belt. Everett has told her so much about Charles in recent days—his boyhood on the farm, his love for Ellen, his rapid decline after her death. Along with the research she did before coming to Gilded Creek, it feels like Gretchen knows Charlie's grandfather well enough that visiting him might be like seeing an old friend. And she also recognizes the tension in Charlie's face and . . . she wants to be there for him. Because she's trying to prove that she can be a good person, and good people are supportive of others. Right? That's the reason she suddenly can't stand the idea of not being there. The sole reason.

"What happened to you staying in the truck?"

"I'll be good, I promise."

He sighs as he steps out of the cab, and it's such a heavy movement that it would do serious damage if it landed on someone's toes. "Doubt it, but let's go."

Charlie isn't exactly enthusiastic about the idea of her joining him for this errand, and maybe she's a jerk for exploiting the way his concern for his grandfather takes priority over fighting with her. It's not going to stop her from opening the door and leaping down from the truck's cab onto the pavement. No, it's actually her concern that the jump while wearing her heeled boots for the first time since she hurt her ankle will aggravate the injury that gives her pause.

Charlie walks around the truck and glares at Gretchen, still sitting sideways in the passenger seat. "What's the holdup?"

"It's . . . kinda high?" she says. "And I'm wearing these stupid boots. Last time I was in the truck, I didn't have a heel to worry about, and—"

"For fuck's sake, Acorn. I don't have time for this." He grabs her wrist and pulls her forward. Her arms instinctively wrap around his neck, and Charlie's hands come to Gretchen's hips to steady her. It can't take more than a second for him to lift her, transfer her from the truck's cab to the ground, but it feels like she's made of memory foam, the press of his fingers imprinted on her body the entire walk into the building, the elevator ride up to the third floor, the short distance from there to the nurses' station.

A middle-aged Asian woman behind the desk looks up from writing something on a clipboard. "Oh, Mr. Waybill, thanks so much for coming. I know it's late . . ." Her eyes subtly bounce from him to Gretchen and back again, as if she has questions but knows it isn't her place to ask them.

"Hi, Wendy. Not a problem," he says. "So, what's going on?"

"Charles is asking about Ellen again." She frowns. "We've been taking the usual approach, telling him that we'll check on when she's coming, that we're sure he'll see her soon, but it doesn't seem to be calming him down tonight."

"All right," Charlie says. Gretchen watches him swallow before he continues. "Has he said anything about me? Is he going to know . . . ?" *Who I am* hovers in the air.

"Well, we told him we were calling his grandson, and he said that was good. He said . . ." Wendy adopts a gruff old man voice that sounds especially funny in contrast to her natural, high-pitched one. "'Good. The boy will sort this out.'"

Her impression of his grandfather brings the slightest smile to Charlie's face. "Okay. Thanks."

"Of course. Let us know if you need anything."

Gretchen follows Charlie down the meatloaf-and-bleach-scented hall to his grandfather's room.

"Wait here," he says, turning to block her from the open door.

His tone and the way his eyes don't meet hers until he's finished giving the order warn her not to argue. This is something he wants to do alone. She nods, agreeing.

There's a moment of hesitation. His eyes close and he takes a deep breath, preparing himself before he slips into the room. Even from where Gretchen stands, Charlie's voice sounds strange, forced, when he says, "Hi, Grandpa."

"Charlie! Am I ever happy to see you, boy!"

"Happy to see you too. How's everything?"

It feels wrong to be eavesdropping like this, but it would actually take more effort not to listen when she's standing right outside in the hallway. Presumably, Charlie wouldn't have let her come this close if he minded. At least, that's what Gretchen is going to tell herself as she slides an inch closer to the open door.

"Oh, awful! They won't tell me where Ellen is. I ask them and they tell me she'll be here later, they'll find out what's keeping her, but they won't tell me where she *is*. They won't tell me where my wife is, and I deserve to know that, don't I?" The senior Mr. Waybill becomes more distressed as he talks, his volume increasing with each iteration.

Charlie's voice is a soothing, soft counterpoint. She recognizes it as the one he uses with the animals, and with her when she needs it. "Grandpa, it's okay. It's okay. I'm here now. I'll tell you anything you want to know."

"Ellen should be here."

"Grandma's back home," Charlie says. "Resting."

"Resting." Mr. Waybill says it as if he's testing the word, weighing it to check if it's right. Apparently, it isn't, because he becomes agitated again, accusing Charlie of lying to him too.

"Grandpa, please—"

"Where's Ellen? Where is she? I miss her. I miss my wife." The unmistakable sound of Mr. Waybill crying breaks Gretchen's heart clean in half. Tears make a regular appearance in her spirit medium work, but usually they're the quiet, sad tears of someone who wishes more than anything to believe their loved one is still somewhere out there. Occasionally, when she's lucky, they're tears of joy because she convinced the client that their wish has come true. But Charlie's grandfather's sobs are full of frustration and worry and a grief that lurks just under the surface where he can't quite grasp it. She knows Charlie is going to be so mad at her for involving herself, but Gretchen can't resist; she can't bear to let Mr. Waybill feel this pain when she knows how to make it better. More than that, she can't let *Charlie* feel it.

So she slips inside the room.

The old man sits on the edge of his bed, head bowed. He's so slender, fragile-looking. His hair has the same natural wave as Charlie's, the stark whiteness of it like a snowdrift atop his head. Charlie sits in a chair pulled beside the nightstand, his hand resting on his grandfather's back, rubbing and patting without any real rhythm.

"Hello," Gretchen says. The sound of a new voice prompts Mr. Waybill to raise his head. Reddened blue eyes—nearly the same shade as Everett's, she notes—study her. But it's Charlie's that have Gretchen's attention, because when they find hers, the displeasure there is as clear as it was that first day she arrived at Gilded Creek. *Leave*, they demand. *Right now.*

Instead, she takes a step closer and puts on a smile. She's about to say that she has a message to deliver from Ellen, the way she would if Mr. Waybill were a client. He doesn't remember that his wife is dead, but it doesn't matter. She'll just talk about Ellen as if she's back at the farm instead of having gone Up, as Everett calls it. She's home at Gilded Creek, busy trying out an Ina Garten recipe, maybe, working on another one of her eclectic afghans, visiting a sick neighbor—what was the name of the woman Everett told her lived across the street until a few years ago? But before she can speak, Mr. Waybill's face brightens and he reaches for Gretchen's hand.

"Ellen, sweetheart! There you are! About time." She thinks back to the photo in the farmhouse's upstairs hallway, how Everett said that Gretchen looks a bit like a young Ellen Waybill. It wasn't *that* close of a resemblance in her opinion. But apparently, it's close enough.

She can't very well admit she's *not* Ellen and kill that look of relief on the poor man's face. So instead she says, "Yes, I'm here now," as Mr. Waybill wraps her in his arms. From the picture she saw and the stories she's heard, Gretchen knows he used to be as brawny as Charlie. Now he's so frail she worries she might break him with one wrong touch.

Charlie moves to rise from his chair, his expression thunderous. He's going to kick her out. As is his right. God, what was she thinking?

"I was getting real worried, El. I don't know why I'm here instead of at home, and they said they didn't know when you were coming to get me, that they were going to call you, but then they said they hadn't been able to reach you yet . . . These people make me feel like I'm losing my marbles sometimes."

"I'm so sorry you were worried," she says, pulling away and patting Mr. Waybill's arm reassuringly. She isn't sure what the right thing to say is here, what the nurses tell the patients to keep them content, so she aims instead for distraction. "We've had our hands full with the new kids at the farm. Isn't that right, Chick?"

Charlie's eyes go wide and he sinks back down into his chair. It's as if she's disarmed him with the use of his childhood nickname. She can see the flicker of belief that flashes in his eyes. He may have seen through her more easily than anyone else ever has from the moment she arrived, but now he's looking at her with curiosity. Like maybe he's realizing there might be another layer to her that he missed upon first glance.

"I remember the time we had six kids born on the same night, back when Charlie was little," she says, recounting what Charlie told her as they sat vigil over Sleepy Jean and the other goats in the little outbuilding.

Mr. Waybill grins, recognition and humor lighting up his eyes. "What a night that was. The first time you helped with the kidding, right, Charlie?"

"Yes," Charlie says, swallowing visibly again. "That was . . . I helped deliver one. Everyone was busy with the others, so you let me take care of it on my own."

"That's right. You named her . . . Stu! And we teased you about naming her after what she was going to become." Mr. Waybill cackles, taking great pleasure in the memory.

"S-T-U, not S-T-E-W," Gretchen whispers, flashing a small grin at Charlie, who looks closer to tears than to smiling himself.

"And you let me give her a proper burial when she died," Charlie says, clearing his throat twice as he fights for the words. "So she never did become stew anyway."

"You can thank your grandmother for that." Mr. Waybill reaches out and ruffles Charlie's hair the same way Gretchen has seen Lori do. "That soft heart of yours is her weakness. Always has been." He looks to Gretchen. "Isn't that right?"

Lean into the truth whenever you can. She looks Charlie in the eye in hopes he'll see how honest she's being as she says, "It's my favorite thing about him."

Mr. Waybill reaches for Gretchen's hand again and gives it a light squeeze. Charlie stares at the floor, as if he can't bear to look at her. It's all becoming too much, this poorly thought-out plan having snowballed into something for which she wasn't prepared. Charlie's soft heart that she needs to break and mend at the same time. Her own heart is decidedly harder, but it feels erratic, as if its beats are syncopated. She searches the room for an excuse to escape and finds it in an empty plastic water jug sitting on the nightstand.

"Let me get you more water. I'll be right back." Gretchen grabs the pitcher and hurries into the hallway, avoiding eye contact with Charlie on her way out. Wendy, still at the nurses' station, points her to a small kitchenette and invites her to help herself. After the pitcher is full and she's nabbed a cup of ice cream from the freezer, she steadies herself and walks back to Mr. Waybill's room.

"I brought you a treat," she says, balancing the spoon on the ice cream cup in one hand and the pitcher in the other. "Would you like some ice cream?"

"Oh boy! The answer to that is always yes," Mr. Waybill says. "Thank you."

"You're very welcome." Gretchen tears the top off the ice cream cup and stabs the plastic spoon into the middle where the chocolate and vanilla meet.

"Forgive me, but . . . do you work here, darlin'? I don't remember your name."

She looks to Charlie, who pauses in refilling his grandfather's cup with some of the replenished water to say, "It happens." He meets her eyes for a moment to emphasize the message hidden in his nonchalant response. *He sometimes forgets from one moment to the next*, he means. *He doesn't think you're Ellen anymore.*

"Oh, sorry, I forgot to introduce myself. I'm Gretchen. I'm a friend of Charlie's." It feels like quite a stretch to call herself a *friend* of Charlie's. Probably more accurate would be "the current bane of his existence," but there's no point in explaining everything going on with Everett and the curse.

"Only a friend, eh?" Mr. Waybill asks as he digs into the ice cream. "Thought my grandson was smarter than that."

"Grandpa," Charlie warns, but his voice is light.

"Come on, boy, she's very pretty."

To Gretchen's immense surprise, Charlie replies, "So I've noticed." Her cheeks heat at the words. Charlie thinks she's pretty? No, not just pretty. *Very* pretty. And there's that telltale blush of his, the one she can't get enough of inciting. *Gotcha*. The euphoria spreads through her fingers, into her toes.

"I'm just saying . . ." Mr. Waybill pauses. "It might be nice to have a great-grandchild."

Charlie claps his hands together. "And on that note, I think we better get going. You're feeling all right?"

"Of course. Why wouldn't I be? I've got ice cream."

Charlie plants a kiss on the top of Mr. Waybill's snowy hair. "Have a good night. Listen to the nurses."

"Will do," Mr. Waybill says, saluting with his spoon. "Now, you gonna take that girl out on the town or what?"

Charlie gives Gretchen a quick sideways glance. "Something like that. Night, Grandpa."

Mr. Waybill takes another big bite of ice cream, then flashes a smile and nods in dismissal.

They walk from the room to the elevator in silence. Charlie's fists are clenched at his sides, and any remaining pleasant tingling promptly vacates Gretchen's extremities. Is he going to yell at her when they get to the truck? He's never yelled at her before, no matter how angry he's been. No, Charlie has always held his anger close to his chest, letting Gretchen see just enough to communicate that he's choosing to spare her from something darker and punishing. That his benevolence is limited and she shouldn't push. Maybe this time, though, it won't be just a warning. Maybe she already dashed way past the point of his patience with this stunt. So much for convincing him of the curse; she assumes she'll be in a car back to DC within the hour.

Everett is going to be so disappointed in her. Hell, she's disappointed in herself.

The moment they're on the pavement outside the building's

automatic front doors, Gretchen takes a deep breath, stops, and turns to Charlie. "I overstepped."

"Yes," he says, refusing to fully face her. "You did."

"I'm sorry. I didn't know he would—I thought I could be useful."

Charlie nods, then stares up at the sky. It's a cool, cloudless night, and the stars are as vivid as glow-in-the-dark plastic cut-outs pressed onto a child's bedroom ceiling. Is he biding his time, building up to the yelling? Gretchen wrings her hands as she waits to discover her fate.

He turns to her at last, lips pressed together in a stiff line before they part. "I don't know how you know things like that," he says quietly. The anger she was expecting isn't anywhere to be found. "Like that they used to call me Chick when I was a kid."

"Everett told—"

But Charlie holds up a hand. "I don't want to— It doesn't matter, okay? Not tonight."

"Okay," she says, unsure if the word is even audible with how softly it comes out. They continue to the truck. Charlie unlocks the doors, and Gretchen does her best to climb into the cab without exposing herself to anyone who might happen to walk out of the building and glance this way. Her dress is shorter than she remembers it being, probably thanks to shrinkage after the mud puddle incident, and the truck is really quite high off the ground.

In the passenger seat, she spreads out the fabric, pulls it down closer to her knees. She's spent so much time in overalls lately that having her legs exposed like this feels strange, almost inherently erotic. Like she's a nineteenth-century lady flashing some ankle.

When Charlie joins her in the cab, his hands clutch the steering wheel, but he doesn't turn the key in the ignition. She's about to tell him it's okay if they don't go anywhere else tonight, if he wants to head back to the farm, or even drop her off there and head back out on his own. But he clears his throat and stares out the windshield. "I don't know how you did it, and I don't think I want to know. But . . . it helped him. So thank you."

"Oh." She's unable to keep the surprise from her voice. "Um. You're welcome."

"It's hard sometimes when . . ." He trails off, tangled in the complexity of the thought. "It's just hard sometimes."

"Yeah." She understands without him saying more, about how all this weighs so heavily on him. Her fingers tremble ever so slightly as she reaches out and places them on his forearm, timid to touch him, worried he'll bite. He allows it, though, and even lays his own hand over hers for a second, barely more than a pat, but enough to engulf Gretchen in head-to-toe heat.

The man is a flame. But maybe she is too. Hopefully, she doesn't misstep and burn it all down.

20

"TIPSY LOU'S? IS THIS A BAR?" GRETCHEN IS HONESTLY
bemused; she expected the mystery of where Charlie spends his
free time to have a more interesting answer. Or at least one that's
more *him*. Like a knitting circle or a book club, maybe. Certainly
not a black-painted cinder block cube of a building off Route 15
that has more motorcycles than cars in its parking lot.

He parks below a window that houses a large neon BAR sign.
"Seems so," he says with a touch of humor she's barely heard
since he asked if she was an undercover pork chop. He gets out
of the truck and comes around to her side. "Want help down?"

Yes, please touch me again. "No, I can manage." Gretchen slips
to the very edge of the side of the passenger seat and kind of . . .
slides like a two-by-four falling off a ledge. Her hands clutch at
the hem of her dress to hold it in place, which prevents her from
flashing anyone but leaves no way to steady herself as she lands
in an awkward crouch.

"That was some dismount," Charlie comments, and his crooked smile makes her almost lose her balance again as she stands.

Once upright, she straightens her clothes and tucks her hair behind her ears. She hasn't worn it down for a week, and the way it brushes against the bare skin near her collarbone keeps startling her. Strange how quickly the way she dressed every day for years has become so unfamiliar, almost uncomfortable. The relative steadiness of her spirit medium gig in DC made her forget how instantly she can acclimate to things when the need arises. "So are you going to tell me what it is we're here for, or am I going to have to wait and see?"

He shrugs and smiles again as he walks ahead of her toward the entrance. *Wait and see it is.*

Inside Tipsy Lou's, the din of dozens of different conversations fills the space almost as claustrophobically as the actual people standing around. It's a swarm-like buzzing that gives Gretchen an immediate headache. She hasn't been in a packed bar like this in years, not since her first few months in DC when she supplemented her then-paltry séance income by scamming drunk government consultants at some of the local power dining hot spots. The whole crying by the bathrooms and claiming her boyfriend just dumped her and left her without any money to get home act was never something she enjoyed pulling off very much; too little artistry involved (and a high risk of being groped). So once she didn't need the extra money to survive anymore, Gretchen happily became a homebody. The intensity of being surrounded by so many people now is enough to make it difficult to breathe, and she finds herself clutching at her chest as if she might be able to coax her rib cage to expand.

"You okay?" Charlie has to yell down at her for her to hear him.

"Yeah, I'm good. Just a bit . . . overstimulated," she yells back up.

He takes her hand, which would be something she would enjoy very much if she were not currently sweating profusely, and Gretchen follows in his wake as he ushers them through the crowd toward— *Oh, thank goodness.* They've come to a separate room in the back that only has a handful of people, most of them gathered around three pool tables. The noise from the main area of the bar still reaches back here, but it's muffled enough that the clack of balls ricocheting off one another is at the forefront.

"Yo! Waybill!" An olive-skinned man with a bushy black mustache and shoulder-length hair looks up after taking his turn at the table to the right. "Didn't know if we'd see you tonight." The man strolls over, and he and Charlie clap their hands together in a bro-style shake. Then he turns to Gretchen and, with eyebrows raised in interest, asks, "And who is this?"

"Hi, I'm Gretchen." She holds out a hand, and to her surprise the man takes it but doesn't shake it so much as drop into a goofy, exaggerated curtsy that startles her into a giggle.

"I go by Dutch," he says, rising again. Dutch flashes a sparkling smile. "And I am *so* pleased to meet you, Gretchen. We heard quite a bit about you last week."

"Oh?"

Charlie clears his throat. "Any tables about to be free?"

"Yeah, Bobbi and I just finished up. You can grab ours. I'd offer to play you, but I assume you'd rather hang out with your date."

"Acorn isn't my date." He says it quickly enough to sting a little, a rubber band snapped on her wrist. A good reminder.

"Hm. Well, whatever she is, you'd be a fool to ignore her to play with *me*. Bobbi's already bled me dry anyway. That woman is an absolute menace. Here, take this." Dutch hands Charlie his cue. "Now, if you'll excuse me, I'm gonna go ply the lovely Roberta with tequila shots and see if I can convince her to be my plus-one for my cousin's wedding in May." His thick, dark eyebrows jump as he looks back to Gretchen. "Careful with this one. He's a menace too," he tells her before strolling away, and she laughs, assuming it's a joke. Of course, there's the extreme sexual tension that has her staying awake much later than she'd like, imagining all of the dirty, dirty things she'd like to get up to with Charlie, and the way he makes her fight-or-flight response kick into overdrive. But she can't imagine anyone else thinking Charlie Waybill is in any way dangerous.

He chalks another cue and hands it to her. "You know how to play?" he asks, gesturing toward the pool table with a nod of his head.

Gretchen's father used to make an extra buck or two hustling in places they were passing through. But he only played when they needed quick cash. It wasn't something he did with any real passion. Just another trick up his sleeve. One of the many he taught his daughter. Or, in this particular case, one he *tried* to teach her—Gretchen never did get the hang of it. She looks over the table's green felt as if her memories might appear there, growing larger like ink stains. "Not really."

"Gotta admit I'm surprised," he says, walking over to where she's standing. He places the cue ball on the table and leans in closer to her ear. "A con artist who can't play pool? Thought it was basically a requirement in your line of work."

In response to her subsequent silence, he gives a few clicks of his tongue and a shake of his head—playful admonishment. Not hostility. So maybe this is okay. Maybe things really have changed between them after what happened the other morning and with his grandfather tonight.

"Seems like a real oversight," he adds.

Not an oversight, just a lack of talent. She bites back the admission.

Charlie pauses for a moment and studies her. Then he takes a step back with a sly smile before he strolls to the opposite side of the table. He grabs the black plastic rack and fills it with the balls from the pockets nearest to him. She rolls the ones from her side over, unable to resist studying the way his body moves, how his shoulder flexes beneath his clothes as he stretches to reach one that doesn't quite make it. Balls all in the rack, he points to the top of the triangle. "The one ball here; eight in the middle; a stripe in one corner and a solid in the other; the rest doesn't matter. Do you want to break?"

"Umm . . . Sure?" As soon as she attempts to take aim with the cue, she realizes she truly has forgotten more about this than she remembers. The angles are all wrong, her grip too tense, the hole she's made with her fingers as a bridge too tight. Discomfort in her wrist confirms she's way off, nowhere close to the correct position. But she also doesn't know how to fix it. Her first attempt misses the cue ball completely. Her second sends it leaping off the table. Charlie catches it in one hand with reflexes that would make an MLB scout stand up and take notice.

"Jesus," he says, the ball safely ensconced in his palm. "You weren't fucking with me? You really don't know how to play?"

Gretchen's ready to spit back something about how maybe he

should believe her when she tells him things, but the words get caught in her throat as Charlie moves closer, wrapping his fingers around her cue. He leans in to whisper in her ear, "I probably shouldn't teach you this. You're already too powerful as it is."

This is like when they first met. Like standing on the farmhouse's porch and hearing him describe her in nearly the same terms with which she thinks of herself. There's less disgust in his voice this time though as he acknowledges that Gretchen's damn fucking good at what she does. And it's nice to be recognized for her skills, as unsavory as he may find them. *He sees me.*

She lifts the cue into a horizontal position again, and Charlie's touch is both forceful and guiding as he persuades her right hand to loosen slightly and lower to correct the angle. He pushes her left palm flat against the table, then adjusts her fingers into a simpler bridge. One of his palms lightly presses her shoulder blade until she's bent over, chin closer to her cue. Meanwhile, his body is pressed so close to Gretchen's that she finds herself subconsciously matching the pace of his breathing. And god help her, all she can think about is if this is what Charlie Waybill would be like in bed, demanding things from her in this way that somehow still feels soft beneath it all.

"Try again," he says, his lips closer to her neck than she realized. The moist heat of his words near the sensitive skin below her ear makes her knees go a little weak, and she has to lean into the table to remain standing when he abruptly takes several steps back.

Gretchen aims the cue and hits the white ball with as much force as she can. It gives a tiny hop in the air before hitting the one, the force too weak to send the rest of the balls very far.

"For a break to be legal, you have to either pocket a ball or hit at least four off the cushions," he says, gathering the few she scattered back into the rack. "Again."

The proper position seems to be part of her now, seared into her muscle memory by Charlie's guidance. But she says, "Can you . . . can you show me again?"

Another shot, this one much better. Something low in her stomach flutters when Charlie says, "Yeah, there you go. Nice job."

He takes aim next. "Watch me." As if Gretchen needs to be told. As if she could do anything except take note of his every move. He hits the cue ball into one of the solids, which bounces off another and sinks a stripe into the left center pocket.

"You're pretty good at this. Pick this up from your grandma too?"

Gretchen meant it as a joke, but Charlie says, "Yeah. And Grandpa. Both played. They had a table in the basement for a time. Taught me down there. I liked it. Played a good bit through college, but had to take a break while I was at sea. Been getting back into it the last year or so."

"You mean you didn't play pool on the tall ships?" She imagines it would be challenging to keep the balls from rolling around.

"Ha. They do have gyroscopic tables on some big cruise ships, but not the windjammers I worked on." He aims and takes his next shot—another seemingly effortless one that Gretchen knows requires immense skill. "And I couldn't play in most ports because I didn't speak the language enough to figure out what rules we were playing by, and I didn't want to get my—"

"You Waybill?" someone interrupts from behind Gretchen.

"Uh. Yeah. That's me."

"I heard you're pretty good."

Who's this chump interrupting their game? (Or whatever it is she and Charlie are doing, since it's less an actual game and more him running the table while she tries not to be too transparent in her ogling.)

She thought Tipsy Lou's was an odd choice for Charlie "I'd like to be a librarian" Waybill's night out, but he's nowhere near as out of place here as the twentysomething guy in an oxford shirt and fleece vest standing beside a tall, slender woman wearing a body-hugging red dress and sky-high heels. His face is flushed from alcohol, and she has the high cheekbones and wide-set eyes of a high fashion model. After years in the city, Gretchen can clock a DC consultant bro from a mile away. It's clear that's what this guy is, though she can't begin to imagine how he and his date found their way to a dive bar in the far, far, *far* suburbs.

"I'm all right," Charlie answers, although the modesty sounds more obligatory than sincere. She can see by the few shots Charlie has taken that he not only has raw skill, but the discipline to have honed it into something formidable.

"Prove it. A hundred dollars," the man says, taking a step forward. Gretchen clocks that his vest has DELOITTE embroidered on the chest. Yep, consulting bro. *Called it.*

"Pardon?"

"I bet you a hundred bucks I'll beat you."

"Not interested," Charlie says without hesitation, then directs his attention back to Gretchen. "Your turn, Acorn." Which, it isn't, not technically, because Charlie still hasn't missed a shot. But getting closer to the cue ball will also get her closer to Charlie, which is where she wants to be. And maybe . . . maybe where he wants her to be too?

"Aw, don't be a pussy, man," Mr. Deloitte says, chuckling as if that was actually a sick burn.

Oh, how Gretchen's always hated consulting bros. How *right* taking their money always felt. There are countless ways she could clean out this one's pockets, easy peasy. Just like the good old days when she first arrived in Washington. But she can't do that here, not in front of Charlie.

"Maybe we should go find Dutch and Bobbi," he says, his hand coming to the small of Gretchen's back. Charlie has it in him to stand his ground; she knows because he does it with her all the time. But she's glad that he's not the type to take this asshole's bait.

"Yeah." Too bad the nice time they were starting to have together is sure to come to an end as soon as they reenter the loud, overwhelming main part of the bar.

As they start to move away from the table, Mr. Deloitte sighs. "Fine. Five hundred."

Charlie pauses, turns. He has a strange fake smile on his face, one that Gretchen's never seen him wear before. "Five hundred? That's a lot of cash, my friend."

"To some people, maybe." The guy glances at the model, raising an eyebrow as if to say, *I make a lot of money, please be impressed.* She mostly looks bored, as she has the entire conversation.

"Okay. You're on. Eight ball, winner breaks," Charlie says. "Three-game race?"

"Charlie—" Gretchen starts, but he takes her hand and gives it a firm squeeze. Which is unexpected enough to silence the rest of her objection.

"Found your balls, huh?" The consultant hands the beer he's holding to his companion, who takes it without any acknowledgment or change in her expression or posture. "Let's go."

And then . . . Gretchen watches Charlie play pool against a DC bro. *It's like watching my present fighting my past.* She sets down the pint of beer she's been nursing since Dutch delivered it a moment ago, as if the few sips she's had may be to blame for that ridiculous thought.

Charlie wins the first and second games, but not by much. And then he fouls by pocketing the cue ball on his first shot during the third. He shakes his head as if disappointed in himself, but when his eyes meet Gretchen's across the table he . . .

Charlie fucking *winks.*

And that's when it hits her. She has to admit, Charlie puts on a good show, making it look like he's just not quite skilled enough to carry out his shots. Anyone who isn't watching the way his shoulders shift ever so slightly as he takes aim would have no reason to suspect a thing. But Gretchen's eyes have become so attuned to his movements that it's now clear as day to her that he is intentionally throwing this game. He's *hustling.* She knows this playbook, grew up reading it, wrote a page or two of it herself, even. But *Charlie* following it feels like she's in a bizarro world.

"What the actual fuck are you doing?" she whispers when he comes close to her to take a sip of his beer after officially losing the third game.

He shrugs, but that crooked grin on his face tells her that he knows exactly what she means. "Playing pool."

She watches as Charlie sinks a ball, then miscues on his next shot. He's good at pretending not to be good at this. *Have I ruined this man?* But no, her influence isn't enough to account for Charlie knowing how to hustle. He's done this before, she realizes. And then has absolutely no clue what to do with that information.

"Shit," Charlie mutters after he loses the fourth game too.

His opponent nods, his grin smug. "Keep playing, man. Practice makes perfect."

"Yeah, good advice." Charlie glances over to Gretchen again and presses his lips together. To anyone else he might look frustrated, disappointed. But she spots how the corner of his mouth struggles not to rise. He's hiding something like giddiness as he grabs the back of his neck, turns to Mr. Deloitte, and says, "I'm feeling like my luck's about to pick up. What do you say we change this to a race to four, double or nothing?"

The asshole weighs the proposition, no doubt thinking about the first and second games versus the third and fourth, trying to determine if Charlie's luck might actually return. Guys like this always err on the side of arrogance, though, so it's not surprising when he nods and says, "A thousand bucks? Sure a hick like you can afford that?"

God, Charlie picked a perfect mark. Gretchen really has to hand it to him.

He makes a show of checking his pockets, then says, "I might need to hit up an ATM. But I can scrape it together."

The next game goes just like the last one, though. Charlie is missing more than he's making, and he loses again. "What are you doing?" Gretchen hisses when he comes over to partake of the nachos someone dropped off a few minutes ago.

"My best," he says out of the corner of his mouth as he chews.

"Are you, though?" Gretchen wants to tell him that if he's in over his head, she can help. She can find a way to intervene before he loses a shit ton of money—money she knows he desperately needs. But offering to lie on the spot would definitely add a large tally to the pro column of his *Is Gretchen Acorn a fraud?* accounting. So she keeps her mouth shut.

Charlie bends down as he puts his beer back on the high-top table and whispers, "Trust me."

And then he goes back to eke out a win. They're tied at three games apiece now. The next game will be the last. Some might think the two players are evenly matched. But Gretchen knows better, just from those few shots she watched Charlie take when they were playing around earlier. The relief when *that* Charlie returns! It's like watching a completely different person as he runs the table after the break. The feigned timidity and the hesitation disappear. There are no slight adjustments after he takes aim. He's on fire—the way he could have been this entire time if he felt like it—and Mr. Deloitte can tell he's been had. His face gets redder and redder with each sunken ball. Charlie shrugs and smiles, as if he can't believe just how powerfully his luck has come charging back.

His opponent looks like he's going to burst a blood vessel when it's finally his turn, and his anger interferes with his concentration, causing him to miscue.

Charlie gives him a sympathetic look that Gretchen is surprised doesn't immediately get him punched in the face. "Eight ball to bottom right corner," he says, going in for the kill. It's a complex shot with one of his opponent's balls in the way—not something an amateur should be able to make. Of course, Charlie Waybill is no amateur.

Gretchen gathers up their jackets, because her Eichorn DNA is whispering to her to plan for a hasty exit.

The cue ball jumps over the obstacle in its way, hits the bumper, and careens into the eight, sinking it into the bottom right corner. Several people have gathered around to watch as the game progressed, and now someone lets out a whistle of appreciation.

"Damn, Waybill," Dutch says. "That was *fiiine*."

The voluptuous purple-haired Black woman standing beside him—Bobbi, Gretchen assumes—raises her drink in the air. "Gorgeous, honey. Absolutely gorgeous."

The asshole's anger takes a back burner for a moment as the complexity of the shot registers, but soon it comes roaring back.

"You're a real motherfucker, you know that?" he says to Charlie with a humorless chuckle.

"Yep," Charlie says, holding out his hand. "Pay up."

The guy glances around as if weighing the likelihood of getting away without handing over the money, realizes he's surrounded by people who have been cheering for Charlie, and snarls as he pulls out his wallet to reluctantly toss ten crisp one-hundred-dollar bills onto the table. As if that's a normal amount of cash to have on one's person. Gretchen shakes her head. *Consulting bros.*

"Thanks." Charlie pockets his winnings. "But hey, good game. You should definitely keep playing, man. I've heard that practice makes perfect."

Gretchen's lips part to yell a warning when Mr. Deloitte makes a fist and pulls it back, but she's not the only one who notices; Bobbi effortlessly grabs the guy's wrist from behind and keeps him in the uncomfortable position of being about to throw a punch. "Now, I don't think that's a smart move, buddy," Dutch says from beside them. "Maybe take a second to reconsider."

The furious, tipsy spoiled brat of a man blinks a few times, then nods. Bobbi releases him but stays close, just in case.

Charlie tosses one of the hundreds back onto the table with a casual arrogance Gretchen never imagined he might possess. "Next round's on me."

Then he downs the rest of his beer in one big gulp, takes Gretchen's hand, and leads her through Tipsy Lou's and into the crisp, dark night.

21

IT MIGHT BE A SECONDHAND VERSION OF THE GOTCHA euphoria, or the adrenaline response of their escape, or maybe even just the thrill of Charlie and her being on the same side of a confrontation for once, but Gretchen's heart pounds against her rib cage with the same urgency as someone locked out of a house. She can't seem to stop grinning, even as a slight ache spreads through her cheeks.

When they come to a stop around the side of the building, she stares at Charlie. Could this truly be the same man who called her a charlatan when they met? She should probably be angry, or at least annoyed, that he's been condemning her for tricking people into giving her their money when it's something he's apparently quite skilled at himself. But for some reason, she can't muster any negative feelings toward him right now. All she feels is a little bit of awe and a whole lot of attraction.

It's a problem. A really big problem.

"You," she says.

"Me?" He points to himself, feigning innocence that would be much more convincing if he weren't smiling back at her. "What about me?"

"You just fucking *hustled a guy*!"

"Hmm," he says, expression unchanging.

"Where did you learn to do that?"

"I think maybe you've been a bad influence on me. I've never done anything like that in my life."

"Oh, bullshit," she laughs, ignoring the first part even though she had a similar thought earlier. "There's no way that was the first time."

He chuckles lightly before admitting, "You're right, it wasn't. First time in a while, though." He glances back the way they came, double-checking that no one's followed them outside. "Look, I enjoy playing pool. I like coming out here to play with friends. We never bet beyond who's gonna cover the next round. But when I was younger and stupider, I would sometimes play for money and maybe . . . when the mood was right . . . *encourage* strangers to bet larger amounts than they might otherwise."

"'Encourage' them. That's a pretty way to say it. Mm, and how often did those strangers try to beat the shit out of you?" If he acted anything like he just did in Tipsy Lou's, she can imagine college-aged Charlie was often at the receiving end of some guy's fist, but she hates to think of it. Perhaps it comes with the territory of trying to save his life, this feeling that she wants to keep him safe from not only the curse but every form of harm, and somehow that extends into his past too. Even if he probably would've deserved it.

"Well, I was usually a little more subtle about it. They'd almost always walk away thinking it was close, that I was just lucky," he says, punctuating it with a chuckle. "But that guy was really annoying me, so I kind of stopped caring."

Charlie's chuckle turns into a full-blown laugh, and Gretchen laughs too, and she's not quite sure what they're laughing at, but it feels incredible to be sharing this moment. The comedown from running a con can sometimes feel a lot like the minutes immediately post-orgasm. Full of emotions that don't make much sense but flood you anyway. She leans back against the cool metal of the truck's passenger-side door, memorizing that wave in Charlie's hair as he bows his head to collect himself.

"And to think . . . you've been so goddamn sanctimonious ever since I showed up at Gilded Creek," she says through her laughter. "Meanwhile, you—"

He plants a palm against the door beside her and leans in closer. For once it doesn't feel like he's looking down at her so much as meeting her where she is. "Sanctimonious? Me?"

"Yes! You've called me a thief and a con artist and a scammer and whatever else based on nothing but the assumption"—he raises his eyebrows—"the *assumption* that I'm not being honest with my clients. Meanwhile, you go out and hustle people in bars with the skill of a professional grifter like it's no big deal."

It's . . . fascinating. The way he can turn this part of himself off and on. Gretchen is always on. She grew up thinking that was the only way to be. That if you had skills of the lying, cheating, stealing variety, you had no choice but to make them part of you. Part of your life. It never occurred to her that there are people in the world who can do what she does, and simply . . . choose not to.

"And you would know," he says, as if highlighting the ignorance she's only just discovering.

"Oh, please." She shakes her head. "You're a fucking hypocrite, Charlie Waybill."

Her smile falters for a moment as she registers the bite to her words. She isn't sure when that indignation crept into her tone, but it's certainly there. Disguising the hurt that would otherwise slip out. The hurt she tries to deny whenever Charlie accuses her of being a fraud. Because for some reason, she wants him to think the best of her and he's only ever thought the worst. Anger about it is safer, but that it affects her at all has been weighing so heavily on her over the past week. He can see through her so well; she wonders if he can also see how much she craves his approval.

Maybe he can, because Charlie moves his hands to Gretchen's upper arms, and his eyes lock on hers. The regular hazel is closer to a uniform gold in the dim, pink-tinged light of the bar parking lot. There's no question about what's making her heart pound now. It's definitely the way Charlie's body is a mere inch from hers, how his heat radiates into her bones. His quick breaths encourage hers to come faster too, as if they're testing whether she can keep up.

And this is her moment, she realizes. This is the moment to make her move, to do what needs to be done. Everett is right that time isn't on their side, and if not now, then when?

"You pretend you're so honorable. That you're such a *stand-up guy*," Gretchen says quietly. The back of her head rests against the truck's window as she looks up at Charlie, so very close, knowing it's a matter of seconds before he caves and kisses her. "But deep down, you're as flawed as the rest of us. You're just better at hiding it."

"Not always," he whispers.

His lips crash against hers, forceful and hungry. Gretchen makes a needy sound she isn't exactly proud of as his tongue slips into the opening she offers. His hands travel down to grasp her hips, pressing her between him and the truck, enabling her to feel every inch of his body, including the ridge of his growing erection. This evidence of his arousal drives her wild, the success of winning him over in at least one way a delicious hum that reverberates through her bones.

Her fingers scramble over his arms, his back, digging nails through his shirt and into his muscles in hopes she'll make a mark. She wants to leave a reminder of what it's like to give in to her so that he'll want to do it again and again. She bites his lower lip, soothes it with the tip of her tongue. That's the extent of her artful seduction, though, as her brain succumbs to overwhelming, uncontrollable feeling. Gretchen wants—needs—Charlie to pour all of himself into this, into her, and she wraps one leg around his, making small sounds of approval when he squeezes her thigh and pushes up the hem of her dress. The truck is cold against her ass without the extra layer of fabric until his warm palm cups one cheek low, fingers playing at the seam of her underwear (and oh, how she's glad she chose one of the lacy pairs tonight even though the ones he bought her are frankly much more comfortable) as he lowers his head further to lick along the side of Gretchen's throat, and oh god, she's going to let this man fuck her right here in this dive bar's parking lot, isn't she?

She cants her pelvis forward, desperate, trying to find a source of friction to relieve this ache that's building inside her, and Charlie moves one of his muscular thighs between her legs, giving her something solid to rock against as he finds her mouth again. It's still not nearly enough.

It isn't supposed to be this way. She's vaguely aware that she's supposed to be in control, the one to bring him to his knees. And yet if he didn't have her pinned to the truck's door, she's fairly certain she would be kneeling on the asphalt.

"Charlie," she sobs. It's as if his name is synonymous with the swell of need threatening to overtake her and a plea for rescue all in one.

Yet he doesn't hear it that way. Or maybe he does and simply returns to his senses. Everywhere Gretchen is pressed against him goes tense. He pulls back, looking at her wide-eyed, like a deer on high alert after hearing a twig snap.

"I . . ." Charlie shakes his head. "I'm sorry."

"No, don't be sorry. I wanted, I want—"

He holds up a hand, stopping her from saying more. "No, I mean that we . . ." Then both hands come to his head, gripping at his hair as he turns his back to Gretchen. She reaches out to touch his shoulder, but he shrugs her away. "That won't happen again," he says, the declaration gruff and final-sounding.

"Charlie—"

"It won't, and . . . and it's getting late. We should get back to the farm."

Gretchen sighs, hoping it might expel some of the frustration and hurt he's left her with. Not to mention the bafflement at how quickly she forgot herself—and the point of what she was supposed to be doing—as soon as he kissed her. "Okay," she says as she opens the truck's door and climbs into the passenger seat.

THE SILENCE DURING THE THIRTY-MINUTE DRIVE BACK TO
Gilded Creek is so thick Gretchen worries she might choke on it.
The miasma is like another passenger, shoved between them in
the front seat, hoarding all of the extra oxygen. A few times, she
opens her mouth, the courage to try to push through it on the tip
of her tongue. But ultimately, she can't help but swallow it down
again. It's the determined set of Charlie's brow, the tightness in
his jaw that tells her it isn't worth attempting right now. So she
says nothing, and he says nothing. *This is how rejection feels. This is
how failure feels.* As much as she tries to divorce herself from the
actual sensations, they linger stubbornly in the corners.

She isn't sure what she'll tell Everett when she gets home. *Charlie and I almost banged in a bar parking lot and I forgot my own name much
less what I was supposed to be accomplishing, and then he got mad at me and
I'm not sure what to do now?* Not exactly a conversation she wants to
have with the ghost tonight. Or ever.

The long, winding driveway seems six times longer than when
they left, but it eventually delivers them to the farmhouse. Gretchen
clumsily slides down from the too-high passenger seat again. This
time, she forgets to hold her dress down and gives any goats awake
in the barn quite a show. Bonnie and Clyde bark in greeting. It's
a cloudy night, only a few stars visible but still many more than
she ever saw in the city. As picturesque as Gilded Creek is during
the day, something about the darkness makes it otherworldly. Beautiful in a way Gretchen wishes she could bottle and take back to DC
to somehow use in her séances.

Charlie walks straight to the door, inserts his key, and opens
it. She follows him inside, where they observe their progress in

removing their shoes with a feigned sense of fascination that keeps them from having to make eye contact. The TV plays an episode of *Taxi*. Everett doesn't poke his head up from the couch to greet them, so Gretchen assumes he's either elsewhere or ignoring her too. Well, if no one in this house is going to acknowledge her existence right now, she might as well head up to her bedroom so she can be sexually frustrated in peace.

She's halfway up the stairs when Charlie clears his throat. "Acorn?"

Gretchen clutches the banister, suddenly a little dizzy. Probably from the half a pint she had at Tipsy Lou's. "Yeah?"

"Um, thank you again for earlier. With my grandfather, I mean. And I'm . . . I'm sorry again for . . ." He trails off. "Anyway. Good night."

"Good night," she responds, perplexed. Because it seems like what she assumed was anger toward her might actually be anger toward himself.

Anyway, so much for peace. Everett is waiting on her bed. "My, my, my," he says, looking her up and down from where he hover-lies prone with his legs in the air like a possessed preteen girl at a slumber party. Gretchen hasn't seen herself in a mirror or any other reflective surface since making out with Charlie outside the bar, so who knows what her hair looks like, how swollen her lips might be. "*Someone* looks like she had a good time."

Gretchen face-plants onto the mattress beside Everett and groans.

"Or . . . maybe . . . not?"

She groans again.

"Why don't you tell me all about it, doll?" he says, leaning closer to her. His ambient chill gives her goose bumps. "I'm a very good listener. It's mostly what I did around here until you got here, you know."

"Literally none of our interactions corroborate your ability to listen to anyone other than yourself," she says into the afghan.

Everett stands and brings a hand to his chest as if she's wounded him. "Ouch."

"Sorry. I just think I'd rather be alone right now, Ev."

She doesn't particularly feel like talking at the moment. Not when her cheeks are still hot with the embarrassment of rejection and the ache between her legs refuses to subside. She's going to need to take care of that as soon as Everett gets out of her room or she'll never get to sleep tonight.

Yolanda was right. She should have packed her vibrator.

"Fine," Everett says. "We can discuss this tomorrow."

"Can we, though?"

"Yes. You owe it to me, Gretch. We're supposed to be a team. How are we supposed to work together to keep Charlie here if you don't keep me informed about what's going on between you and him?"

"*Nothing* is going on between us," she snaps. "So there's really nothing of which to inform you."

"Oh. Oh, I see." Everett flashes her his crooked smile. "You struck out, huh? Well, now. Unexpected, I have to say. But this is something I can help with." He winks. "I was a real cake-eater in my day, you know."

She narrows her eyes at him. "Gross."

"What? It just means I had a way with the ladies."

"Still gross. And I don't need your advice. I'm not you, and Charlie isn't one of the horny farm girls you fooled around with behind the chicken coop."

"Doesn't mean I can't—"

"Yes, it does," Gretchen interrupts. "Please, go away."

"You need to figure this out soon."

"You think I don't know that?" But Everett is through the wall before she finishes shouting the words.

22

GRETCHEN NEVER DID GET TO TALK TO CHARLIE ABOUT HER ideas to increase Gilded Creek's profits, and apparently they are avoiding each other today. It's fairly easy to accomplish, considering her mornings have settled into a routine—wake up at five thirty; eat a bowl of flavorless fiber cereal; help corral the goats for milking, reunite the babies and their moms for the day; refill the goats', dogs', and barn cats' food and water; and head back to the house for lunch—so it's not particularly challenging for Charlie to ensure he's anywhere else but around her. He even dismissed her from the milking room as soon as she got the goats in line, presumably hoping to avoid even the possibility of any minor non-animal-related interaction between them.

As she crests the small hill on her way to run down the checklist Lori left for the cheesemaking room while she's with her daughter this weekend, she spots Charlie at the far end of the pasture, inspecting the fence. Pretty much as far away from her as physically possible without leaving the property.

Well, fine. It's not like I particularly want to talk to you either.

Want to or not, though, Gretchen does need to talk to Charlie soon. She has plenty of ideas, but she's running out of time to implement them before she goes back to DC. And if she can't make this work . . .

Everett's teasing while she ate her lunch bounces around in her skull: *Charlie and Gretchen sitting in a tree, K-I-S-S-I-N-G. First comes . . . Well, first comes you, doll, if you'd let me give you some advice.* She never should have admitted anything about what happened last night to that stupid ghostly jerk.

When she finishes up on the barn's second floor, she looks back out into the pasture, her eyes once again immediately drawn to Charlie. And maybe his gaze feels her pull as well, because he looks up just then and sees her. It's quite a distance, but Gretchen's certain she spots his eyes go wide before he ducks his chin and pretends he's inspecting the tool in his hand.

Really. And Everett believes seducing Charlie will help win him over! If this is any indication, Gretchen thinks, had things in the parking lot managed to progress any further, Charlie would probably have walked into the woods and kept on going until he reached the Atlantic Ocean. Then he would have hopped on a boat, sailed to Europe, and continued walking for extra insurance.

"This is ridiculous," she says to herself as she makes for the pasture. Her eyes comb over the luscious spring-green expanse, dotted with the few bright yellow dandelions and gorgeous purple wood violets that haven't yet been munched away. She ensures the goats are all browsing at the far end and none will attempt to escape (or try to eat her, which she's still not fully convinced isn't a thing that could happen after spending more time with them), and that the dogs are occupied with the herd, then opens the gate and marches through. Gretchen Acorn is a woman on a mission. And that mission is to help save this stupid, beautiful goat farm and its stupid, beautiful farmer.

"Hey!" Gretchen realizes her mistake as soon as she shouts; she's still a good fifty yards away from Charlie, and she's prematurely alerted him to her presence. But who would have thought, truly, that a grown-ass man would pretend not to hear her and walk with purpose in the opposite direction? "Charlie Waybill!" It comes out as an angry grunt as she picks up speed. She has to jog in order to keep up with his quick strides, and it isn't particularly easy in cheap rain boots with an iffy ankle. He glances over his shoulder as he continues to put more distance between them.

"I'm busy!" he calls back to her.

"Doing what?"

"Fence . . . stuff."

"Good! Great! I'll help. I'm excellent at fence stuff."

That absurd statement gets Charlie to at least stop and turn toward her with his hands on his hips. "Oh, and I thought your crime of choice was fraud."

"What?"

"Like fencing . . . goods? Selling stolen shit? Never mind."

"Yeah, that's a deep cut," she says, slightly bent over to catch her breath. "But I appreciate the attempt to take your insults to new creative heights." Gretchen straightens, still panting a little. "Why are you running away from me?"

"I wasn't running."

"Fine, then why were you speed walking—" A cough interrupts her sentence, so she throws out her arm to gesture the concept of *away from me*. Then she does a brief check for anything objectionable before lowering herself to the grass. "Please don't take off. I can't . . . can't chase you again."

"Are you okay?" Charlie asks with a begrudging concern that Gretchen can't help but cling to.

"Been better."

He kneels in the grass beside her. "In. Out. In. Out."

"I know how to . . . to fucking breathe," she snaps. But she's also following his lead, adjusting her breaths to the pace of his words and the rise and fall of his shoulders. Their eyes remain locked. She looks at him like he's a lodestar, but he looks at her as if he's a scientist and she's a living demonstration of the Krebs cycle. The passion from last night suddenly feels very one-sided. Whatever. That's not why she's here, Gretchen reminds herself. This should be about the business. Making it easier for Charlie to stay. To *want* to stay.

"Good?" Charlie asks.

Gretchen nods.

"Now, what was so important that you felt the need to give yourself an asthma attack?"

"I don't have asthma," she says. "I'm just out of shape."

"Guess I better work you harder, then." They seem to both register the double entendre at the same time and look away in opposite directions—a silent agreement not to discuss what happened outside Tipsy Lou's.

"I, uh, wanted to talk to you about some business stuff. We were supposed to chat last night, but then with visiting your grandfather and . . . everything . . . we never got around to it."

"Okay. Well. Like I said, I'm busy with the fence. That wasn't me making excuses. So if you want to talk, you gotta walk." Charlie stands and offers Gretchen a hand.

She takes it, letting him pull her up, forcing herself to ignore the heat between their palms. Charlie backtracks to the area of fence he was inspecting before Gretchen spooked him like a scared little rabbit (he would object to that simile, of course, even though that's exactly what he looked like trying to get away from her) and shoots a new staple into where the wire mesh meets the wooden post.

Gretchen follows him around the pasture's perimeter, laying out her plans: social media to spread the word about the farm, events to bring people in, partnerships with other local businesses to reach new customers. By the time she comes to the end of her informal proposal, the goats and dogs have wandered over to them, and Charlie has also reached the end of the fencing. He takes his hat off, smacks it against his leg three times, then replaces it on his head. "And who is going to be doing all of this extra work?"

"Me," she says, as if that's the most obvious part of this plan.

"I thought part of our deal was that you would help out around the farm. Taking pictures and messing around on your phone all day isn't particularly helpful to me."

Gretchen came prepared for almost any objection Charlie could throw her way. She pulls up Instagram on her phone and shows him the profile for a goat farm in Ohio. "This place is only a little bigger than Gilded Creek, and it's doing a lot of the stuff I want to do. They're a relatively small dairy operation, but they make a ton of extra money through events. Goat yoga. Cheese and wine tasting date nights in partnership with a local vineyard. Based on how much the tickets cost, I bet they're making five hundo a weekend on baby goat cuddling sessions."

Charlie narrows his eyes. "'Hundo'?"

She brushes away the question. Gretchen can't be certain, but she thinks she might have picked that up from Everett, which is frankly upsetting. "I know this is a lot of work, but it's the kind of work I'm good at," she says, weighing her next words. "I know you don't respect the *what* of what I do, but as I've said before, it's a business. And I do run it really well."

He frowns, scratches his beard. It doesn't take him as long to respond as she expects. "Okay. But you're doing this on top of everything else I need you to do. Don't even think about trying to use all this to get out of your chores."

"Wouldn't dream of it," she says, surprised to find it isn't a lie. Somewhere along the last week or so, Gretchen realizes, she began enjoying farmwork. The way it forces her to use her body and lets her mind take a break. How she can see many of the results of it immediately and concretely. Even being around the animals has turned into something she doesn't mind so much, now that she has a better idea of what to expect. As if to prove this, she plucks a cluster of leaves from a tree and holds it out toward a nearby goat, forcing herself not to flinch as it takes the snack from her hand.

Charlie doesn't acknowledge this act of immense bravery. "I'd rather not have pictures of me on the Instagram."

"Oh, there are definitely going to be pics of you on 'the Instagram,' babe. A tattooed and bearded goat farmer? It's gonna be a virtual panty-dropping spree."

"I hate everything you just said."

"Fine, fine, we'll focus on the babies for now." Gretchen scrolls through the Ohio farm's photos. "Some of their most popular posts have the kids dressed in little outfits. They call them *goat coats.* That's cute. I wonder how much it would cost to get some of those."

Charlie lets out a forbearing sigh. "Come with me."

GRETCHEN'S NEVER BEEN IN THE ATTIC BEFORE. SHE wasn't even aware the farmhouse had one until Charlie leads her into his office and opens a small door, behind which is a narrow winding staircase. It takes them up to a musty, angular space filled with boxes and plastic storage bins. Everett must have seen them come up here and thought it would be fun to join them, because he's now hover-standing beside Gretchen, asking a million questions. Not that she can answer without having to tell Charlie that his ghost ancestor is around. She isn't about to start another fight when they've come to a tentative accord. Instead, she subtly shakes her head and mouths, *Not now.*

Everett replies, "Hot cow? What about a hot cow?"

Charlie browses the mountains of storage bins until he finds the one he wants buried at the bottom of a stack. He lifts the top two bins in one go, his biceps bulging beneath his T-shirt, and Gretchen has to resist the urge to fan herself. "Warm in here," she mumbles to cover herself in case she accidentally gives in.

"Heat rises," Charlie says absently. He pulls the last bin toward him and unsnaps the lid.

"Oh!" Everett exclaims, standing chest-deep within a credenza missing its drawers in order to look over Charlie's shoulder. "I haven't seen this stuff in . . . who knows how long, but it feels like a while!"

"What is it?" Gretchen asks.

She's momentarily confused when Charlie is the one to respond. "Some of Grandma Ellen's knitting projects." He holds up a tiny, colorful striped . . . something. "This the kind of thing you meant?"

"Is that . . ." She doesn't finish the question, because it's obvious that it's a tiny sweater meant for an animal—most likely, she assumes, a baby goat. Gretchen moves closer and tests the texture with her thumb and index finger. "Whoa. How many of these do you have?"

Charlie does a quick visual count of the bin. "Probably . . . forty? Grandma and I made them back when the herd was a lot larger, so more than enough to cover the kids we have now. You can take your pick. Figure out which ones are most photogenic, I guess."

Gretchen dives in with an excited gasp, sorting the tiny sweaters into piles on the bin's discarded lid. Some are a little wonkier than others. "You said you helped make these?" she asks.

Charlie's response isn't verbal, and she doesn't look up to see if he nods. But Everett chimes in, "Oh, I remember this! It was the week of Christmas, and Charlie's parents were, I don't know, off somewhere or another for work like always. So Charlie stayed here with Charles and Ellen. He was fifteen and all broody over some girl. Ellen told him she needed to make sweaters for kidding season and taught him how to knit so he would help and stop being so insufferable."

Gretchen swallows, knowing this is a risk. But it's specific enough that she decides it's worth a shot. "Christmas when you were fifteen," she says quietly, watching Charlie for a response.

He stares at her for a long time.

"You were annoying everyone, pining over a girl. Was it still Brittany Studebaker?"

He slowly shakes his head, and Gretchen is relieved when a small smile plays on his lips. "Brittany Romero, actually."

"Wow, you really had a thing for Brittanys, huh?"

She reaches for another sweater, less colorful than the rest. It's a dark gray-blue that reminds her of a storm cloud. As she pulls it out of the box, she's surprised to find it keeps going and going.

"Oh, that's not—" Charlie lunges toward her, but the abrupt movement makes Gretchen instinctively pull away, keeping it out of his reach.

When she yanks the rest out of the bin and holds it up, she finds that it's not a goat sweater at all but a . . . well, she supposes it's a person sweater. Except . . .

"Wow, I don't remember *that*," Everett says, "and I feel like I would." He lets out a little whistle. "I definitely would."

"I . . . I, uh, tried to knit a sweater as a present for my grandpa after we finished the ones for the goats." Charlie palms the back of his neck. "But um, my skills weren't exactly there yet."

Gretchen holds up the misshapen, oddly proportioned garment. "No, no, I've met your grandfather. And he definitely has four-foot-long arms. So this is perfect." She bites her lip so as not to laugh. Everett, now float-sitting atop a child-sized wooden rocking horse pushed so far under the angular slope of the wooden-beamed ceiling that his head must be somewhere outside, doesn't bother holding back and lets out a full-throated cackle.

A small window lets in enough of the late-afternoon sunlight to reveal the pink on Charlie's cheeks. "I got the gauge wrong. And, um, some other stuff probably."

"It might be a bit rough"—Gretchen looks again at the sweater and realizes that's an almost comical understatement—"but it's still really sweet that you tried."

"That's what Grandma said too." And now Charlie lets out a little chuckle of his own, his embarrassment shifting more toward amusement. "Still, I'm surprised she bothered keeping it. Probably planned to frog it to reuse the yarn but never got around to it."

"The sweaters you wear sometimes . . ." Gretchen says, keeping herself from reaching out to touch Charlie's arm—especially because he isn't wearing one of the sweaters right now so she can't even play it off as relevant. "Ellen made them all?"

"Yeah. A few were birthday or holiday gifts, but I actually found a bunch in my grandpa's closet that he—well, he didn't remember she made them. He said someone must have broken in and left them there." He lowers his eyes. "So I figured it would be okay if I . . . I know this sounds ridiculous, but it's like I can feel . . . her love . . . when I wear something she made. And I didn't want all that love to go to waste sitting in the back of a closet."

"That doesn't sound ridiculous at all," Gretchen says softly.

Charlie clears his throat and taps his fist against the top of a stack of nearby bins. "Anyway, hope these work for whatever nonsense you're planning. I need to do a few more things before sundown. Make sure you leave the cedar balls in there and close up the bin when you're done. Moths. They eat things." He frowns at his words as if unsure why he said them, then turns and leaves the attic.

Gretchen waits until she can no longer hear Charlie's retreating footsteps. "You were right, Ev. He's a good egg, and his yolk's real runny." But Everett isn't on the rocking horse anymore. He must have climbed out onto the roof, because she hears him shouting something above her head. Perhaps he wanted to give Gretchen and Charlie some privacy, although she doubts he was being that considerate; more likely, he went out to get a closer look at a bird.

She realizes after a moment that she's clutching the dark gray sweater to her chest. *Charlie put so much of his love into this sweater,* she thinks. And even though she knows it wasn't meant for her, she slips it over her head. It would be a shame if it went to waste.

23

GRETCHEN PACES HER ROOM, EVERETT WATCHING FROM the bed.

"What's with all the back-and-forth, doll?"

She stops momentarily to bite her lip, but then continues her window-to-door, door-to-window journey. How to explain what's been bothering her since she first had the idea last night? "I need to ask someone for something, but I'll be asking them as a personal favor instead of a business one, and I don't . . . I try not to do that."

He taps his chin. "What is it you need and who do you need it from?"

"I got the farm's website and social media accounts set up a few days ago, and they're gaining a bit of traction. What we need next are events to bring attention to our existence, and I was thinking goat yoga might be a good place to start. My roommate—my business associate, Yolanda, she works at a yoga studio and she's involved with a yoga teacher . . ."

"I don't know if I know for sure what yoga is, but this sounds . . . not complicated? Just ask this friend of yours to help."

"But it *is* complicated because she *isn't* my friend." Gretchen throws herself down on the bed beside Everett, careful not to get too close. She's managed to go a whole five days without his extreme chill pummeling her body, and she's not particularly eager for a thoughtless outflung arm to break the streak.

"So she . . . doesn't like you?"

"No, she does! That's why it's a problem."

"I'm . . . really not following here."

"The thing is, Yolanda is my roommate, but she's mostly my employee. She collects information for me to use in my séances. If it weren't for me giving her a steep discount on rent in exchange for information, I'm not sure she'd be in my life at all. So, when our business arrangement stops making sense for her, she's going to leave, and it will be way easier if it feels—if it feels like—"

She isn't leaving *me*. Gretchen has never actually articulated this aloud, and now that she's on the precipice of doing so, she realizes how much emotion is obscured inside of it. "I don't like mixing my business and personal life," she says instead.

"Hmm." Everett crosses his arms over his chest, considering her nonsensical explanation. "Can I tell you a story?"

"I have a feeling you're going to regardless. So go ahead."

He pauses, thinking, before he begins: "Once upon a time, in a small rural area of Maryland called Derring Heights, there was a very handsome farmer turned very handsome spirit. He was bound to the land that had been in his family for generations because he angered an old bat who cursed him for following his dreams."

"I think I've heard this one before," Gretchen says.

"No, you haven't," Everett says. "Just listen."

Gretchen rolls her eyes and gestures for him to continue.

"When he was alive, the very handsome farmer didn't have many friends. In fact, he didn't have any at all. Sure, there were men who might give him the time of day, and there were certainly women who appreciated his extremely beautiful face and chiseled, perfect body—"

"Everett."

"Anyway, there were often people around him, but they weren't *friends*. They were just . . . people. The very handsome farmer never could seem to get anyone to, well . . . to like him. They simply tolerated him. Oh, it wasn't their fault. Not really. The very handsome farmer didn't exactly make it easy. He lied and he cheated and sometimes he took things that didn't belong to him. One time, he stuck a finger in an apple pie cooling in a neighbor's window. And another time, he stuck a finger in the neighbor's wife—"

"*Everett!* Did you really?"

He looks to the side, neither confirming nor denying. "The point is, the very handsome farmer was often lonely. And he couldn't blame anyone except himself for it. But as he grew a bit older, a bit wiser, he started wishing he had someone. Someone true, someone to care for him—flaws and all. A friend. And that's why, when he got an offer to sell the farm to a fella from the railroads, it felt like a gift. He could move somewhere new, somewhere no one knew about the selfish things he'd done, and maybe he could find what he was missing. So even when the evil old bat warned him of the consequences of leaving, he decided to go anyway. Because he thought maybe he'd rather be dead than alone any longer." His voice peters out into a whisper by the end of the last sentence.

Gretchen shifts to her side to stare at Everett. It's almost as if the swirling clouds beneath his skin have become imbued with emotion. Vulnerability. She never expected . . . She has to stop herself from reaching for his hand.

"Well, splat!" he says with a rueful chuckle. "The very handsome farmer died and became the very handsome spirit. And he was even more alone than before, because now he didn't even have anyone to give him the time of day or admire his good looks. It gave him a lot of time to think, and he started to realize that perhaps the reason no one cared about him when he was alive was because he didn't care enough about others. Perhaps this was the lesson the evil old bat hoped he would learn. Or maybe she was just a mean, vindictive little . . ." Everett narrows his eyes and purses his lips before bringing himself back to the story. "Then, one day when the very handsome spirit was quite resigned to being alone, something amazing happened: This woman showed up at the farm, and she could *see him*. Really . . . see him." Everett turns his head and looks Gretchen in the eye. "And there was something . . . something kind of sad about her. Like maybe she understood how he felt. From that moment, he wanted more than anything in the world for her to be his friend. And to be a friend to her."

"You are my friend," Gretchen whispers. "Even though you're . . . a lot sometimes. You're my friend, Ev." It's true, she's surprised to realize. Somewhere along the way, Gretchen forgot to hold a part of her back when it came to Everett. Maybe because, subconsciously, she's aware that he's stuck with her as long as she's at Gilded Creek. Or maybe it's that his charm is a slow, creeping thing—like the ivy on the barn that surely started as a single unthreatening leaf but quickly and quietly grew into something formidable, something encompassing. But it's undeniably there—affection, friendship.

He smiles that slow, crooked smile that Gretchen has no

doubt hypnotized many a young farm girl—and neighbors' wives, apparently—back in his day. "Oh, you thought that story was about me? No, no, just something I saw on TV."

"Riiight." Gretchen smiles back.

"Loving people . . . can hurt," he says slowly. "I understand that. Maybe better than anyone." There's a melancholy undercurrent to the chuckle with which Everett punctuates this, and for the first time, Gretchen thinks about how many people have come and gone from Gilded Creek during Everett's time here. What it must be like for him to live with all of the various Waybill family members, growing to care for them, being responsible for their well-beings, knowing they'll never reciprocate and that he'll still be here long after they're gone. Then here Gretchen is, the first person with whom he can communicate in decades, planning to leave at the end of the month. And Everett has befriended her nonetheless. It's . . . brave. And it's . . . well, it's also stupid, in her opinion.

"Why do it, then?" she asks. "Why do something that's probably going to hurt?"

"Oh, doll," he says, sounding for the first time like the much older—and perhaps wiser?—soul he actually is. "Because it hurts so much more not to."

Everett presses his palm against his lips, then hovers his hand an inch from Gretchen's cheek. Her shiver makes them both smile again.

"Now," he says, springing up. He claps his hands together noiselessly. "I heard Charlie say that another prospective buyer's coming, so I'm gonna go plan something extra spooky." Before Gretchen can respond, he adds, "*Without* almost killing them. Obviously. Catch you on the flippity flip!"

She rolls her eyes, not bothering to ask where Everett picked that one up. He disappears through the wall.

Gretchen grabs her phone from where it's sitting on the nightstand and texts Yolanda, asking her to call when she's free. What Everett said was nice (and way more sentimental than anything she ever expected from him), but their friendship is built on mutual loneliness. Yolanda isn't lonely, though; she has a girlfriend (despite what she may say), coworkers, cousins, and all sorts of other people in her life who adore her. She's busy. Which is why Gretchen is surprised to find her phone ringing right away.

As soon as she picks up and says hello, Yolanda launches right into it. "You have a lot to answer for, girl. One text and a vague email two weeks ago about you being gone for a month, then nothing till now?"

The familiar voice fills Gretchen with something she's taught herself not to trust—that deep craving for affection, so strong it makes her want to cry. But instead of trying to shed it like a too-warm coat, she allows it to settle over her. "I know, I know," she says. "I'll tell you everything in a second. But listen, I need a favor. It's . . . sort of personal, though. Not business."

"Of course. Anything for you," Yolanda replies without a moment's hesitation. "Now, explain what's going on."

"Right. Yeah. So . . ." Gretchen takes a deep breath as she mentally organizes the chaotic last couple of weeks into something approaching a coherent narrative. "So you know how I've been . . ."—she lowers her voice just in case Charlie is walking by her room at that very moment—"pretending to talk to ghosts? Well, uh, funny story . . ."

24

GRETCHEN IS PRETTY SURE THE GROANING IS COMING from the kitchen.

She can't imagine why Everett would be making that sound since he can't feel pain (and it's definitely an in-pain sort of noise). But whoever *is* making it has a deep voice, and both Charlie and the delivery guy should be outside unloading bales of alfalfa from the truck. They still had quite a bit to go when she left them, and despite Charlie's claims that she's going to dry up the well, her shower really didn't take that long. Maybe it's the wind, she tells herself as she drags a comb through her wet hair. Hesitantly, she cracks the bathroom door and sticks her head out. "Ev?"

No answer. But another groan, this one louder, travels upstairs as she steps out into the hallway.

For a moment she wonders if it could be an intruder and considers arming herself with something heavy. But any intruder making *that* sound is already injured enough to pose little threat. Besides,

Gretchen thinks, who would bother breaking into a farmhouse in the middle of nowhere? It's not as if the rusty seed drill—Charlie finally explained what it was to her a few days ago—along the driveway screams, *We have things worth stealing here!*

"Charlie?" she tries when she reaches the bottom of the stairs.

"Yeah," he gasps.

And it's like something else takes control of her body, hurrying her into the kitchen and over to where he's hunched over, bracing his hands on the table. It's reminiscent of when they had their first conversation here, when Gretchen tried to tell him about Everett and the curse. Except this time there's no anger in his expression, only frustration and pain. She looks him up and down, searching for blood, but thankfully finds none. Still, it's obvious something's wrong. "Are you okay?"

He winces as he shakes his head, a deep line between his furrowed brows. "Back spasms. Happens . . . once in a while . . . lifting stuff."

"What do you usually do for it?"

"Ice pack. Came to get one, but . . ." Charlie trails off, breathing hard.

"Let me help. Sit."

He groans again, but manages to lower himself backward onto a dining chair when Gretchen directs him with featherlight fingers on his shoulder. She pulls the ice pack out of the freezer and folds a flour sack towel around it like he did the morning he brought it out to her when she tweaked her ankle.

"Your shirt . . . ?" Her voice trails off before the sentence can find its verb.

Charlie attempts to lift the hem of his T-shirt, but comes to an abrupt stop without making much progress. "Can't," he says, glancing up at her from where he has his head bowed over the back of the chair.

She reaches for him, then her hands drop again as if the memory of his rejection in the bar parking lot last Friday swats them away. *Better ask first.* "Do you want me to . . . Can I . . . ?"

He puffs out a breath. "Yeah. Yes. Please."

What is the least sexual way to take someone's shirt off? Should she start at the back or the front? Gretchen's hands are up in the air as if she's found herself in the middle of a stickup. "Okay, I'll just—"

"Okay."

But she doesn't move.

"Acorn." Her name comes out as a frustrated growl, which is familiar enough to snap her back into reality. Right. This is Charlie, and he doesn't even particularly like Gretchen. He literally tried to *run away* the other day rather than have a conversation with her. So she has to touch him—big whoop. It's not exactly the scene of a grand seduction. He's hurt, she's helping, it's *fine*.

She makes a decision, grabs both the front and back hem of the shirt and jerks it up, revealing his muscular, lightly furred torso and that strong but apparently troublesome back of his. "Arms," she says, "like this," and adjusts his hands so he's clasping the back of the chair, making the shirt easier to peel off with minimal movement on his part. Charlie lets out another groan once it's done, and Gretchen finds herself spilling apologies and placing a hand in the middle of his bare back before taking it away as if he were a cast-iron pan she forgot was still hot.

"No, I—" He swallows. "That actually felt kind of nice. Can you . . . put your hand there again for a second?"

"Like this?" she asks, trying to find the same spot.

"Yeah."

"Would it make it worse if I pressed, very gently?" Gretchen adds light pressure into her fingertips as she talks, and Charlie's groan sounds slightly less pained in response.

"Oh, that's . . . that's actually kinda good," he manages.

She adds her other hand and uses her thumbs to trace either side of his spine, pressing more when she feels some resistance. Massage therapy has never been one of Gretchen's skills, but she recently absorbed a bit of information about the human muscular system thanks to Yolanda's tendency to talk to herself while studying for the physiology portion of her in-progress yoga teacher training, and she tries to remember the names of the muscles she's kneading as a way to make this more clinical. Because this touch feels too intimate, and Charlie's responding noises are way too reminiscent of the ones he made when he had his hand up her dress outside Tipsy Lou's, and she needs something—science, she needs *science*—to get her back into the right headspace.

"Yes," Charlie sighs as she makes her way down toward the waistband of his jeans.

"Yes?" she responds, and her voice comes out equally breathy.

Oh no. *Where is Everett to kill a mood when you need him?*

"A-again."

Gretchen closes her eyes tight, as if she's the one in pain. The right thing to do here is to take a large step back and suggest Charlie try the ice pack now. Instead, she lets her fingernails drag lightly up the length of his back, her thumbs starting the journey downward again from his neck this time, the place where his gold-brown hair meets his skin, and when she presses harder there it prompts an actual *moan*.

Gretchen finds herself leaning forward until only an inch of space remains between her and the hunched expanse of Charlie's back. "Yeah?" she whispers, and watches as his skin responds to the sensation of her breath on it.

"Please," he says.

Gretchen isn't sure when or how she makes the decision; it doesn't register at all. It's as if her mouth simply finds its own way to that spot on his spine right between his neck and shoulder blades, like a bird coming to rest on a power line.

He inhales sharply before whispering an exhale: "Gretchen." It's so quiet she would doubt her own ears, believe she imagined it, if she hadn't felt the vibration of her name travel from his body to her lips.

"Hey, hey, party people!"

Well, if quickly jumping as far away as possible from a man's bare back that you were previously kissing were a sport, Gretchen Acorn would definitely now hold the world record.

"Jesus!" she shouts, her hand flying to her throat as if she might somehow hide her pounding pulse.

"What?" Charlie attempts to look over his shoulder, lets out a small whimper when the movement causes him pain, and returns his head to the cradle of his arms on the back of the chair as Everett simultaneously points at Gretchen and says, "Oh, shoot, did I interrupt? Sorry, carry on."

"I . . . There's nothing . . . Go away, please. Just go," Gretchen snaps, extending a finger toward the doorway.

"Um." This from Charlie.

"Not you."

Everett holds up his hands in contrition as he slowly backs out of the room. Then he reaches back through the wall to give her a double thumbs-up.

"Everett just came in and—"

"Time for more bullshit now. Got it." If Everett's sudden appearance weren't enough of a cold bucket of water on the moment, the derision in Charlie's voice certainly is.

She buries her head in her hands. "Sorry, sorry, I . . . I shouldn't have—" Although she's not sure if she's saying she shouldn't have mentioned Everett or that she shouldn't have kissed his naked back. *I kissed Charlie Waybill's naked back. Holy shit.*

"Don't you think I feel it too?" Charlie asks abruptly, less irate and more . . . pleading? "Of course I . . . I feel whatever it is between us. But I don't trust it, I can't. Because I don't trust *you.* And I think you understand that. So please don't . . . please don't test me."

"I wasn't. I swear, I wasn't trying to—"

"You should probably hand me the ice pack and . . ." He spares her the words, but she knows they're *leave me alone.*

So she does.

25

THANKS TO YOLANDA AND PENNY'S ASSISTANCE IN GETTING the word out through the Balasana mailing list and social media, tickets for Saturday's goat yoga event sell out within seventy-two hours of Gretchen posting the link on Gilded Creek's nascent Instagram (two hundred followers and counting!). Yolanda tells Gretchen to open up a few more spots to allow some of the waitlist to register, and those fill promptly too. As Gretchen hoped, the farm is set to make a nice chunk of change off city folks' love of doing bougie things in the countryside.

Since the weirdness in the kitchen, Charlie has again attempted to avoid Gretchen. This time she agrees that it's for the best. She isn't sure she could handle a third round of his rejection. That last one was . . . oof.

She didn't realize it was possible to be this despondent while dressing baby goats in tiny sweaters, but she's certainly managing it. Sleepy Jean lets out a surprisingly loud bleat when Gretchen wrestles her into a neon-pink and mustard-yellow polka-dotted one. "You are gonna be an internet sensation, SJ, I know it," she tells the black-and-white goat, who is already triple the size she was when she was born two weeks ago.

While chasing one of the more ornery kids into the pen surrounding the little stone outbuilding where they've decided to keep the babies today instead of bringing them to their moms, Gretchen spots Charlie on the farmhouse's porch, crunching into an apple. *He can see right through me, and what he sees is that I'm my father's daughter, deep down.* All this time she's tried to tell herself she's different from the man who raised her, better than him, but is she really when she's allowed her desire for Charlie—for his body, but also his approval—to overshadow saving his life? *Maybe I do lie to myself after all.*

"Are you almost done?" Everett asks, standing with one foot tapping impatiently half-inside a large oak tree's trunk.

She straightens the wonky red sweater (probably one of Charlie's) she put on the kid whose paper collar labels him as Waluigi. "That was the last one. What's up?"

"Have you gone up the driveway today?"

"No, why?"

His crooked smile stretches across his blue-white face. "I gotta show you something."

Together, they head over the little hill and down the gravel-and-dirt drive toward the main road, joined by one of the barn cats that's recently appointed Gretchen as its favorite provider of chin scratches. She has to admit that being chosen feels pretty great.

"Can't you just tell me?" Gretchen asks, one eye on the cat weaving in and out of her legs to avoid tripping. "I still have a ton of stuff to finish up before the event, and Yolanda just texted that she and Penny will be here in twenty minutes."

Everett shakes his head. "No, no, you have to come see."

A few yards later, he stops abruptly and motions with his head in the direction of the old broken-down seed drill and the dead tree. Gretchen follows the gesture and sees . . .

Flowers?

She approaches the formerly unsightly hunk of metal to find the open top filled with dark, moist soil, in which is planted an assortment of pansies and petunias. Nailed onto the tree's stump is a piece of wood, painted white with large, black block letters: GILDED CREEK GOAT FARM. Underneath, slightly smaller: EST. 1793.

Gretchen sucks in a breath. "Charlie did this?"

"Must've," Everett says.

"But when?"

He shrugs. "Overnight, I would imagine."

"But . . . why? What does it mean?"

"Geez, enough with the questions. I'm very smart, Gretchen, but I don't know *everything*."

She rolls her eyes.

"But if I had to guess," Everett continues, "maybe this is Charlie's way of saying he's hoping you'll be able to help him stay."

"DON'T YOU DARE THINK ABOUT TRYING TO RUN AWAY from me this time, Charlie Waybill," Gretchen warns as she approaches the farmhouse. Charlie's eyes are wide, as if that's exactly what he would be doing if she hadn't issued the warning. She comes to a stop at the bottom of the three stairs leading up to the porch, which puts her a safe foot or so away from where Charlie sits on the top step. Definitely not close enough to accidentally kiss any part of his person. "I thought you went to Tipsy Lou's to play pool last night."

"Didn't make it out there," he says, and looks at the apple core sitting beside him as if urging it to regenerate and give him something to stuff his mouth with to get out of this conversation.

"The flowers in the seed drill. The sign. It looks great."

He shrugs. "You've been complaining about it being an eyesore, and it seemed easier than moving it."

"But your back," she says. "You could have hurt it again."

"It's feeling much better, and bags of soil aren't that heavy. I'm fine."

"Well, then thank you. It'll be a perfect photo op for the people who come today. It'll help us get the word out about the farm."

"Yeah, I know. You're not the only one with business sense, Acorn." Apparently, accepting that the apple isn't going to save him, Charlie clasps his hands together and rests them between his splayed-out legs, leaning on his thighs. "Besides, it'll help with curb appeal. The real estate agent called yesterday. Someone's supposed to come check out the place at four thirty. Yoga will be over by then?"

Gretchen feels her stomach drop. "Yeah."

An incline of his head is his only response.

"Well," she says, "I just wanted to tell you it looks great."

"Thanks."

She moves to leave, then turns back around. "We sold out, by the way," she says. "Forty people now. Penny's going to bring an amp and a mic since it's a big group. I think it's a Bluetooth thing. Will that work out in the pasture?"

"Should. Lori's good at tech stuff, and she's got a ticket for this, right? She'll be around if you need help. Off the clock, though, so don't bother her too much."

"Where will you be?" Gretchen asks. "You know, if someone has a question about the goats or something."

"Oh, I think you can handle it," he says, giving her a smile that reads almost like a snarl. "You know a lot about this place now, and for anything you don't know, I'm sure you can make up the perfect response. That's kind of your specialty anyway."

She puts her hands on her hips, but her voice comes out more curious than angry. "You don't need to do that, you know."

"Do what?"

"The whole being-a-dick-to-keep-me-away thing. I'm already away. You've expressed very clearly how you feel, and I'm not that desperate, babe. I'm not going to keep lusting after someone who doesn't want me back." Thank god lying comes as second nature to her, or that would have been extremely hard to say.

"Not wanting you isn't the issue," he mumbles.

But before Gretchen can respond to that, Everett runs toward them with his arms waving as if he's trying to shoo away a flock of seagulls. "They're here! Your friends are here!"

Sure enough, a blue Volkswagen is making its way slowly down the long driveway.

"That's Yolanda and Penny," Gretchen says to Charlie. "Try to be nice."

He brushes a blade of grass off his knee. "Aren't I usually?"

"I suppose you are. To everyone who isn't me."

"Yep, that's right," he says, and strolls to the car to introduce himself and help unload.

26

HUGS HAVE BEEN A RARITY IN GRETCHEN'S LIFE FOR A while now. Yolanda tries, every now and again, and occasionally Gretchen caves like she does with her other attempts to keep her roommate at arm's length. But those instances only make her feel more hollow after the fact, more alone. It's easier to forgo that kind of friendly intimacy, she thinks, than to trust herself not to crave more of it.

Yet today, when Yolanda bursts from the car and throws her arms around her with an excited scream, Gretchen accepts the embrace without a second thought. Everett's words about loving people have been buzzing around in her head over the past week, and while she isn't completely convinced that friendship is a luxury she can afford to indulge in, she's at least willing to admit that she's happy to see Yolanda. Having her at the farm is like her two worlds colliding, but it's . . . well, it's kind of nice, actually.

As they part, Yolanda holds Gretchen's shoulders and takes

her in like a doting aunt observing her niece's growth. "My god, girl, you're looking . . . so different!"

"I am?"

"Good different!" she quickly adds. "Healthier. Stronger. Less like someone who spends most of her time in a basement with no natural sunlight."

Gretchen examines her arm, noticing for the first time that she has the same stark divide between pale and the lightest brown on her biceps that Charlie has. The thought of their matching farmer's tans makes her remember him shirtless in the kitchen, and the warmth of that skin between his shoulders against her lips. *Stop that.* "Ha, yeah, I guess that makes sense considering."

"I can't believe it! Gretchen Acorn thriving as a goat farmer." Yolanda laughs.

"Honestly, I'm surprised too." Because really, Gretchen *is* thriving. After getting over the learning curve, building up a bit more upper-body strength, and falling into a routine, she began genuinely enjoying so much of her work at Gilded Creek. Especially this past week as she started incorporating some of her business improvement ideas. It almost feels like she . . . belongs here. "Everything good back ho— back in DC?"

The abandoned word—"home"—felt wrong in her mouth. The one bedroom plus den above the tiny belowground storefront where she does her séances doesn't cause any sense of longing; it's just another place she's lived, no different from the other apartments and motel rooms and houses across the country that held her life for short periods of time and then were left behind. No, Gretchen has never had a place that felt like her home.

Not until now. Here.

She tamps down the thought.

"Yeah, I paid the rent and the bills with the money you sent, like you said in the email," Yolanda says after a brief pause that makes Gretchen tilt her head ever so slightly. *Interesting.* Yolanda glances around as if looking for someone. "So where's the . . ." She mouths, *G-H-O-S-T.*

"Everett is . . ." Gretchen does a quick scan of the area, finding a booted foot sticking out of the Volkswagen. "He is currently inside Penny's car, watching the solar-powered dancing flower on the dashboard."

Everett notices her looking his way, thrusts his head out of the (closed) window, and shouts, "Look at this thing! It's moving on its own! Technology has come such a long way!" He mimics the flower's movements, swaying his shoulders to and fro.

Gretchen sighs. "And now he's dancing along with it."

"Ha, that's so fucking weird." Yolanda leans closer so no one will overhear. "It's kinda freaky that you can actually see and talk to ghosts now, Gretch. It's like you pretended your way into it being true or something."

It's refreshing to finally talk to a live person about this. Someone who believes her without any hesitation whatsoever. Maybe she should have gotten over herself and called Yolanda sooner. "Ghost, singular. I have no idea if I would be able to see or talk to other ones. Or how many are actually out there in the world. They're sorta rare, apparently."

Yolanda's dark eyes shift over toward Charlie, who, after introducing himself to Penny, was immediately loaded down with things to carry as if he were a human hand truck. "And that's the guy?"

"The guy I'm trying to save from being eternally stuck on this farm? Yep, that's him."

Yolanda looks again at Charlie, who now has four yoga mats tucked under one arm, a wicker basket held in one hand, the handle of an amplifier in the other, and two towels draped around his neck. "Hmm. He's cute. No Daniel Day-Lewis, of course, but—"

Gretchen gently nudges her roommate in the side with an elbow. She hasn't even finished chiding herself for the overly playful gesture before the words burst out of her: "Doesn't matter anyway. He hates me."

Oh, great, apparently she's just saying whatever the hell she's feeling now. It's as if the lapses of judgment she keeps having around Charlie are a disease spreading into the other parts of her life. She's going to need to find a way to treat that, and quick.

Yolanda smiles as she looks somewhere over Gretchen's shoulder in the direction Charlie walked with Penny. "What's that saying? There's a thin line between love and hate?"

Based on Gretchen's own experiences, that sounds about right. Most of the people who have grown to hate her loved her first. Maybe it works the opposite way too. "It's whatever," she says. "I don't even care if he likes me as long as he listens to me about this place."

Hopefully, she can pretend her way into that becoming true too.

THE GOAT YOGA EVENT GOES OFF WITHOUT A HITCH. WELL, for the most part. There is an incident involving Waluigi peeing on not one, but *three* people's yoga mats. Plus another person's back. Thankfully, most of the peed-upon victims take it in stride, and the one who starts fussing in the middle of Savasana is quickly quieted when Lori marches over and reminds her in a Lori-like fashion (i.e., a teensy bit menacing) that the event's disclaimer warned that Gilded Creek is a working goat farm and that anything brought onto the property may be ruined or soiled. "At your own risk," Lori whispers, jabbing a finger in the woman's direction. "Those are the *key words*, lady." Of course, since Lori is there as an attendee and not an employee, the scene winds up being somewhat awkward and confusing until Penny requests in her calm, singsong voice that everyone return to their own mats and has Yolanda deliver one of the extras they brought to the upset woman to restore the peace.

Everett followed along with the class for a while, standing next to Penny and showing off his surprising flexibility (whether a remnant of his living days or a weird bonus of being a spirit, Gretchen can't be sure). Somewhat expectedly, he quickly got bored and started meandering through the grid of yoga mats and people, providing commentary on both their efforts and outfits.

Minor hiccups aside, Gretchen is pleased with the way it all turned out. They made $1,200 from ticket sales alone, and several attendees have stopped by the cheese and soap table to make purchases before leaving. She figures that with events like this every weekend throughout the spring and summer, along with everything else she has planned, Gilded Creek Goat Farm might actually generate a profit. Except, of course, there won't be events like this every weekend. Because Charlie doesn't have time to do all of the extra stuff—the marketing and the planning—that yoga or cheese tastings or baby goat cuddling require. And Gretchen won't be here to help much longer. The proof of concept was so exciting, she forgot that it would need to be sustained for it to do any good.

She only has a week and a half before she goes back to DC. Back to pretending to talk to the dead to make rich old women's privileged, depressing lives more manageable. The thought of it makes her feel like she swallowed a bunch of pennies. And it's not just because she hasn't convinced Charlie not to sell yet that she's worried; it's that she's grown attached to the farm, and the work, and to him. Even (or maybe especially) to the ghost currently entertaining himself by hover-sitting atop vehicles' roofs as they bump down the driveway, screaming like he's on a roller coaster each time they reach the edge of the property and an invisible force knocks him off.

He's so fucking ridiculous, Gretchen thinks. *And he's the best friend I've ever had.*

The idea of losing any of it is like her heart's being haphazardly chipped away, a block of wood in the hands of an overeager novice whittler.

At least she'll still have Yolanda. Maybe she'll even figure out how to reach out a little more, ease into friendship. Test the waters to see if Everett's right, if it hurts any less than what she's been doing—less than the loneliness, which, she now admits to herself at least, has started hurting an awful lot.

As Gretchen sells some herb chèvre to a woman who's asked four times now if she's *certain* it's gluten-free, she notices Yolanda and Penny approaching. They come to a stop a short distance away, turning to face each other. Because Yolanda is so much taller, she has to look down while Penny looks up. Their fingers intertwine, Penny giving Yolanda's a squeeze before lifting up on her tiptoes to plant a small kiss on her jaw. Then Penny walks in the opposite direction, and Yolanda continues her approach to the table where Gretchen has finally dispatched with her customer, looking for all the world like she's about to cry.

"Gretch," Yolanda says.

"What's wrong?" Is it possible Gretchen just witnessed Penny breaking up with Yolanda? Seems unlikely; based on their few encounters, she's always found the petite woman Yolanda insists is not her girlfriend to be a mixture of calm and practical. Not the type to welcome the chaos of dropping that kind of bomb before having to ride in a car together for the next hour. But even though she doesn't know Penny all that well, Gretchen is an expert on Yolanda after years of living together. And the way she's worrying her bottom lip before responding means she's either deeply upset or nervous about something.

"I—" But then she changes course. "Can we talk?"

"Uh, yeah. Sure. Let me just put this stuff away."

Yolanda helps Gretchen carry the cheese cooler and box of soap up to the second floor of the barn. Wordlessly, they go back down the stairs and walk toward the creek, postponing what is apparently going to be an emotional conversation.

She's going to tell me she's quitting, and I'm never going to see her again. The realization hits Gretchen like a goat headbutting her in the solar plexus. And it hurts. She thought she would be safe from it, that she kept enough distance, but all she can think about is how much she missed out on by not letting Yolanda in. Three whole years that she could have had hugs and laughter and companionship with this wonderful person, all wasted in some foolish attempt to prevent herself from having to feel this pain again. Pain that's come for her regardless.

Was Everett right? It's hard to imagine that letting herself love and be loved would have made this hurt *less*.

At least this, she knows from experience, she can survive. Yolanda is far from the first person to leave her or be all too happy to see her go. Her mother, her father, Lawrence Biller. Supposed school friends who forgot her as soon as she left town. Lovers who enjoyed her company for an hour or two, then merrily sent her on her way. Clients like Mrs. Van Alst, who all stop coming around after a while in bittersweet confirmation that she's done her job well.

"It's okay," Gretchen blurts out when they reach the sparse shade of a giant weeping willow that grows right where the creek starts to curve. "It's okay. I knew this would happen one day." Because it always does. Things come to an end. People you care about leave you. That's life.

Relief smooths Yolanda's features, and then she throws herself at Gretchen again, wrapping her arms tightly around her upper body. "I should have known you wouldn't be surprised. You predicted it, after all. I thought you were just teasing, bullshitting like usual. But I don't know, maybe you do have a gift, because I never said a word to Penny, and yet, when it happens at the end of April, it'll be almost exactly a month, like you said."

Gretchen feels vaguely lost for a moment before she remembers the last conversation they had before she left for Gilded Creek. "You're moving in with her. That's great."

"I wanted to tell you earlier, when we first got here and you asked about things at home, but I chickened out." She drags the toe of her sneaker through the grass. "I'm happy, Gretchen. So happy. And excited. But I'm also . . . I'm also kind of heartbroken."

"Heartbroken? Why?"

A tear slips out of the corner of Yolanda's eye and she swipes it away. "God, I'm sorry I'm so emotional. But I just . . . love you so much, you know? I'm going to miss living together."

For some reason, this hurts even more. This hammering home

that there was always the possibility of affection between them, there for the taking if only she had been brave enough. She didn't have to spend the last three years feeling so alone. And now that she's finally willing to admit that the friendship is mutual and always has been . . . well, it's the very definition of too little, too late. "I'm sorry I've always been so—" Gretchen shakes her head. No, no point in bringing it up now. *Lean into the truth whenever you can.* She tightens her grip around Yolanda and coerces a bit of honesty from deep inside herself. "I love you and I'll miss you too, but I'm really happy for you and Penny."

"I can still work for you," Yolanda says as the hug comes to a close. "I plan to quit at the salon once I finish my yoga teacher training, but I'll still keep up my connections there, and we can meet for lunch, or I can call you every single day, tell you what I've heard so it isn't in writing—"

"We'll make it work," Gretchen assures her, even though she's unsure if that's true. She probably can't afford to pay Yolanda if it's not in the form of a substantial discount in rent. Not to mention the few hundred Yolanda did contribute covered most of the utilities. The ten thousand from Mrs. Van Alst—if she even gets to keep it—is only going to last so long, and then what?

And if they aren't working together, will Yolanda really make time for her? Her past tells her no, but she wants so much to believe . . .

That's a problem for later. "Remember," Gretchen says, "name the cat Mitsy."

Yolanda rolls her eyes and lets out a wet chuckle. "Now, *that's* still not happening."

"I was right about you and Penny. And I do talk to a ghost for real now. Maybe my powers are actually legit and the real con was convincing you they weren't?" She widens her eyes at Yolanda until she gets another laugh out of her. It feels . . . so good. And that goodness is absolutely gut-wrenching.

"So all that info I've given you over the years?"

"Just wanted you to feel useful." Gretchen smiles, though it doesn't feel particularly sticky. It might slide off her face at any second. "Can I take the two of you out to dinner to celebrate?"

Yolanda checks her phone. "Ah, shit. Rain check? I'm supposed to sit in on a prenatal class at the studio tonight as part of my training, and Penny says we have to get going now if we're going to make it back in time."

It's tempting to allow that familiar twinge to overwhelm her, to tell her that Yolanda isn't only leaving the farm now and their shared apartment at the end of the month, but *her* and *forever*, but she fights through it enough to accept one last hug. "Okay. When I'm back in the city," she says, aware that that feels like a hundred years from now instead of a couple weeks. "Maybe that fancy pizza place you like where they give you attitude if you ask them to slice it for you."

Yolanda's smile is so big and genuine that it bolsters Gretchen's.

"You want to walk back with me?" she asks, but Gretchen shakes her head.

"I'm going to stay here for a minute. Besides, it's almost four?" She checks her phone to confirm. "Charlie has someone coming to look at the place soon, and I don't feel like fighting about it."

"Good luck with him," Yolanda says. "Whatever you want that to mean."

"Thanks. Be safe."

Yolanda stares at her for a moment, then plants a noisy kiss on her forehead. "Love you. See you soon."

And as she watches Yolanda walk away, Gretchen wishes she could hear those two sentiments placed back-to-back like that and truly believe it.

27

GRETCHEN SLIPS OFF THE SNEAKERS YOLANDA THOUGHT-
fully brought her from the apartment, then takes off her socks. The
grass here under the weeping willow is spring-new and cool. It's
feathery beneath the soles of her feet and between her toes. She
didn't grow up a country girl, yet being barefoot in the grass under a tree beside a burbling creek feels like it aligns just right with
something inside her soul, something she didn't know was there
until recently.

Then again, there's so much she didn't know was there until
recently. (Or, at least, didn't want to acknowledge was there.)

Maybe that's what happens when you spend most of your life
using your feelings instead of *feeling* them. All those years of treat-
ing her emotions like models in a figure drawing class—memorizing
their shape and shades so she could accurately replicate them on
cue—have made it so uncomfortable to sit still with them now.
Working on the farm and living with Charlie have given her a

better tolerance for discomfort, though, and she's determined to allow herself to simply *be sad* for a moment without her heartache needing to be molded into something more practical.

Yet when the tears come, Gretchen can't help but notice that they're like those tears from the first day she arrived. They generate somewhere deeper inside her than the ones she usually produces on demand, down somewhere where the ache of loneliness rests against her ribs like a bad chest cold. She lies back now, letting the wispy grass cradle her, and closes her eyes, wondering how she might replicate that depth at a future time when it would come in handy. Instead of forcing herself to cry, she could learn to make herself feel this horrible sense that she's never meant to keep anyone, and the tears will simply come on their own. Another way to make her lies a little more true.

So much for feeling her feelings without trying to make them useful.

A jangling sound approaches, quickly followed by a warm, wet tongue between her toes. "Arghhh!" Her eyes spring open as Clyde's big, drooly mouth heads for her face next. "No!" she shouts as she hoists herself up to a seated position in order to better resist the dog's overly zealous affections.

"He's just checking if you're alive," Charlie says from a few feet away.

Gretchen's attempts to fight off Clyde's tongue are unsuccessful, and he gets in a good, long taste of her salty cheek. "I am, I am; god, make him stop."

With a hint of a smile, Charlie whistles a sharp command, and the giant marshmallow barrels off, back toward the herd.

"Did you need me for something?" she asks as she swipes a forearm over the grossly wet part of her face.

"Yolanda told me you were here and that you might need a friend, so I . . ."

"So you came. To be my . . . friend?"

Charlie pulls off an excellent nonchalant shrug, but the way he glances away as he speaks tells Gretchen that he understands this is the equivalent of declaring a cease-fire between them. "Yeah. Plus I figured it would be smart to keep an eye on you while that prospective buyer is checking out the place."

As if Gretchen is the one who is going to get up to mischief. She considers going to find Everett to ensure he doesn't do anything dangerous again, but she isn't quite ready to leave her spot beneath the willow tree's ethereal canopy. Besides, she's lectured the ghost enough on not engaging in attempted murder that she's confident he'll stick to his usual spooky shit instead of getting handsy. Well. Moderately confident.

Charlie kneels on the ground in front of her. He reaches out to wipe residual moisture—tears or dog spit, who knows—from her jaw with his thumb, and her attention jumps back into the moment. *Charlie is here to be my* friend. And god, he's certainly the type of man who knows what friendship means, and doesn't take it lightly.

"Yolanda is moving out at the end of the month," Gretchen lets herself say. "So she can live with Penny. And I'm really happy for her, I am. They're great together. But, well, Yolanda also helps me out a lot with the business." A flicker of suspicion flashes in Charlie's eyes, and she hurriedly adds, "Admin stuff. Scheduling, bookkeeping. I compensate her through a reduction in her share of the rent. I'm not sure I'll be able to afford to keep her on after she leaves." She swallows. "And I don't know if I can do it all alone. Or . . . if I even want to."

Charlie rubs a thin blade of grass between his thumb and forefinger. "I get it. It's hard. To do things alone. Especially when you've grown accustomed to having someone around."

He might be talking about his grandparents, and how much he misses helping them run the farm instead of doing it all by himself. But he might, she realizes, be talking about *her*. *Will he miss me when I go back to DC?* Has she made herself useful enough to miss?

She looks out toward the creek, watches the way a big gray rock in the middle forces the water to part around it. But it all winds up in the same place despite the detour. Maybe that's what her time at the farm has been—a big gray rock in the middle of her life, something that forces her to take a different path but will ultimately lead nowhere else than where she was already heading. But maybe . . .

"I like it here," Gretchen says, as if trying to feel out the universe.

Charlie's gaze drifts to the same rock in the water. "Me too. It's my favorite part of the property."

Here was supposed to mean Gilded Creek as a whole. And, well, near Charlie. But this exact spot also happens to be Gretchen's favorite part of the property, so she doesn't bother correcting him.

He adds, "I played over here a lot as a kid. I liked to wade into the creek, catch the frogs and minnows. Dry out on the bank and then roll under here to take a nap in the shade."

"That sounds wonderful," Gretchen says, surprised that she genuinely means it.

"It was. Growing up here was wonderful and . . . fantastic. In the true sense of the word. Like a fantasy." He leans back, propping himself up on his hands, and crosses his legs. "Grandma used to plant a massive field of sunflowers every year, and come the end of summer, there were rows and rows of huge, gorgeous blooms."

Gretchen recalls the sunflower tattoo, beneath the one of Stu, right over his pulse point on his wrist. She's grateful when he continues, "People came from all around to see them, to take pictures. I spent hours sitting in the middle of that field, surrounded on all sides by massive flowers, pretending I'd been shrunk down to the size of an ant and that no one would be able to find me to make me go back to the city come September." One side of Charlie's mouth kicks up in sheepish amusement. "I'm going to miss this place," he says. "When you got here, I was so eager to go, to wash my hands of it. But now I think . . . I think I'm going to miss a lot of things once I leave."

"Charlie . . ."

"I know. Curse, ghost, haunting for eternity." His tone is flippant, but his tensed jaw makes it come out stiff. Then his voice goes quieter, almost conciliatory, when he says, "You know that it would be a stretch for me to believe in all that even if I could trust you."

Even if. "And you can't trust me."

"No, I can't."

"Well, what do I need to do to change that?" Gretchen asks. She thinks it manages to sound light enough, but it's as if her desperation has become something tangible and lodged in her chest. Her time at the farm is running out, and she's growing more and more anxious about Charlie's fate. And her own.

"I think you know," he says softly.

"No, I don't *know*, Charlie!" The intense irritation that suddenly overtakes Gretchen urges her to her feet. She flings her arms out. "I've been here for weeks now, trying to prove to you that I'm not out to screw you over. What will it take to convince you? What do you want from me? A fucking signed and notarized affidavit?"

He rises until he's standing too. He moves slowly toward her. Not like he's worried about startling her, but like the air between them is thick and requires some effort to get through. And then he's there, close enough that when Gretchen's hand twitches, it grazes his. "I just want the truth." It comes out as a whisper.

"I've been telling you the truth. Everett is real, and there's a—"

"That isn't what I mean, and you know it. I want *your* truth." Charlie leans down, their lips as close together as the fingers that keep brushing against each other. And if their mouths follow suit, Gretchen isn't sure she can survive it. Her desire is a rubber band pulled to its limits, ready to snap given the smallest encouragement. "What is your endgame, Acorn? Because I keep trying to figure it out, what you stand to gain from me not selling this place, and nothing makes sense. What do you hope to get out of this? What's in it for you?"

"What's in it for me?" she repeats, taking a step backward. "What's *in it* for *me*? For fuck's sake, Charlie. For someone who thinks he can see through me, you're missing something really fucking huge here."

He simply stares at her, his eyes a little too wide. Gretchen suspects he's trying to reshuffle all of the pieces of the puzzle to see if he can work it out before she continues. But no, he doesn't see it. And god, Gretchen has done her fair share of morally gray shit in her life, but the fact that her punishment so exactly fits the crime is too much. Just too much. Aunt Lucretia Thorne and

Everett–level irony. She launches a strange laugh toward the slender leaves that break up the light gray sky above their heads.

"So, you took one look at me when I arrived on your doorstep and thought you had me all figured out, that you could see everything I am. But you don't see anything, Charlie, if you can't see what's right in front of your stupid, handsome face." She jabs a finger into his sternum, then lets her hand collapse on his chest until her palm is resting over his heart. "How do you not see what I can't help but show you? How do you not see the way my heart is absolutely *breaking* with how much it needs to keep you safe?"

They stand there like that for what feels like hours. And then Charlie gently says, "I do. I do see it," and brings his hand up to cover hers. "But with you, I just can't risk believing everything I see." His hand drops and he takes a step away, breaking the contact. He turns and walks toward the pasture without looking back.

28

GRETCHEN PACES BACK AND FORTH, BACK AND FORTH IN her bedroom, the sleeves of Charlie's Frankenstein's monster of a sweater hanging a good six inches past her fingertips and swaying with her movements. Everett is prone atop the bed, reading Agatha Christie.

"Page," he says without looking up. After a few seconds of Gretchen failing to respond, he lifts his head and repeats louder, "Gretch. Page."

"Sorry." She stops pacing just long enough to flip over the paper in the large hardback collection they found in Charlie's office.

He pitches his voice higher, a rudely accurate imitation of hers. "'You watch too much TV, Everett,' she said. 'Why not read a book for a change,' she said. 'I'll turn the pages for you,' she said."

Gretchen gives him a quelling look.

"What has you so distracted anyway?" he asks, not bothering to look up.

"Oh, I don't know, maybe the fact that the only person who

has been a steady presence in my life in recent years is moving out and taking a large part of what makes my business successful with her? Or maybe that I have less than two weeks to figure out how to make this farm profitable while simultaneously convincing a man who still very much doesn't trust me to change his life plans based solely on my word?"

"Page."

Gretchen reaches over and slams the book closed.

"Hey!" Everett protests.

She resumes walking, absentmindedly flapping the sweater's dangling sleeves like a baby bird trying to gain purchase in the air. "I knew Charlie didn't trust me, but I'm not sure I comprehended the depth of it. I thought maybe if he saw that I care about him, he would believe me. But he doesn't. He still doesn't. He thinks I might be faking that too."

Everett sighs and rolls onto his back.

"Oh, I'm sorry, am I annoying you with my problems? The ones that I wouldn't have if not for you?"

He frowns. "Well, excuuuuse me for complicating your life with my tragic death. If I knew back when I left Gilded Creek that the resulting eternal curse would be inconvenient for Miss Gretchen Acorn, well, surely, that would have changed things."

"I don't appreciate your tone," she says. With a huff, she flops down beside him on the bed. At some point, the chill that emanates off Everett's weird cloudlike skin became a comfort (as long as they make no actual contact), so she scoots slightly closer for the reassurance that someone is there beside her. Even if she is annoyed with him right now.

He turns his head to look at her. "Sorry."

"Me too." Gretchen presses her fingertips into her eyelids through the thick sweater. "Maybe I should just tell him everything. But then . . . What if he hates me even more? What if I tell him who I am and what I do, and it just makes everything worse?" It's certainly backfired on her before.

"What if it makes everything better?" Everett sits up. "Look, we're running out of time here, doll. Tell him the truth, kiss him into oblivion, whatever you think is best. I leave the how up to you. But you gotta do something, and soon."

At that moment, the white noise of Charlie's shower suddenly ceases, making them both all too aware that Gretchen's mark is right next door, as naked and wet as any sitting duck.

Everett tilts his head in front of hers, grabbing her attention again. "Tonight. Make a move tonight. Or I make it for you."

"And what are you going to do, exactly? Make him shiver a little?" She shakes her head incredulously. "I don't have to listen to you, you know."

He widens his eyes mockingly.

Before Gretchen can respond with her next quip, Everett swipes his arm over the nightstand, knocking the lamp sitting atop it to the floor with a crash. The base and bulb shatter into a hundred pieces as Everett poofs into the Nowhere.

It's only seconds until Charlie's footsteps come charging down the hallway and the door flings open, hard enough that it bounces off the wall. "Are you okay?" he asks, keeping his eyes averted as he enters. He's wearing a pair of gray sweatpants and nothing else, a dark stain near the hip where he tugged them on without fully drying off first. His hair is damp and disheveled, and a drop of water rolls down his shoulder, drawing attention to the tree branch there with its slender, drooping leaves. *Oh.* It's the weeping willow by the creek, Gretchen realizes. The same one they were under this evening when she told him her heart needs to keep him safe.

The thought is pushed away as she takes in his concerned expression and recalls that she needs to respond. "Yes, I— Everett, he got mad at me and he . . . he knocked the lamp onto the floor. I'm sorry, I'll clean it all up and pay for a replacement. Let me go get the broom and—" She stands and makes a move toward the mess.

"No," Charlie says, grabbing her shoulder to stop her from stepping forward. "You're not wearing shoes. You'll cut yourself. Wait right there, don't move."

She doesn't bother pointing out that he isn't wearing shoes either. Instead, she stays put as ordered. Attempts to regulate her breathing while he's gone are mostly fruitless, and she's still struggling by the time he returns with the whisk broom and dustpan from the laundry room downstairs.

From her standing position slightly off to the side, she watches Charlie clean up the mess Everett made. The muscles of his back flex deliciously, and he remains in a squat as he works, leaving Gretchen unable to think about anything except the probable strength and firmness of his thighs.

Just tell him. Tell him everything. Tell him now.

"Charlie, I need to . . ." she starts.

"Tell you the truth, I always hated that lamp." He talks over her, as if he might not have heard her.

"Really?"

"Yeah. It's been in this room since I used to sleep in here as a kid. Always thought the texture of it looked a little like a clown face watching me at night." He shudders.

Gretchen lets out a small surprised laugh, though Everett did tell her about Charlie's coulrophobia. "Why'd you keep it, then?"

"Bad memories are still memories, I guess. And it gets harder and harder to let go of any of them."

"True. Very true." She has plenty that she clings to fiercely enough, though probably less for sentimental reasons and more because they feel like lessons she's had to learn and can't afford to forget. "And since we're talking about the truth . . ." Gretchen cringes at the less-than-smooth segue.

But as Charlie sweeps the last large hunk of porcelain, the part attached to the plug, into the dustpan, his eyes travel up Gretchen's bare legs and he blinks a few times. "What . . . are you wearing?" he asks, his voice quiet.

"Huh?" With the hullabaloo of Everett smashing a lamp and Charlie's appearance as topless cleanup crew, Gretchen forgot that she's dressed in something deeply sentimental that she pretty much stole.

"Is that the sweater I made?"

She lets out a tired laugh. "Do you really think there's more than one sweater that looks like *this* in the world, Charlie?" But Gretchen immediately regrets the flippancy of her response when he stands and looks down at her, his hazel eyes so intense they feel like a threat. "I'm sorry I took it from the attic without asking."

He tilts his head as if considering, examining the fit. "Too late to object now, I guess."

"Still, I'm really sorry."

"No, it's okay," he says, laying the dustpan and broom carefully atop the now-clear nightstand. "I think I sort of . . . like you wearing it. I mean, I like that someone's getting some use out of it. And it looks . . . it looks nice on you."

The intensity of Charlie's gaze fades into something else, something fragile and sweet. It's honestly terrifying. Because Gretchen has been here before. Standing in front of a man who looks at her like she might be something special, some*one* special. And the last time she let herself be honest in the way she wants—needs—to be with Charlie, that look transformed so quickly into disgust and hatred. She didn't lose everything back then. But she did lose everything that mattered.

Arguably, there's even more at stake now. Yet, as she weighs what to say next, it isn't her spirit medium shop or money that she's afraid of losing. It's this place. It's Charlie.

But she's definitely going to lose him if she keeps holding back. So she can't anymore.

Still, she inclines her head, not quite brave enough to look at him, to watch his expression shift. Gretchen takes a deep breath. *Lean into the truth whenever you can.* "What you said about the sweaters being full of the love of whoever made them . . . Charlie, I—I think I took this one because I wanted to feel what it would be like to be surrounded by yours."

"Oh," he says quietly, simply. There's a long silence before he asks, "And?"

"And?"

"How does it feel?"

Her voice is wobbly when she finally answers. "Warm. Warm and . . . safe. Right."

"Oh," he repeats, with a small nod. Then: "What—" Charlie clears his throat. "What if I asked you to give it back?"

Said in any other tone, Gretchen might take this as a reprimand. But his question is full of heat, and his eyes have changed yet again, now darker, his pupils large. *Not wanting you isn't the issue.*

Those words from this morning clatter around her head like a dropped metal bowl on ceramic tile. She wants him too—so badly it makes her ache in every hidden corner and crevice of herself. Gretchen has already chosen honesty, and is there anything more honest than simply *wanting*? She bites her bottom lip. "Then I guess I'd be naked."

"God, Acorn." He closes his eyes as if it might keep him from picturing her bare body beneath the misshapen wool. By the rapid rise and fall of his chest, it's clear that this strategy isn't particularly effective.

She doesn't want this to be too convenient. If they're going to do anything now, Gretchen wants it to be incontrovertibly clear that Charlie made the decision of his own volition. So she gingerly pads over to the dresser and hoists herself atop it, putting more space between them—one small, final obstacle he'll need to overcome before anything else happens.

Not that she particularly wants him to change his mind. "You can check, if you don't believe me," she says, and parts her knees an inch—just enough to be a suggestion, an invitation.

Charlie moves cautiously toward her. Not out of hesitation, though. More like a big cat approaching its prey. And then he's there. Being on top of the dresser decreases their height difference, and Gretchen savors the way he looks straight ahead at her instead of down.

"I'd be a fool," he says, wrapping his right hand around her left calf, "to believe anything that comes out of that scheming mouth of yours." But even this is imbued with hunger and something almost like a sense of wonder. His fingers coast up her leg, leaving a trail of tingling heat in their wake. Gretchen shivers despite being the opposite of cold, and goose bumps rise up on her skin. When he reaches the crooked hem of the sweater draped over her upper thigh, his other hand joins in on the opposite side to slowly, slowly draw the wool up. As he nudges the sweater higher, Gretchen lets her legs fall open wider, and Charlie nestles between her knees. His breath is ragged and hot in her ear as the hem continues its painstakingly unhurried journey toward her hips, calloused hands warm and slightly abrasive on the skin of her thighs right below.

Everything is hot anticipation. The moment feels like it could go on forever. Gretchen wonders if she might never escape it, sentenced to be eternally enthralled and unsatisfied. But she doesn't want to hurry him, doesn't want to make a wrong move and break this fledgling accord between them. So she digs deep into her patience reserves, remaining calm even when he pauses for a second as he reaches her hips, finding no fabric beneath his fingertips.

"Guess you were telling the truth this time," he says at last.

But while his tone is full of swagger, his cheeks are flushed. The special brand of gotcha euphoria she experiences only around him rushes through her, almost painful in its intensity. And Gretchen can't take it anymore. She throws her arms around his neck and kisses him, muttering words of approval when his hips meet the dresser as he pulls her to its edge.

"I've tried so hard to not want this." Charlie closes his eyes as Gretchen slides her hands over the work-hewn shape of his stomach, his chest, as she kisses and nips at his jaw. "And I can't do it anymore," he says. "I give up. I know I might regret it, but I give up."

His words echo Gretchen's feelings so exactly that it's like they bounce around in her chest, ricocheting off her ribs and smacking into her heart. "You still think I'm a liar?" she asks in between frantic bites and licks at his bottom lip.

He matches her aggressiveness, digging his fingers into her hips the way she likes so much. "I don't know what you are anymore."

"Believe me. This thing between us is far, far from a lie, Charlie," she says, taking one of his hands away from her hip and moving it to the apex of her thighs. "Do you feel how much I want you? I can't fake that."

His fingers part her, and one slides through her slickness, testing, as he lets out a quiet curse. Charlie runs the finger back and forth through her folds, then brings it up to paint Gretchen's bottom lip with her own desire. He watches, rapt, his eyes hooded, as her tongue darts out to sweep over the evidence of her truthtelling.

Before she can register being scooped up, Gretchen is deposited on the bed. Charlie crawls up her body until she's flat beneath him. She reaches for the hem of the sweater, lifting up slightly to take it off, but his hand comes to her shoulder and lowers her again. "Leave it on."

He takes her arms and directs them above her head, then ties the too-long sleeves together around one of the wrought iron posts in the headboard.

Gretchen stifles a laugh, trying not to ruin the moment. "You know I could just slip right out of this if I wanted, right?"

"I know. But you're not going to, are you?"

She bites her lip and shakes her head. This is exactly how she hoped he would be—this mixture of rough and soft that she's been drawn to from the moment they met.

"Good girl," he says, sending a new, even sharper jolt of desperation through her.

Charlie moves back down her body, inching the sweater up toward her chest in the process, which unfortunately obscures her view of him as he takes a minute to suck and lick at her nipples before continuing downward. In a way, not seeing him is almost better, allowing her to focus on the sensation of his warm breath and his hot mouth and . . . oh god, yes, his wicked tongue. Because beneath how good it all feels, Gretchen is still terrified that all of this marks the end. That despite his willingness to overlook it right now, Charlie will ultimately be able to see how much she's still holding back. What if he thinks she's only doing this to win him over, and not because it's truly what she wants with every fiber of her being? Once upon a time, Gretchen would have been okay with him thinking that, thinking whatever, as long as he gave in to her. But now she needs him to know that she's in this for the right reasons. She needs to tell him that—

Oh god. His mouth is a fucking miracle, and his beard brushes deliciously against her inner thighs, and it's like he's slowly unraveling the ball of need low in her stomach while simultaneously getting it more and more tangled up in her feelings.

"Please, Charlie," she hears herself beg. She isn't sure if she wants him to stop or keep going. As the pleasure climbs, it feels unlikely she'll survive either outcome.

Then one finger slides inside her, soon joined by a second. He isn't exactly gentle as he moves faster in response to the sounds she makes, and Gretchen wonders if Charlie is aware of what he's asking of her. Because it feels like he's asking for not just her release, not just her honesty, but her whole heart too. And she wants more than anything to hand it over on a silver platter, let him examine it, and decide if it's worthy.

He crooks his fingers and finds the right angle to reach the spot that sends electricity shooting through her limbs. It's the exhilaration of cresting the hill on a roller coaster, almost too much sensation but all of it thrilling. Yet she knows that this roller coaster is destined to crash instead of seamlessly pulling back into the station, and everything she's held inside her for so long is going to release with the physical tension. It'll spill out all at once—the loneliness, the guilt, the desire to be seen and wanted for who she truly is, and, most of all, the fear. The fear of not being enough, of being left, of Charlie never believing her about the curse—and she finds herself arching, twisting the sleeves of the sweater as she fights against the inevitable. He lifts his head, and his eyes latch onto hers over the bunched sweater, watching her inch ever closer to that precipice, as if he also suspects that they're on the edge of something bigger than an everyday orgasm. Gretchen shuts her eyes, hoping that it will somehow save her.

His head dips back down, and she gasps, "Wait. No. Stop."

Charlie immediately ceases and sits up. "You okay?"

"Yeah, I'm good. I'm great. I just . . ." *Don't want to be alone anymore. Especially not in this.* "I need to have you inside me."

He hesitates for only a moment before he moves his way up her body and frees her from the sweater, leaving it tied to the headboard. His mouth falls on hers as he kisses her deeply, the taste of her honesty on his tongue kindling a newer, more intimate desire. His words are a whisper against the sensitive skin beneath her ear: "You're sure?"

"Yes. I'm so sure. Please."

Her eyes flutter open to find him watching her. "Okay. Wait here."

When he returns with a box of condoms from his room, he kisses her again, hard, making her moan, before slipping out of his sweatpants. Gretchen takes in the delicious sight of Charlie's naked body, all of the parts of him she's dreamed about finally there for her eyes to feast upon. He's beautiful, with colorful art climbing up one arm, those willow leaves draped over his shoulder like a signal that this is a place where she can rest. And it hits her anew: This man, so strong and full of life, so stubborn and goddamn *decent*, is in grave danger. That rise and fall of his chest as he prowls over to her again? The thump of his pulse that she feels against her hand when she lays it on the side of his neck? Those things are so much more delicate than he understands.

She imagines the tanned skin beneath the bright colors of his tattoos transformed into blue-white clouds. He would be so miserable haunting this place. And he wouldn't last a week with Everett as his sole companion, much less an eternity. For an absurd moment, she imagines them dividing the property down the middle with pretend duct tape, Charlie declaring that they'll be keeping to their respective sides for the next several centuries.

She can't let him come to harm. She has to do whatever it takes to make him believe her.

Except, she realizes suddenly, that this has never been about what she's willing to *do*. It's about what she's willing to give up. Is she willing to lose everything to keep Charlie safe?

Yes.

She took a gamble on Lawrence and lost, but she understands now that it's because he never truly saw Gretchen. He saw the person she pretended to be, and finding out that wasn't who she was deep inside was a shock. But with Charlie . . . he spotted the real her beneath all of her strategic outer layers the moment they met. And yet he's still here with her, touching her, wanting her.

Charlie positions himself behind her on the bed, running his rough hands over her body, raining kisses over her skin. His hard cock nudges against her as he guides her to her knees. Warm lips rest on the spot between her neck and shoulder for a moment. "Are you sure?" he asks again. His voice is so gentle that it breaks Gretchen's heart into slightly smaller pieces than it was already in.

She doesn't know if he means about the sex, or about what she's decided she's going to do, but the answer is still the same: "Yes." It's as if he reads her mind or hears it in her tone how much more difficult this will be if she has to look him in the eye, so he eases her down onto her stomach, flat against the bed, parts her legs, and enters her from behind.

The slow, tight slide of him into her, the weight of his body pushing hers into the mattress, makes her reconsider for the briefest second. There's a chance, of course, that he will stop, that he will leave, once she starts talking. He has every right to change his mind at any time, but she hopes with everything she's got that he won't. She would hate to lose the delicious sensation of Charlie Waybill inside of her so shortly after discovering it. But this is more important than her pleasure. It's worth the risk. Something she wants to give him even more than she wants to give him her body.

"My name isn't really Gretchen Acorn."

She finishes the sentence just as he's pulled halfway out. He stills.

"It's Gretchen Eichorn. Legally, at least."

No movement. Her heart races in panic. *He's going to stop. He's going to leave me. And then this place. And then this mortal plane.* Except he doesn't stop. Charlie bends his head forward and kisses her shoulder. Once. Twice. And thrusts back in with enough force to send her an inch up the bed. The sensation of him so deep inside her paired with the friction of the knitted afghan against her bare skin makes her gasp.

Again, he stills. And it takes a moment for her to realize that he's waiting for her. It's a request for more.

"You were right about me from the beginning. I'm a fraud. A con woman. A bullshit artist."

The answering thrust is even harder and she moans. *Okay.* So this is how they're going to do this: She gives him information, he transforms her honesty into their mutual pleasure. It might feel transactional with someone else, but with Charlie it feels almost like absolution. Her reward for opening herself up fully to him at last is this physical validation that she's done something good. Something right. He's wordlessly praising her with his every movement. It is, without a doubt, the hottest, most intimate moment of her entire life.

So she gives him more.

"Back in DC, I pretended to talk to the dead in exchange for money."

And more.

"Yolanda uses her jobs at local businesses to gather information and gossip for me."

And more.

"I do a bunch of research on my own too. Google, social media, and yes, Ancestry dot-com. And I do write off the annual subscription on my taxes."

More.

"I've been running the spirit medium scam for years."

. . . Nothing for that one.

"And I'm . . . I'm really fucking good at it. The best."

Ahh, there we go. She clutches the afghan as she's pushed farther up the bed.

"Being a bullshit artist is in my blood. I lied my way through my entire life until I met you— Oh. *Oh.* Charlie! God, yes!" That one gets a moan out of him too, and it's a moment before she can say anything else because now he's moving into her without waiting, like he can't hold back anymore. He surrounds her, blanketing her body the same way his sweater did, his lips and tongue and teeth on the back of her neck, her shoulder, and that delicious spot in between. He mutters things against her skin that she can't quite catch in full, but she makes out a "yes" and a "so perfect" and a "such a good girl" and she clenches around him.

"I'm— I'm—"

"Yeah," he whispers into her ear. "Yes. Come for me."

This time she doesn't fight it. She lets the sensations overtake her, almost not even registering when Charlie picks up the pace before stilling and letting out a long, ragged groan. And yes, she does feel a little like she derailed from her track and slammed into a brick wall at high speed. But something tells her that, if Charlie will help her sort through the wreckage, she might be able to put herself back together even stronger than before.

29

THEY STAY LIKE THAT FOR A MOMENT: STILL CONNECTED, his weight atop her. Then Charlie pulls out and rolls to the other side of the bed. The only sound is the duet of their breaths, heavy and still racing to deliver enough oxygen to their satiated bodies. Gretchen is vaguely aware that Everett is very likely back from the Nowhere and could come barging in at any minute, but she's too wrung out to move. Or to care.

The most she can manage is to turn her head, to rest her cheek against the pillow that muffled her screams as she came. She studies Charlie's profile, trying to memorize it. This is, she realizes, the first time she's had an opportunity to really look at him without pretext.

"I've been wanting that since the very first moment I saw you," he says to the ceiling with a little sigh of satisfaction as he removes the condom, and that pleases Gretchen immensely. It's possible he's talking about the sex, but it's equally likely, she thinks, that he's referring to hearing her tell him the truth about herself.

"The feeling's mutual." This isn't a lie at all, no matter what he meant. Something started subtly tugging at her as soon as Charlie opened the door that first afternoon, and only now does she realize it was her intuition telling her that this was a place—a person—where she might find a temporary respite. Not forever, but at least for a little while. And she needs that. The weariness crept up on her over the years, and now that she's noticed its presence, the thought of going back to DC and pulling out her bullshit paintbrush again for a bunch of grieving rich people doesn't hold the appeal it once did.

What if I don't have to go back to that? It's a fleeting thought. A ridiculous thought. What else could Gretchen even *do* after she leaves Gilded Creek? She isn't exactly qualified for most legitimate jobs . . .

"When did you change your name?" he asks.

The question pulls her from her train of thought, and the lack of hesitation in her answer surprises her. For not having a lot of practice with telling the full truth, it somehow comes easily here, with Charlie.

"Six years ago, I think?" Well, she might as well explain. Save him having to ask, which she's sure he will. "My father and I . . . we're estranged now, but we were working together up until then. Our last job—I didn't even know it was a job. Or maybe I did know, but . . ."

Charlie turns onto his side and slides his fingers through her hair. The sensation grounds her, encourages her to continue. More of that wordless praise. "There was this guy. Lawrence. An investment banker. It wasn't . . . it wasn't a romantic thing. I was . . . I showed up claiming to be his daughter from a past relationship, and he just . . . immediately took me in. Became my dad . . . Not my actual dad—Lawrence Biller was about as far from Ned Eichorn as you can get—but Lawrence felt like the dad I would have had in an alternate universe. Or the dad I would have wanted as a child if I'd known to want something different. Anyway, we got close. Closer than I've ever been to . . . to anybody. I pretended to be his daughter, yes, but I wasn't pretending otherwise. I was just myself. And he loved me, so easily, like there was no reason in the world not to."

"And then?" Charlie prompts.

"And then my dad told me the mark he'd been working for the last three months wasn't going to pan out, and we were running low on cash, so it was time to get as much as we could out of Lawrence and skip town." Gretchen sucks in her lower lip as she remembers the night it happened, the things her father said before he kicked her out of the Hyde Park apartment they had scammed their way into that autumn. *What did you think we were doing here? Biller was always meant to be our insurance policy. If you've started thinking of him as anything more, that's your fault. I know I taught you better than that.* "I told him I wouldn't do it. That I cared about Lawrence and that he cared about me, and I wouldn't betray him. He asked if I was really choosing a mark over him, and I said yes. So he told me that I was of no use to him anymore if I wasn't willing to do what it took. That if I was going to suddenly get up on my high horse, I could ride it off into the sunset alone until I wised up. And that's what I would be—alone. Because Lawrence would never keep me around if he knew I wasn't who I claimed to be." Her father had certainly been right about that. She sniffs, holding back the tears that threaten to spill over. "Anyway, my dad got caught pretty soon after, trying to blackmail a Wisconsin state supreme court judge. Wasn't his usual type of job. I don't know why he did it. He must've gotten desperate."

Gretchen pauses for a moment, thinking (not for the first time) how that call from jail when he was arrested felt like being contacted by a stranger. Some people say the moment you grow up is when you realize your parents aren't perfect; for her, it was realizing that her father wasn't as smart of a criminal as she always believed him to be. Which, given the values with which she was raised, is sort of the same thing.

"So I went to Lawrence, and I told him everything, thinking he would be . . . proud of me? God, I don't even know what I thought. He just looked at me with such *disgust*. And he told me that if he ever saw me again, if I ever tried to contact him, he'd go straight to the cops." She closes her eyes and forces out the words she's never before admitted to herself. "I'm still glad I didn't take his money, but sometimes I wish I'd never told him the truth. Then he could have kept loving me."

"And that's when you moved to DC and set up shop as a spirit medium?" Charlie asks quietly.

"Eventually. There were a few places before that while I tried to figure out what was next, scraped together some money. My father's name started showing up in the newspapers right around when I got to town. Mine never made it in, thank god, but I couldn't risk anyone making the connection, especially since I was starting my business and knew I would be dealing with the DC upper crust. So my last name became Acorn for all intents and purposes. And honestly? Gretchen Acorn feels more real to me than Gretchen Eichorn these days anyway."

"Acorn suits you," he says after a brief silence. His fingers continue combing through her hair, periodically tugging on a strand, making her body buzz all over again. "A little thing, tough on the outside, a world of potential within." Charlie's words wrap around Gretchen's heart like the warmest hug. "You're good at what you do," he admits. "The fake-medium thing. Very, very good. Don't think I don't recognize that. I see the skill behind it. It's what I find so interesting, so damn infuriating about you."

This is all too much, Gretchen thinks. Someone seeing her and appreciating her skills. Someone *wanting* her for the actual her. *Too much.*

She turns on her side too and kisses him, letting their lips rest against each other for a moment after it ends, an echo of earlier.

When they part at last, he looks into her eyes. "When you said . . ." Charlie hesitates, then starts over. "When you said that 'back in DC' you pretended to talk to the dead for money . . ." He pauses. "Does that mean . . ."

"Yes. That I'm not pretending here. I can actually talk to Everett. See him too." She realizes by his reaction that she's really downplaying the absolute bonkersness of what she is saying. "It's all, um, really fucking weird, actually. Please do not take my nonchalance at face value. It's just the only way I know how to deal with it."

He's quiet again for a long time. "So you admit that your career as a spirit medium is completely based on lies, and that you conned countless people before that. But you're still telling me that Everett, the curse—that those things are real?"

"Yes," Gretchen answers, ensuring she doesn't turn away from his gaze despite how uncomfortable it is to have him searching her eyes this intensely. *He thinks I'm still lying to him. I told him everything and he still thinks I'm lying.* Panic rises up in her throat. "I know it's hard to believe—"

"It is. It is hard to believe. But . . ." He releases her and brings his palm to his forehead. "But you haven't given me much choice, have you?"

"Charlie . . ."

She watches him retreat into deep thought. After a few moments, he says, "You have no reason to tell me all of those things—to give me enough information to absolutely destroy your life if I wanted—and then lie to me about this. So I . . . I guess I have to believe you? That there's a ghost. And you talk to him. And I . . ." His eyes go wide. "I have to live here for the rest of my life? I can never leave Gilded Creek?"

There's a distinct tinge of panic in his voice as it all fully hits him at last. It's heartbreaking, really. Even after everything, Gretchen's instinct is to say something untrue that will make him feel better. But he's not one of her clients. That's not what he wants from her. "I know it's a lot," she says instead.

"Uh, yeah, it's a lot. It's . . . it's a lot."

She sits up and reaches for his hand. "I want to help you with this. However I can."

"Thanks," he says, but his mind is obviously miles away. "Um. I need to . . ." He moves his hand away abruptly. "I'm sorry. I need to be alone for a while. To think about what this all means."

"Oh. Okay. Yeah. Go . . . go do that. I'll be here if you need me."

Charlie stands and pulls on his discarded sweatpants. It's strange to go from having him completely surrounding her, *inside* her, to this distance—both physical and emotional. He's silent as he leaves her room. She tries not to let it get to her, to tell herself it's natural for him to need space to process this bizarre, life-altering reality. But even if it's for a perfectly legitimate reason, it still feels like another abandonment in a long line of abandonments.

She unknots the sweater from the headboard (more challenging than she expects, probably thanks to Charlie's sailing experience) and slips it back over her head. It's tempting to tell herself she simply doesn't want to be cold, because that lets what happened between them be purely sexual. But the real reason is because it's the closest she assumes she'll get to sleeping in his arms tonight.

Except later, when her room is pitch-black thanks to the new moon, she's awoken by warm fingers brushing over her shoulder, followed by hot lips that soon find hers in the dark. "You said you're here if I need you?" He whispers it into her ear.

"Yeah?"

"I need you."

She answers with soft kisses wherever her lips can reach, her fingers threaded through his silky hair.

This time they move slowly, gently together, Charlie's mouth only leaving hers long enough to whisper thoughts that vacillate wildly between dirty, grateful, remorseful, and scared. Their kisses turn salty, and she isn't sure whose tears they are, but she licks them from his lips and mutters reassurances that she'll figure out how to help him. She isn't sure she can guarantee that, of course. But god, she's going to try.

30

IN THE MORNING, GRETCHEN WAKES UP ALONE, THE SPACE beside her in the bed cool to the touch. She (mostly successfully) resists the urge to panic. There were a lot of emotions flowing last night, but even though everything between them has changed, it doesn't mean they've changed that way. It would have been nice if he stayed, sure, on a physical level. But it's not like she expected him to. Gretchen isn't about to start doing something as stupid as *expecting things* from someone just because he's hot and good in bed and vulnerable with her in a way she finds both a little terrifying and a lot attractive.

She grabs her phone from the nightstand, hoping its clock will tell her she can linger here for a while before having to get up and get ready for the farmers market. Instead, she finds a text from Charlie: **Grandpa fell early this morning. I'm with him at the hospital. Can you handle market solo today?**

No problem, she responds, both because she feels even more strongly about showing up for Charlie than she did before and because the idea of Gilded Creek missing out on a couple hundred dollars in this crucial penultimate week of her stay makes her feel itchy. Then she asks: How is he?

Broken wrist, keeps forgetting how it happened but otherwise in good spirits. Resting now.

And how are you? she asks next.

She doesn't receive an answer for several minutes. But then: I'm ok. And another minute later: Thank you. Which may be a "thank you for asking," or a "thank you for taking care of the market," or a "thank you for last night." Whichever it is, it sends warmth into Gretchen's chest that, in the light of day, she tells herself is a close cousin of the gotcha euphoria, nothing more.

Charlie proceeds to send the address of the parking lot where the market is held, the location of the spare set of keys for the ancient station wagon she's to drive there, and a bunch of instructions for how to pack up and transport the cheese and soap. She, of course, already knows all about the cheese and soap, having helped out with the market the previous two Sundays. But she figures he's trying to distract himself. So in that spirit, she asks him questions about other things she already knows, smiling when he texts back entire paragraphs about cheese flavor profiles and soap ingredients with only a brief I thought you already knew this but . . . to acknowledge that he sees what she's doing.

He always sees what she's doing. And seems to like her all the better for it.

Once she's dressed and ready to go, she opens her door to find Everett hover-sitting cross-legged on the floor of the hallway.

"Um, hi," she says.

"'Um, hi,'" he mimics with a grin. "You look . . . refreshed. Sleep well?"

"Very." The sleep she did get was certainly restful, a nice chunk of it spent as the little spoon to Charlie's big spoon. "When did you get back from the Nowhere?"

"Oh, somewhere around when you were like, 'Ahh ahh mm-mmm ooh'? The first time, I mean. Not when you made the same sound during round two in the middle of the night. Though obviously I was around for that one too." Gretchen's outraged expression has him quickly adding, "Hey, don't give me that look. I wasn't *trying* to listen. You two were just really loud. I could hear you from the couch."

She narrows her eyes at him but doesn't say anything. It's embarrassing to learn that their intimate moments weren't, strictly speaking, all that intimate.

"So where do we stand on the whole convincing-Charlie thing now?"

She takes a deep breath, the reality of it all hitting her anew. "I told him everything. And he believes me about you and the curse."

"Really? So he's going to stay? Crisis averted?"

Gretchen goes into the bathroom to brush her teeth. "I don't know. We didn't discuss that part of it. But I'm assuming so. As long as we can make it financially feasible."

Everett does a twirl, following her in. "Gretchen Acorn, I could kiss you!"

"I'm really glad you actually can't," she says around her toothbrush.

They make eye contact in the mirror, and Everett gives her one of his crooked smiles, but this one is small and affectionate instead of intended to charm. "I know how hard it was for you to do that. Thank you."

Gretchen nods ever so slightly, touched by the genuine gratitude in his voice. It's easy sometimes to think of Everett as immature, impulsive. A tad prurient. But maybe there's some depth to him after all.

AT THE MARKET, GRETCHEN CATCHES HANNAH EYEING HER as she sets up. *Looking for Charlie, I bet.* "Just me today!" she calls over to the Johnny Bee Goods booth with an overly wide smile that Hannah tentatively returns.

"Oh, that's . . . nice?" She tries but can't fully hide her disappointment, and Gretchen is perversely a bit satisfied.

But after everything is out and ready and Gretchen is standing there behind their table (which now has one of Ellen's least clashy afghans acting as a tablecloth, among other small aesthetic improvements), waiting for customers to appear, she has an epiphany. How did she not think of it before? It's tempting to smack herself in the forehead. Such an easy way to boost the farm's business. She checks her phone—ten minutes still before the market officially opens. Just enough time.

She does a quick online search, then walks across to where Hannah is making minor adjustments to her display. "Those are really pretty," Gretchen says, nodding toward a group of beeswax candles with various herbs and flower petals pressed into the top.

Hannah straightens, wispy strands of hair Gretchen assumes were strategically left out of her French braid swishing with the movement. "Thanks. It's something new we're trying."

"I'm sure they'll be a hit." This is intentional flattery, of course, but it's also true. Which is one of the reasons Gretchen came over here in the first place: From the artfulness of her display to the lovely smile Gretchen has watched her deploy each time a customer approaches, Hannah is an excellent saleswoman. *Like recognizes like.* But unlike Gretchen, Hannah will be around for the foreseeable future. "I actually wanted to talk to you about a business proposition, if you have a second. Charlie was planning on bringing it up with you today, but he had a family emergency. I told him I'd discuss it with you on his behalf, since it's somewhat time-sensitive."

"Oh gosh, I hope everything's okay. I'm free for a bit. What's up?"

"How many farmers markets do you do a week?"

"Two during the winter, five in the summer," Hannah answers.

"Wow. Busy bee, huh?"

Hannah smiles politely at the pun.

"And you do wholesale?"

"Yeah, we work with a few gift shops in Maryland and Virginia, bed-and-breakfasts, places like that."

"Any arrangements with restaurants?"

"Just a farm-to-table place here in Leesburg right now, but I'm planning to really focus on expanding that this summer."

Of course, Gretchen already discovered much of this while skimming the Johnny Bee Goods website, but it's nice to know the information is current. Having someone dedicated to sales and marketing has given Hannah's family's operation a much wider reach than Gilded Creek Goat Farm, but Charlie doesn't have the time or money to replicate that business model, especially once Gretchen goes back to DC.

So why reinvent the wheel?

"I don't know if you were aware, but Charlie actually had to put the farm up for sale back in February."

Hannah's fingers fly to her lips. "Oh my. I knew it wasn't easy lately, but I didn't realize . . ."

"Yeah, that's one of the reasons he took me on as a, uh, an intern this spring. I'm working on an MBA and he's letting me use the farm as a case study." Being honest with Charlie doesn't mean she has to be honest with *everyone*. Baby steps. "Part of the problem is that he doesn't have the time or resources to sell his products widely. This is his only farmers market right now. And he does well here, but he's missing out on a ton of profit by not being able to get his stuff in front of more customers. So he thought maybe you could sell some of Gilded Creek's cheese and soap at your table at the other markets you do, maybe talk to your gift shops and B and Bs on his behalf? In exchange for a percentage of the profits, of course."

She tilts her head. "Interesting proposition."

For some people, it would make sense to lean into the potential financial benefits of this arrangement, but Hannah's crush on Charlie Waybill is clear—painfully clear—to Gretchen. So, even though it annoys her, she says, "Charlie thinks you're such a fantastic saleswoman, you know, and that you would represent Gilded Creek with professionalism and charm. That's why he wanted to ask *you* for this favor."

Hannah's cheeks pinken. "Oh. I . . . Well, I'm very flattered. And you can tell Charlie I would love to help him out however I can. Really no problem. My pleasure."

Gretchen laces her fingers together and holds her hands under her chin in an exaggerated gesture of gratitude. "Thank you so much. He's going to be so relieved. This will make a huge differ-ence, maybe even help him keep the farm."

"Well. Anything for a friend. And we'd hate to see him leave." Hannah drags the toe of a red cowgirl boot over the parking lot's asphalt, watching its progress in order to hide her smile.

Of course, Hannah means that *she* would hate to see Charlie leave. For a split second, Gretchen wonders if the chance of suc-cess here is worth the possibility that Hannah and Charlie wind up growing close. Dating . . . getting married . . . having children. Wow. The thoughts really keep escalating. *I'm jealous.* It's strange how the realization doesn't bother her the way it would have be-fore. Just a fact of life now: Water is wet, grass is green, and she doesn't like the idea of Charlie with anyone that isn't her. Yet, at the same time, she knows someone else—someone more like Hannah—is who he will probably wind up with one day.

She hopes. Jealousy aside, she'd hate for him to have to be alone too.

WHAT GRETCHEN DIDN'T COUNT ON IS THAT CHARLIE would come join her at the farmers market after he left the hos-pital.

"You didn't think I could handle things?" she asks when he strolls over and sits down in the empty folding chair beside where she's standing. Part of her appreciates that he doesn't even seem to think about kissing her hello. *Better to keep this uncomplicated. Easier when I have to leave.*

"Never said that." He folds his arms over his chest. "They discharged Grandpa, so I made sure he got settled back in at Meadewood and then figured I'd check in with you here since it was on the way." Gretchen doesn't know this area super well, but she does know that Meadewood is not even in the same state. Certainly not "on the way." "All good here?"

"All good," Gretchen confirms, although it comes out slower than she'd like because at the same moment, she catches Hannah giving Charlie a little wave and a brilliant smile from across the way. "Um, but I do need to tell you . . . I did something—"

"You— What did you do, Acorn?"

But before she can answer, Hannah appears in front of their table. "Hi, Charlie."

"Oh, hey, Hannah."

"Didn't expect you today, but glad you're here. Gretchen already told me what you were thinking, and it's a great idea. I'd love to help. Do you want to maybe, um, grab a coffee after we're done here? To discuss the details?"

Charlie's eyes are daggers, flaying Gretchen alive. "Uh, sorry," he says, turning back toward Hannah. "I—"

"Don't forget, you're supposed to meet Deborah at one," Gretchen says. She hopes he doesn't mistake the rope it's intended to be as a snake.

"Ah, yeah. Deborah. Right. So, maybe another time?" Charlie glances sideways at Gretchen very briefly, as if checking if this is the right response.

"An email is probably best when working out business stuff anyway," Gretchen says before Hannah can suggest dinner instead. "Good to have things in writing, right? That's what they're always saying in business school, at least!"

Hannah reluctantly agrees, "Yeah, definitely."

"We'll send you something early this week," Gretchen says.

"Great. Well. I'll just be getting back to my booth, then."

Hannah points over her shoulder with her thumb. "Again, really glad you could make it today after all, Charlie."

"Thanks, me too. And um, Hannah?"

She stops mid-turn. "Yeah?"

"Your hair looks really nice."

Her cheeks pinken even more deeply this time. "Oh. Thank you."

Once she's out of earshot, Gretchen leans in toward Charlie. "'Your hair looks really nice'?"

"She seemed disappointed. I figured a compliment might help."

"You've never once complimented *me*." Gretchen feels like a bit of a petulant child as soon as she says it.

"That isn't true."

She shrugs. The fact is she has remembered every single nice (or even almost-nice) thing Charlie Waybill has said to her since she arrived at Gilded Creek. Some of them have been compliments. Some of them, last night, were sexy as hell. But not one of them has ever been said in that charming, almost boyishly awestruck tone he used on Hannah just now.

"Fine," he says. "Your hair looks nice today too."

He tugs on her ponytail and, even though he isn't rough, a tingling sensation travels from her scalp down, down, down. She lets out a small whimper, and Charlie freezes.

"Don't *do that*," he warns, his voice quiet. "Or I'm going to have to bend you over this table and take you right here."

"Well, then don't do *that*," she counters, "or I'm going to have to let you."

Gretchen is gratified to see the bulge growing in his jeans. He clears his throat and shifts in his seat. "Speaking of Deborah," he says, apparently reaching for the first guaranteed boner-killer topic he can think of, "she called this morning to let me know she's staying in Provence a few weeks longer, so she won't be playing in next month's bridge tournament. Apparently, she's met someone. A vineyard owner named Michel."

A genuine smile stretches across Gretchen's face. "That's great. I love that for her."

"She asked about you. About the exorcism."

"And?" Gretchen's heart flings up toward her throat as she waits for his answer.

"I told her I was very . . ." Charlie gives her a sideways look. "Satisfied with you."

She bites her lip, fighting back laughter as heat sweeps over her neck and face. Leave it to Charlie to figure out how to lie to Deborah without actually lying.

Clearly pleased with her reaction, he leans back and says, "So are you going to fill me in on whatever business dealings we apparently now have with Hannah?"

"She's going to sell some of your products at other farmers markets around the region and help with wholesale, in exchange for a portion of the profits. And maybe a small flat fee to cover the cost of using their booth. That would probably be fair."

"Oh. That's actually . . . that's not a bad idea. And she agreed?"

"She did. Especially when I told her how highly you think of her sales technique."

"I do think highly of her sales technique." He watches the beautiful blonde talking to a customer. "She's got nothing on you, of course." Charlie nudges Gretchen's arm. "See? Compliment."

She rolls her eyes, but his praise nestles between her ribs, a bird settling into the nest it's meticulously built twig by twig.

31

THEY MANAGE TO MAKE IT TO DINNERTIME WITHOUT acknowledging the elephant—or rather, the specter—in the room. With a spoonful of chicken noodle soup raised to his mouth, Charlie asks, "So, what's he like, then?"

"Who?"

"Everett," he says around his food.

"Oh." This isn't what Gretchen expected would top Charlie's likely very long list of questions about this whole situation. But despite his casualness, she suspects this is a deliberate choice, the least overwhelming part of an extremely overwhelming development in his life. *Imagine the ghost haunting your property being the* easiest *thing to comprehend.* "Well, to be honest, I've grown to really love him, but he still kind of suuu—rprises me with how cool he is," she manages to change course just in time for Everett's appearance in the kitchen. "And he is now in the kitchen with us."

"Wait, are you talking about *me*?" Everett asks. He strides over to the table and perches atop it, the bread they bought at the farmers market half inside his butt.

"Yeah. Charlie was asking about you. What you're like," Gretchen says.

"Oh! Have you told him yet that I'm very handsome?"

"I have not told him that, no."

"Oh, well, what are you waiting for? Tell him," Everett says, overlapping with Charlie's, "Tell me what?"

Gretchen sighs. "Everett would like you to know that he is very handsome."

"Um," Charlie says.

Everett huffs, "Why'd you say it like that? That I wanted him to know. Now he'll think I'm vain."

"You *are* vain, babe."

"Now tell him—" Everett starts, but is interrupted by Charlie dropping his spoon into his bowl with a clang.

"I don't know if I was ready for this," he says, dabbing at a droplet of broth that hit the table. "Now that I know he's *here* . . . it's really fucking unnerving to watch you talk to him." He rubs his hands over his face. "Sorry. Sorry. I'll be okay. I just need a minute."

Gretchen has taken it for granted that, no matter how absolutely bananas this all is, at least she can *see* Everett. She knows where he is, can communicate with him. How would it feel to find out that, since you were a young child, you've been under random surveillance by someone you will never formally meet or talk to? That has to be more than a little disconcerting.

"Do you think it might help you acclimate to all of this if you could interact with him directly in some way? Would that help you process that he's really here?" she asks.

"I . . . I don't know. What would that even entail?" Charlie asks.

"Well, he *can* touch things. It just takes a lot of energy and he disappears for a while afterward. It's not something he could do all the time or anything, but right now, if it would make you feel better, I'm sure he could tap your arm or something as a kind of 'hello.' Right, Everett?"

The ghost groans. "Ugh, Gretch, do I have to? I just went to the Nowhere last night and it *suuuucked*."

She gives him a look that brooks no further argument. Gretchen missed her calling as a tough-but-fair middle school teacher, because she's gotten that look down pat over the last few weeks.

"Fiiiine," Everett concedes, hopping off the table and going to stand behind Charlie, stretching his fingers out like he's a concert pianist about to take the stage. "Where does he want it?"

"Don't make it weird," she admonishes before turning back to Charlie. "So, do you want him to touch you?"

"I . . . guess? Maybe? Does it . . . hurt?"

"A little. I get painfully cold whenever he so much as brushes against me, and it's even more intense when he actively touches me. But I also might be more sensitive to it than most people."

Charlie takes a moment to consider this. "Okay," he says at last. "We can try it."

"Where would you like him to—"

"Surprise me." He sounds almost annoyed, which Gretchen is starting to recognize means he's actually nervous.

"Whenever you're ready, Ev."

"See you later, I guess," Everett grumbles, before reaching out slowly toward Charlie's face. He boops him on the nose.

Everett disappears immediately, and Charlie jerks his head back, surprised to have been touched on his face of all places.

"Holy fuck," he gasps. "*Holy. Fuck.*"

Gretchen reaches for his hand across the table. "You okay?"

"I guess. A little cold. A lot . . . freaking out."

"That's okay. Freak out all you need to."

"I think . . . I might have felt him before? Once when I was a kid, it felt like someone poked me while I was playing pool alone downstairs, but I figured . . . And he's gone now? He . . . what did you call it? He poofed?"

"Yeah. It seems to be the more energy he uses, the longer he's gone, and all he did was tap you, so he should be back soon." Gretchen returns to her soup. "But like, last night, when he broke that lamp, he was gone for almost half an hour."

"Oh god, he wasn't . . ."

"There while we . . . ? No. Besides, he knows better than to come into my room without asking first. We established that early on. And also, he was really invested in us having sex, so he wouldn't have risked interrupting."

"Why was he invested in us— You know what? Never mind. I don't think I can handle all of this information right now."

"Fair enough," she says.

They eat in silence for a while longer. Eventually, Gretchen decides to change the subject, hoping to drain the shock off Charlie's face. "So, market was good today. We pretty much sold out."

"Yeah. Nice weather brought a decent crowd," he responds, obviously thankful to take part in a superficial conversation. He stands and takes his bowl over to the sink. "If I haven't already said it, I appreciate you reaching out to Hannah about distributing for us. It'll help a lot."

"It will, but probably not enough to make a real difference."

Gretchen stands too, joining him at the sink with her own dishes. "The cash flow is a real problem, Charlie. You're what? Fifteen thousand in the hole right now? That's a whole lotta cheese to sell."

He sighs and leans into the counter. "Maybe I could look into a loan again. Last time I talked to the bank, the interest rates were too high, which is one of the reasons I decided to sell instead. But if I can't do that, then—"

"What about Mrs. Van Alst? I'm sure she would be more than happy to help you out. And she certainly has it. Especially since she won't be seeing me anymore." Because at some point over the last twenty-four hours, Gretchen decided that whatever her future holds, it cannot include exploiting Mrs. Van Alst. Which is what she would be doing if she continued seeing her when she's no longer helping her all that much.

Charlie looks at her for a moment, as if deciding whether or not to talk about Gretchen choosing not to enforce her part of their original bargain. Eventually, he shakes his head. "I can't ask Deborah for money. What if I can't pay her back?"

"I'm not sure she'd even expect you to, to be honest. When I talked to her, she seemed eager to help you out, no matter what that meant. No matter the cost."

He scoffs. "I'm not you, Acorn. I can't just *take* from her because she's willing to give. I have my pride."

"Ouch," Gretchen responds. She turns away so he won't see how that comment crash-landed in her chest.

Charlie's hand comes to her shoulder, then his other finds her waist. "I'm sorry. That was shitty of me. I don't . . . That isn't really what I think about you."

"Yes, you do," she counters, letting herself melt into his heat.

"And it's fine. It's no less than I deserve. You were right when I showed up on your doorstep. I'm a fraud, Charlie. I take advantage of people when they're at their most vulnerable."

"You give them hope."

She looks over her shoulder at him, surprised.

"I'm not saying I agree with it or that you should keep doing it. But . . . I do believe that you've done more good than harm overall since you struck out on your own. And that your heart's been in the right place. Mostly. Probably. Sometimes." Charlie flashes that rare smile of his, so rakishly lopsided. Then he leans closer, and his lips brush against her ear, sending a light shock through her system. "I can't know what it was like for you, why you've made the choices you have. But I want to understand. If you're ever ready to tell me."

She turns in the cage of his arms and runs her fingers up through his hair. "Maybe one day." *And maybe never.* The entirety of her life is a story she isn't sure she's ready or willing to tell, even to Charlie. Just him giving her the benefit of the doubt, that maybe she isn't a total monster driven by pure greed, is so much more than she ever expected to get. No reason to press her luck now, when their time together is almost up.

He pulls her closer, and the intimacy between them is too much, way more than Gretchen ever signed up for, really. So she kisses him hard, forcing the moment into purely physical territory so that she can better navigate it. Charlie has both straps of her overalls undone and his hand down the back of them when Everett Kool-Aid Mans into the kitchen from somewhere outside.

"I'm baaaack!" he sings, then notices that he's interrupted and starts slowly reversing out of the room. "Oh, interrupting again. Whoopsie. Don't mind me!"

But Gretchen lets out an exasperated sigh into Charlie's neck.

"What's up?" he asks.

"Everett. He's back."

"Ah." Charlie closes his eyes for a moment. "He still here?"

She glances over his shoulder to find about half of the ghost still protruding from the wall. As if she wasn't going to notice. "Somewhat."

"Will he follow us if we head up to my room?"

"Not if he knows what's good for him," she says, her eyes meeting Everett's in warning.

32

THEY ROLL APART, SWEATY SKIN PEELING AWAY FROM
sweaty skin, hearts racing and chests heaving. There's a shallow
crescent of indentations on Charlie's left shoulder, where Gretchen
sunk her teeth into the weeping willow's leaves as she came. She'd
feel guiltier about it if she wasn't certain she would have a row of
fingertip-sized bruises on each of her hips tomorrow.

It was exactly what she needed, physically and mentally. She's
been telling herself all day that whatever that was between them
when Charlie came back to her room in the middle of the night
last night, that slow, gentle, tender . . . *lovemaking* . . . was an anom-
aly. In *no way* indicative of how things are between them now.
When they first went up to Charlie's bedroom tonight, she worried he might do something to make her doubt that. Soft kisses,
sweet caresses, whispered confessions—those would all be like a
big splatter of white paint launched onto the picture she's created
of the situation, interrupting the narrative she needs to show herself. So it was a relief, such a relief, when he closed the door behind

them and pressed her up against it. His first kiss was hard, rough, and Gretchen almost laughed at how comforting she found it.

Charlie sighs, flinging an arm over his head. "Guess that wasn't very good."

"What? Are you kidding me? That was amazing. I came so hard I almost bit your arm off."

"Couldn't have been that amazing since it didn't get you to confess to any crimes."

Gretchen turns her head to give him a look.

"I figured that's the gold standard," he says, trying to suppress a smile.

"First of all." She props herself up on her elbow and gives him a light shove on the shoulder, which then turns into a light tracing of the mark she left there. "I haven't technically confessed to *any* crimes. Nothing I told you is strictly illegal. Just morally . . . iffy."

He barks out a laugh. "Okay. Sure. What's second of all?"

"Oh, right. And second of all." *I can't tell you all of my secrets, because then you'll know me better than anyone in the world. And what will I do without you then?* "Do you really want a confession? You sure?"

He looks to be considering her question, and then his voice comes out quietly, like he expects his world to be upended again. "Yeah. Tell me something."

There's a moment where something strange almost slips out of Gretchen's mouth, something horribly inappropriate and . . . not even true. Something like "Every moment here with you feels like the happiest of my life." That's so absurd she almost laughs at herself, then pivots to her real, much less revealing, and definitely more factually accurate confession. "One time, last summer, Yolanda came home early from work and caught me masturbating while watching *There Will Be Blood*."

There's a pause as he contemplates this. "Which scene?" he asks.

"What?"

"Which scene were you watching?"

"I don't remember," she says. But Gretchen definitely remembers.

Charlie urges her on with a small smile that questions if this is really how she wants to break her honesty streak.

She rolls her eyes and sighs. "The one where he's slapping Paul Dano a bunch in the mud and oil." She hurries to add, "I feel the need to say that I'm not . . . It wasn't anything about the scene in particular that turned me on. I just happened to be turned on for unrelated, hormonal, biological reasons at the time I was watching it. I figured I would multitask. You know."

"Hmm," he says. "Did Everett really push you into that puddle the day you got here, or were you actually attempting to live out your unconventional sexual fantasies on my property?"

She gives him a playful nudge, and he grabs her hand and kisses it. The moment turns soft and warm, as if it's wrapped in one of Grandma Ellen's Magic Eye afghans. It's too sweet for Gretchen to sit with, so she wrestles her hand away from his and lets it wander down his body.

He sucks in a breath through his teeth when she reaches his stomach. But then his fingers thread through hers, joining their hands again and delivering them to the spot over his heart as if saying, *You won't get away from this that easily.*

His heartbeat is strong but slowing under her palm, and his breaths even out and become deeper. Along with his continued silence and closed eyes, Gretchen wonders if Charlie's drifted off to sleep. She's not far from dreamland herself. Should she stay, or untangle their fingers and head back to her own bed? The latter, for sure. But then he says, "So . . . it's just Everett, then?"

"Hmm?"

He turns over to face her. "He's the only ghost here?"

"Oh. Yeah. Just him. Apparently, becoming a ghost is a super rare thing. Most people simply . . . go Up, according to him."

"Oh."

Gretchen knows the pensive look that takes over his face. It's that of a person coming to terms with the fact that they'll never speak to someone they've lost ever again. Usually, her job is to obliterate that look, turn it into shining, comfortable hope. But that isn't what Charlie wants from her. It may not even be what she wants from herself anymore.

"Charlie . . ." She shifts, pulling the covers to her shoulders in hopes she might feel less exposed. "The crux of my business back in DC is saying the right thing, the thing the client's loved one would want them to hear, at the right time. There were lies involved too, yes, but . . . that part, giving reassurance, never felt like lying to me." Her fingers worry the sheet's seam as she builds up her courage, the truth still a somewhat complicated thing for her to access after a lifetime of hiding and twisting it to better suit her needs. "What I'm trying to say is that I didn't consider it a lie when I told you Ellen is proud of you. I don't need to be able to talk to her to know that that's how she would feel."

"How can you be so sure when I've basically destroyed her and Charles's legacy?"

"You haven't destroyed anything. In fact, it's because of you that this farm has hung on for the last two years. You take care of everything and everyone around you, even the people like me who don't deserve it, and you make a mean spaghetti with meat sauce. Of course Ellen is proud of you. *I'm* proud of you and I barely even know you." She feels her face heat at this confession.

"That's funny," he says, reaching to tuck her hair behind her ear. "Because it feels like you might know me better than anyone."

It hurts as much as it flatters, that sentiment. Knowing that Charlie has been lonely too. And no matter how uncomfortable the realization makes her, he certainly does know her better than anyone. Sure, she's told Everett a lot of things, and she has shared history with Yolanda, but Charlie is the only person who's ever taken one look at her and recognized the artist behind the painting she attempted to present to him. Telling him that would make her more vulnerable than she wants to be right now, so she instead says, "I did some math today while I was at the farmers market."

"Yes, I heard you calculate the price of three soaps plus two cheeses plus tax when someone asked. I was quite impressed."

"I meant bigger math. About profits and expenses and shit."

"Ah. And?"

"If Hannah can sell a hundred dollars' worth of product at each of the markets she goes to, and you continue having events throughout the summer including maybe a wedding or two, and you can get a couple local businesses to buy wholesale . . . I think you could break even in a year."

"Oh, is that all?" he asks, sounding both amused and exhausted by the thought.

"It would be hard. But it's doable. And I could . . ." What? Help out when she's able to get away from the city? The suggestion would be like offering a drowning man a foot-long piece of rope attached to nothing.

He sighs. "Maybe I should just sell off the herd completely. I have no idea how I'd make any money living out here in the middle of nowhere and not farming, but at least the land would stay in the family."

"Let's not get ahead of ourselves. I mean, I obviously don't know much about how this works, but could you switch to a different type of animal or crops or something?"

"No, the start-up costs would bury me even deeper." Charlie presses his palms against his eyes. "Look, Acorn, I really appreciate you trying to help me. I do. I admit that when you showed up, I had my doubts, but you've proven yourself to be stubborn and smart as hell. It's possible, though, that even you can't solve this problem. That what you're doing won't be enough. And I need you to understand that if that's the case, it will not be your fault. Whatever happens to me—it's not your fault."

I just wish I could take your place. It's not the first time the thought has drifted across her mind. But this time it doesn't drift so much as linger. It's not a cirrus cloud urged along by a brisk wind, but a fog that settles heavily. Part of her surely feels this way because she wants to help Charlie, and part because it would be the ultimate way to prove to herself that she's not her father; he would never in a million years do something so selfless. Except is it really selfless when she's grown to love Gilded Creek? The idea of staying here until she dies is intimidating, of course, like any permanent choice would be. But it doesn't sound like all that much of a hardship when it means she would get to stay in this place that feels like home and leave her old life—her bullshit artist career, the weight of her family's history—behind.

She smiles at Charlie, realizing she's gone too long without responding. "Too bad I'm not a Waybill. Then I could stay and run things here while you go do whatever you want."

Unless you're volunteering to become a Waybill . . . Everett said that to her once, the day she first arrived. And she sort of forgot about it, because it seemed as absurd as his flash mob idea back then. But now . . . now . . .

"Holy shit," she says, springing up in bed. "Wait here. I need to talk to Everett."

33

EVERETT SITS BESIDE THE PILE OF BABY GOATS IN THE corner of the small outbuilding, quietly singing the theme song to *Welcome Back, Kotter*. He looks Gretchen up and down, taking in her hastily donned outfit consisting of one of Charlie's T-shirts, a pair of his sleep shorts, the flannel, and her rain boots. He raises his eyebrows.

She preempts his criticism of her fashion choices with a wave of her hand and comes to sit on one of the hay bales. "I have some questions for you."

"Oh, I see how it is. It's all 'Everett, scram' till you need something from me." Gretchen opens her mouth to either argue or apologize—even she isn't sure which it will be—but Everett sighs and says, "Go ahead."

Gretchen leans forward, propping one elbow on her knee while she pets the supersoft floppy ear of a kid who makes its way over to nibble on the hem of her flannel. She should probably figure out what has Everett in such a funk, but first things first. "When

I got here, you said something about me becoming a Waybill. How would I do that?"

"Ah. Well, the usual way. Through marriage."

"And that would work? Do we have evidence that the curse will accept someone who marries into the Waybills and takes the name as a full-fledged family member?"

"I don't know. I hadn't fully thought about it when I said it, but I'm pretty sure . . ." He presses his finger to his chin, thinking for a moment. Then he snaps his fingers; like all of his other gestures, it doesn't make a sound. "Enid," he says, pointing at Gretchen.

"George's wife?"

"George died before her, and Gilded Creek went to Enid until Charles took over."

"And it wasn't some technicality, like that Charles or one of his sisters were still on the property?"

Everett shakes his head. "Nope. There was a time when it was just Enid here. The twins both married and moved away at the beginning of that summer, I think, and Charles joined the Navy and planned to make a career of it soon after. That was until he met Ellen. She loved the idea of living on the farm, so . . ."

"But the curse counted Enid as a Waybill even though she wasn't born one."

"Mhm. At least I guess so, because nothing bad happened to Charles when he shipped out."

"So I would count too. If Charlie marries me and I take his name. I would count as a Waybill."

Everett rises to his feet and grabs for the wall to steady himself. He instead falls halfway through it. Once he's fully inside the building again, he holds up both hands. "Hold on, you're considering marrying Charlie?"

She leaps up and begins pacing. Sleepy Jean bleats when she gets close to the cuddle puddle, and Gretchen pauses to smile at the kid, who just keeps getting cuter and cuter, in her opinion. "Yes. Maybe. I mean, not *marrying* marrying him, just . . . taking his name in an official capacity so that I'm technically a Waybill and can stay at Gilded Creek, freeing him to leave and pursue something else. There wouldn't need to be anything to the relationship except a piece of paper. Which should still be enough to satisfy the curse's criteria, right?"

"Gretchen, that's . . . that's . . ." He throws himself onto the hay bale she vacated, again moving too briskly and winding up partly inside it.

"Ridiculous? Shortsighted?"

"Brilliant," he says. But it sounds doleful, and his eyes focus on the straw covering the floor, devoid of their usual spark.

"What's wrong? You don't wanna hang out with me for the rest of my natural life?" She forces a small chuckle.

Everett's head shoots up then. "I do. I do want that."

The vehemence in his voice takes her by surprise and fills her with a lovely warmth. "Okay. So what's the problem?"

"For starters, Charlie will never go for it. He'll never let you sacrifice yourself."

"That's just it. It isn't a sacrifice," Gretchen says. "I actually like living here. And he really, really doesn't want me going back to doing the spirit medium thing. Neither do I, to be honest. I'm tired of having to lie all of the time, having to constantly worry about slipping up and ruining my own life. Charlie appreciates my honesty above everything, so if I just tell him that this is truly what I want, I think I can convince him that it's more like he's doing *me* a favor."

"And how are you going to run this place on your own?"

"I wouldn't be on my own, not really. Lori would still take care of the cheesemaking, and once we start making enough money, I can hire someone to take the lead on operations so I can focus primarily on the business side of things. Maybe we could bring in a few more part-time people. Find some real interns." Gretchen notices Everett's expression falling further and further as she talks. "What? Just tell me. Why are you so against this?"

He hangs his head. "I just never expected this to happen when I asked for your help. I don't want you to be . . . to be unhappy because of me."

"Oh, *now* you have an attack of guilt. A little late for that, babe," she says teasingly as she sits back down beside him, getting close enough to feel his chill. "I appreciate that you care, Ev. It's been really nice to have someone around who I know will be there no matter what. And not only because you literally cannot leave."

She expects a laugh or at least a smile, but it never comes. Instead, he stares at her, more serious than she's ever seen him. "You're a special person, Gretchen. I don't deserve your friendship."

"Probably not, but you have it anyway."

Everett's mouth finally curves ever so slightly at the corner. They sit there in silence for a moment, until Everett asks, "Do you love him?"

Gretchen considers the question for a long time. What she feels for Charlie is a strange, selfless thing. There's lust, of course, but there is also a fierce affection crossed with the profound need to do anything in her power to ensure and support his happiness, even if it does mean making herself *un*happy in the process. Is that love? "Does it matter?" she responds at last, dodging having to answer both Everett and herself.

"It might. What if you told him how you feel? What if it made him want to stay too? Then you wouldn't need to marry, you could still leave if things were to change . . . He probably feels the same way, you know. Or will. Charlie doesn't generally get involved with someone if he doesn't think it could turn into something serious."

Hope blooms in her heart, and she quickly tramples it. She doesn't want to know how Charlie feels, because what if it doesn't change anything? That's the last thing she needs—yet another person who supposedly loves her but will still wind up leaving. Best to send him on his way now, before either of them mistakes this practical solution as anything more.

She shakes her head. "I'm doing this because I don't want it to be his burden anymore. He didn't ask for it, he doesn't deserve it. This farm has become an albatross around his neck. It doesn't bring him joy to be here anymore. There's no point to this if he starts feeling an obligation to stay for any reason—including me or my feelings."

"Gretch, I just don't want you to be . . ." *Unhappy*, she assumes he'll say again. Everett throws off his cap in a burst of emotion. It immediately reappears on his head.

"Why are you so against this? You're the one who came up with this plan, remember?" Gretchen throws her hands up in frustration and stands again, resuming her pacing. Two of the kids think she's playing and run past her, stumbling over a resting Waluigi, who lets out an indignant bleat.

"I'm not," he says. "I'm not against it. But things are different now. I care about you. And I just think you're being a little hasty here, wanting to sacrifice yourself for a guy you didn't even really like a few weeks ago."

"Well, I didn't really like you a few weeks ago either, and look

at us now!" she shouts and throws her arms out, accidentally flinging one through Everett's body. Gretchen folds into herself for a
moment, trying to ease the resulting frigidness. *Serves me right*. Everett frowns at her, expressing the same thought. She sighs. "Look.
I was taught to listen to my instincts. My instincts tell me this is
my best option for saving Charlie. And if you're worried I'm being completely selfless here, I promise you I am not. I'm getting
plenty out of it too." Her hands come to her hips. "If there's a
reason I shouldn't go to Charlie with this idea, something I'm not
seeing, tell me now."

"Or forever hold my peace, huh?" He stares at her a long while,
then back at the ground. "There isn't any reason."

"Okay. Great! Good." Gretchen nods. "All right. I'm going to
go . . . well, propose to Charlie, then."

"Okay. Good luck."

"Thanks. Do you want to come with?"

Everett shakes his head. "I'll give you your privacy."

As she leaves the outbuilding, Gretchen tries to figure out what
about that whole conversation with Everett felt so off. The wrong-
ness of it was all vibes, nothing concrete she could put her finger
on. Is it possible that *Everett* is in love with her? No way. *He thinks
of me as a hot sister*. Besides, a marriage of convenience that results
in Charlie leaving Gilded Creek wouldn't exactly be a problem in
that situation. No competition for her attention then.

So what *is* the problem? Is it really just that Everett cares about
her happiness and isn't convinced she'll enjoy living here for the
rest of her life? It's impossible, she assumes, for anyone to know
for sure if they'll be happy in any one place until they die. Or with
any one person. But that doesn't mean people don't make those
kinds of commitments all the time anyway. Besides, she spent a

good chunk of her life without any real permanency. Maybe the staying-put-long-term thing will grow old, but she doubts it.

Maybe Everett was counting on Charlie having to stick around and now he's disappointed that may not happen. That's the only reason she can think of that makes any sense, and she isn't unsympathetic; Everett has known Charlie since he was a baby. He cares about him, likes having him here. They're (technically) family—the only family Everett really has left. But if Charlie leaves, surely Everett could do worse than having the farm in the care of someone with whom he can actually communicate. Someone who will leave the TV on for him without question. If Gretchen knows anything about her spectral friend, it's that he loves a good gab session and a *Hogan's Heroes* marathon. She can provide him with both to ease his sadness about Charlie leaving. If he's worried about being lonely, he doesn't need to be. At least this way they'll have each other. *We can miss Charlie together*, she thinks.

When she reaches the farmhouse and heads upstairs, she finds Charlie snoring quietly in his bed. It's tempting to wake him up . . . maybe with her mouth? But as she silently pads toward him, her lusty intentions disappear. Instead, she watches him sleep, her eyes following each curve and angle of his face, observing the peacefulness of his rest. The next time she glances away and finds the alarm clock on the nightstand, twenty minutes have somehow passed. Neither of them will be able to function in the morning if she wakes him now, and there's plenty of work to do bright and early.

Her proposal can wait. Something inside her loosens, glad for a temporary reprieve. As excited as she is to have potentially solved their conundrum, it's not as if she's eager for all this to change. She's only just barely gotten sort of used to it.

The empty space beside him seems to call out to her—*you don't have to sleep alone.* It's a lie, of course. An enticing one, but a lie nonetheless. Because Gretchen knows she will have to sleep alone. Maybe not tonight, but for all of her future nights now that she knows how to give Charlie his freedom. Still, she climbs into the bed and snuggles against his warm, strong body. Just this once, she promises herself. Just until morning, when the light of day will highlight the brushstrokes and remind her that none of it is real.

STRETCHED ACROSS THE BED THAT STILL SMELLS LIKE Charlie despite his having vacated it sometime before she woke, Gretchen decides her idea to marry him and take his name so that she can, in essence, take his place at Gilded Creek still feels like the right one deep inside her bones. It isn't her Eichorn DNA whispering to her, but something else, something less mercenary and sneaky that's gently guided her to this conclusion. But the practicality of getting Charlie to agree to the scheme has suddenly hit her in the face like an errant flailed arm. "How do you propose a marriage of convenience to the cursed man you're having sex with?" Googling that on her phone, unsurprisingly, does not give Gretchen any answers. Instead she tries: "How do you propose?" She clicks on the first result.

Make it romantic.

Okay, well this isn't going to be helpful either. Because this proposal has to be the opposite of romantic. It has to be . . . businesslike. This is, in essence, a business decision. It's a career move for both of them. Her from bullshit artistry to goat farming. Him from goat farming to librarianship, or whatever it is he's going to do with his life once he's no longer tied to Gilded Creek. This has nothing to do with the love she may or may not feel for him and everything to do with the most mutually beneficial solution to the problem at hand. That's what she's going to tell herself. That's what she *has* to tell herself.

So Gretchen goes back to her own room and dresses in her usual white undershirt and the train engineer overalls, rolled up high on her calves to make space for the rain boots she'll put on before heading outside. She wrangles her hair into a messy bun atop her head and goes downstairs. Her heart thuds so hard she feels it in her skull as she enters the kitchen and finds Charlie sitting at the table there, eating his breakfast. He's wearing another of Ellen's sweaters, this one rust, fuchsia, and sky blue. For a moment, she has the ridiculous thought that if she could crawl inside it too, they could live there together in peaceful, ugly Technicolor contentment.

"Running late today?" she manages, heading for the cabinet that holds the twiggy cereal she's somehow grown to look forward to in the mornings.

Charlie swallows the bite he was chewing. "A little. *Someone* has kept me up late the last two nights." He gives her an accusing look, but it's mixed with a playful smile that makes her heart feel like it's melting, dripping drop by drop into her stomach like an ice cream cone in August. "It's starting to catch up with me."

"I'll try to be more conscientious going forward." She smiles back as she pours some cereal into a bowl.

He finishes his last bite of breakfast and leans back in his chair, eyes on her as if she might make a good second course. "I think I'd rather adjust my schedule to allow for a later start."

Gretchen isn't sure if it's desire or nerves threatening to creep up her throat. She swallows whatever it is down and forces herself to start the conversation they need to have. "I want to talk to you about something. Something important."

His face goes serious instantly. "Is everything okay?"

"Yeah, everything is fine. Great, actually. I think . . . well, I think I came up with a way around the curse. A loophole so you can leave Gilded Creek."

He stands and joins her by the counter. His head tilts, showing he is skeptical but ready to listen.

"Everett and I figured out that the curse treats Waybills by marriage the same as Waybills by birth. So, if you marry someone who then takes your name, and *they* stay at the farm when you leave—"

"It technically keeps the property in the family."

"Exactly."

"I'm . . . I'm not really following, Acorn." But by the firm line of his mouth and the tension in his jaw, Gretchen thinks this isn't completely true. "What are you trying to say?"

"I'm trying to say . . . I'm trying to say that you should marry me, Charlie."

34

CHARLIE BLINKS A FEW TIMES. "REPEAT THAT, PLEASE."

"You should marry me."

"I should . . . marry . . ."

"Me. Yes. Because then I can be a Waybill, which means you can—"

"Leave Gilded Creek. Yes. I understand that part." He runs his fingers through his hair. "What are you— This is absolutely— Marry you?"

"I know it sounds drastic, but—"

"*Sounds* drastic? It *is* drastic."

"But worth it," she says. "You could have your freedom, go live your life however you want, away from here."

"I cannot believe you think I would be okay with this. With getting my freedom at the expense of yours."

"Look, babe, I've had my freedom for years and I haven't used it all that admirably." He gives her a look that warns he's not in the mood for her to be flippant. "Okay, fine. The truth is that

I've grown to really love . . ."—*you*—"this place. And the manual labor still may not be my strong suit, but the business side of it all is. The ideas I have . . . they're *good*. This is an opportunity for me to do something I enjoy, something I have the skills to do well, and for once it's all completely aboveboard. I want to do this for you, yes. You deserve it, Charlie, after everything you've done for your family. But it would also be for *me*. You get your freedom, and I get a boring, safe life full of honest work. It's good for us both. And you won't have to sell the farm."

"But even if you can turn things around, it will take time. Gilded Creek won't be immediately profitable, and my father still won't pay for Grandpa Charles's care."

"I have the money," she says. "I have the ten thousand from Mrs. Van Alst, plus the payments she's sent this month. I'll find the rest somewhere. We'll turn a profit soon enough."

"Gretchen." Charlie runs his hands through his hair again. "I can't let you do that."

"Consider it an investment. That's what we can tell your dad. That you found a business partner. He doesn't need to know the details. Once you show him the farm isn't in the negative, that we have a business improvement plan to ensure continued profits, he'll have to pony up the cash for your grandfather."

Charlie looks deep into Gretchen's eyes, the way that makes her feel completely exposed. He frowns. "You know I think you're brilliant, but what happens if you fail? What happens if you can't keep Gilded Creek in the black and we *have* to sell after all? Your life isn't less important than mine."

"No, it's not. But Charlie, you haven't done anything to deserve any of this. I have," she says. "I've done things that I should probably pay for somehow. Hopefully not that way, but . . . if it happens, if I'm forced to leave and I die . . . well, at least I'm already acclimated to living with Everett." She forces a small smile. "I understand if you're worried this is a scam, that I'm trying to get something from you. We'll get an ironclad prenup—"

"God, Acorn. How could you think, after everything, that *that's* my issue with this plan?"

She shrugs, hiding her surprise at the emotion in his voice. His trust is still so new, such a fragile thing in her mind, it was only natural that she consider the best ways to protect him legally, to provide him some proof that she wasn't up to any tricks. If that's not the crux of his objection, then . . .

"We could see other people, of course. I wouldn't expect— There would be zero obligations between us. We could stay in touch if you want. Or not. It doesn't . . . it doesn't really matter to me."

He takes a step forward and brushes his fingertips over her jaw, making her shiver, then settles his palm against her cheek. "Is that what you want?"

"Yes." She resists leaning into his touch, keeping her eyes locked on his instead. If she looks away, he'll know she's lying. "That's what I want."

"And if you regret it one day? If you want to leave?" he asks, his voice quiet. "What then?"

"I won't."

Charlie shakes his head. "What then?" he repeats.

Gretchen swallows. "No-fault divorce is a thing in Maryland. We can just agree to dissolve the marriage, you can come back here, and I can go. No harm, no foul. Same situation as now. But that's not going to happen. I've thought this through, I promise. It's . . . it's the only way. The only way around it. And we both get what we want."

"Do we?" His gaze drifts from her eyes to her lips, and he presses his thumb lightly right beneath the bottom one before stepping away and breaking contact. Charlie turns his back to her and braces his hands on the counter. His strong back heaves with the deep breath he takes. "When do I need to decide?" he asks at last.

"The name change could take anywhere from a day to closer to a month. So it would probably be best to get the wheels in motion sooner than later. Get your dad to pay for next month's bill from Meadewood."

"I'll have an answer for you by tonight."

Gretchen nods even though he can't see her. *I'll have an answer for you by tonight.* *Surely, what everyone who proposes marriage hopes to hear.* "Okay." She grabs her abandoned cereal, which is already soggy from sitting in its milk through their conversation, and dumps it into the trash. In about two hours, she may regret not eating, but right now her stomach is roiling too much for her to care. "I better get out there and get started."

Wiping her hands together, she heads for the kitchen doorway but freezes when Charlie says, "Acorn."

"Hm?"

He turns his head to look over his shoulder at her. "Does it really not matter to you? If we stay in touch?"

"I've enjoyed our time together, Charlie. But if we do this . . . I truly don't need anything in return. Not even your friendship." The smile on Gretchen's face feels more wistful than she intended, which she's certain he'll notice conflicts with her matter-of-fact tone. So she continues out of the kitchen, slips on her rain boots, and heads out into the crisp spring morning—into the life she hopes Charlie will cede to her.

IT'S A LONG DAY OF REMINDING HERSELF THAT SHE'LL BE okay, regardless of what Charlie chooses. If she has to go back to DC and pick up her spirit medium business where she left off, she certainly could. Her clients have been sending her emails and leaving messages inquiring when they might be able to book her services again since basically the day after she left. Mrs. Easterly, the woman who looks like the human embodiment of the luxury goods opportunity shop in Georgetown, has left three messages requesting Gretchen make another attempt at contacting her late husband. A few of her most ardent customers have even suggested they'd be happy to pay a premium in order to be the first on her schedule when she returns. So yes, she'll manage if she needs to return to her previous life. She can scrape together enough of an income until she figures out how to transition into something less morally fraught. Because she's no longer particularly interested in her previous line of work as a long-term plan.

But she'll be okay.

She's had a lot of practice being okay.

And if she gets to stay at Gilded Creek, she'll still lose Charlie, but at least she'll have Everett. And Lori, whom she could see herself growing closer with over time (especially once she tells the older woman that she can actually talk to the farm's resident spirit). There's even Hannah at the Leesburg farmers market, who Gretchen thinks could maybe turn into a friend, once the jealousy she feels isn't quite as sharp. And there are the goats she's learned to enjoy caring for, and the barn cats she likes to pet, and the dogs she's still nervous around but appreciates, and the birds in the trees, and the tadpoles in the creek, and who-knows-what-else come summer when this place will surely explode with color and sound. She looks toward the bright, overgrown woods bordering the north of the property that the goats will probably have cleared by mid-spring, and the low, rolling mountains farther in the distance. She imagines it all crimson and amber and copper in the autumn. Snow-dusted in the winter. That first year here would be spectacular and surprising, discovering the landscape in all of the seasons. Then it would become a comfort—reliable in a way she's never truly known before. She tells herself that staying here will be enough. It will be enough to ease this ache in her chest. To quiet the whispering voice that tells her the yearning she has isn't for a place, but a person.

She finishes up her daily chores as the sun begins to set. Everything's turned golden—gilded, even—and ethereal. She decides not to head to the farmhouse just yet. Besides, Charlie's due to deliver his verdict soon; avoiding him for a little while longer might be cowardly, but she's never claimed to be particularly brave, so whatever.

"I think I'm going to go for a walk. Do you want to come along?" she asks Everett. He's been hanging around for the last hour, attempting to rank his favorite *Night Court* characters (Harry first, of course, but he can't settle on the rest of the order). His chatter is even more incessant, more frantic than usual, as if he too is nervous about what Charlie will decide.

The ghost glances back at the house, where a light shines in the living room window. "Nah, Charlie's home. Maybe he'll put *Jeopardy!* on."

"I don't know why you like watching that when you know almost none of the answers."

"I *learn things*, Gretchen, gosh. Don't ridicule me for trying to better myself."

She rolls her eyes, then blows him a kiss. He blows her one back and heads for the farmhouse, two of the barn cats following close behind, sensing if not seeing him.

Gretchen considers going down to the creek, beneath the willow tree, but her heart can't handle it right now. Instead, she walks up the driveway until she reaches the old seed drill. Its flowers sway slightly in the light evening breeze. It's tempting to get stuck thinking about Charlie here too, to get philosophical about how their relationship is like this—an apparent blight that turned into something beautiful practically overnight. But Gretchen knows that if she's going to live here for the rest of her life, she needs to break herself of the habit of thinking that way, and quickly, or she'll lose herself in missing him. So she pulls out her phone and takes a few photos until she gets one she's happy with. She posts it on the farm's Instagram account, which she's pleased to see has gained more followers since Saturday's goat yoga event, and writes a caption about how beautiful sunsets are a farmer's reward for hard work and long days that she knows will go over well with city people who romanticize living in the country.

She ambles back to the house, but again hesitates. Instead of entering, she sits on the stairs leading up to the porch. *Like I did with Charlie after Everett pushed me.* So much for not connecting everything back to Charlie.

Gretchen isn't sure how long she sits there on the steps, but it must be a while because it's now fully dark, stars spread thick over the clear night sky like spilled powder. Considering how late it likely is, she isn't surprised when she hears the front door open behind her.

"You planning on coming in soon? It's getting cold."

"Yeah. Soon," she answers.

There's a soft grunt as Charlie lowers himself to the ground behind her, scooting forward until he's pressed against her back and the insides of his legs hug the outside of hers. His warmth surrounds her, and she can't resist—she leans against him, gives in to his gravitational pull.

And Charlie allows it. At least at first. Then something changes, his body going tense in all of the places Gretchen feels the contact. She thinks he'll stand, put distance between them. Instead, he slowly draws his right index finger from her wrist up her forearm until he reaches the slightly too-long sleeve of her T-shirt. He hesitates there for a moment before reaching for the buckle of her overalls and disconnecting the strap from the bib. His hand slides inside and cups her breast.

"Yes," Gretchen finds herself whispering, although he hasn't actually asked a question.

In response, Charlie unfastens the other side of the overalls, allowing him access to her entire chest. After teasing her through the cotton of her T-shirt and the light padding of her bra, he untucks her shirt and reaches under it for more direct contact. She twists her head, desperate to find his lips, to kiss him, but he turns his face away.

Is he . . . angry with me?

"Charlie?"

He doesn't respond, only undoes the two side buttons at her hip and drifts one hand lower until it's inside her overalls, playing over the front of the ridiculously unsexy but comfortable under-wear he bought for her. Gretchen's willpower would be useless right now even if she wanted to engage it. She tilts her hips as much as she can while sitting on the step, trying to urge the contact he's teasing.

"Charlie," she repeats, this time less a question and more a desperate plea.

"You want this?" His voice is deep, calm, a vibration in her ear. It has that intensity that signals he's furious with her, and it's unexpected, startling, even.

Her curiosity and concern battle with an intense and exponentially increasing need for release. The latter wins out as soon as his fingers dip under her waistband, and she gasps out her assent; she doesn't think she'll ever be *that* good of a person, no matter how much she attempts to reform.

She nearly sobs when he finally touches her where she needs him. Her arm reaches up, circling his neck in some desperate subconscious attempt to ground herself in the moment, ensure she doesn't float away on the sensations he sends throughout her body. Then he buries two fingers inside her and she cries out as he curls them and strokes over the spot he's already learned will send her over the edge within a matter of seconds.

"I need you to remember this," he says, his other hand still cupping her breast. "I need to know you're going to crave this every single time you walk up these steps for the rest of your life."

The rest of my life. He's going to marry me. Gretchen never spent much time imagining the moment she would officially become engaged, which is probably for the best because she certainly never would have thought it would happen while she was being pleasured on a farmhouse porch.

"Tell me you're going to remember, Gretchen," he says. His tone has shifted, she notices, and it doesn't feel like he's ordering so much as begging her. As if the pleasure isn't even the point, just the only way he thinks he can make himself important to her. She hates to think that she hurt him when she said she didn't need anything from him, but it's for his own good. If she's going to leave Charlie better off than she found him, she cannot let whatever this is between them turn into something that keeps him tethered to a place he no longer wants to be.

That doesn't mean losing him won't haunt her, of course. But she's used to that by now.

"I will, I will," she answers, closing her eyes against the truth of it and against the release that's coming at her fast, a massive wave that will take her out no matter how much she braces herself for it. "I'll remember, always."

Charlie lets out a sigh, his breath hot on her neck. Relief? And then he rewards her for her honesty, because he understands that's what she's giving him, and this is the exchange rate. His fingers find a somehow even more perfect angle as they move into her again and again, and Gretchen lets out a long whine that crescendos into a moan as she comes, the stars behind her eyelids joining the ones in the sky when she finally blinks back into awareness.

His hand slides out from her underwear, from the overalls pooled around her waist. He presses a soft kiss to her temple that lingers longer than she expects. It feels distressingly like a good-bye. As he shifts backward and stands, Charlie's shelter is immediately replaced by the night's chill. Gretchen knows she should also get up, go inside, but she's too overwhelmed—by pleasure, by emotion—to move yet, even though she's shivering.

As her brain begins to function fully again, she remembers Charlie's words. *The rest of your life.* "So we're . . . You've decided, then?"

"I'll pick up the marriage license Thursday, and we can go to DC on Friday to pack up your stuff and deal with any other business you have there. An ordained friend is going to stop by Saturday morning to do a quick ceremony. You can file the name-change paperwork by next week."

"Charlie—"

"Go inside before you freeze." And he stomps down the stairs and heads in the direction of the barn. Gretchen watches as he disappears into the darkness. *I did it. I convinced him. It's done.*

But the gotcha euphoria she expects never arrives. All she feels is empty.

35

WHILE CHARLIE DRIVES TO FREDERICK TO PROCURE THEIR
marriage license on Thursday afternoon, Gretchen is busy wrapping and rewrapping bloomy rind cheese until it meets Lori's exacting standards. At one point, she's scolded for her use of excess plastic wrap and told her job was to package the stuff, not make it look like Kathy Bates in *Fried Green Tomatoes*.

Has Charlie told Lori yet that he'll be leaving and that Gretchen will be taking over Gilded Creek? Probably not. It's unlikely Lori won't have opinions on the changes, and she isn't the type to keep them to herself. So this current, almost companionable silence points to her not knowing about their plan. Or, well, it's silence to Lori. Everett followed them here and has been talking about *The X-Files* for the past half hour, but Gretchen's gotten pretty good at blocking him out.

Not that it doesn't eventually get to her.

"Now, in the episode I watched before you got home, they almost kissed. Almost. But then it wasn't actually Mulder! You know who it was? Guess. Gretchen. Guess. *Guess*. All right, fine. I'll just tell you. It was a shape-shift—"

"Hey, so, what would you think about . . . me staying here awhile longer?" Gretchen tries, her voice a little too loud in order to drown out Everett. It's as good a time as any, she decides, to take Lori's pulse on the subject.

"Oh, so you'll talk to *her*," Everett says with a frown at the same time Lori shrugs and says, "Sure. Why not. You're helpful enough, I suppose."

Gretchen bows her head to hide her grin. That's actually extremely high praise coming from Lori. She's quite proud to have proven herself *helpful enough*.

"Besides," the older woman continues, "you and Charlie are an item, ain't ya? Figured you might wanna stick around."

Gretchen tries to laugh, as if the notion is absurd, but instead chokes. "I— We— No. We're not . . . we're not an item."

"Ha!" Everett barks.

Lori raises her eyebrows. "Does Charlie know that?" Her voice sounds a bit more foreboding than usual, like she's completely ready to move Gretchen to her shit list if need be.

"Yes. He's aware," she responds quickly. "It was, uh, a mutual decision."

"Hmm." Lori's hum overlaps with Everett's scoffed, "Yeah, sure it was."

"Now, what does that mean?" Gretchen asks both of them. She moves to put her hands on her hips but remembers she's wearing plastic gloves that aren't supposed to come into contact with her person. Instead, she stands with her arms awkwardly out to her sides, which isn't quite as successful at demonstrating her annoyance, but it's the best she can do.

Her defensiveness (or more likely her weird stance) gets a chuckle out of Lori. "It *means* that whatever is going on"—she catches the look Gretchen is shooting her way and placatingly adds—"or *not* going on between you is far from settled, whatever you may think, hon. I have a gift, remember? Sensitive to energy and whatnot. And the energy around you two is crackling."

Everett points to Lori. "Smart lady. I've always liked her."

Gretchen waits until the older woman is looking away, then points to the door and mouths, *Out*. Everett blows a raspberry at her but complies, leaving instead through the wall and—if his subsequent yelp is any indication—plummeting from the second story to the ground only to never actually hit it.

Lori tosses the ladle she was using into the sink and crosses her arms. "Look, I don't know what your deal is. You showed up one day dressed like some Stevie Nicks wannabe and suddenly Charlie's introducing you as an intern. That's, as my daughter would say, extremely sus. But whatever it is you're really doing here, it's clear that you and Charlie got it bad for each other. And take it from a grumpy ol' gal like me: You two are complete knuckleheads if you don't grab the opportunity to be happy when it's standing right in front of you." Before Gretchen responds, Lori holds up her hands. "I know, I know. None of my business. I'll shut my trap."

"No, I . . . I appreciate that you care enough to say something." Having someone meddle in her personal life like this is a new experience, for the most part, and it's weird how nice it feels to have someone insert themselves this way with her well-being in mind. Maybe this is what it would've been like to grow up with a mom.

Lori's laugh is like an owl hooting—a sound Gretchen has

grown quite acquainted with now that sleep has become somewhat elusive. "Oh, I don't *care*, hon. Not about you, at least." Her
smile tells Gretchen this isn't entirely true. "Charlie, though, he's
a good boy. He deserves happiness."

"Yes, he does," Gretchen agrees. Even though it will come at
the expense of hers. Her honesty with Charlie is contagious, she
supposes, because it's getting harder and harder to believe that
they're both getting what they need out of this arrangement. She
wants to live at Gilded Creek. Of course she does. She's spent the
past few days imagining the life she's going to build here, the quiet
routine of work and rest she wants to fall into as she settles in for
good. But the brushstrokes of the picture she's painting are still
too hard to ignore, distracting from the reality of it. As is the
empty spot in the scene where her heart wants to add a farmer in
a bright travesty of a sweater, and knows it can't if they're both
going to walk away from this with what they each truly deserve.

THE TRIP FROM THE MARYLAND COUNTRYSIDE INTO DC
takes almost two hours, thanks to Friday morning rush hour, but
it feels even longer. Ever since Charlie accepted Gretchen's proposal of a marriage of convenience the other day, an almost fu-
nereal mood has seeped into their (increasingly sparse) interactions.
Their only physical contact since he left her on the porch Monday
night was an accidental brush of their hands yesterday morning
when Gretchen gave Charlie a Post-it with her full legal name and
social security number for the license, which prompted him to
scowl and her to apologize.

"What is going on with you two?" Everett asked last night

when Charlie walked by Gretchen folding laundry in the living room without acknowledging her.

"What do you mean?"

"There's tension again, but it's definitely no longer bomb-dot-com tasty."

She shrugged. Years of keeping her problems to herself, recycling her emotions into cantrips she could use in her work, made it too difficult to articulate the intense feeling of loss nestled close to her heart. She knew, of course, that the whole point of this plan was that Charlie would leave. But she never expected to lose him before he even stepped off the property.

They've been silent inside the truck for so long that Gretchen startles when Charlie speaks at last. "So, uh, we should probably discuss the plan," he says.

Gretchen looks out the passenger-side window, pretending to check the side mirror. "What do you mean?"

"Like, when do you want me to go? Right after the ceremony, or . . ."

What about never? "Probably wait until the name change officially goes through, I guess. To be safe." She takes her hair out of its ponytail and redoes it as she talks. "I filled out all of the paperwork already, just have to submit it along with the license. I asked about processing time when I called yesterday, and they said it should be done within three days given the current queue."

"So we're looking at end of next week, then."

"Most likely." Gretchen wants to ask what he'll do after he leaves—if he'll go back to working on the tall ships for a short while or look into a library science degree or maybe pursue something else altogether. But it will be easier if she doesn't know. Then she won't be able to definitively picture where he is or who he's with or what he might be doing. She won't be able to miss *him* so much as the idea of him.

The way she misses everyone else she's ever cared about who left.

As he parks the truck in the space behind the duplex that holds Gretchen's spirit medium shop and apartment, she wonders what he'll think of her after seeing the behind-the-scenes of her life. Unless he's done thinking about her at all.

Without discussion, they agree to start with the apartment. Gretchen pulls out her keys, unfamiliar in her hands after nearly a month of never needing them, and unlocks the front door. Charlie, holding a bunch of flat boxes under his arm, follows her up the stairs to the two units on the second floor. She opens 1A and gestures for him to go on inside.

Since Yolanda agreed to handle selling off the furniture in both the shop and the apartment, Gretchen assumes this won't take all that long. Moving around a lot as a kid taught her not to accumulate too many belongings, and she's thankful now that she never broke that habit even after staying here for a few years. She supposes she no longer has to embrace minimalism now that she'll be living at Gilded Creek for the rest of her life. Maybe she should start collecting something as a way to celebrate her newfound permanence. Something extremely inconvenient to move, like geodes or antique doorstops.

"This should be quick," she says, looking around the sparse space. "Yolanda's already taken her stuff, so anything left that isn't furniture can go in a box. Can you cover the kitchen and living room? I'll work on my bedroom. Oh, and we should take the TV. I'll put it in the guest room for Everett."

The evidence that Gretchen ever lived here at all takes less than twenty minutes to collect into three large boxes.

After stacking the contents of her apartment in the truck's back seat, they head downstairs to the small basement space from which she ran her spirit medium business. The lingering scent of incense makes Charlie sneeze as soon as he walks inside, and he almost drops the next batch of flat boxes he's carrying.

"I'll take care of the back room," she says.

Charlie gestures to a bunch of crystals laid out on a side table. "Do I need to do anything special with those? Wrap them up or . . . ?"

She can't help but smile at how seriously he's taking something she told him she doesn't actually believe in. "They're just rocks I bought in bulk on Amazon, babe. Throw 'em in a box."

As she parts the curtain to the tiny back room, there's a loud *kathunk* followed by several smaller *kathunks*, which she assumes is Charlie sweeping the entire contents of the table into a box in one go.

In this closet where she ate so many Cup Noodles over the years, Gretchen makes for the plastic case that holds her important documents (she might be a bullshit artist, but her business's official recordkeeping has always been *meticulous*), then works her way through the assortment of cleaning supplies, papers, and bric-a-brac on the shelves. She saves the part that holds the unopened envelope she left behind for last. But she won't be able to avoid it forever.

Just like she won't be able to avoid her father. Moving to Gilded Creek will give her time—he'll have to track her down all over again. But he will. She knows he will.

Except now, when he shows up, he can't take anything away from her. She's giving it all up on her own.

Gretchen retrieves the letter from the pile, slips a finger under the edge of the seal, ready to tear—

"Almost done in here." Charlie's voice startles her into tossing the envelope Frisbee-style into the nearest box. *Another time*, she tells herself, flexing her fingers in an attempt to calm her nerves. In all honesty, she's glad for an excuse to further delay opening it.

They finish packing, the shop transformed from velvet enrobed and dimly lit to ivory walled and sparse. Maybe the next renter will be a lawyer or a one-person nonprofit. Or one of those optometrists who rent out office space in residential buildings, making your visit feel somewhat like going to a random elderly man's run-down house to try on glasses.

"I think that's everything," Charlie says, coming back in from his latest trip to the truck. "You ready to head out?"

Gretchen glances around the space one more time, both feeling her connection to it and barely recognizing it. *I grew a lot here. But now I've outgrown it.*

"Yeah. I'm ready."

On the way out of the building, they run into the landlord, Mr. Smolak. Gretchen might not recognize him, having met him only twice in person previously, except that it's hard to forget a man who looks like if John Waters had a mortician twin brother.

"Mr. Smolak," she says, flashing one of her sweetest smiles at the pencil mustache resting on his upper lip. "So good to see you."

"Likewise," he says without even a hint of sincerity. He looks at his watch. "You're moved out?"

"We are. Other than the furniture, which my roommate will be taking care of over the next few days, everything's cleared."

"Excellent, excellent."

"Have you found a new tenant?" she asks, part of her simply wanting to make conversation and another genuinely interested in the fate of the place where she lived and worked for so long.

"Not yet, but there's a lot of demand. One gentleman's called nearly every day to see if the space is available to show yet."

"Oh?" Gretchen asks. "He wants to rent the basement?" She swallows her growing suspicion.

"Basement and apartment, like you. Seems really interested in how you had everything set up. Even asked for your contact info so he could ask some questions."

"Did you give it to him?" She can't hide the panic in her voice, and Charlie notices. His brows narrow and his mouth goes tight, concern clear on his face.

Mr. Smolak shakes his head. "Nah. I've got plenty of other interest, people practically begging me for the spaces. Felt like the guy was asking me to jump through hoops to get him to rent, and I didn't appreciate it. I don't have time for high-maintenance tenants." He looks at the watch on his wrist as if it's meant to emphasize the point.

"We need to be getting on the road," Gretchen says, managing to keep her smile in place despite the little butterfly wings of panic flitting around her chest. "I'll send you my new address for the security deposit refund."

She continues toward the building's back door, pulse pounding in her head. Her father. Her father was trying to find out where she'd gone. Weasel his way back into her life with more than just a letter. A deep breath reminds her she doesn't have anything to worry about; everything she has now—this new life she's building—she earned with honesty and hard work. She's made herself not only useful, but essential. The only person who could take that away is looking at her with such concern that she wants to throw herself into his arms and weep.

"Acorn?" Charlie asks. He moves to put his hand on her arm, then stops himself and tucks it into his pocket.

She smiles and shakes her head. "Let's just go home."

36

THAT NIGHT, GRETCHEN SITS AT THE KITCHEN TABLE AND
sorts through the boxes, organizing the contents into things she
wants to keep, things she'll probably donate eventually, and
things to store in the attic. The letter sits right at the top of the
next box she opens. After learning that Ned was so desperate to
find her that he tried to get her information from Mr. Smolak,
her initial panic has eased into something more like curiosity. If
Gretchen's changed so much in the last month, how much could
her father have possibly changed over several years? What if the
letter isn't another rebuke but an apology? She picks it up and
slides her fingernail under the corner of the envelope's flap once
again, then loses her courage and tosses it back on the table in
front of her.

"What's that?"

Her head shoots up at Charlie's voice. "Nothing," she says
reflexively, covering the envelope with both hands. As if that's
not the most suspicious thing she could possibly do.

He studies her for a moment, even though it must be extremely obvious to him that she's lying, and shakes his head. "I guess it doesn't matter anymore," he says quietly as he turns in the doorway to leave.

The unspoken part of that sentence, Gretchen is certain, is: *if you tell me the truth.* Over the last few days, she thought she couldn't feel any worse. And yet! More air gusts out of her, deflating her further.

"Charlie, wait." Her chair skids out behind her as Gretchen leaps up and goes to him. She grabs his hand. They both stare at her fingers wrapped around his palm as if equally startled by the texture of skin on skin. "It's a letter from my father. It arrived the day before I left." She replaces her hand with the envelope.

He looks it over, as if searching it for clues. "You haven't opened it."

"I thought there wasn't a point, that I already knew what it said. But now I'm wondering if maybe it could say something different." She stares at him until he meets her eyes. Something tells her that this is her last chance to show Charlie she can be real with him, and she wants more than anything to do that for him. And for her. "I don't know. I don't know which would be harder."

"Well, would it change anything?" he asks, his voice soft. "Whatever that letter says, would you want your dad in your life again?"

"No." The one good thing that will come of losing Charlie is the opportunity for her to stay at Gilded Creek, to have a fresh start here. Her father, no matter how much potentially reformed, is part of her past. A past she's more than ready to leave behind.

Charlie takes a step forward and hands the envelope back to

her, their hands brushing gratuitously in the process, as if Gretchen's touch opened the floodgates to these little bursts of micro-contact. She turns away, clutching the letter, staring at the handwriting that spells out the name she now goes by. It feels like it was written with sarcasm instead of ink. *Oh, too good to be an Eichorn now, hm?*

And yeah, maybe she is too good for the Eichorn name if it represents what her father stands for (or, at least, stood for)—lying, cheating, getting his no matter the cost. She became Gretchen Acorn in order to create distance during the drama of the trial, but the alias also allowed her to be her own person. To draw her own lines, ones she could feel good about. Now she's going to become a Waybill. Another opportunity to remake herself into the person she *wants* to be, instead of the one her father molded her into.

Gretchen goes back to the table and the pile of things she plans to keep. A lighter sits beside a box of incense from her studio. She takes it and the envelope over to the big farmhouse sink. But she can't seem to get the lighter to light, her thumb fumbling over the mechanism with each attempt. Then Charlie is there, behind her. He gently takes it from her hand and clicks the flame alive.

"Wait!" she hears herself say.

The flame goes out.

Gretchen stares down at the envelope. "Do you . . . want to read it first?"

"Do you?"

"No, no. Definitely . . . definitely not. I just . . . If this letter is what I think it might be, my father isn't going to pull any punches. He's going to be blunt about who I am. About the things I've done. And you deserve to know. We aren't going to be *married* married, but you should still know. If you want to."

"Why would I care?" he asks. But his voice holds no harshness. "Why would I care what your father has to say about anything when I already know you, Acorn?" The hand that isn't holding the lighter comes up to tuck her hair behind her ear. "I already know that you pick the peas out of your vegetable soup, and you don't know how to whistle." Their eyes lock in the reflection of the window above the sink, the darkness outside making it almost mirrorlike. "That you take ridiculously long showers no matter how many times I remind you we're on well water. I know that you're still a little nervous around the dogs, but that you've really taken to the cats. That you sing goofy made-up songs to the goats when you think no one can hear you, and that you've started bringing them almonds after lunch every day." His voice goes quieter as he bends toward her ear. "That you always bite your bottom lip right when you're about to come."

Gretchen swallows, heat flooding her as she takes in the words. "Do I?"

"You do," he whispers. "And I know that you care intensely about people, that you hate to see anyone suffer when there's something you can do about it."

"We don't have to pretend I'm a good person, Charlie," she says, looking away, his eyes in their reflection seeing too much.

"How could you think— Jesus, you're not a good person, Acorn, you're the *best* person. You could have easily walked away from all of this and left me to die, but you didn't. You refused to give up on this place. You refused to give up on me." Out of her peripheral vision, Gretchen can see that Charlie's focus is still entirely on her face, watching her as he speaks. "You have such a big heart.

It isn't your fault that your father exploited that from the moment you were born. That he taught you how to wield it to benefit him."

"But I still decided to do the things I did. Maybe not as a child, but I was in my twenties by the time I stopped working with him. I knew better, and I conned people anyway. And I really fucking enjoyed it. You don't need to pretend I'm some sort of saint, or a . . . a *victim*."

After a moment's pause, Charlie replies, "No, you're certainly neither of those. But the part that matters is that you stopped. As soon as you understood just how much you were hurting people, you stopped, even though it meant losing the only life you knew. And you found a way to use the tools you were given to make people's lives better. You have consistently tried to find your way to what is right, Gretchen. You have given up *so much* to do that. You *are* giving up so much. That's what I know, and I don't give a fuck what your asshole father has to say about any of it."

At this, she turns her head. Her cheek brushes against his jaw and she closes her eyes, savoring the wiry softness of his beard on her skin. Possibly for the last time. *At this point*, she thinks, *almost everything could be for the last time.*

"Okay," she says. "Yeah. Okay."

Charlie straightens behind her, breaking the contact, and flips on the lighter again. Gretchen holds the envelope in the flame until it catches, then lays it in the basin of the sink. She knows, due to a misadventure while cooking a frozen pizza last week, exactly how much smoke will trigger the fire alarm in the hallway. So once the paper is curled and black, she turns on the faucet and douses it. The soggy mess sits there like the world's largest and most disgusting spitball.

She turns around and is surprised to find Charlie still standing so close; she thought he would have moved back after lighting the envelope. Cautiously, she leans forward until her forehead rests against his shoulder. He doesn't touch her in response, but he doesn't step away either. "He'll find me again," she says. "Eventually."

"How?"

"Oh, it'll be super easy. He'll find the marriage license within a week. Won't be hard for him to do the research from there, uncover your connection to Gilded Creek, realize I'm living here. I'm good at that kind of thing, but my father is next-level. He would've made a hell of a private investigator had he ever wanted to go straight."

Charlie's silence prompts Gretchen to peek up at him. She finds him frowning down at her.

"It's okay. He'd never hurt me. Not physically. And I could always sic the dogs on him. You know how absolutely vicious they are."

The corner of her mouth kicks up, matching his. Both probably thinking about Clyde snoozing in the sun the other afternoon, barely reacting as baby goats climbed and jumped all over and around him.

Charlie's hand hovers momentarily before it settles on her upper arm, his thumb brushing over her skin. "I don't want—" He cuts himself off and changes direction. *What was he going to say?* "I don't feel great about you being here alone."

"I won't be alone," she says without a moment of hesitation. This is, of course, the mantra she's used to reassure herself over and over the last few days. "I'll have Everett. He almost killed someone once, by the way. I'm sure he'd be willing to give it another shot."

The joke falls painfully flat. Charlie stares at Gretchen with something in his eyes that she can't quite identify. She suspects whatever is behind it isn't particularly complicated, just too unfamiliar for her to parse. Because no one has ever once in her life looked at her quite like this.

"You don't need to worry about me," she says, sliding her fingertips into the short hairs of his beard. He tenses, then permits himself to relax into her touch. "Really, Charlie. I promise I'll be okay."

"But what if I'm not?" he whispers.

"What do you mean?"

Instead of answering, he lowers his mouth to hers.

Gretchen always wondered what it would feel like to return somewhere and feel like she was home. Like she belonged to a place and it belonged to her. She thought that she was close to feeling that way about the farm. But when Charlie kisses her, she realizes that it's this. *This* is the feeling she's wondered about her whole life. *This* is what it feels like to be home at last.

And it's yet another place she can't stay.

She breaks the kiss and takes a step backward, then another, until there's nothing between them but empty space. Then Gretchen turns and runs for the stairs.

SHE ISN'T SURE HOW LONG SHE'S BEEN SOBBING INTO HER pillow. But when she finally turns her head to gasp for air, Everett is lying in the bed beside her.

"What are you doing here?" she asks. Her voice stumbles as

she attempts to work through the congestion her tears have generated, so it mostly sounds wet instead of annoyed as she intended.

Everett looks down at himself, then around. "Um. Laying? Or is it lying? I've never understood that."

"You aren't supposed to come into my room without asking first."

"I did ask first. I said, 'Knock, knock, can I come in?' like usual, and then I did it again, and then I said, 'Gretchen, sweetheart, you're gonna drown in your tears if you don't ease up.' And you didn't answer, so I thought maybe you *did* drown, so I—"

Annoyingly, the reminder that she was sobbing prompts another round of it.

"Oh, Gretch, please don't cry anymore," Everett says. A coolness over her back makes Gretchen suspect he's hovering a hand over the spot in a futile attempt to soothe her. "It makes you so splotchy."

She manages to give him a withering look through her swollen eyelids.

"Tell me what's wrong. What's eating you? Is it cold feet? Are you rethinking this whole marriage thing?" He sounds almost hopeful. "You don't have to go through with it, you know. It's Charlie's burden, and I'm sure he won't hold it against you if you don't want to take it on—"

"It isn't that. Not really."

Everett sits up and crosses his legs. "Then what? I'm here for you. You can talk to me."

Gretchen studies him. There's genuine compassion in his eyes, something close to what she saw in Charlie's in the kitchen earlier (though without the underlying heat). She rises to sit facing

Everett and buries her face in her hands. "I love him too much. I love him and that's why he has to leave."

"Oh. Wow. Okay. I mean, I knew you were stuck on the guy, but I didn't realize it was so serious," he says after a moment.

"I didn't either, but . . . it is. I know that love means giving him his freedom, and I thought I could be selfless enough to do that, but I'm not sure now. How am I going to live here without him? I know I don't deserve to keep him, but I *want* to. I want to so fucking bad." Her sobs make her shoulders heave, her whole body shake.

"Shh, shh." Everett inches slightly closer to her, careful not to let their knees bump. "I . . . I wish I could hug you. I wish I could do something, anything . . ." He trails off into a silence that lasts uncharacteristically long enough to pierce through Gretchen's sorrow as something notable. She wipes her eyes with her arm as she looks up, and catches an odd expression on his ultra-pale face.

"Gretchen, I have to tell you something," he says at last, his voice quiet and his gaze dropping down toward the bed. "It isn't forever."

Something about the way he says it doesn't sound as if he means, like, this too shall pass. "What?" she asks. But her Eichorn DNA has already provided an explanation; she recognizes Everett's expression now as the same one she must have worn when she decided to tell Charlie the truth.

"It isn't forever," Everett repeats. "The curse. It'll expire. In a few more months, a year or two tops, you can leave. Find Charlie if you want. It's not . . . You don't need to be upset anymore."

As the ghost's words fully register, it's like one of those extremely sharp knives they advertise late at night on TV, slicing through her sadness so cleanly her tears abruptly stop. "I don't need to be upset."

"No, doll. Just . . . just patient." He smiles nervously.

"Patient," she repeats. "Because it isn't forever. The curse has an expiration date."

"Yep," he says, the smile turning into an even more nervous grimace as he does half-hearted jazz hands. "Surpriiiise."

"Which means you've been lying to me. Since the moment we first met."

Everett abandons his attempt at lightheartedness as he notes her aggrieved expression. "Well. Yes." He swallows hard. "But . . . good acting, right?"

37

THERE'S A LONG PAUSE BEFORE GRETCHEN CAN GET A word out again. But the look she gives him speaks volumes—practically an encyclopedia of her fury. He doesn't even need help turning the pages.

Everett puts his hands up and backs away, falling off the bed. From where he's splayed out a few inches over the floorboards, he says in a hurry, "Before you get too sore, let me explain."

"Oh yes, you definitely have some explaining to do."

"Was that supposed to be an *I Love Lucy* reference?"

"No."

"Good, because it sounded absolutely nothing like Desi Arnaz."

"Everett Jebediah Waybill," she says through her teeth.

"It's kinda funny, actually . . ." He drums his fingers on his lips. "That I conned a con artist. You can see . . . how that's funny . . . right?"

"No. No, I don't currently see the humor in the fact that you . . ." Overwhelmed by the rage bubbling up inside her, Gretchen can't find a way to articulate the full scope of his offense, and settles on a gritted-out, understated, *"lied to me."*

"It's not like I meant to! Or, I mean, I guess I did. I just never expected—"

"Jesus, Everett. Is there even a curse at all?" she asks, flinging her arm out.

He dodges it, as if sensing that an inadvertent bone chill is not going to make Gretchen any calmer. "Yes! Everything else I told you was true. Charlie and I are indeed both in quite a jam here, it's just not as . . . eternal as I led you to believe. The real terms of the curse are that if I can keep the Waybills at Gilded Creek for a hundred years, then I get to leave. If I don't, I'm stuck here for-ever. I think. Probably." He smiles again, this time going for ador-ably contrite.

She seethes. "And Charlie?"

"He's still in danger. If he left now without your whole mar-riage plan, he and I'd *both* be stuck here forever. But after the hundred-year anniversary, as long as a Waybill is still around, the curse will be lifted. Then he'll be free to do as he pleases. Or you will, I guess, if you still want to take his place."

"Fucking hell, Everett. Why didn't you tell me that from the beginning?! You don't think 'Hey, Charlie, you just gotta hold off another few months and then you can do whatever you want' wouldn't have been an easier sell than *the rest of his life?*"

"Well, you know how wobbly time is for me. I figured I must be coming up on a century of being dead, but from one moment to the next I never know exactly how close to the hundredth an-niversary we are. When Charlie put the farm up for sale, I thought I could simply scare off prospective buyers for a bit, and then, when it was time, I would go Up, he would finally sell, it would all be hunky-dory. But he got a lot of interest in the place as soon as he put it on the market, and I couldn't be certain if we were talking days or months or even years." His head pops up, eyes bright. "Say, could we get a calendar? To hang on the icebox? You could cross it off at the end of each day. I bet that would be helpful."

"No," Gretchen snaps.

"Right," Everett continues, realizing the calendar idea isn't up for further discussion at the moment. "Anyway, so when you came along, and you could see me—well, you were a gift I never even thought I might receive. I . . . I couldn't just let you walk away. Which, must I remind you, you were very eager to do."

"That still doesn't explain why you lied. Why you didn't just tell me from the beginning that the curse would expire and all I had to convince Charlie of was to wait it out."

Everett lifts one shoulder. "I needed you to take things seriously, and maybe I got a little caught up in the drama. And then it sort of . . . snowballed? Because we became friends, and it started to seem like maybe you'd *want* to stick around, or at least keep coming by on occasion, and how was I supposed to tell you then?"

"How about 'Hey, Gretchen, you've been planning the rest of your time on this mortal plane based on *a lie*'?" She throws out her arms again in anger.

He swiftly dodges once more, then squints as if not sure what part of this she isn't getting. "But then you would've been mad at me."

"*And I'm not now?*" she shouts.

"Come on, it's not like you've never lied about stuff! Shouldn't you . . . what's that saying? Respect the hustle?"

"No, I absolutely should not 'respect the hustle'!" Except . . .

she sort of almost does. She doesn't *like* it, of course, but looking back, she's impressed by the way Everett stuck to his story, never letting on that he was hiding something from her. In retrospect, there were tells, but nothing that ever led her to suspect . . . And it's not as if she truly has the moral authority to be mad about his deception, does she?

People in glass houses, et cetera, et cetera.

Gretchen once again cradles her head in her hands. "I cannot believe this," she mutters. "You were going to let me and Charlie get *married*. You were going to let me live here without the person I love, only to, what? Poof away one day and never return? And then I would have been stuck here, alone, wondering what happened to you, still believing I'd die if I left?"

That's the crux of her anger, she realizes. Not that he lied, but that Everett was going to leave her. That he had every intention of abandoning her to a life of loneliness, knowing his presence—his friendship—was the one thing she felt she could count on remaining steady.

"I did try to talk you out of it. A couple of times, actually. Which I should get credit for, because I really do want you to stay," Everett says. "I also feel the need to point out that I did wind up telling you the truth."

"The day before I was going to enter into a legal institution in order to save someone who doesn't even need saving if we just wait it out!" Gretchen takes a few deep breaths, calming herself. He cut it close, sure, but Everett did ultimately confess. She knows from experience how much courage that takes. Still, his deceiving her has shattered everything she thought she knew about him. About their friendship.

"What about us being friends, Everett? Is that a lie too?"

"Hey. No. How could you even ask that?" He moves in front of Gretchen. "That was all the *truth*. Cross my heart and hope to— Well, just trust me, okay? You really are the best friend I've had in my entire, well, life and afterlife combined. That was my downfall, I suppose. I started to care about you, and you started to care about me. I've never had that before, with anyone. So when I saw how much you were hurting, I thought, 'Gosh, I would do anything to stop her pain,' especially since I felt a *teeeeeensy* bit responsible for it. I didn't want to see you hurting anymore because of something I did. So I knew I had to tell you." He pauses. "Geez. It was really easier not having all these emotions. I didn't realize how *uncomfortable* they can be. Like wearing a slightly too small union suit."

There's a beat of silence before he adds, "I do feel some remorse about misleading you. But I can't be truly sorry, because it meant we got to spend this last month together. And I'd like to think you got something out of being here. So maybe . . . you're welcome?" he says, flashing a nervous smile.

"Ha, yeah, no. I'm not . . . *We* are not cool, babe."

Everett's smile falls. "Oh, come on! Haven't you ever heard that you're not supposed to hate the player, you're supposed to hate the game?"

"Where did *you* hear that?" She crosses her arms. Not to close herself off but to hold everything in. Because she's angry, so angry, but she's also . . . kind of touched. Like, in a really fucked-up way, of course. It's just that this is so opposite of everything that's ever happened to her—someone *wanting* her to stay to the point of actually conning her into it. Anger is still the main thing Gretchen is feeling, but now it's tinged with these bright edges, like the sun peeking out from behind a storm cloud. "Look." She sighs. "One day, possibly, I will be able to forgive you. Because you might be a devious little fucker, but so am I. Or I was. So I can't hold it against you forever, as tempting as that might be."

The corner of his mouth lifts, and he's about to say something—probably a smart-ass comment about how he won't actually be around forever anyway—but Gretchen cuts him off. "You were a friend to me when I needed one. But whether I'll be ready to forgive you before you're gone, I don't know." She pauses. "When are you gone, anyway?"

"I died December fifth, 1924," he says. "So December fifth, 2024. That's . . . soonish? It's what—like, May 2023?"

"It's April twenty-sixth, 2024. We've got about seven months." She pauses, wondering if it makes it better or worse that he was intending to let his deception go on for literal years if that's what it took.

"Are you still going to go through with the marriage thing?" Everett asks after a moment.

"I don't know," she says. There's currently a lot she doesn't know. Her brain feels like it's filled with scrambled eggs. "I have to say, it's awfully tempting to marry Charlie, send him on his way, and then leave myself, knowing it would mean you're stuck here for eternity. I think that would really serve you right."

"But then you'd be dead and have to stay here too." He tilts his head and smiles, as if declaring a checkmate.

"Which is why I'm not going to do that. Because I'm not willing to sign up for an eternity with you. Plus, if I'm alive, it'll be much easier to make the rest of your afterlife a living hell."

Everett scoffs. "How do you plan on . . ."

His voice disappears as Gretchen strolls over to the TV she brought back from DC, now sitting on the dresser. She reaches for the plug and pulls it out of the wall. "Downstairs too," she says.

"Oh," he says, eyes wide and his blue-white Adam's apple bobbing.

"Now, if you'll excuse me," she says, "I need to go figure out what the fuck to do now."

38

THIS IS SUCH AN ABSOLUTE MESS, GRETCHEN THINKS AS she stabs a stick into the ground beneath the willow tree. Charlie's ordained friend is supposed to arrive in less than twelve hours to marry them. And now she's going to have to go tell Charlie that it's not necessary after all, he just needs to hang out until December and then he's good to go. Then Gretchen will . . . Well, she's not sure what she'll do, since she's already given up her apartment and emailed all of her clients in DC to let them know she was retiring from the business.

She pulls the stick toward her, annoyed that it doesn't move more than a fraction of an inch. It would have made sense to find a shovel, probably, but she was too discombobulated as she left the house to think that far ahead. At least the bag of sunflower seeds was right where she remembered seeing them the other day.

She could, of course, reinvent herself in a new city, set up shop there. Except the idea of that holds no appeal whatsoever. Maybe she could still give Charlie the money to keep him afloat, then go try to work on another farm somewhere. Although she suspects that no other farm will feel the way this one does (or be so willing to accommodate her inability to lift more than twenty-five pounds).

Giving up on digging with the stick, she pokes a finger into the largest of the holes she's made and uses it to pry the earth away. Ah, much more efficient. Sunflowers grow to be pretty big, she thinks, so she presumes the hole also will need to be on the larger side.

As the cool, claylike soil buries itself beneath her fingernails, her mind returns to the problem at hand. What if . . . what if she doesn't tell Charlie about this new development at all? Does the change in timeline even matter? Why make him wait for his freedom when he could have it now? Then they could still get married. Gretchen could stay at Gilded Creek. She could reveal everything in seven months, after Everett is gone. Claim to be absolutely shocked that Everett misled her, or simply chalk it up to some strange nuance of the curse of which no one had been aware. Charlie could sell the farm then if she hasn't made it profitable, or even if she has. They could get divorced and sever the small thread of legality binding them together. But in the meantime, at least, she'd get to stay.

It's so tempting to lie. To ensure she'll still get the things she's put so much effort into telling herself will be enough. To give Charlie the freedom she promised him without delay. Her body buzzes with the thrill of it. One last con. Who would it hurt?

But then Gretchen imagines standing under this tree tomorrow morning—they never discussed it, but she's been picturing that this is where they would do their little perfunctory ceremony—beside her freshly planted sunflower field, and exchanging the very basic vows required by Maryland law to make Charlie her legal spouse, and . . .

Oh god, she can't do it. Gretchen's spent the last week telling herself that she's giving Charlie what he wants most—his freedom. Except that's never been what he's asked of her. All he's ever asked Gretchen to give him is the truth. How can she deny him that now? She can't foist freedom upon him in some twisted attempt to keep her own heart safe. She doesn't want to trick him into thinking that he never cared for her, or that she never cared for him.

The chilly late-April nighttime breeze flutters her sleeve. A jacket would also have been a good idea, but she left the house so flustered and angry and sad that she didn't even think to grab hers from the hook by the door. She claws again at the soil, determined to get this done. It's intended to be part of her grand gesture, although what she's gesturing toward she still isn't sure.

And then, suddenly, she is.

"I have to tell him everything," she says aloud. Everything. That's the scary part. Because if she's going to be honest, she'll need to tell him that she's in love with him. And then when he inevitably tells her to leave, or decides to leave himself, she won't be able to console herself with him not being aware that he was breaking her heart.

She thought that living at Gilded Creek without Charlie for the rest of her life was meant to be her punishment for all of her previous misdeeds. But maybe *this* is actually the punishment intended for her: to crack open her chest and hand her heart over to someone else to do with as he pleases. If she's going to do that, be so exposed, what does she have to gain by holding back? Why shouldn't she beg him to love her too? To be her partner in . . . well, not crime. But her partner in life? To ask him to please, please let her stay and see what they can make out of all this?

Movement out of the corner of her eye has her turning her head. Lori once said something about coyotes, and Gretchen doesn't know anything about their habits, but her heart races in anticipation of getting gobbled up. But as her eyes focus in the deepening dark, she sees that it's a person, that it's Charlie, making his way from the house to the willow. As he gets closer, she spots something thrown over his arm—the deformed sweater she stole from the attic.

"There you are," he says, ducking under the tree's low-hanging branches.

"Here I am," she answers, her voice barely above a whisper. Her heart, which slowed a bit when it realized it wasn't in immediate danger of becoming coyote food, speeds up again.

"What . . . are you . . . doing?" he asks, now close enough to see the small trench Gretchen has excavated beneath the tree.

"Planting." She tries to keep her tone casual, but the need to sniffle at the end of the word undercuts her efforts. "Sunflowers. I wanted to . . . needed to . . ." What had driven her to do this again? It's difficult to remember exactly what was going through her mind when she came out here, so frazzled by Everett's confession and what it meant for her and Charlie's plan. All she can recall is the strong, almost overwhelming urge to do something that might communicate to Charlie even a tiny sliver of the expansive affection that she feels. A parting gift, whether he decides to stay or go. "Because of Grandma Ellen," she concludes, even though she hasn't actually communicated a whole coherent thought.

"That's . . ." His smile is especially wonderful coated in the blue hue of the night. "Acorn, this isn't how—" Charlie's eyes land on the bag of seeds, and his words fall apart into laughter. "Where did you get those?" he asks.

Gretchen stares, unsure what's so funny. "The pantry."

He covers his mouth, trying to hide his amusement. "This is . . . this is very sweet," he says. "But it's . . . You aren't going to grow anything. Not with roasted seeds thrown into a single pit in the shade."

She looks at the five-by-three-by-six-inch hole she dug beneath the weeping willow, then at the dirt covering her hands to the wrist, then at the half-empty resealable bag of David Original seeds. She doesn't know much about planting anything, but she can now see how at least two or three of the choices she's made are probably not strictly correct.

Tears threaten to fall again as she stands. *I need to tell him. Now. Everything.* She takes a step closer. "Charlie, I—"

Her words are interrupted by his wrapping the sweater around her shoulders, tying it into a knot in the front. It's such a thoughtful gesture, so tender, that it takes her breath away, and the rest of her confession gets lost in her throat.

"And please stop going out at night without a sweater or a jacket or something." And the fact that he cares enough to lecture her undoes her further.

"Charlie, we need to talk," she says.

"Yes, we do," he agrees. "That's why I came to find you." Charlie sticks a hand into his hair, his fingers dragging through the golden waves tinged with the night's blue-blackness. His eyes won't meet hers. "I need to tell you I'm not marrying you tomorrow."

Oh. She figured that might be the case after she told him that the marriage wasn't necessary if he was willing to wait a few months before selling the farm. But that he's saying he isn't going to marry her now, before she's even told him about the reality of their circumstances . . . Well, that stings a little. "Oh. Okay. I . . . Okay. That's—"

"I've decided I want to stay at Gilded Creek."

She nods. He'll be glad to know that it won't have to be forever. "I underst—"

"No, you don't," he interrupts, sounding annoyed with her already. "Please, let me finish. I have a lot more to say."

Charlie takes a moment to turn his head, as if studying the land around them. When his eyes arrive back on Gretchen, he studies her the same way before speaking again. "When I was growing up, this place was so full of all the things I thought made a good life. A life I wanted for myself when I got older. But after my grandmother died, after my grandfather couldn't live here anymore, and I took over . . . it wasn't at all like I remembered. It was so hard, and it was . . . god, it was so fucking lonely. All of the happy memories I had turned bittersweet. I went from feeling like I belonged here to the farm becoming this thing that was constricting me, squeezing the life out of me. And along with the money troubles, I thought . . . I thought it was time to give up. Accept my failure and move on. That the life I thought I could have here didn't actually exist."

Charlie reaches out and adjusts the sweater around Gretchen's shoulders, smoothing out a stray piece of yarn. "But then you showed up."

Her eyes narrow and she tilts her head, requesting he continue.

"I told you once that the family part of this being a family business is what made me love it. Working with you, seeing you care so much about the farm's success, rising to every challenge, appreciating all of the beautiful parts of Gilded Creek I'd been taking for granted, it started to feel like it used to. I started to love the work again, love this place again. I felt like I belonged. Life got . . . better."

The tears she's been holding back fall from Gretchen's eyes, and she doesn't bother studying to see what kind they might be or how to use them. She wants her brain completely focused on the man in front of her as he parts his lips to continue speaking.

"I tried to tell myself it was just a coincidence. That it wasn't you making me feel that way, but . . . Acorn, I need to apologize. I've called you a liar. More than once. Demanded your honesty. But I haven't held myself to that same standard. I'm sorry that I haven't been truthful with you. Or with myself."

Oh god, Gretchen thinks. She doesn't think she can handle finding out Charlie has been keeping a secret too. "Really, you don't need—"

"You said you didn't want anything from me, not even my friendship. But I want something from you. And it isn't some ridiculous marriage of convenience." He looks down at his boots, as if he's shy. It reminds Gretchen of all the times he broke eye contact with her in those early days. All the times he blushed. Charlie slowly lifts his head and takes her hands in his, not caring that they're mud-caked. "The truth is this: I want to stay here. And I want you to stay with me. I want to work together every day. Sleep together every night. Plant a field of sunflowers together, one that will actually grow. I just want to be together for as long as we can. I want you to be my family. And even if it doesn't work out and I wind up stuck at Gilded Creek for the rest of my life, it'll have been worth it." He pauses and takes a deep, slow breath before continuing. "Loving you . . . loving you will always be worth it. And I do love you, Gretchen Acorn. I do."

Swallowing past the lump in her throat, Gretchen whispers, "Charlie . . ."

His eyes close as if she's dealt him a blow. "You don't want to stay with me."

The absurdity makes her let out an inappropriate bark of laughter. "No, I do! Oh my god, I do want to stay with you. And to be your partner, in every sense of the word. More than anything. But it won't be forever. Or it won't have to be forever. If you—if we—don't want."

"Sorry, I don't follow." And, really, how could he? Without context, this sounds like absolute nonsense. It goes against everything she's been telling him. But there's no suspicion in his expression. Nothing that indicates he won't believe everything she says, once she stops botching it. That's a relief. Such a relief.

"Everett lied," she says. "He told me the curse was eternal, but it's not. It's only until the hundredth anniversary of his death. Which is December fifth of this year. As long as you stay until then, he'll get to go Up, and you'll be free to leave."

"I— But why? Why did he . . ."

"At first, he figured exaggerating the curse's terms was the best way to get me to take it seriously, and then he kept rolling with it because it got me to stay. And because he kind of sucks, like as a person."

Charlie's grip on Gretchen's hands momentarily tightens. His jaw tenses. "So after all of this . . . I can . . . I can just leave whenever?"

"Yes. I mean no. Not whenever. According to Everett, leaving now would still mean death and spending eternity as a ghost. But anytime after December fifth should be fine."

"I . . . Holy shit." Charlie pulls away from her to rake his fingers through his hair again, no doubt transferring some dirt there in the process. "Gretchen."

"I know. I'm never letting him watch TV again." She pauses and kicks at the small pile of soil on the ground. "I'll understand if you . . . if this changes things and you don't need me—"

He shakes his head vehemently and says, "This does change things, but not that. I still need you to help me with the business. And . . . well, I also just need *you*." His hand comes to cup her cheek. "I will always need you, Acorn. And not for what you can do, but for who you are to me."

"I promise I'll try to be useful," she says, trying to make a joke of this desperate need to assure him this will be worth it. That he isn't making a mistake loving her.

"Why are you always talking about being useful, making yourself useful? Useful, useful, useful," he says, exhaling in amusement as the word starts sounding like nonsense with repetition. "I've never wanted you because you were useful, Gretchen. I want you because you're you."

The way he says it is so earnest that she can't find it in herself to doubt him. Gretchen bows her head, trying to hide the embarrassing wideness of her natural grin. "You were really willing to be stuck here for the rest of your life . . . for me?"

His responding smile drains some of the tension from his features. "I mean, I was hoping we would be able to make things work so that I wouldn't be in it by myself, but yes. When I stopped lying to myself about how I feel, I realized I don't want freedom half as much as I want you." He laughs. "Don't look at me that way. Weren't you willing to be stuck here for me too?"

Gretchen doesn't know how to do this, to love and be loved without ulterior motives. It's all so new and tenuous that she's terrified already that she'll break it. So when she kisses him, it's soft, gentle, almost cautious. As if sensing her trepidation, Charlie takes her face decisively in his hands and kisses her back with an intensity that says: *We can be rough with each other, imperfect and messy and ourselves, you don't need to be afraid of losing me.*

When they finally part and Gretchen's eyes flutter open, they connect not with hazel eyes but the blue ones directly over Charlie's shoulder.

"Oh, I do love a happily ever after." Everett sighs contentedly. "I suppose you could say that without me, you two never would have wound up together at all. Hmm, it's almost as if I did you a favor by lying . . . Almost like I left you off better than I found you . . . Something out of your own playbook, really. Which means you can't be too mad at me, Gretch, right? Right?"

Gretchen buries her face into Charlie's neck and groans even as a smile pulls at her mouth. It's going to be a long, long seven months.

EPILOGUE

SHE CAN'T GET OVER HOW QUIET IT IS.

That's the main thing Gretchen is having trouble getting used to. It's December twelfth—one week since Everett went Up—and she can't help but miss the ghost's incessant chatter. There was a time (or many times, actually) she would have given anything to relax on the porch with a hot cup of tea and hear nothing but the soft *meh*ing of the goats huddled in the barn, an occasional bark from one of the dogs, the distant rumble of traffic on the main road. But now, doing just that, her ears near-buzzing with the relative silence, she finds herself wishing Everett would appear and give her a rundown of his latest television obsession.

They weren't certain how it would all happen. Would it be right at midnight? Or in the afternoon, closer to when the newspaper article they found reported Everett's time of death? And would he simply disappear, like when he poofed into the Nowhere, or would he slowly fade until there was nothing left of him?

Around ten at night on December fourth, soon after she settled into bed with Charlie, he leaned over and kissed her, then whispered, "Go. You should be with him tonight." So Gretchen went into the guest room (which had once again become Everett's space now that she shared a bed with Charlie) and lay down beside him.

Gretchen thought about the weeks immediately following Everett's confession, and how her attempt to give him the silent treatment lasted barely four days before she started to miss his company. She hated that he'd done it, of course, but it was hard to keep her anger active. Especially when she so intimately understood both the loneliness that caused him to cling to the lie in the first place and the deep affection that caused him to abandon it. Things were back to normal between them, more or less, but the knowledge that this would be one of her last-ever conversations with him prompted Gretchen to say, "I've forgiven you, you know. For lying to me about the terms of the curse."

"Thank you." Everett hovered his hand over hers, just close enough to make her shiver. "I'm sorry I did it, you know. But I can't say I regret how it all turned out." He gently poked the small diamond engagement ring that once belonged to Ellen Waybill, taking great care to only allow his fingertip to go through the stone and not through to Gretchen's skin.

"All's well that ends well, I suppose," she said with a sigh. Another few beats of silence later, she asked, "Do you think Aunt Lucretia knew it would go down like this? That you'd need to become a better person on the way to keeping the Waybills here, and that was the real goal all along?"

Everett touched his chin, considering. "Nah," he said. "I think she just wanted me to suffer."

Gretchen chuckled, then turned to face him. "Are you scared?"

"No," he said immediately. "I'm . . . a bit sad, maybe? But not scared." A wistful smile, still a little crooked, spread across his face. "You know, when I died, they had a little service here at Gilded Creek before they buried me in the family graveyard. So of course I hung around, wanting to see how people were taking my untimely and tragic death. Wanting to watch sweet little Betsy Chandler shed tears over my grave, hear the stories the boys I used to go into town with to raise hell would tell about me. But no one came. No one. Except cousin George, of course, who I suppose felt obligated, and Aunt Lucretia, who smiled evilly the whole time. It hit me then that I wasn't a fella anyone was going to miss. Not really." He rolled his eyes, showing more of the cloudlike whites, and sniffled, though he hadn't had the biological capacity for tears in a very long time. "Listen to me, so maudlin! But I just wanted you to know that it means . . . well, it means *everything* to me, Gretchen, that this time, there's someone who might miss me."

A tear rolled down Gretchen's cheek. "Of course I'll miss you, Ev. You're a huge pain in the ass, and there have been times I have genuinely researched how to do an exorcism, but I love you. You know that I love you."

"I do know. And I love you too."

"Like a hot sister?" she asked with a laugh.

He smiled, then whispered, "Like a best friend."

Everett's reassuring chill eventually lulled Gretchen to sleep, and when she woke up sometime in the early hours of the morning, he was gone. She only realized later that it was a Thursday—perhaps a significant day of the week in the spirit world after all.

The sound of the front door opening and closing snaps her

out of her memories, and Gretchen whips her head around. Charlie steps out onto the porch, holding his own mug of tea in one hand and the shawl he knitted for Gretchen's birthday last month tucked under his arm. He places the mug atop the railing before carefully draping the soft lilac-colored fabric over her. It's not perfectly symmetrical, but his knitting has much improved since he made the Frankensweater—which Gretchen still wears to bed on occasion.

"Thank you," she says, smiling at him as he takes his usual spot beside her.

He shakes his head, feigning annoyance that she once again didn't dress appropriately for the weather. She's pretty sure he knows that she does it on purpose at this point, because she still gets a thrill from each little exasperated gesture that proves how much he cares. Love, she's found, is a lot like the gotcha euphoria she used to experience, but steadier. Reliable. Something she can hold on to for longer than one rapturous moment.

"You're missing Everett again," Charlie says. It's not a question. He can see it on her face. He's gotten even better at reading her with practice. Actually, he's so good at it now, she doesn't think she could keep something from him even if she put all of the power of her Eichorn DNA into it. And it's nice, so nice, to be known that well. To no longer have to hide anything.

"It's too quiet here without him."

Charlie takes a sip from his mug, probably disagreeing with her declaration, considering all of the bizarre one-sided conversations he no longer has to endure. "Enjoy it while it lasts," he says, then gestures with his chin toward the construction equipment in the property's far northeast corner. "They're pouring the foundation tomorrow."

It was Gretchen's idea to turn a portion of Gilded Creek Farm into a nonprofit. It was also her idea to approach Mrs. Van Alst with the proposal. She loved everything they wanted to do and promptly donated enough money to cover their start-up costs and then some. They broke ground on the Rachel Van Alst Education and Community Center shortly before Thanksgiving. In partnership with an organization that matched them with their new part-time farmhand, Raul, they're going to start hosting formerly incarcerated people interested in agricultural careers for paid seasonal internships. That's just the first step, though. Day camps for kids, cheesemaking classes, barn dances, local school visits with the goats—Gretchen and Charlie have big plans to make Gilded Creek Goat Farm a place that welcomes everyone where they are (and ideally leaves them a little better off than when they arrived).

"You could go somewhere, you know," Gretchen says, resting her elbows on the railing, mug cupped between her hands.

"I could," he agrees, not bothering to look at her.

"Move to Taipei. Make your living playing pool." Her game face isn't what it used to be, and she cracks a small smile, knowing he'll respond the way he has each time she's brought this up in the last few days, concocting different fantasy lives for him— part insecure, part joking, maybe part serious.

Charlie smiles as he turns, one side higher than the other, and Gretchen's heart breaks and mends simultaneously. "Well, Acorn, as fun as that sounds . . ." He wraps his arms around her from behind and rests his head against hers. "I'm already right where I belong."

Gretchen leans into him as she looks out over the land. The distant mountains, the now-dormant sunflower field that bloomed big and bright at the end of summer, Sleepy Jean and the rest of the herd browsing the pasture. It's such a perfect scene that she could almost mistake it for one of her old paintings. Too good to fully trust. But the warmth radiating in her heart (and her body, thanks to the shawl and Charlie's touch) reminds her that it's all real—no bullshit anywhere to be found.

ACKNOWLEDGMENTS

Much like this project as a whole, I planned to make this silly, but it turned out earnest instead. Whoops! Anyway . . .

First, this story—and I, myself—have benefitted immensely from the expertise of my incredible editor, Sareer Khader. The pride I've grown to feel in this book is all the result of your support and guidance, Sareer, and I truly cannot thank you enough. I also must thank Jessica Mangicaro, Kim-Salina I, Kristin Cipolla, Stephanie Felty, Tina Joell, Vikki Chu, George Towne, Megha Jain, Christine Legon, Jessica McDonnell, Craig Burke, Claire Zion, Jeanne-Marie Hudson, Christine Ball, Ivan Held, and all of the other wonderful folks at Berkley and Penguin Random House who had a hand in making *Happy Medium* and getting it out into the world.

Enormous thank-yous as well to agent extraordinaire Taylor Haggerty, and to Jasmine Brown, Alice Lawson, and Heather Baror-Shapiro.

Thank you to the many authors who have been extremely generous with their time, advice, and support as I navigated both my debut and the dreaded sophomore novel, but especially to Jasmine Guillory, Ashley Poston, Carley Fortune, and the other incredible people who recommended *Mrs. Nash's Ashes* in interviews or in their newsletters, and also to Sarah Hogle, Ava Wilder, India Holton, Kerry Winfrey, and Martha Waters for always being so kind whenever I elbow my way into their inboxes to ask questions/complain.

So much love and gratitude to my Bad Cats—Amber Roberts and Regine Darius, who steadfastly cheer me on as I write (and also, more commonly, as I languish); to Alexandra Kiley and Jenn Roush, who helped me coax my first draft into something turn-in-able; and Rachel Runya Katz, Esther Reid, and Amanda Wilson for performing quality assurance on the finished product.

Getting to research this book was a lot of fun. Thank you to Molly at Georges Mill Farm for giving me a crash course in dairy goat farming, and also to the "medium" I visited for (inadvertently) showing me some of their tricks.

Immense thanks as well to friends and family who have gone out of their way (sometimes quite literally!) to show their support—especially Ambriel, Madeline, Ariel, Megan, Claire, Jill and Ryan, Chuck and Joyce, and Nan. Not to mention a *lifetime* of thanks to Scott and Terra Adler, who are wonderful and supportive and the subjects of this book's dedication. And to Houston and Hazel—I am always, always beyond grateful for you.

I'm constantly bursting with appreciation for those who have championed my work, especially librarians, booksellers, and bookish influencers. Every time you recommend *Mrs. Nash's Ashes* or *Happy Medium* to your patrons, customers, and followers, I feel like the absolute luckiest (and most thankful) duck.

And last but certainly not least, thank *you*, my dear reader. It is an immense honor to get to share my words with you, and one I never take for granted.

HAPPY MEDIUM

SARAH ADLER

READERS GUIDE

BEHIND THE BOOK

ON A DARK AND METEOROLOGICALLY UNEVENTFUL NIGHT according to online weather records for October 21, 2021, I accidentally summoned the specter of this book in the form of a Twitter joke. "A medium inherits a historic goat farm and falls for the spirit of the farm's former owner. It would be called I AIN'T AFRAID OF NO GOATS," I posted, completely, naively unaware of what I'd just punned myself into.

It's funny, being haunted by a joke. It didn't particularly care that I was already twenty thousand words into drafting a different project. I found myself swiftly losing interest in what I had expected to be my second novel, the one my agent had already okayed. The professional writer part of me wanted to troubleshoot what had caused me to stall, to find a way through the wall I'd hit. But the part of me that the joke was starting to wrap itself around— dare I say, possess—mostly wanted to think about the 1990 film *Ghost*.

Here's a brief summary of the movie in case you haven't seen it (though you really should at your earliest convenience): Patrick Swayze and Demi Moore are a young married couple who spend their time making love and also pottery until Patrick Swayze is murdered during a mugging and becomes a, well . . . you know. He's obviously really bummed out about this, especially when he realizes that the mugging may not have been random and his widowed wife is in *peril*. So, he finds Whoopi Goldberg, who is a con artist posing as a spirit medium, and basically annoys her into helping him warn (and also sensually touch and dance with) Demi Moore.

In the original tweet thread, I'd responded to my critique partner's enthusiasm toward the idea with the comment, "The vibe would be *Ghost* if Patrick Swayze and Whoopi Goldberg were the couple." But the more I considered it, I realized that, if I *were* to try to write this idea into an actual, real story, I wasn't actually that interested in that dynamic. Paranormal romance is a great subgenre, but it's challenging to do well, and I wasn't confident enough to play on hard mode by having main characters who couldn't kiss each other. Because, traditionally, ghosts and living people aren't capable of prolonged physical contact. That's why we got the bizarre yet sexy scene where Patrick Swayze uses Whoopi Goldberg's body to have one last tactile moment with Demi Moore. It's easy to forget in the poignancy of that moment that, while as the audience we are seeing Patrick, in the reality of the scene it's actually Whoopi caressing Demi's mouth with her thumb. Which, weirdly hot, but not what I was after.

Except, maybe, it sort of was. *What if*, the joke whispered while I was folding laundry, *it isn't Patrick Swayze and Whoopi Goldberg who are supposed to be the couple in this idea?* And then, because jokes have little respect for boundaries, it followed me into the shower and continued, *What if it's actually supposed to be Whoopi and Demi Moore?* Hmm. Now that was a path my brain was happy to follow! Besides, it wasn't like I knew what to do with my stalled project, and I was starting to need a contingency plan.

Something I've learned over the course of several years of trial and error as a writer is that a good (or ridiculous) premise isn't enough; there also needs to be a plot behind it. So, I spent some time focused on logistics, the joke becoming part of what drove everything forward. Could I actually turn a stupid pun into an entire book proposal? Apparently, the answer is yes, because my agent and editor both wound up approving it and then I was on the hook to actually write the dang thing.

Something that's less funny about being haunted by a joke is that, if you let it hang around awhile, the cartoonish sheet with the eye holes cut out eventually slips off and reveals what's actually underneath. In my case, that was depression! Imagine my surprise as I began drafting what I thought was going to be a goofy-ass story, only to find phantoms of things I thought I'd buried lurking between the lines, making themselves known through characters who were sadder and lonelier and more complicated than any I'd written before. The same way that the intense yearning for brightness and hope I had while drafting *Mrs. Nash's Ashes* left its mark on those pages, the anxiety and isolation I was feeling was creeping like ecto-mist into my drafting of these.

When I was a teenager, I used to work in an old train station that local ghost hunters swore was haunted as heck. I was almost always there alone, and I didn't want to take any chances. So I would always say *hello* and *goodbye* to whoever may or may not have been hanging around, hopeful that this small courtesy of acknowledgment and my strong affection for the building would be enough to keep any potential spirits from targeting me for any spooky shit. I have no idea if there were any ghosts there or not, but accepting their possible presence did help me keep my fear at bay.

After fighting with this book for a while, trying to cast the heavier stuff out of it but only managing to drive it even deeper, I remembered those days of walking into the train station and saying aloud, "Good morning, just here to work today." And I thought, hey, maybe I could try something similar with this. So that's what I did. I said hello to the discomfiting thing beneath the joke. I recognized that I was never going to be able to hide it beneath its cartoon ghost sheet again—not completely. And I decided that was all right. That it was okay if you saw the occasional shadowy spectral limb peeking out.

That's why, when my editor asked if I had any other title ideas (and really, I was honestly shocked they let me keep I AIN'T AFRAID OF NO GOATS as long as they did), my friend Jenn's suggestion of *Happy Medium* felt so right. Because this book helped me discover the exact balance of humor and vulnerability I needed to act as a sort of emotional exorcism. And now the joke can (hopefully) rest in peace.

DISCUSSION QUESTIONS

1. As a fake spirit medium, do you think Gretchen really helped more than she harmed her clients?

2. Do you think Gretchen should have read the letter from her father? What do you think it said?

3. Which television show would you most want to binge-watch with Everett?

4. Does his history of intermittent hustling make Charlie's criticisms of Gretchen hypocritical or more valid?

5. Do you think Gretchen ever tells Mrs. Van Alst the truth about her (in)ability to communicate with her daughter? *Should* she tell her?

6. What is the worst color combination you can imagine for one of Grandma Ellen's sweaters or afghans?

7. Why do you think it matters to Charlie so much that Gretchen be honest?

8. Do you believe in ghosts? Have you ever had an encounter with one?

9. What do you think would have happened to Everett and Charlie if Gretchen never came to Gilded Creek?

10. Do you think Gretchen will ever encounter more ghosts?

A FEW BOOKS THAT INFLUENCED THIS ONE

Welcome to Temptation by Jennifer Crusie

Cold Comfort Farm by Stella Gibbons

Just Like Magic by Sarah Hogle

A Notorious Countess Confesses by Julie Anne Long

Will They or Won't They by Ava Wilder

The Code of the Woosters by P. G. Wodehouse

H. D. Kimrey

Sarah Adler writes romantic comedies about lovable weirdos finding their happily ever afters. She lives in Maryland with her husband and daughter and spends an inordinate amount of her time yelling at her mischievous cat to stop opening the kitchen cabinets.

VISIT SARAH ADLER ONLINE

SarahAdlerWrites.com